THE RIPPON SPURRIER

C. J. RICHARDSON

ONE MAN WILL STOP AT NOTHING

THE RIPPON SPURRIER

Published in 2021 by

C. J. Richardson

Copyright © 2021 C. J. Richardson

ISBN (paperback) 978-1-7399238-0-8
ISBN (ebook) 978-1-7399238-1-5

Cover Design and Interior Layout by designforwriters.com

For John

Acknowledgements

As EVER, I WOULD like to thank The Next Chapter Writing Group for their never-ending support and encouragement during the writing of this book.

Thank you to family friend Daniel Herth for his help in spotting errors and advising on some of the religious terms I have used.

I would also like to acknowledge two principal book sources and their authors from the beginning.

Kesselring, K. J. (2010). *The Northern Rebellion of 1569*. Palgrave Macmillan.

and

Sharp, S. C. (1975). *The Rising in the North THE 1569 REBELLION Being a reprint of the Memorials of the Rebellion of the Earls of Northumberland and Westmorland edited by Sir Cuthbert Sharp in 1840*. Shotton, Durham, England: J. Shotton, 3b Old Elvet, Durham City.

I have based the contents of this novel on actual events that happened in 1569. The principal protagonists are fictitious, but some characters are actual historical figures.

It is not possible to know the temperaments, motivation, and voices of those actual historical figures. I have portrayed them in a way that fits with my interpretation and view of the actual events and the parts they played.

Foreword

I WAS FIRST DRAWN to this story while researching local history at Ripon library close to where I live. I came across the name of a local resident, Thomas Markenfield of Markenfield Hall, who was heavily involved in the rebellion's instigation. Intrigued, I visited the Hall, one of the most intact medieval manor houses from that period. By the time I left Markenfield, I knew I wanted to write this novel.

I made several research trips to Durham Cathedral, Brancepeth Castle, and Barnard Castle to gain an insight into the layout and feel of such splendid buildings. John Speed's 16th-century atlas of all the counties of England, Scotland and Wales was an excellent resource when trying to visualise the topography of the time.

Cuthbert Sharp's book on the rebellion of the North was a superb source for letters sent between Bowes of Barnard castle and William Cecil in London, written in the language of the time.

And

K. J. Kesselring's book on the same subject provided the whole timeline for my novel with some very clear insights about the political and religious situation at the time. Her word-for-word citations for the Proclamations made by the rebels brought a great sense of realism to the novel.

During the time leading up to the rebellion, the population of England had suffered several years of poor crops because of harsh weather, raised taxes and land enclosures. Crime became rife as vagrants wandered the streets of towns and villages, no longer able to turn to the monasteries for food and shelter since the dissolution some thirty years earlier. Queen Elizabeth was slowly eroding the power of the northern earls and landowners, who were still devout followers of the Catholic Faith. She removed them from certain offices of high standing, replacing them with those of the Protestant faith. The tipping point came when Mary Queen of Scots fled from Scotland, seeking shelter from Elizabeth, but found herself imprisoned and held captive instead.

November 1558

ESCAPE WAS IMPOSSIBLE. THE *falcon pursued her. She could not run fast enough, and he was nearly upon her. He swooped down, his eye getting bigger and bigger, looking straight through her. He grabbed her with his talons, pulling her within the span of his enveloping wings. Something hit her face. So hard. She fell like a stone. Then blackness. Nothing.*

Robert

THE RUT HAD STARTED. In the far distance, across the many fields the Markenfields owned, and toward the ruins of Fountains Abbey, the fallow deer gathered. I could hear the insistent, deep-throated, repeated belching of the stags. The surrounding air was damp, and a mist lay low on the ground as I rode up to the front of Markenfield Hall. I was glad I had worn my wadmol cloak. The leaves on the trees lining the road were turning red and gold – a sign of the winter to come.

The drawbridge was down, and the guard standing outside the gatehouse on the far side of the moat signalled for me to cross. I entered the courtyard and dismounted, untying a soft leather bag from my saddle before a young groom took the reins and led Mutton over to the stable block on the left. The smith was busy at his anvil; the familiar ring and smell of hot metal drifting out into the sharp morning air made me feel at home. I could almost imagine that if I should but put my head around the door of the smithy, I would see my father striking the iron. I had spent the first seven years of my life here with my father. He was the smith, and they had employed my mother in the kitchen. My eyes misted. I wished he could have been here to witness this day. The day his son was on the cusp of marching alongside the Master of Markenfield on a pilgrimage, just as his father had done with the old master many years ago.

Smoke billowed from the kitchen chimney, and the rich smells emanating through the open leaded windows made my stomach groan. I had already broken my fast with bread and cheese, but I could always find room for good food at any time of the day. I knew the cook, Goodwife Green, and a broad smile and a quick compliment about her cooking skills before I left would almost certainly buy me a fresh piece of bread with a dollop of butter or goose fat.

I looked up at the grand house before me. The creamy York stone was blackening with age but showed the strength and thickness of its walls. The buttresses and high crenulated roof gave the appearance of being in a castle's confines rather than a gentleman's home.

I felt a sense of awe whenever I came back, even after all these years.

A man appeared in a doorway to the right of the kitchen and came over. I recognised him. Samuel Fenton.

'Good morrow, Samuel. Fare thee well?'

He nodded. 'The Master is expecting you. Come this way.'

I followed him and entered the door that led to a dark stone staircase, which took us up to a level above the undercroft. Another heavy wooden door awaited at the top, and Samuel opened it to reveal the Great Hall.

'Goodman Gray to see you, Master,' he said before retreating to stand by one of the large, ornate leaded windows.

A massive fire roared in the cavernous hearth at the western end of the Hall, making the vast space feel warm and welcoming. Thomas stood up, abandoning his breakfast of stuffed pheasant and bacon. Tall and slim, his neat beard framed his narrow face, and his steel-blue eyes sparkled with confidence.

Another man was sitting at the long oak table in the centre of the room. I immediately recognised Richard Norton. He was the high sheriff of the whole of Yorkshire and Thomas's uncle. Although elderly, the man was by no means frail but well-built with white hair that fell onto his shoulders. He had sharp, beady eyes and carried with him an air of authority and high standing. He was also one of the men my father had marched alongside on the Pilgrimage of Grace in '36. I hoped my dream of marching alongside these two men would be fulfilled soon.

'Come. Sit with us, Robert.' Master Thomas patted the chair next to him.

I felt ashamed standing before them, they in their fine doublets, me in my coarse woollen cloak and leather jerkin. I took off my felt hat and bowed low before walking over to the table and taking my place beside them. The sight before me made me drool, knowing there would be no need to butter up Goodwife Green after all.

'Help yourself. There is plenty,' said Thomas, slurping on a flagon of ale.

I did not need telling twice and pulled my knife from my belt. Cutting myself a large slice of pheasant, I ate hungrily. The fowl tasted heavenly on my tongue, rich and flavoursome. Samuel came over to the table and poured a jug of ale, placing it in front of me.

'I hear you have fashioned my nephew with a set of spurs fit for a king,' said Richard. He pointed at the soft leather pouch. 'Come now. Do not have us wait. Let us see your work.'

'As you wish, my lord.' I wiped my hands on my cloak and opened the strings of the bag, lifting both spurs out and passing one to each of the gentlemen. The spurs gleamed from the hours of polishing, the solid silver inlay worked into and bold against the glossy sheen of the leather straps; delicately engraved in miniature with the Five wounds of Christ, each hand and foot showing where the nails had punctured the skin. The crown of thorns was so exquisitely intricate and as sharp to touch as the barbs on a rampant sloe. The rowels were true and straight, each spike evenly spaced.

'By Jesu, Robert. You are an excellent spurrier and silversmith,' said Richard. 'I have not seen this quality of workmanship outside of London. You will make Rippon famous.' He turned to Thomas, adding, 'And you, my nephew, will wear spurs charged with Catholic spirit when we ride out. We cannot fail in our noble task now.'

'Indeed, Uncle,' said Thomas. 'I will ask my close friend Nicholas Morton to bless them before we march. A priest of such high standing will surely have His ear.'

My shoulders widened as I pulled myself upright, sitting straight-backed with pride at the high sheriff's compliment. My cheeks burned hot, and I could not temper the broad smile on my face. Master Thomas patted my arm and spoke. 'You have served me well, Robert. I hope to have you at our side when we commence our crusade.'

'Of that, you can be sure, Master,' I said, still basking in the pleasure of their praise.

Thomas took a purse from his belt, counted out two pounds in silver and gave it to me.

Knowing our meeting was at an end, I stood and bowed to both men again. 'I am grateful for your generosity, Master; I will pray every night until you send for me.'

I took my leave, and Samuel led me back down the steps. I collected my horse from the stables and rode back over the drawbridge and down the broad road. The silver coins jingled in my purse, and I made sure I was out of hearing distance before I threw my cap into the air and cheered my good fortune. Catherine would have her beautiful feather mattress sooner than she knew, and I would follow in my father's footsteps and march alongside my master. I decided not to tell her of the coming rising just yet. There was no point in causing her to worry in her condition. At that moment, a cloud covered the bright sun, casting a shadow over me, and a darker thought crossed my mind. What if I could not be with her for the birth of our child?

Richard Norton

RICHARD NORTON STOOD AT the window. He was looking out across the fields and the village. 'Your trust in Goodman Gray is touching, Thomas, but is it well founded? There are enough loose tongues to get us sent to the Tower. Sussex has spies everywhere.'

Thomas got up from the table and joined him. They both saw Robert bending down to retrieve his cap from the ground before mounting the old-looking nag he had been riding when he arrived.

'The Grays have been loyal to my family for generations, Uncle. I would trust Robert with my life. Surely you remember Gray's father. He marched alongside you and my father in '36. Northumberland and Westmorland will find their most faithful followers in my manor.'

'Of course, I thought I knew the name. I can see the resemblance now. It's the hair. The last time I saw Robert, he was naught but a thin whippersnapper. All skin and bone. He has turned into a mountain of a man like his father.' Richard stared out across the landscape, watching as Robert Gray became smaller and smaller. He certainly did remember the lad's father, with hair the colour of a beech tree in autumn. It was not the happiest of memories. Turning, he glanced over to the manservant who was replenishing the pewter flagons with ale. He signalled for Thomas to dismiss him.

When they were alone, they both sat down and Richard raised the flagon to his lips, drinking his fill of the yeasty liquid. He wiped his mouth with the back of his hand.

'Is your friend, Dr Morton, still in England?' asked Richard. 'I thought he had returned to Rome?'

'No. He is on the pope's business, travelling about the country. He tries to gauge the mood of the people. Telling them to be strong and hold faith. He will be a great asset when it comes to the muster.'

'I need to tell you that Northumberland's becoming nervous. He talks of abandoning the cause.'

'God's blood!' Thomas slammed his flagon down on the table. 'What is he thinking?'

Richard recognised his nephew's quick temper and laid a hand on Thomas's arm. 'Sit, and I will explain.'

Thomas complied, though his eyes sparkled with frustration and impatience.

'Sussex has sent word that we are to appear before the council at York yet again to explain ourselves.' said Richard. 'Northumberland fears arrest on appearance there. If Rome does not excommunicate Elizabeth, Northumberland and Westmorland say we cannot march against her. It will be treason. Speak again to your friend, Morton. He may be able to persuade Pope Pious to act more quickly.'

Robert

Rippon, Yorkshire, Wednesday 15th October 1569

THE SWEAT POURED FROM my forehead. I pulled the glowing bar of steel from the forge, using the tongs my father had bequeathed me. Each time I used them; I saw the muscles roped down my father's arms; the mass of flaming hair tied back with a woven braid dyed red by my mother; the dagger at his waist. Now I was the one placing the molten metal on the anvil, hammering it into shape and creating a fresh pair of spurs.

Richard Norton had commissioned them to match those fashioned for Master Thomas. My mood was not as bright as the fire's flames. Catherine should be more grateful. The opportunity to make such extravagant and beautiful goods was not to be sniffed at by any means. If we did an excellent job of these, work would flood in, leaving us extremely comfortable. It would be possible to take on a second apprentice and create a fine legacy for the son I hoped she was carrying. My thoughts spat forth like sparks from the hammer striking the metal I was forging. I remembered the harsh words spoken earlier that morning. Catherine's fears over my close relationship with Master Markenfield were unfounded. I had tried to reassure her...

'It was old Master Markenfield that gave my father a chance,' I had said. 'He let him use this shop rent-free for six months while he built the business.'

'And his son never lets you forget, my husband,' Catherine had replied, hands on her hips. 'He feigns friendship to gain your loyalty for the war he is planning.'

'He need not feign any friendship. I will be loyal to him as my father was to his master. I will not have you discredit him, Catherine. You are my wife, not my counsellor. You would do well to remember.' I had left the room before I said more and made the rift bigger.

I turned my attention back to the spurs and continued to hammer out the metal bar. To see her tears did ever cause me great pain; it was as if I had held a branding iron to myself.

I remembered the day I met her so clearly. It was a bitter November day eleven years ago, and news had reached the town that Queen Mary had died from the powerful influenza sweeping across the country. I remembered thinking that not even a queen was immune to the terrible disease, as I still mourned my mother's loss two months earlier. All the talk in the town was of Elizabeth. She would be crowned in the coming days, and then all these five years living blissfully as Catholics would end, and we would sink back into Protestant rule and Protestant ways once more. I was glad my mother was not here to witness such grave news.

There had been such a commotion in the street. A child had run in front of a horse on the road outside my shop on the market-stede. It had reared up and kicked out, ripping her forehead wide and plucking her left eye so that it dangled down on her cheek, staring, unseeing and cold. Her father had been in my shop and had rushed out to pick her up and put her in the back of their cart. Her mother cradled the child's body as they rode out of the town to return to their small cottage at Markenfield. The family had come back into Rippon a few months later with the child who had one clouded eye that stared unseeing and a neat pale line of a scar above the eyebrow. The townsfolk had drawn back in fear, saying the child and her mother must be witches. No earthly person could survive such a wound, they had whispered and gossiped among themselves. Her father told me a few weeks later, when I went out to shoe a horse for him, that she had been unconscious for a good month. His wife was a healer and had returned the eye to its socket with a few stitches, but now their daughter only had sight in her right eye. Catherine had never been able to remember what had happened that day. Why she had been running as if the Devil himself was chasing her. After that first trip into town, Catherine's mother had fashioned a patch from a piece of leather to cover the offending orb and plaited a length of hemp to fasten it around her head.

I became very fond of Catherine as she slowly turned from a child into a young woman. She was shy and hardly ever spoke to me, although she always walked proudly as if daring anyone to comment or abuse her with foul words when in town. Each time I saw her, I fell more and more in love with her, and the day eventually came, a year or two later, when I finally plucked up the courage to ask her to marry me. There were many years between us, but she needed a strong, full-grown man to care for her. Never mind that she would argue her own capability. She thanked me for the offer but refused, saying that not a soul on earth could love a face like hers, that her disfigurement would be a barrier to love for all her life. I reached out, and, as she stood there shaking, no doubt in her mind that I would recoil, I gently removed the patch and gazed at her. Tears trickled down her cheek as she whispered, 'I will understand if you wish to withdraw your generous offer.'

Dipping my head to her face, I kissed her just above her right eye, which was the colour of the bluest cornflower. I kissed the scar above the place where her clouded eye stared sightlessly into the distance, and my lips brushed the outline of her nose, kissing away her tears before resting upon her lips.

'You are the most beautiful creature I have ever seen. I ask you again. Will you marry me?'

A delicate, uneasy smile washed over her face as she searched mine for the truth of my words, and, seeing it was so, she answered.

'You need to know something about me, Robert. Something that might make you change your mind.'

'Nothing could make me change my mind,' I said purposefully. 'Nothing.'

'You have not witnessed it yet, but I have seizures. My mother says I go silent and begin to shake.' She took hold of my hand. 'I have visions – I see things I cannot explain.'

I took her in my arms and assured her that nothing about her would stop me from loving her. I meant it, even though something inside me trembled at the thought. Whatever her visions, they must be with God's blessing as she was most surely a good and pious person. 'I will ask you again. Will you become my wife?'

'Yes, Robert. I will,' she said, sliding into my arms.

I picked her up and swung her around, the happiest I had ever been in my life.

Her father was agreeable but said we had to wait awhile and could not marry until she had reached her fifteenth year.

Since that time, we had lived together in harmony. I had worked hard to grow the business, and it had favoured our fortunes.

My life was full of love, and the happier we were, the more my artistry and craft improved. Many townsmen said I was a fool to marry a witch's daughter and that she would put me under a spell and ruin me. They were wrong. Customers became loyal, and I drew business from all over Claro Wapontake and even further afield. My success provided a good excuse for others in the same trade to say that Catherine's powers and magic made people bring their business to us rather than stay with the tradespeople who had serviced their needs for years. Our only sadness came from the lack of children. Catherine could not carry them to term. But now, after several attempts and several years later, it seemed we might, at last, become parents.

I worked all morning, stopping only to pour water from the trough over my head to cool myself. By the time Catherine had appeared to tell me to come and eat, I had worked off my earlier mood. Wiping my hands and face with a rag before joining her in the dwelling room, I turned to my apprentice, John, telling him to watch over the shop, and promising to bring the boy some food on my return.

Catherine

ROBERT DROPPED ONTO A chair. 'I hope not to fight again, Catherine. I am too tired.'

I watched him grab some bread and dip it into the thick pottage, wolfing it ravenously, swilling down great draughts of ale. I ate in silence. Speaking to him before he had sated his thirst and satisfied his hunger was pointless. It was most challenging to keep a still tongue when I feared he would end up dead if he continued to support Master Thomas, who bared his faith to the Catholic church so openly. Every day I clung to the hope that our prayer books would not be found.

It was not so long since that terrible day when the authorities raided the house of the town's blessed curate, Thomas Blackburne, and forced him to burn all his books in public. Now he might not be willing to perform the act of purification for me after I gave birth. Some of our neighbours had burned their prayer books lest they be charged with heresy, but Robert and I had not reached that decision. Not yet. At least we could worship quietly in our own home. It was the pressure to attend the protestant services at St Wilfrid's every Sunday that hurt us most. Hiding prayer books was one thing but plotting to overthrow the queen – Robert may as well go out to the forest and kill himself, leave his body to feed the very trees that supplied his forge.

I stroked the large swelling of my belly. The child was kicking. I prayed the blind woman's prediction had been correct in foretelling the birth of a son. Robert was set on it. Tears welled as I thought about the loss of three of my infants through miscarriages. The blind woman said they had been daughters. This child had survived much longer so far, and I reasoned it was my destiny only to carry sons successfully.

Robert sat back and pushed his empty bowl across the table.

I took a breath before speaking. 'I hear on the market-stede that Sussex has summoned the earls to York again.'

He stood up, leaning until his face almost touched mine, his voice low and deliberate. 'Leave this alone, Catherine. I will not have you interfere. The gossipmongers are not worth your ear.'

I stared back at him, determined to make him listen. 'I only fear for your safety. What will become of our son if you are killed?'

His eyes softened. 'He will remember his father with pride. Someone who stood strong and defended the true faith that looks to Rome for its holy orders.'

I knew it was hopeless and went to my husband. Pushing him back down on the bench, I sat on his lap and held his head to my breast as if I could protect him from himself. The tang of hot metal, thick on his red hair, always made it seem as if his locks must be on fire. His clothes smelled of the sweat that came from hard toil. 'If you must follow the earls, take me with you. I will nurse your wounds and fill your belly each night. Do not leave me alone. What if I should have a seizure?'

Robert pulled himself free of my arms and sat up. He took my face in his hands and planted his mouth on mine, breathing in deeply as if he could not get enough of my scent. I returned his kiss, my mouth welcoming his tongue, knowing all thoughts of a hungry apprentice had disappeared. I did not remind him.

Thomas Markenfield

Markenfield Hall, Yorkshire, Friday 31st October 1569

THOMAS AND ISABEL MARKENFIELD knelt before the altar in the tiny chapel beside the great Hall. They would usually sit in the narrow squint behind the double piscina, but Thomas's Uncle Richard was attending, and there was not enough room. Thomas knew Isabel would miss the warmth of the fire in the squint, but she would have to steel herself, as he was doing, against the cold seeping from the floor and through the cushion beneath her knees. The servants took their places in the little wooden pews behind them.

Dr Nicholas Morton wore a magnificent black and gold chasuble and a large ruby ring on his left hand. He washed his hands in the double piscina's left-hand bowl, elaborately carved with oak leaves, acorns and the Markenfield family crest. The right-hand dish would serve to wash the chalice after the service. He stood before the altar and said Mass for All Souls' Eve in a clear and confident voice.

'Saint Michael the Archangel defend us in battle; be our defence against the wickedness and snares of the devil. May God rebuke him; we humbly pray. And do thou, O Prince of the heavenly host, by the power of God, thrust into hell Satan and all the evil spirits who prowl about the world for the ruin of souls. Amen.'

The Mass continued while the Sanctus bells rang out for the souls of the dead. When all was finished, and we had sent the servants back to their duties, Thomas led the way into the Great Hall.

The table was laden with sweetmeats and pancakes, apples, nuts, soul cakes spiced with nutmeg and raisins, boxty bread, meat pies and roasted fowl. Several jugs of apple cider and wine ensured the diners' thirsts were well served. Scented beeswax candles, standing amongst the dishes, flickered, and added to the perfume of the fresh rushes spread thickly across the stone floor. A log fire blazed in the hearth, casting shadows across the stone walls. Most of the servants had retired to the kitchen for their own celebrations.

Their dinner guests, Richard Norton and the priest, Dr Nicholas Morton, gazed greedily over the feast before them.

Isabel turned to Nicholas. 'I thank you for taking Mass, Father. It is a great honour to have you here on such an important evening. Would you say grace for us?'

Nicholas raised his hands, palms pressed together, and the others bowed their heads and closed their eyes.

The steward, Samuel, remained standing, his expression flat. When grace was done, Thomas dismissed him; directing him to go down to the kitchen where he could help the kitchen staff to hand out soul cakes and whatever was plentiful to all the villagers who might come to the door this evening. 'Make sure you help yourself and feed your family well this holiest of nights, Samuel. I know your losses have been great this year. Bid your wife well as she prays for the souls of her lost children.'

Samuel bowed and took his leave without speaking.

'Churlish fellow,' said Richard. 'No grace or manners.'

'His family has suffered greatly, Richard,' Isabel said. 'This sweating sickness has taken many lives. We give him some leeway until he is recovered.'

Richard harrumphed his displeasure, watching the steward leave.

'When will you go?' Thomas asked Richard when Samuel had left the room.

'Tomorrow evening,' he said. 'Everyone will be sleeping off the festivities. Even Sussex's men will be too full of wine and ale to notice my departure.' He laughed and raised his glass to his hosts. 'May He look down on us and know our cause is just and right. For now, let us celebrate All Hallows' Eve and remember our forefathers.'

The evening passed comfortably and, before they retired, Thomas assured Richard that he would join him at Brancepeth as soon as an opportunity arose. 'We must persuade Westmorland not to back away from his duty, especially as Northumberland sits at Topcliffe, quaking in his boots. John Swinburne is happy to come with me. What about your relatives?'

'Christopher stands with us, and my other sons all pledge their allegiance. My brother Thomas is already at Brancepeth with the Tempests.'

Catherine

Rippon, Yorkshire, Wednesday 5th November 1569

FROM THE SHADOWS AT the rear of the workshop, I listened to my husband talking to Master Markenfield.

'You have worked with a deft hand yet again, Robert. My uncle will be well pleased.' Thomas lowered his voice. 'I am soon to pay a visit to my dear friend, the Earl of Westmorland at Brancepeth. I will show him your handiwork. He may wish to add to your workload soon.'

Robert smiled. 'I would be only too glad to offer him my service.'

I was nervous. It was an honour, of course, to have the master enter the shop personally. It would bring customers from everywhere, knowing that Thomas Markenfield favoured Robert's skills. I was in awe of the master. He had been on a crusade and made a Knight of the Holy Sepulchre in Jerusalem. But I always felt a tightening in my chest whenever I saw him. In my heart, I had ever known he would put Robert in grave danger one day. And now, although I could not be sure, I suspected that day would come soon. I retreated into the kitchen, tiptoeing over the herb-scented rushes covering the floor.

After brushing down my blue kirtle, I made sure my coif was secure over my hair. Robert always said my golden curls reminded him of honey, that and the colour of my eyes was what made him fall in love with me in the first place, but, even now, I could not understand how that could be. I had thought no one could have feelings of love for the daughter of a healer, let alone someone with a face like mine. I felt a tingle, as always, thinking about the first time I had taken notice of him. He had been coming to the strip of land my father had rented from Master Markenfield for a year or two. It had been towards the end of my twelfth year, and I was putting down fresh hay for our horse, Bess. Robert had followed my father into the barn. He kept glancing at me as I led Bess outside and held her while he took off her old shoes and replaced them with new ones. I do not know why I was so much more aware of him that day. I could not stop looking at him. Although he was some years older than me, it did not alter how he made me feel. Tall and broad with muscles rippling down his arms, he had smiled, and his forest-green eyes seemed to bore into me. His hands were large and strong as he pulled the horse's hoof between his knees. I had a sudden urge to have those hands pulling me close. My face flushed so hard, it felt on fire. The memory made my cheeks burn even now.

Wrapping a grey shawl around my shoulders, I took up a basket. I needed bread and cheese and, while the master was here, I would get away and listen to the latest news on the market-stede.

Slipping past the two men, who were deep in conversation, I left the workshop's intense heat and stepped out into the autumn sun, mingling with the crowds on the square. Most were Catholic, but there were many spies among them. All the church officials were desperate to win the queen's favour, reporting anyone who openly showed papal support for our poor, dear Scottish queen, Mary, held captive at Tutbury by the Earl of Shrewsbury.

I passed the ostler who was tending to Master Markenfield's horse and made my way along the row of shops, stopping at the butcher's to purchase a little beef to flavour today's pottage. I was accustomed to the noise and clamour of people shouting their wares, the sound of the hammers ringing out with every stroke. The stench from the tanning yards, the human piss and excrement littering the street, the horse and cattle dung, all of which had made me bilious during the early stages of pregnancy but now had no effect on me.

Strolling past the Unicorn Inn, I stopped outside one of the other spurrier's shops. Harry Gardyner, wearing his usual red felt hat with the pheasant feather, was busy working and did not see me. A familiar figure came out from the door at the rear of the forge.

'Good morrow, Catherine. I see your husband has sent you to spy on us again,' she said.

I laughed. 'Good morrow, Bridget. I can see my husband's skill makes you nervous.'

In fact, we were great friends, as were our husbands. When they were boys, Harry's father had been killed during the Pilgrimage of Grace, and Robert's father had taken Harry in, treating him as a second son and giving an apprenticeship to both of them. Now they had their own tenanted plots and were in friendly competition with each other. The number of Loriners on the market-stede was growing. Along with bits, stirrups, and mountings for bridles, they were now making spurs. There were more smiths and cutlers too. I would report to Robert and talk to him again about considering increasing his complement of wares.

When seen side by side, we could be mother and daughter as Bridget was about fifteen years older than I and showing a little grey at the edges of her coif. She had taken me under her wing when I first married Robert, ignoring the prejudices of other townsfolk regarding their suspicions about my being a witch, and we were almost inseparable now. Through her support, some families had given me the benefit of the doubt. They called on me when their children were ill – or even for my help when giving birth. Bridget and I walked on together, perusing stalls and carts. The quality of goods was poor, and the quantity paltry. Poor harvests, high land rents and the rise in tariffs for market stalls were crippling the tradespeople. It had worsened over recent years. The queen had an insatiable hunger when it came to filling her coffers, and it seemed to me that it was the Catholic population carrying the heaviest burden.

'Is that Master Markenfield's horse outside your shop?' asked Bridget. 'He seems to be a regular visitor.'

'He is here to see how Robert is faring with his order,' I said, hoping for no more questions.

'It must be something extraordinary for the master to spend so much time there. Harry wonders what he does to win such favour.'

I detected a nervous edge in my friend's voice. 'He only does as the master asks, as all of us do. Robert has done nothing more than his job.' My voice trembled. 'Come. Let us see if the soap maker has any fresh scents to tempt us,' I added, changing the conversation. Why had Harry not asked Robert directly about his business? A sudden shiver ran down my back.

We made our way across the market square, and I noticed two church officials talking to the ostler. The men seemed engrossed in whatever he was telling them and continually glanced through the opening at the front of Robert's workshop. I blushed as they looked my way, but soon realised they were not interested in me. Turning toward raised voices growing louder and louder, I saw the bellringer dragging a rough-looking peasant by the scruff of the neck across the square. He was most likely on his way to the Pie Powder Court.

'Someone else bulking their grain with grit, I shouldn't wonder,' said Bridget.

It was not surprising, with such poor harvests again this year. We continued to the stall where a woman was selling herb-scented soap, and we each bought a bar before moving on to purchase bread from the Baxter and returning to Bridget's home.

'Good morrow, Harry!' I shouted. The noise from the workshop was immense. I thought he had not heard. 'Good—'

'Good morrow,' mumbled Harry before putting his hammer down and disappearing inside.

It surprised me. Harry was usually a sociable character, always ready with a smile and a kind word. 'Is there something amiss, Bridget? Has Harry received bad news?'

Bridget blushed. 'No. No. His mother is quite ill. He worries about her. That is all.'

I took hold of Bridget's hands. 'I am sorry to hear that. Let me know if there is anything we can do to help. Mayhap Robert can take on some of Harry's work while you both care for her.'

Harry reappeared, marching over to Bridget, and grabbing her arm. 'We do not need yours or your husband's charity, Goodwife Gray. My wife had no reason to tell you about our private affairs.'

Harry dragged Bridget inside, leaving me stunned and puzzled at such a rebuff.

Anne Percy – Countess of Northumberland

Cock Lodge, Topcliffe, Yorkshire,
Sunday 9th November 1569

ANNE PERCY SIPPED HER wine, enjoying the heat from the fire. It was the only place in the vast room that held any semblance of warmth on a dark and damp day. She inspected the small bread manchet before popping it into her mouth. The yeasty flavour pleased her taste buds, making it the only part of the meal she could stomach this morning. The family chaplain, Father Mudde, sat opposite her serving himself from the platter of salt fish on his lap. The blazing logs lit their faces as they listened to her husband's chuntering. After more than ten years of marriage, three daughters, and a son who did not survive past his first birthday, Anne had heard it all a hundred times before. Father Mudde dabbed the sheen of sweat from his bald pate with his handkerchief.

'The queen thwarts me at every turn, Father Mudde,' said Anne's husband, the Earl of Northumberland. He paced the floor. 'She has no less told the commissioners to ignore me in my capacity as High Steward of Richmond. Am I not an earl? Do I not deserve respect for my high standing?'

Father Mudde nodded, mumbling a response, his mouth still stuffed with fish. Anne felt her stomach turn, her hand flying to her mouth. She swallowed hard and looked toward the tapestry covering the far wall. The colourful scene of horses, dogs and archers hunting deer proved more pleasant than looking into Mudde's gaping mouth.

Northumberland continued to pace the floor, face florid, his barrel chest threatening to burst the gold buttons on his russet-velvet doublet. 'Is it right that I am unable to defend my tenants in Richmond against the Enclosures Act? Whatsoever I do to enhance their miserable lives, she and Cecil bring me down.'

Anne knew his words were valid. Since William Cecil had become Elizabeth's chief adviser, the man could do no wrong, and the queen's ears were intent on listening to his evil counsel. Cecil's greatest wish was to join Scotland and England together as one great Protestant nation.

Northumberland grabbed a piece of trencher bread, stuffed it into his mouth, chewing and spitting crumbs as he continued. 'It is because of that man's ideas on how to fill the royal coffers she stole my copper mines three years ago, Father.'

'My lord,' said Father Mudde. 'I spend my sorry life hidden from view in these sad times.' He sighed, shaking his head as he rose and waddled over to the table. 'My only peace is that I can be the instrument that saves your soul as I serve as your chaplain here.' He slipped a pickled herring into his mouth.

Anne almost gagged as she watched him, mouth open, rolling the herring around on his tongue, sucking and slurping before swallowing. She turned her gaze back to the tapestry.

'It is Cecil,' said Northumberland. 'He is the one demanding our attendance before the council at York. Sussex says he has tried to persuade the queen of our assurances not to march against her but fears Cecil is winning the battle of minds.'

'It is true, my lord. His ambition to clear England of those who kneel before the true God gains momentum every day. We must pray that the true queen and rightful heir will be restored to her beloved Scotland.'

'I am sure God will answer all our prayers,' said Anne, heartily sick of listening to the woeful pair. She turned to her husband. 'Come and sit down. Drink some wine and calm your nerves.'

Northumberland shook his head. 'I fear the queen will not relent in her efforts to find good reason to file a warrant for our arrest.'

A steward appeared in the doorway. 'There is a messenger from the Earl of Sussex, my lord.'

Northumberland stayed the sudden trembling in his legs. 'Show him to us.'

Father Mudde slipped away through the servant's entrance. Anne went to her husband's side. A high ruff of pleated linen framed her powdered-white face and rouged lips. She squeezed his hand.

Sussex's pursuivant bowed to Northumberland on entering the Hall. 'My lord, I have word from my master.' He passed a sealed envelope to the Earl.

Northumberland waved the man away. 'You may wait outside.'

Opening the missive, hands shaking, he read it aloud.

I beg you to beware bad advice and precipitate action. Take heed of the Council of such as I have warned you would show honey and deliver you poison...let not vain delusions abuse you with fear of your own shadow. The

queen summons you to attend court forthwith and make
an account of yourself.

Northumberland collapsed into his chair beside the fire.
'Perhaps we can gain some time,' said Anne, rushing over
to her writing desk. She penned a note swiftly.

> *My dearest Sussex, my husband was loath to comply*
> *with your last request to attend York, having heard such*
> *grave rumours that he and Westmorland would be treated*
> *as captives and sent to court forthwith. As you, my good*
> *friend of many years, have also made plain before, I am*
> *also of the sure mind that time and the risk of inclement*
> *weather will quell any thoughts of hasty action from this*
> *quarter. My husband rightfully feels affronted by such hei-*
> *nous accusations from the court in London, but the long*
> *winter will give him time to reflect on his feelings and our*
> *gracious majesty to realise he means her no harm.*

Anne signed and sealed the note, giving it to one of her
servants and bidding him accompany Sussex's man back to
York.

'His patience is at an end, Anne.' Northumberland put his
head in his hands. 'He will send Oswald Westropp and his
band of horsemen to arrest me forthwith. We must hasten to
Brancepeth and try to restrain Westmorland from this folly.

It was early evening and already dark when Northumberland
and his entourage arrived at Brancepeth. A steward helped
Anne down from her horse and guided her and her maid into
the castle, up a stone staircase and onto the galleried corridor.
Northumberland and Father Mudde followed close behind.
Torches lit the way to where Westmorland was dining, the

sound of raised voices and laughter telling them their host was entertaining several guests in the Baron's Hall.

Anne would typically have enjoyed a leisurely stroll along the corridors to gaze upon the portraits of their host's family and ancestors before dining with them in the grandeur of Raby Castle, but tonight she was here at their stronghold of Brancepeth and eager to hear Westmorland's view before giving up all hope of a stand. Would he be willing to let Elizabeth and Cecil continually strip them of all their assets?

Two soldiers guarded the studded wooden doors of the Hall, each holding a halberd. They bowed to Northumberland and Anne before pushing the doors wide to the sight of dozens of men seated at long tables. Several priests were in attendance to take Mass and minister to their masters' spiritual needs, and Father Mudde joined them. Servants hurried back and forth, serving steaming dishes of sturgeon, venison, beef, and small birds stuffed with sweetmeats. Warm air billowed out to greet the newcomers, the rich smell of food not quite extinguishing the odour from the much-used jakes in the corner of the room.

'Greetings, my dear friends,' said Westmorland, standing up and opening his arms wide in welcome.

'It is good to see you, Charles.' Northumberland bowed to his host.

Anne eyed up Westmorland. He had such an air of grace about him that always made her own husband look ungainly in contrast. Her heart always fluttered when she laid eyes on Westmorland's thick, shoulder-length hair, which was almost as black as his eyes, and his clothes seemed to fit perfectly on his broad shoulders and slim waist. The finely embroidered linen ruff around his neck stood in stark contrast to the fashionable black velvet doublet, inset with green silk. So unlike her husband's clothes, which were lucky to survive a day without tearing. He enjoyed good food, but why it must always stay around his middle and not thicken his long, spindly legs was a constant source of discomfort to her.

'Come, Anne,' said Westmorland. 'You must be chilled to the bone.' He took her arm, leading her to a seat at the table close to the fire.

Anne closed her eyes and sighed as twenty-seven-year-old Westmorland put his hand on her shoulders.

Bowing to Jane, Northumberland seated himself on the other side of the table next to Richard Norton. Anne looked up to find her husband glowering at her. She ignored him, looking around at many familiar friends already surmising, by the look on their faces, her husband was likely too late to turn the tide. Westmorland's brothers were there, Richard Norton's sons, Thomas Markenfield, the Swinburne family, landowners from Chopwell who owned vast swathes of land all over Northumberland and the Tempests, another recusant family who had grown rich through coal mining enterprises.

Northumberland looked across the table. 'I find it strange that my Lord Westmorland is so ready to rise when all good hope is passed. Sussex has sent a messenger insisting I show myself at Court immediately. You must have received the same. He warns the queen's patience has worn thin. I fear we will all be executed should we attend her call. I come to tell you it is too late for us. It would best serve us to make for Scotland in haste. We will take shelter with the good Catholic lords there.'

Some men nodded their agreement, but Anne could see that Thomas and his Uncle Richard were not happy. They were of the same mind as herself and feared their arguments would lose ground. It was apparent they thought little of her husband.

'Are we to listen to this cowardly buffoon,' said Thomas, standing up. 'Are we to sit back and let Northumberland spread fear like rancid butter on toasted bread? Already, your bravado melts into your shaking bones.'

There was a roar of angry voices around the table. Northumberland's hand went to his sword as he rose from his seat and faced Thomas. Anne feared for her husband's safety as much as his pride.

'Be quiet!' shouted Anne, standing up, determined to keep up the challenge from Markenfield but not so her husband be ridiculed. At least not by anyone apart from herself. 'My husband is no coward,' she shouted. 'He speaks much sense, and we do not court death willingly.' She gazed at her husband and smiled warmly, her eyes telling him to let her have her say. 'But now, and my husband would surely agree – looking about us – if we have enough men to count on as I see here tonight, we can most surely continue with our plans in earnest.' Anne's eyes sparkled with fire and determination, the men in the room drawn to the passion and conviction in her voice.

As her gaze settled on Westmorland, she could see the lust in his black eyes as he stared at her. Damn the man for his handsomeness, for his youth. That sharp flutter across her chest again took her breath for a second.

Thomas took up the challenge and said, 'Countess Anne is right. Now the queen has ordered us to court, Sussex will call the muster. We must act quickly and take York forthwith.'

It was common knowledge the Swinburnes and Tempests were among those keen to rise against Elizabeth. They cheered Thomas on, saying Elizabeth had no right to keep Queen Mary locked away in Tutbury Castle all these long months with Shrewsbury and his greedy wife, Bess. The place was fit only for a barracks.

Anne listened to some wealthy landowners who were not so sure. They did not want to risk losing the lands granted by the old queen, Mary Tudor. She looked to Westmorland and his wife for some word that might change the mind of the doubters.

As if Anne had willed it, Jane, the Countess of Westmorland, burst into tears. 'We and our country are shamed forever now that, in the end, we should seek holes to creep into,' she wailed. 'What of my brother, the Duke of Norfolk? Is he to be left to obtain the freedom of the Scottish queen alone? He has offered his hand in marriage to her. Will he say that his loyal friends in the North were all cowards?'

Anne and her husband had long since stopped opposing the idea of Jane's brother, the protestant Duke of Norfolk, marrying the Scottish queen. Fearing it would put an end to his support for their cause, they had been vehemently against the union. In the end, they had been won round when Northumberland received a secret message from Queen Mary, stating that the marriage was of convenience only and was her best chance to get back to Scotland.

Anne went to Jane and put an arm around her shoulder. 'We are with you all the way. Do not fear. These men are honourable and would not desert us in our hour of need.' She looked at the doubters. 'Do you think you will keep your lands by refusing to march? Elizabeth will strip you bare until you have nothing.' Her words made the doubters falter and decide to remain a while longer.

Northumberland went to Anne and took her hand. His own fears swept aside; he bowed to Westmorland. 'We stand beside you, Charles. We will set out on our Pilgrimage together.'

'There then, that is settled,' said Westmorland, swallowing hard and relaxing his shoulders. 'Let your wife rest a little and put your mind to our Proclamation.'

Anne smiled, knowing Westmorland needed the thousands of men she and Northumberland could muster. 'I need no rest, my lord. I am keen to help.' Anne waved her arm to include all there. 'Come, sirs, we have much to plan. I will ride out with you when the time comes.'

The men talked and argued long into the night and deep into the following day. Those, including Thomas Markenfield, who wanted to raise arms against Elizabeth and topple her in favour of the Scottish queen, were shouted down.

'Have you forgotten? We cannot march against Elizabeth; a person chosen and anointed by God,' said Westmorland. 'We can only argue our cause. If the pope had excommunicated her, we would have right on our side, but no one will support a bid to overthrow their monarch.'

'God's blood! Has not Elizabeth excommunicated herself?' asked Thomas. 'I have spoken long about it with the pope's emissary, my friend Nicholas Morton.'

'No!' said one priest. He was somewhat taller than the others, with a beaked nose and shallow cheeks that made him look more like the Grim Reaper than a man of God. 'We cannot make assumptions about such matters,' he added. Some of his fellow priests nodded in agreement. He continued, 'The excommunication has to be formal. Only the pope can pass judgement, and it has to be publicised.'

Thomas dismissed the priest's words, shaking his head. 'According to Nicholas, when the queen refused the papal envoy entry into England, she had, for all intents, sundered herself from the communion of the church.'

Father Mudde stood up, saying that even without Rome's authority, it was lawful to defend the Catholic religion in those doctrines which are the common Christian inheritance.

It was impossible to achieve consensus, and three conspirators were about to walk away, refusing to march without written word from the pope.

'We have not the time to wait for the Holy See's formal response,' said Richard Norton. 'I have heard from several sources that he is totally behind us and intends to label Queen Elizabeth a heretic. If we wait for a piece of paper with his seal, it will be too late; most of us will already have been arrested with our heads hung up for all of York to gaze at. We must act now.' Richard's voice cracked. 'I have memories, as do the older men of you here, of marching alongside our dear friend Robert Aske in the Great Pilgrimage of '36. The sight of Aske hanging from Clifford Tower in York still fills me with rage. Here is an opportunity to avenge his memory.'

'My uncle is right,' said Thomas. 'We must plan our next step in earnest and proclaim our intentions. We can state that we do not march as the queen's enemy, but as her friends who wish only to show her she has been misguided.' Thomas watched as the doubters sat back down. 'Come. We will thrash out this proclamation together. It will include all we wish to make clear and encourage people to join our just and holy crusade.'

'So it shall be,' said Westmorland. He hailed his servants to bring more refreshments.

Anne was keen to have her say on what was in the proclamation. This rebellion was still a possibility. Stroking her belly, she decided to stay her joyful news until they were on the march.

A few hours and several attempts later, Westmorland stood and read aloud:

We, Thomas, Earl of Northumberland and Charles, Earl of Westmorland, the queen's most true and lawful subjects, and to all her highness's people, sendeth greeting: Whereas diverse new set up nobles about the queen's majesty, have and do daily, not only go about to overthrow and put down the ancient nobility of this realm but also have misused the queen majesty's own person…

The Hall doors swung open, and a messenger handed Westmorland a missive. It displayed Sussex's seal. Westmorland read the contents. 'It appears Sussex has now declared us traitors to the queen and liars to all our followers.'

Thomas hammered his dagger hilt into the desk. 'By Jesu! It has not satisfied some men here with our exclusion of Queen Mary's plight thus far. We must no longer curb their will.' There were roars of approval from the Swinburnes and Tempests. 'Elizabeth has brought this on herself.'

It was late the following evening when Westmorland, once again, stood up and cleared his throat.

Whereas it hath been, by the sinister and wicked report of sundry malicious persons, published that the assembly of these noble men, the Earls of Northumberland and Westmorland, hath been to the overthrow of the common wealth and the Crown. Know ye therefore, it hath been faithfully and deliberately considered and devised by Thomas, Duke of Norfolk, Henry, Earl of Arundel, Will, Earl of Pembroke, and the said Earls of Northumberland and Westmorland, with a common consent of sundry, wish to make known and understood to all persons to whom the true succession of the Crown appertaineth. The said nobility hath been prevented thus by certain common enemies of this realm, near about the queen's majesty's person… We have therefore assembled ourselves to resist force by force…

The proclamation was soon on its way to every town and village under the earls' and landowners' jurisdiction through several keen and loyal horsemen. Thomas sat back and grinned. Anne could read the man easily. At every meeting with her and her husband, he had talked of little else since returning from his crusade to the Holy Land. She knew he was relishing the thought of fulfilling his role as a Knight of the Holy Sepulchre and that it was about to be realised.

Catherine

York, Wednesday 12th November 1569

It had taken us the whole morning to reach York, travelling up Ploxwaingate. Two uniformed guards stopped us at Micklegate Bar. One of them, a burly fellow, walked around the horse and cart before asking Robert to state his business.

'My wife enjoys the market. I will need to guard my purse,' he said, with a smile and a wink.

The guards laughed. 'Take care,' said one, gawping at my swollen belly, 'the streets are busy.'

I knew Robert was here to buy the ticking and goose feathers to make the new mattress he had promised. He had that secretive air about him when we set off, humming to himself, trying to make me believe it was a day out for both of us afore the weather turned to snow. Smiling to myself, I decided not to spoil his surprise.

The streets were far busier than usual for a market day; progress slow as we inched the horse and cart forward through hordes of people. I wondered about the number of armed soldiers in the streets and immediately regretted our being there. If Robert said one word about his loyalties to the earls, their lives would be in danger.

More than a few soldiers were falling out of alehouses, drunk and making a nuisance of themselves, accosting women about their daily business. A few less choosy harlots flaunted themselves in front of the drunken men. They blew kisses and lifted their skirts to show the ribbons at the top of their stockings, intending to make some money out of those whose wit had left their heads and found its way down to their breeches. Fights were breaking out, and fists were flying. Amid the deafening noise, terrified cattle, penned up and waiting to be sold, were pushing against the walls of the wattle pens. They pawed the ground with their hooves, sending up clouds of dirt and dust and frothing at the mouth. Their breath hung thick and misty in the cold air as they bellowed wildly, threatening to stampede. Mutton was whinnying. His ears twitched as he tried to shake free of the mouth bit. I could barely hold on. Climbing down from the cart, Robert spoke softly and calmed the horse before taking hold of the bridle and leading him through the crowd.

I pulled my shawl tight around me, covering my belly. 'We need to leave, Robert. It is dangerous here.'

'We will go to the old inn on Stonegate. You will be safe there.'

I had been to the inn before, but it was across the city and would take a good while. Robert knew many of the tradespeople that frequented the place and would not want to miss an opportunity to do some business. There was no use in arguing about it.

The inn was overflowing, but Robert found a seat in a corner by one window and led me over. I could feel the room closing in on me. People were almost standing atop each other. After looking forward to coming to the monthly market, I now felt a great sense of fear. The clamour of the crowd pounded in my ears.

'I'm hungry enough to eat my horse,' Robert said. 'Come now, lass. Let us enjoy our meal. 'Tis a pity we cannot stroll about the city. Mayhap I can bring you again in the spring.' He waved a serving girl over and ordered some beer, a trencher of bread and a wedge of cheese.

'Why are there so many here, Robert?' I asked. 'I have never seen such a crowd of men in one place.'

'Methinks Sussex has called the muster.' He spoke in low tones. 'We must get word to the Master. He has joined Westmorland up at Brancepeth.'

'Who will you trust to go there?' I was frightened of the answer.

'I will travel tonight. If anyone should ask my whereabouts, say I am delivering more spurs to Markenfield Hall.'

The serving girl, dressed in filthy and torn clothes, brought the food and drink and placed it on the table. She held out a grubby hand. 'Three pennies, Sir.'

'How can I refuse such a good price,' said Robert. 'I am surprised, though? Your master usually charges a good deal more.'

'I know, Sir, but they forbid my master and all householders to raise prices during the muster. Sussex needs all the men he can get. Are you here to sign up?'

I held my breath.

'I— Yes, where do I go?' asked Robert.

Relieved at his response, I relaxed my shoulders and breathed out deeply.

'Over yon to the workhouse at St Andrew's Hall on Peasholme Green. There are hundreds of men answering the call. It is a grand sight to see.' The girl's eyes shone with excitement. 'They will provide a sword and dagger. And even a long coat and boots to keep you warm. My father has never owned such before. He says the pay is good too.'

'That is excellent news. We will not tarry with our meal.'

'Mayhap your wife should wait here.' The girl looked me up and down. 'It is not safe on the streets. You will be knocked over in the crowd.'

'My wife accompanies me on our last day together,' said Robert, still pretending he was here to answer Sussex's call. He smiled and winked at the girl. 'She will be sad to see me go.'

'You must hope your good husband can return home before the child is born,' she said to me. Turning on her heel, she answered the call of another customer.

The girl's words struck home. 'She speaks the truth. Change your mind, and let me travel with you and the master when the time comes. Rather I have the child in a field than at home alone.' I wondered if I would have the support of Bridget should I have a seizure in his absence. She always seemed afeared and kept her distance at those times. Robert was so understanding, resting my head in his lap and holding me until I returned from that other world where terrifying dreams awaited me. I could never tell him their content for fear of his reaction, only ever saying I could not remember.

He spoke in whispers, taking my hand. 'Everything will be fine. You will see. I have a surprise for you. Wait here until I return.' Robert stuffed his share of the bread and cheese in his pockets before standing and speaking loud enough for all to hear. 'I shall away to sign up for my Lord Sussex.' Raising his tankard, he added, 'God save the queen.' He drank the beer in haste as others repeated his toast.

I reached for his hand, my voice barely audible. 'Please, do not go. We require naught that risks your safety. The longer we are in York, the more chance of you being recognised. There are many here, including all your so-called friends who know your support for the earls.'

'I will be swift. Do not worry so.' Kissing me on the cheek, he headed towards the door before I had time to protest more. I saw him acknowledge several of his fellow tradespeople on his way out. What was he thinking? Any one of them could betray him to Sussex's men. I looked around the room. There were few other women to be seen. Shrinking back in my seat, I kept my head down.

As I sipped my drink and nibbled a little cheese, I heard a voice I recognised. Harry Gardyner and another man walked past me, deep in conversation as they headed to the door. Why had he not made himself known? Remembering how he had spoken to me and his wife Bridget outside his shop, I realised I had not seen her at all since then. I sensed something was amiss. Something bad.

They must have been listening to what Robert had been saying. Leaving my drink and food, I got up and followed them. As I pushed my way through the crowd, the smell of rank bodies made me gag. Once outside, I could barely see Robert as he led Mutton down Stonegate. There was no way I could catch him up. Harry Gardyner's distinctive red felt hat was heading in the opposite direction, towards Petergate and the cathedral. I followed, threading my way through the crowds, keeping a safe distance from the two men. There was something familiar about the second man, but I could not place him. I continued to follow and saw them turn left at the end of the street, desperate to know what Harry was up to. Quickening my pace so as not to lose them, I managed to keep track. It was challenging while fighting off the pathetic, grasping hands of drunken soldiers and beggars. The clawing terrified me, and my heart beat faster and faster. I needed to take control of my breathing.

Turning the corner, I lost all sight of Harry and his companion. Balancing on my toes to gain a little height, I looked up the street. I scanned the crowd, looking for the red hat. There were many red hats, but not one that held a pheasant's feather that stood upright towards the sky.

I thought to give up, but then it was there again, the red flash and golden feather, going through the Bootham Bar city gate. I arrived there a minute later, and the guard on duty waved me on. Following them through, I strained to see which way they were headed. The red felt hat was visible outside the door of Kings Manor. They were on their way to see Sussex and The Council of the North. I waited and, after a short while, Harry reappeared with two officers wearing swords. Their tunics displayed Sussex's coat of arms. Harry and the other man were talking animatedly and pointing back in the direction they had travelled. Harry must have told Sussex of Robert's loyalty to the Master. They would arrest him and – although she prayed not – torture him for information.

Feeling sick to my stomach, I turned and hurried back in the direction I had come. The guard let me pass back through the great oak doors. How could Harry do this to us? He and Robert had been friends since childhood. I reached the corner of Stonegate and stopped to catch my breath for a moment. I pushed on quickly and fought my way through the crowds. It seemed an age before I reached the inn and leaned against the outside wall for support. The world around me was spinning, the blood pounding in my ears, my pulse racing, and my chest tight. Hearing Robert calling out my name, I turned to see him leading Mutton to a stop. His face was lit bright with excitement.

'What do you think?' he said, nodding at the flatbed of the cart.

Without acknowledging the gift I knew was there, I grabbed his arm. 'Robert. We are undone. We must hurry from here before they arrest you.'

†

We were finally outside the walls. News of the muster had travelled fast, and we passed many men and women heading towards the city. Some eyed us suspiciously as we sped in the opposite direction. I hung on to his arm while jostled and thrown up and down on the hard seat. The wheels kept crashing into deep mud ruts in the road as we raced on, mile after mile. A recent cold snap had frozen them hard. It was easier to travel on firm ground when on foot, but there was a danger of laming a horse or breaking an axle in these conditions.

When we were only a few miles from home and about to come to Boroughbridge, the winter sun began to set.

'I will call at the stables here. Goodman Thorpe is bound to have a trusty mount I can buy. He supports our cause, and I can trust him.' said Robert. 'I will take it home with us and make sure you are safe before setting out.'

I knew the horse would be Robert's only chance to get away and escape arrest. He would hang for conspiracy and treason; there was no doubt in my mind. It was also dangerous to travel through the night, at the mercy of thieves and robbers.

We drew up outside the stables. Robert climbed down and disappeared inside. I turned to look at the flat of the cart. A huge hessian bag was open, several goose and duck feathers scattered across the cart bed, having escaped. Beside the bag was a bolt of finely woven ticking, ready to be sewn up and stuffed after I had aired the feathers. Comfort was the last thing on my mind now as I pulled my cloak tighter around me. Looking down the street, I recognised Goodwife Green. The cook, who worked in the kitchens at Markenfield Hall, was climbing aboard a cart laden with goods from a local merchant's shop. The woman's quatch cheeks were red from both the cold air and the effort required to heft her body. I had not seen the cook since attending the funeral of the children of Marjory Fenton. That poor woman had suffered such a great loss and – Dear Mary, Mother of God – that was who he was. The man who had been with Harry was Marjory's husband,

Samuel Fenton. The master had spies and enemies in his own house. I crossed myself. How many more spies were at the Hall?

Robert returned and tethered the horse to the back of the cart before climbing up and taking the reins.

'Robert,' I said, blurting out the words. 'I have recalled the other man's name. It was the master's steward, Samuel Fenton. The master will be sore to know that someone he has in his house has betrayed him. Warn him. There may be others.'

Robert's face turned pale. 'God in heaven. Is there no one we can trust?' He shook his head. 'Who, if any of our friends are true to us, Catherine? You must be careful whom you speak to from now. Do not trust anyone; I beg you.'

The rest of the journey was in twilight, and the stars flickered and sparkled like candles across a cloudless indigo sky. A full frost moon smiled down at us as an icy wind rose and stabbed through my shawl, making me shiver. Having barely eaten any of my meal at York, I felt faint with hunger.

'Not long now,' said Robert. He snapped the reins, but Mutton was tired and did not respond, no longer as tough as the meat Robert named him after. He urged the horse again, speaking softly to him. Mutton plodded on, his head hanging down.

As we came over the river bridge and made our way up the hill toward the market-stede at Rippon, the night sky was alive with the sound of St Wilfrid's bells ringing out. They sounded strange until Robert told me that the bells were rung backwards so that everyone knew it was a call to muster. Masses of torches lit up the square. A dense crowd was gathered by the obelisk, cheering and waving their weapons in the air. Many were carrying bows, pikes, and all other manner of sharp farming implements. Gentlemen, too, in their fine doublets, mounted on warhorses, swords at their sides, helmets and armour reflecting the torch lights. Robert pulled the cart to a halt and asked what was happening. A man told us a messenger had come into Rippon that morning and read the earls' proclamation aloud. He repeated the speech's essence to us, adding that some townsfolk had taken over the church to ring the bells and turf out the heretic priests.

Robert leaned down from the cart and slapped the man on the back. 'We will soon worship in our beloved church again,' he said, joining in with the cheering. Hugging me close, he added, 'It has begun. The pope will excommunicate Elizabeth, and the true queen, Mary, will be brought to the throne. We will march to London to claim what is rightfully hers.'

Bridget Gardyner appeared from within the crowd and approached the cart. 'Robert – Catherine. Have you heard the news? I looked for you earlier, but you were not at home…' She looked at the cart and saw the bundles of feather and ticking. 'Ah. I see you have bought a new mattress. You are lucky to afford such things.'

Robert's face lost its smile. 'We buy our goods from the money we have earned honestly. Where is Harry? I did not see him in the crowd. Does *he* come by money honestly?'

Bridget's face coloured. 'What do you mean? Why would you say such a thing?'

I answered my friend, my tone dull. 'Your husband was in York this day, spying on Robert and me. He works for Sussex, Bridget. He has betrayed us.'

Bridget trembled, speaking in earnest. 'I begged him not to follow you, but he would not listen. His mother died last eve.' She looked so pitiful, gazing up at us.

'I am sorry for his loss,' said Robert, his voice a little softer. 'But what has that to do with his betrayal?' Robert climbed down from the cart and took hold of Bridget's hands. 'Why would Harry do this to us, Bridget? I need to know. We have always been as brothers.'

'His mother made a dying declaration, talking about Harry's father and how he died on the Pilgrimage of Grace,' said Bridget, sniffling. 'She said that it was your father and the master who deserted him in his hour of need.'

Robert threw down Bridget's hands. 'It is not true,' he said, spitting out the words. 'My father was an honourable man. That cantankerous woman was lying. She did say naught but hurtful words to my father, always trying to put him down.' Robert was shaking with rage, wagging his finger in Bridget's face. 'My father told me Harry's father had been shot by mistake. Someone had taken him for an enemy. Harry's knows that to be true. Why would my father lie?' He turned from her, climbing back onto the cart. 'Your husband is a traitor. If I see him again, I will kill him.'

Robert snapped the reins, and Mutton started out towards home. I looked back at Bridget, unable to say a word.

†

It was the still dark hours before dawn, and I could not sleep. My body shook with fear as I wondered whether Robert had made it safely to Brancepeth. Since our wedding day, Robert and I had never spent a night apart. The hessian bag, full of feathers, and the bale of ticking lay untouched on the floor. Why did we have to go to York? If he had not been so keen to buy me the new mattress, we would not know of the Council and Sussex calling a muster to arms. He would be here beside me. Trying to block thoughts of him being far away, I turned my mind to more pleasant memories, of my home, of our wedding, of the day Robert had come to claim me…

My father, a cottager, had been out on his small strip of land, smaller still now that he had to use part of it for his cow and a small herd of sheep. He could no longer graze them on the common land since the Enclosures Act. He still had to pay the same rent to Master Markenfield, made up by a share of the harvest and some coin. Casting down the high ridges, set up in the winter to allow the water to drain away, he had been preparing the soil in readiness for this year's crop. The oxen were being driven by my younger brother Jack while my father guided the plough. The spring morning was bright, the sun rising early into a cloudless sky. I was impatient to see Robert and remembered how I had fidgeted on the three-legged stool, my hands clumsy, pulling the teats hard, making the cow kick out and bellow as I milked her.

By the time the sun was high, I had fed the geese, washed my father's second shirt, scrubbed the soiled rags for my baby sister and was draping them on a bush to dry. I looked up the rough track to see a cart and horse in the distance. I ran inside the cottage where my mother was feeding vegetables into the large pot hanging over the fire. 'Come, Mother. Call Father and Jack for their dinner.'

'Slow down, my girl,' she said, bending down to pick up baby Nell from the floor. Hitching the child up onto her hip, she added, 'He will not come until his furrows are done.'

I took my mother's hand, impatient and excited. 'But you must be outside to greet Robert as he arrives. At least wave to Father, so he knows he is come.'

My mother chuckled. 'Be patient, Catherine. Your father is not blind. Robert will not ride away again if your father is not at the door. Besides, your father would not miss this time with his eldest daughter before she starts life as a woman.' Baby Nell wriggled, trying to fight her way through the faded smock so that she could suckle at my mother's breast. Mother winced, so I lifted the baby from her and pushed a finger into its small pink mouth. Nell suckled in vain but seemed comforted.

The afternoon went well. Both Robert, Jack and my father drank to our happy union most heartily. I could not stop smiling. Sitting down on the packed earth floor in front of the fire, I rested my back against Robert's legs as he squatted on a low stool. I felt his muscles tighten as my mother explained how he should not move me if I had a seizure but cushion my head with his hands or a blanket; how he should lie me on my side and check I am breathing. When I wake, he should wait with me until I feel able to sit up. He did not speak or ask questions, becoming quiet and distant. I asked him to walk outside with me, and as we strolled, I explained it would not be as difficult as my mother had said, telling him I only needed someone nearby for comfort. He was more relaxed at that, explaining he had worried that he would let me down and cause me harm.

As the sun was setting, my father said it was time for us to journey back to Rippon. He handed Robert a willow crate containing a young gander and a goose so that we might start our own flock. My mother made up a bag of herbs from her garden so that I could plant them as soon as we arrived at our home. It felt strange to think of not calling this place home anymore.

'Plant them the way I have shown you. Always remember to dry enough to last through the winter,' she said, pulling me to her. 'I have given you something for every illness and condition. You know well enough how to prepare them.' I did, for she had been teaching me for as long as I could remember.

After many hugs and well wishes, Robert and I boarded the cart and set off up the lane. A little while later, we passed a man dressed in rags and staggering along the path. The man's face was a mass of pus-filled scabs, his ragged clothes covered in vomit. It made my stomach turn. Robert steered the cart clear, knowing it would be foolhardy to help the poor soul.

It had been the last time I had seen my family alive. If only I had gone back sooner to pay a visit. I might have been able to save them. Robert said the outcome would have been the same if I had been there. If only I had been there.

I got out of bed, pulling my rosary beads and prayer book from their hiding place. Kneeling on the icy floor and praying, I worked the beads between my fingers. I prayed for my dead family. I prayed Robert had made it safely to Brancepeth. What should I do now? If the shop did not open today, there would be questions. Robert would want me to carry on as usual. Going over to the fire, I poked the embers while feeding them with kindling. The flames soon started to flicker and rise.

Robert

Brancepeth Castle, Northumberland,
Thursday 13th November 1569

IT WAS THE SCREAM that alerted me. Pulling hard on the horse's reins, I brought it to a halt. Jumping down, I cautiously approached a small bundle of rags that was yelping as pitifully as a whipped dog on the floor. Scared animals could still bite. The shape of the heap, and the upturned bucket beside it, told me this particular animal was of the human variety.

'Are you hurt?' Bending down, I touched the child's shoulder. The boy shrank himself further into a ball. 'Here, let me help you, lad.' Holding my hand out, I waited.

The boy's eyes were wide, his voice a squeak. 'I thought you would kill me. I am a good worker, Sir. My mistress needs me.'

I could not help but laugh. Taking hold of the boy's hand, I pulled the thin and frail child to his feet. 'I am not in the habit of killing small boys. I did not see you in the dark. It would be better to carry a light in future.'

'Yes, Sir. I will, Sir.' The boy rubbed his knees. Still shaking, he picked his bucket up and limped away.

I followed. 'What is your name, boy?'

'Edmund, Sir.'

'Where is the night watch, Edmund?'

'He is sleeping with all the others in the stables,' said Edmund, as he drew water from a nearby well. 'We have been abroad most of the night.'

'That's no excuse in these dangerous times. Now, show me where I can stable my horse. He needs to be rubbed down and fed.'

Edmund filled his bucket and heaved it up, slopping water each time he moved. 'My mistress, the cook, will scold me if I take longer.' There was a whine in the boy's voice, and his bottom lip was trembling.

'Do not worry. I will explain to your mistress.' I took the full bucket from him. 'Show me the way.' Edmund hung his head and led me to the stable. I followed close behind. 'Tell me about your mistress, the cook. What is her name?'

'Mistress Oswyn, Sir.'

'And what is her best dish?'

'All she makes tastes good to me, Sir. I am always hungry.' The boy smiled up at me.

Laughing out loud, I said, 'Then we must be much the same. My stomach forever reminds me it needs feeding.' I ruffled the boy's fair hair, all stuck up and stiff with grease and dirt, as we entered the stables.

'Quiet boy!' shouted someone from within. 'Cannot a man sleep in peace?' More raised voices grumbled and swore at the man who had shouted out, breaking the calm so that the horses snorted and whinnied.

Edmund led my horse and me over to the part of the stable where he usually slept. The farting and the usual smell of horse dung, along with the ripe tang of sweat and unwashed bodies, created a malodorous warm fug.

'You can tie your horse here next to this mare. She is gentle and will not make a fuss.'

I unbridled the horse, tied him to a halter and put a nosebag on the tired animal. Edmund handed a soft leather rag to me and picked up one for himself. While we rubbed the sweat from the horse's flanks, not wanting to cause another uproar, I whispered to the boy, 'How old are you, Edmund?'

'About eight years, Sir. I hope to start my apprenticeship soon.'

I could hear the excitement in his voice. 'What sort of apprenticeship?'

'Blacksmith, Sir. My father has nearly paid enough to the earl, and I work as a pot boy and stable hand to help pay for my lodgings while I wait.'

Setting my rag down, I put my arm about the boy's shoulder. 'I was right then. We are much the same. I am a spurrier and smith. Come, fellow tradesman, let us see if we can convince your mistress to feed us.' The boy straightened himself up, pulling back his shoulders. It pleased me heartily to see Edmund's response to a little kindness. I guessed there had been scarce time for a small boy in a busy castle.

'She is not in such good humour,' said Edmund. 'We have been working most of the night to feed my master and all his guests. We are all tired.'

'Leave it to me, young Edmund. I fancy I have a way with the ladies.'

I led the way into the kitchen, and Edmund stayed close behind me. The cook looked up. 'About time too, you lazy, worthless—'

I smiled at the shocked look on the woman's face. 'Good morrow, Goodwife Oswyn. Pray, do not scold the boy.' It was difficult to ignore the large boar on a spit in front of the fire. Swallowing my saliva, I continued. 'It is I that made him tarry so. I almost killed him in my haste to arrive at the castle in goodly time to see the earl and Master Markenfield.' Great globs of fat dripped into the wooden trough beneath the boar. Goodwife Oswyn, it occurred to me, looked not unsimilar to the beast and seemed to melt at a similar rate. The fire in the hearth was a great blaze of good oak logs and kept its heat well. I tried to concentrate, forcing myself to look directly at the cook with her small beady eyes and heavy jowls. 'We have been settling my mount in the stable. I have been riding all this long night, and the horse was tired and in need of attention. I beg forgiveness for causing such an inconvenience, but I have news for my master and the earl.'

'Aye. Well. The earl and his guests are still abed. You must wait until they rouse.' She turned her attention to the boy. 'Best get on with your duties, Edmund.'

Edmund went over to the enormous hearth and began feeding the fire with birch and hazel to give it a boost before turning the hog slowly on its iron spit.

The cook looked me up and down as if she were trying to decide whether I was trustworthy or a spy here to glean information. Who could blame her? It was difficult in these times to know who to trust.

'A steward will inform his lordship of your presence in due time, Goodman...?'

'Gray. Robert Gray at your service.' I took off my felt hat and bowed in an exaggerated fashion. 'May I compliment you on the aromas in your kitchen? You must be a fine cook indeed to make a man's mouth water so.'

She turned away as if shy. 'I... I. Well. Come and sit. I am sure you must be hungry, having ridden all the way from York.'

Smiling broadly, I sat down at the large wooden table. If Westmorland were not yet risen, a little time could not hurt. I looked to Edmund over by the fire and gave him a conspiratorial wink. It was barely minutes before she placed a wooden flagon of beer and a generous wedge of freshly baked bread and butter before me.

Goodwife Oswyn disappeared through an inner door. I tore a piece of bread and held it out to Edmund. The boy ran over and snatched the offering, stuffing it into his mouth, all the while watching the door for his mistress's return.

The steward led me upstairs and along the galleried room to the Baron's Hall. The guards opened the door, and the steward stood aside, signalling for me to enter. The smell hit me; stale beer, stale piss, and body odour were even worse than the stables' aroma. Gentlemen and priests lay on the floor; some were still sitting with their heads resting on the wooden banqueting tables. It must have been some gathering last night. The Earl of Westmorland and Master Thomas stood in front of the great hearth, warming their hands before the blazing fire. A finely dressed woman stood close by. I bowed to each in turn. I had never met the Earl of Westmorland and, though he looked half asleep, it struck me how tall and handsomely dressed he was. No wonder his name always came up in connection with ladies when the gossipmongers in the market-stede at Rippon were in full voice. I had heard that all young maidens swooned in his presence, and even Northumberland's wife, Anne, was smitten by him. Master Thomas stood at Westmorland's side, looking relatively slight against the other man's broad stature. I bowed to them all in turn.

'My lord, Countess Anne,' said Thomas. 'This is Robert Gray, my spurrier and smith.' He turned to me. 'Come, Robert. I hear you carry news.'

I was interested to see for myself how the countess would behave around Westmorland. I told them of my visit to York with Catherine, explaining how many men were gathering; what Sussex was offering to encourage them to stand with him; the money, the clothing and even a sword. It was enough to bring men running from all the neighbouring towns and villages. 'There must be a thousand or more already, my Lord Westmorland.'

'You have done well to get here so quickly with your news. I thank you for your trouble. Make sure you rest well before your journey home.' Westmorland waved a hand to dismiss me.

'If it pleases, my lord, Countess, I pledged to Master Markenfield that I would be at his side when he marches out. I would like to fulfil that pledge and remain if you would allow it, sire. I have my father's sword and my own bow.' A sudden rush of pride ran through me. In time I would pass it down to my son – God willing.

'Goodman,' said Westmorland. 'What is your trade?'

'A Spurrier and Smith, my lord.'

'This is the man who made my own and my uncle's spurs,' said Thomas. 'He is a master at his craft.'

'And you doth shoe horses?' I nodded as Westmorland continued. 'Your skills will be useful on the march, Robert. My smith is taken ill, and it would be a blessing to have you with us. I will make sure you are well furnished. Rest now. Ask the cook to feed you.' Countess Anne's eyes never strayed from Westmorland as he spoke, and I concluded the gossips were indeed correct.

'Thank you, my lord. If it pleases, I would speak further with my master.' I turned to face Thomas, not comfortable being the bearer of bad news. 'You have a spy in your midst at Markenfield, Master. Samuel Fenton was in York yesterday, and when I left my wife at a local inn so that I could attend to some business…' I hesitated for a moment, knowing how Thomas would respond. 'She saw Fenton and another man leave the inn directly after I had gone. They had been listening in as I told Catherine I would come and warn you. Catherine followed them and saw them go to the council at King's Manor. We had to leave York in haste. We feared arrest for treason.'

Thomas's face grew red, his eyes blazing. 'Samuel? After everything my family has done to comfort him over the loss of his children.' He paced the floor before his head jerked up, and he asked me, 'Has anyone warned my wife? I must send word.'

'Wait,' said Anne, taking hold of Thomas's shoulder. 'He will sit quiet so that he may hear more news to report to Sussex. My husband will send a fresh rider, Thomas. We can use this to our advantage and send false news of what we intend. A note to your wife to say we hold back until we have sufficient support in these parts would have Sussex caught off guard. He will not expect an immediate assault on his beloved city.'

'Of course, my lady.' My master's face lit up. 'We must feed him titbits tasty enough to make Sussex believe he has the upper hand.' Having settled the matter, he questioned me further. 'Who is the other man that has betrayed me?'

I knew it would hurt my master, but I could not lie. 'I am afraid it is Harry Gardyner, Master.'

'What? The ungrateful—' Thomas almost drew his sword from its sheath now. My breath caught as I stepped back. 'The bastard shall pay for this. I will have him flogged… I will… I will see him and his family out on the street as beggars.'

'I do not understand his actions, Master,' I said, trying to calm him. 'Mayhap he has a troubled mind…his mother is recently passed away.' I surprised myself. Why on God's earth was I trying to defend the man?

'Devil take his mother; the man shall not betray his master and walk away. No one shall get the better of Thomas Markenfield. Not he, not Fenton. No one.'

'What is all this racket?' groaned one gentleman at the table.

'It is naught; rest your head again, good fellow,' said Westmorland. He took hold of Thomas's shoulder. 'Come, sir. Do not carry on so in front of a servant. We will discuss this in private.' He turned to me. 'Go now and get some rest. I will send for you in due course.'

'My lord. My lady.' I bowed and took my leave, relieved to be dismissed. I had never seen my master so angry. It was with good cause, but what would Bridget do? Surely he would not see her turned out onto the street. Was my father to blame for what was happening? I searched my memory again. No. I could not – would not believe what Harry's mother had said. My father was a hero. Harry Gardyner deserved the master's wrath – if the master got to him first…

Robert

Brancepeth Castle, Northumberland,
Friday 14th November 1569

THE YARD WAS HEAVING with men and horses, and the atmosphere celebratory. A stab of regret flashed through me as I wished Harry had been here. We had both dreamed of being soldiers when we were small boys. How proud our fathers would have been to see us march beside their master. Now, we were sworn enemies and I would stand alone, determined to avenge my father's name when Harry and I next met.

Horsemen held banners aloft, their armour pristine from polishing, while the low rising sun bounced off their helmets. At the head of the crowd was Richard Norton, his white hair blowing in the wind and a great gold crucifix hanging around his neck; his banner of the five wounds held high. To Norton's right, Westmorland made a grand sight in his fine, gleaming armour. His wife, Jane, and his uncles were mounted beside him. To Norton's left, Northumberland had drawn his sword as if in readiness to fight that very minute. His wife, Anne, was at his side. I thought she looked magnificent in her cape of Murrey-cloth, trimmed in ermine. Her white face looked stunning in contrast, and a broad smile played on her lips. I had heard she was as keen as her husband to restore the Catholic faith.

Riding amongst such high-standing men and women made my heart soar with pride. Behind Northumberland, Norton's sons gathered. Alongside them were Thomas Markenfield, the Swinburnes and the Tempests. I mounted my horse and joined this group, eager to show my worth.

Outside the main gate were up to 300 armed horsemen who had mustered at the castle in the early hours. Many farmers, yeomen, and peasants, carrying sickles and pikes, stood up, ready to march with them. Foresters carried axes; wore daggers at their belts; quivers of arrows and bows slung across their backs. I saw others had swords and wondered if they had been passed down from fathers who had marched in The Pilgrimage of Grace.

Richard Norton raised his sword to bring the men to order. The shouting died down to a few mutterings before silence descended. Only the clatter of hooves, showing the impatience of steeds eager to be on the move, interrupted his words.

'Be patient, good men. For this day, I need only horsemen and a number of priests. We ride to Durham to take the city and return the cathedral away from its heretic services and restore the altars for a great Mass. Whence it is done, we shall return with the men of that city who will take the oath and march alongside us. All you fine fellows left here, gather supplies for the long journey ahead. Tomorrow we head south.' A great roar went up as we set forth under blue skies and a fine day.

The pace was steady as we travelled out across the moors. The vast open sky framed isolated trees, and, here and there, high rocks jutted from the earth like sentinels from a long, forgotten past. Heather, a startling purple just a few weeks before, was now grey and wiry and lay in great carpets. The bracken was thick and crowned with a hard morning frost that crunched and gave way to expose brown and curled fronds before turning to dust under the horses' hooves.

I rode alongside, chatting to other horsemen of a similar rank to myself. Many were yeomen and tradesmen and, as the miles passed, we discussed lost business opportunities in hushed tones. These grumbles were tempered occasionally with loud bragging about the honour of riding alongside our lords and masters.

I could see Durham cathedral atop a distant hill from several miles away, the towers of stone golden in the sun, a beacon of light and sanctuary. The tiny houses of the city beneath were clutching at its ankles like children. The River Weir snaked below, defending all that rose above its deep and swift-flowing waters. I looked around to see all other faces as awestruck as me at the sight. My thoughts turned to home and St Wilfrid's. I longed for my church and town to be saved from the heretics, as this army would surely save this one.

On reaching the city's gates, we met many cheering townsfolk standing outside the houses and shops that straddled Elvet Bridge. The people made way, letting the horsemen pass onto Fleshergate before following us up the hill towards the cathedral.

I followed closely as Westmorland rode at the side of Richard Norton, my master close behind. ''Tis well if Dean Whittingham keeps hidden this day,' said Westmorland. 'He plies his heresy with all zealousness such that the people are right sorry to have to listen. I look no further than to chase him from his sanctuary and let the people do as they will. He would look well enough if someone should bind him and roll him down the hill towards the river.' I and my fellow riders laughed loudly as we imagined such a sight.

The explosive clatter of the hooves of around thirty horses on the cathedral's stone floor made the worshippers cry out.

The thunderous noise ricocheting off the church walls sounded like the cannonball and shot of a siege. It took the worshippers a while to realise what was happening. The townsfolk who had followed us up the hill pressed their way in behind the lead horses, cheering and crossing themselves to show allegiance to Westmorland and his followers. There was barely room for anyone to move.

Westmorland brought his horse to a standstill in front of the communion table. He shouted down at the young priest who was taking the service. 'Where is your dean? Bring the churl here, heretic.'

The priest stood his ground as other priests came hurrying over to join him. He looked up at Westmorland. I could see his eyes were cold and challenging.

'My master is away. Take your men and leave this holy place. You are not welcome here.'

Westmorland laughed. 'Most readily, sir. I am your humble servant.' He twisted around on his saddle to face his men. 'This young man wishes us to leave. What say you?'

The cavernous nave echoed with the sound of our laughter and jeers from horsemen and townspeople. Two of the towns-men took the young priest by the arms and dragged him away, while most of the other priests that had initially gathered around him remained in the cathedral.

Westmorland spoke again. 'Those of you here who are of the same mind, bring down these symbols of heresy, and we shall hold Mass and bring this church back into the arms of our Holy Lady. Those of you who do not support us may leave freely and without harm from any of my men.' He leaned down from his saddle and snatched a prayer book from one priest. 'Now, good people, find every one of these, build a fire with their false words and take warmth from their destruction.'

Cheers filled the air as the crowds set about pulling down the communion table and any other Protestant relics and altars. People formed a line and passed down all the prayer books. It was not long before the smell of burning paper drifted in from the cathedral close outside. As if from nowhere, Catholic altars, supposedly destroyed during the changeover from Mary Tudor's reign to Elizabeth's ten years before, were being carried into the magnificent church and set back into their rightful places. A woman cradling a pair of gold candlesticks approached West-morland. Her eyes were gleaming; her mouth curled upwards into a broad smile. 'We have waited long for you, my lord. May God and the pope protect you in your noble cause.' She hurried towards the altar to return the candlesticks to where they originally stood. The priests who had remained were joyful for the chance to return to the old ways. I helped them to recover copes, chasubles, and rosary beads from hiding places around the cathedral. Looking about me, I wondered if Westmorland found it hard to stomach the whitewashed walls once covered in colourful paintings. The beautiful stained-glass rose window had been desecrated and broken, leaving sharp gashes like open wounds. The sun, shining through, cast coloured daggers of pattern across the stone floor. At least the magnificent columns that held up the vaulted ceiling were still intact; the pillars, with their carved spiral twists, towered above them.

Westmorland dismounted and walked over to the family tomb where his ancestor Ralph Neville lay. It did not appear to have been vandalised, all the ornate carvings and family shields still plain to see. Northumberland, and others of appropriate standing dismounted, removed their helmets, and took their places, kneeling before the altar beside Westmorland. Countess Jane and Countess Anne joined them. Guards stood at the end of each row, ready to fend off any would-be attackers. I stood in the aisle at the end of my master's row. The rest of the horsemen, waiting outside, dismounted and came inside on foot to take their places. Many people filled the rest of the nave as the Mass started. Hundreds more gathered outside to listen to the service and revel in the sound of prayers said in Latin for the first time in years.

The Mass had been a complete success, and we could all see the strength of support for the cause. We left the cathedral, apart from several guards who were to maintain its security now we had returned it to Catholicism. Westmorland directly led the way to the Town Hall. He was met with smiles and open arms by the mayor and his councillors. They all swore allegiance, and Westmorland left several more horsemen to maintain order and guard the city.

It was late afternoon when we rode back over the bridge with several hundred more supporters. The mood was high as we made our way back over the moors, arriving back at Brancepeth late in the evening. I wished Catherine could have seen what we had achieved in just one day. Imagine what could be done by the time we arrived back in Rippon.

It was not yet dawn, and the cobbles in the yard sparkled with frost in the moonlight. Torches hung from the surrounding walls. I loaded Westmorland's military forge cart, complete with kiln, with equipment from the smithy. I had always longed to own such an asset, to travel to customers and provide a better service. Mayhap it would be possible to make one. It looked simple enough.

Entourages hurried about me; maids and stewards were running back and forth, loading carts with provisions, ale, wine, wool blankets, chairs, and carpets to assure comfort for the earls on their travels. Archers wore chain vests and carried full quivers and longbows on their backs. Several priests emerged from St Brandon's church, having already said Mass for the earls and saying prayers for the journey ahead. They kissed the crucifixes hanging on chains around their necks. Holding staffs that would serve as walking sticks during the march, they took their places beside their respective masters.

Edmund had helped me lead a pair of oxen from the field and harness them to the cart. 'Will we have to fight, sir? I have not said goodbye to my father. I hope he understands there was not time.' The boy was wick, skipping and jumping about, fighting a mock battle with an invisible enemy. He thrust his tiny dagger through the air. 'Will I be given a sword?'

The sight had me roaring with laughter. 'I think you best to hide under the cart if there is any fighting to be done. You could not lift a broadsword. A soldier would pluck you off your feet in a second and swing you round on the end of his blade like a rabbit.'

Edmund's smile slid from his face. He shuffled off to the smithy to collect tongs, pliers, and a variety of hammers while a couple of Westmoreland's servants helped me haul the anvil onto the rear of the cart. I had not meant to upset the lad. When he returned, dragging the sack of heavy tools behind him, I patted his head. 'I will be most glad to have such a brave boy alongside me. We can look to each other's backs for safety.' Taking the sack from him, I flung it up on the cart before smiling down at my new friend. The boy's eyes were as wide and shiny as a silver church plate. I doubted Edmund had ever travelled further than the castle and Brancepeth village, and now we both might have to journey a great distance.

'I heard London was hundreds of miles away. It must sit at the end of the world,' said Edmund.

'It is a goodly way,' I said. 'Away, we must prepare my horse.'

Edmund reached out and took hold of my hand as we walked over to the stables.

'Good lad. You hang on to me.'

As we were saddling up the horse, a man approached us.

'Edmund,' he said, brow furrowed as he wrung his hands in front of him.

Edmund turned and grinned at the stranger. 'Ben,' he said. 'What brings you here?' Then Edmund stopped smiling. 'Is my father still not recovered? Is he worse?'

The man, Ben, placed his hand on the boy's shoulder. 'He's gone, Edmund. The sickness took him. We buried him beside your mother.'

Ten minutes later, Edmund and I waited at the rear of Norton's group, my horse tied to the back of the forge cart. The boy had not cried. He had not followed the man called Ben back to the village. He had continued with the job we had started and not spoken at all. Ben told me he was a neighbour to Edmund's father and had thought it best to let the lad know. They could not delay the burial for fear of contagion. All I could think about was how I had felt when my father died. Edmund would need time. He would talk to me when he was ready. I was more than a little sad that I could not ride out with Master Markenfield instead of having to travel at a snail's pace with the forge and the oxen.

Catherine

Rippon, Yorkshire, Saturday 15th November 1569

I OPENED THE SHOP as usual. The apprentice, John, was keen to help me until he was needed for the march. At thirteen years, he had learned how to shoe horses, fashion bits and stirrups, and make a set of iron spurs. It would not be long before he would return to his own family, who owned the silversmith's across the market-stede. Robert had been wise to offer John an apprenticeship in return for instruction for himself in working silver. Four years on, and her husband was now benefiting from learning such a skill. Trade was brisk, and time passed quickly as men from outlying villages and farms flocked into Rippon to serve their masters. The earls had promised good money for their services, and they were in high spirits. The Unicorn and one or two alehouses were also doing profitable business, and some travellers had set up stalls to sell their wares.

At noon, I fetched John a bowl of pottage and a trencher of bread. 'It should be quiet at this time,' I said, 'but you must call for me if the need arises.' Glad to go back behind closed doors and away from prying questions about Robert's absence, I slumped down at the table and toyed with my meal. It was difficult to eat when all I could think about was whether Robert was safe. People had even asked me if it was true. Had Harry's father been left to die? What would happen to my friendship with Bridget? A rush of anger sparked inside me knowing Harry had killed everything good in mine and Robert's life. I could not stand by and let him spread such lies about my husband. Grabbing my woollen shawl, I marched back into the shop. 'I will not tarry, John, but I have something to do that will not wait.' I said, leaving John gaping after me. I marched across the market-stede and straight into Harry's shop. No one was working, and the forge appeared to be without fire or flame.

'Harry Gardyner, are you within? I would speak with you at once!' I shouted. There was no reply, but passers-by stopped to see what was happening. 'Harry Gardyner,' I repeated, banging on the closed inner door. 'Hast thou become deaf? I will speak to you before I leave this place.'

The door opened slowly, and Bridget peered through the gap. Her face looked gaunt, and the purple bruising beneath her eyes showed a lack of sleep. 'He is not here, Catherine.' She opened the door wider. 'Will you come inside?' I stepped over the threshold. The small crowd dispersed, whispering and gossiping as they went.

Bridget led me through to the dwelling room. The empty cot, where Harry's mother used to sleep by the fire, had been removed. The room looked sparse without it, and I felt a fleeting pang of guilt for not having been there for Bridget. I turned to the woman who had been a dear friend for all of my married life.

'Where is he? How could he betray us so?'

Bridget looked to the earthen floor. 'It was his mother. She said terrible things about Robert's father. Harry was so angry, his mind full of grief. He believed all she said.'

'And you? What do you believe?' I waited for some word that might make things easier between us.

'I do not know. Who would tell a falsehood on their death-bed?' Bridget looked at me, her eyes pleading. 'What must

I believe then? That someone would sell their soul and risk staying in purgatory for all their afterlife?'

I had no answer. What Bridget said made sense. It would be foolish to do such a thing. Did that mean Harry's mother spoke the truth? It would destroy Robert's memories. Destroy all that he thought he knew about his father. Slumping down onto a wooden bench, I put my head in my hands.

Bridget placed her hand on my shoulder. 'Dearest friend, have faith in that I would never betray you. Harry has not returned from York. I fear he has taken up arms for the queen. We both have reason to fear for our husband's safe return.'

I reached up for the warm, familiar hand resting on my shoulder, covering it with my own. I could not help but take comfort from my oldest friend. What purpose would it serve to be enemies? I thanked God we still had each other. None of this was Bridget's doing. We must help one another through these dangerous times.

Robert

Northallerton, Yorkshire, Monday 17th November 1569

WE MARCHED THROUGH DARLINGTON and Richmond, celebrating Mass, gathering more troops as we travelled. As we entered each town and village, I travelled with the horsemen to help empty churches of all heretic symbols and participate in each Mass we held for the locals. They cheered us on at every stop, men and women eager to help, desperate to return to the old ways. Westmorland always ensured a contingent of men to guard each town as we moved on. By the time we left Richmond, our throng had numbered over 6,000 men and 200 or so women. Edmund and I brought up the rear alongside carts of flour for bread, vegetables, cured bacon, salted beef, casks of ale and several rolled-up canvas tents for the earls and gentlemen.

That night we made camp on the fringes of Northallerton, and I fired up the forge in readiness to make new shoes for the horses. Edmund worked hard, pumping the bellows, and stoking the fire, so it would remain hot enough for forging. There was no need to repair any weapons as so far they had been little used. Watching Edmund made me imagine what it would be like to have a son working alongside me, remembering my father working late into the night to fulfil orders. I dug the soft pads of my thumbs into my eyes. Dear God. Why can I not remember without bawling like a baby? And now, I cannot believe Harry has betrayed me. This pained me just as much. Surely, he cannot believe what his mother told him. Was not my father the kindest he could be to them both? Indeed, while growing up, he had shown more patience to Harry than to me – his own son. I had not minded. I had been sorry for Harry's loss.

When the shoeing was done, Edmund and I joined the other carters at one of the many fires around the camp. They offered us beer and bowls of steaming-hot pottage as we listened to stories and tales of other marches told by older men who had taken part. I wondered whether to ask if anyone had known my father, yet something held me back. The reason was not apparent to me, but there was a slight churning in my belly as a faint memory flitted across my mind: my father kneeling, head in his hands and crying. Where did that come from? I could not fathom what it meant as I tried to hold on to the vision. Somehow, I knew it was important.

One day, many years after the Pilgrimage of Grace, my father had gone hunting alone. He had gone before dawn and asked me to take care of the shop. Harry had moved out to his own premises across the square by that time, having completed his apprenticeship and earned his guild papers. Father had seemed lost in his thoughts for days and left me to run our shop without him. Although I sensed he was down in spirit, I had relished the responsibility. A day's hunting would do him much good, my mother had said, but when father had not returned in the evening, she worried. We sat up all night, but he still had not come home by daylight. I went to find Harry and asked other townsmen for help, searching, setting off in pairs to cover more ground. There was still no sign when Harry and I got back as the sun was setting. Mother was pale and tired, kneeling on the floor praying before our little altar. Her eyes looked red and sore; tears had dried on her face, leaving trails down her cheeks. I took her hands and pulled her to her feet.

'They will find him,' I had said, making myself believe it as I held her close. An hour or so later, there was a knock at the door. Harry went to answer, and one of the men who had been out searching was standing on the threshold, head bowed, felt cap in his hand. He asked Mother to come outside where they could speak to her privately. She told Harry and me to stay inside, refusing to let us hear the news. I did not understand and argued, but she was firm, and the two men also insisted we do as she had asked. When Mother came back inside, she was trembling. She would not speak of it, saying that Father was dead and that was all there was to it. She would not say how he had died, where his body was. Nothing. It was not until one night a few weeks later, after incessant questions from me, that she snapped and said there had been signs of plague on his neck and he needed to be buried quickly. There had been no service at the church because it was too dangerous.

'Please. Can we?' Edmund's voice penetrated my thoughts.

'What's that?' I tried to concentrate.

'Can we walk about the camp? There is much to see.'

'Aye. When we have eaten.' I looked about the men around us and smiled, listening again to their tales.

Having sated our hunger, we set off on our stroll. Edmund's eyes were bright with wonder as he looked about him. Men and women were gathered in groups – pennants raised to show who their masters were. Older women cooked food while the younger women danced and sang. More than a few men were eager to snatch them up and carry them away to the surrounding woodland. Some men were unmarried, but many gandermooners were making the most of a wife's lack to keep them warm at night. Since marrying Catherine, it had never crossed my mind to betray her in such a manner. I turned Edmund away, and we moved on through the centre of the camp where Westmorland, Northumberland and other men of high status sat outside their colourful marquees eating at tables while servants dashed back and forth. The priests had set up camp at the edge of the throng. All Edmund and I could see was a brown huddle kneeling in prayer, many bald pates reflecting the dancing flames of the firelight. Even though we showed irreverence by laughing at the sight, the low murmur of their chants was soothing to hear.

Edmund asked me if he could spend some time with the horses.

'I would like to help the ostlers groom and feed them,' he said. 'Chestnut will be missing me.'

'Chestnut?'

'Oh.' He looked sheepish. 'Your horse. You did not tell me his name. I call him Chestnut. His coat shines so.'

I laughed. 'Chestnut is a good name. I like it.'

Edmund let out an enormous sigh – obviously relieved I was not angry with him. I agreed he could go and told him to head straight back to the forge cart when he was done. When he had gone, I walked over to watch the harquebusiers. Their weapons fascinated me, and I longed to know how they worked. One man let me clean his harquebus, but I could not charge or fire the lethal weapon. The man explained that the horses were skittish enough during the day, and a shot in the dark would set them into a panic. He said he and his comrades were under strict orders not to use the weapons unless necessary. When sent out on skirmishes, their mission was to rout out gentlemen, local landowners and yeomen who were loath, or most likely too scared, to join them.

The man laughed. 'We need only to point the guns to change the doubters' minds. Sometimes they come voluntarily, sometimes without a say in the matter.'

On my way back to the forge cart, I stopped to watch Master Thomas laughing at Richard Norton, who was staggering and swaying about with a sword in his hand. It made me smile. Other gentlemen joined them at their table, a few that I had not seen before tonight. They were all merry indeed and falling about with laughter. A young serving girl, who looked no older than Edmund, came by. She tried to pass the drunken men, but one of them grabbed her arm and pulled her close. He was a large man with broad shoulders, long greying-black hair, and a beard. He wore a silver-grey doublet, matching paned slop with gold lining, hose, and a grey velvet cap – obviously someone of great wealth. The girl screamed, but the man silenced her, planting his mouth against hers. She looked like a tiny bird in his grasp. I turned to see my master's reaction, but he did nothing to stop the brute. In fact, he and the other men were urging the man on and banging their pewter cups on the table. The girl struggled but could not escape. Norton stopped his imaginary sword fight and looked over at the struggle. He grinned, saying, 'Beware, Shinclyffe. Your wife will have much to say at your antics.'

I hurried over. As I tapped the man's shoulder, he turned to face me while still holding tight to the girl. He was taller than I had imagined from afar. 'Sir, I think the maid is too young,' I said. 'Her mother is waiting for her.'

The man stared down at me; his charcoal-coloured eyes were flashing. 'Away, churl. Mind your business here.'

I pleaded with him again. 'She can be no more than eight years, Master. She cannot—' A fist hit me full in the face, and I found myself on the floor.

'Know your place, churl. Get back to your own business,' said the man, staggering as he looked down at me. The girl broke free and scampered away into the darkness. Scrambling to my feet, I looked to Thomas, but my master turned his back and continued drinking and laughing. Dusting myself down, I walked away, my fists clenched at my side. Laughter chased after me. I could hardly see my way for the fury in my head but knew it would mean certain death to strike a man of that standing. My face burned with embarrassment.

Edmund was already curled up and fast asleep when I got back to my hearth. I sat by the fire until I felt more in control. I had never seen the man before, and I was sure he had not been on the march before today. Norton seemed to know him. Perhaps he was local to Northallerton. I would not forget this night. How could my master allow this to happen? I sighed, grateful at least that the child had escaped. I crawled under the cart to lay beside Edmund, watching the boy's chest rise and fall a while before turning over and closing my eyes. A few minutes later, Edmund shuffled closer and put his arm around my waist. Despite my foul humour, it made me smile. The boy did this every night. 'To gain some extra warmth', he always said, but I knew the boy was afeared of the dark and what might be out there in the forests.

Catherine

Markenfield Hall, Yorkshire, Tuesday 18th November 1569

IT WAS LATE MORNING, and the air was chill when I pulled on the reins, bringing Mutton to a halt. Bridget and John were sitting beside me at the front of the cart. Rippon had begun to burst at the seams with volunteers, beggars, and chancers as word had come that the earls were less than a day's march away. I found the town watchmen and paid them to watch over the shop while I was away, offering them half payment now and the balance when I returned. They knew Robert well and were happy with the arrangement, understanding the balance of monies would be honoured. I did not think it safe to leave Bridget there on her own, and John's parents had already left by the time he had helped me load the cart. The early fog had lifted, and a pale-yellow sun shone over the fields around Markenfield Hall and village. A sea of people, campfires and tents, horses, and wagons were all laid out before us. The sight was like nothing I had ever seen before.

'There are many times more people than I saw at the muster in York,' I said. 'It is good to see such support for the master.'

We had drawn up near to families we recognised as being from Rippon. It would feel safer among familiar faces. Having brought enough food, blankets, and goods such as would fit on the cart, I jumped down to unload the kindling. John and Bridget were still gawping at the vast scene in front of them. 'Bridget, you find some stones to mark out the fireplace,' I said. 'John, can you unload some logs?' We set to, and I took out a large iron pot and a tripod.

Within a couple of hours, we had set up camp, and the iron pot was bubbling with a thick pottage flavoured with strips of bacon rind. When we had finished eating, I noticed John shading his eyes as he looked out across the fields.

'I wish to see if my parents need any help to set up camp, Mistress. Is it well that I go?' he asked. 'I will not tarry.'

'It is well. They will be glad to see you. You may return this evening when Robert arrives with Master Markenfield.' I hoped the apprentice would not have to search among the army of people for too long before finding his family.

Bridget sat quietly by the fire, head in her hands, shoulders hunched over. She had barely touched her food. I was worried about her and, after laying some blankets down under the cart, went and sat beside her. 'Tell me what troubles you.'

'Our neighbours' tongues are wagging,' she said, nodding at a nearby campfire. 'They know what Harry did.'

Putting my arm around Bridget's shoulder, I hugged her close. She was too thin, her bones hard under my hand. 'Let them wag. You are not to blame for your husband's doings. The gossipmongers will soon have someone else to satisfy their idle talk.'

'What of Robert? When he returns, he will not want me here. Methinks I should leave now.' Bridget's eyes glistened, and she wiped them with her sleeve.

'Robert will understand. He knows I could not leave you alone back there. Lie down under the wagon. Try to rest.'

Sitting beside the fire and thinking about all that had happened in the past few days, I realised Master Thomas's wife, Lady

Isabel, might puzzle on her steward Samuel Fenton's whereabouts. He was most likely still with Harry at York, where I followed them and saw them report Robert to Sussex and The Council. My mistress needed to know of his betrayal, so I decided to go to the Hall. Before leaving, I went over to where Bridget was resting under the cart. 'Try to sleep. I will not be long.' For now, it would be better not to make Bridget privy to all my intentions.

Making my way up the road until I reached the Hall's outer gate, I told the armed guards on duty that I had important news for their Mistress. One of the guards took my name and told me to wait there until he brought an escort. He disappeared across the courtyard and into a door at the far end. I waited, looking through the open gate. At last, he came out with another man. My breath stopped short. It was Samuel Fenton, and he was looking directly at me. I felt sick, unsure of what to do. I hurried off the road and in amongst the campers. My heart raced as I threaded my way through them, tripping over everything in my haste, all the time praying he would not find me. A hand grabbed my shoulder. 'No. Let me go,' I squealed, shaking myself free before facing my captor. 'John. Oh, John. Thank the lord.' As I leaned against the young apprentice, my heart raced.

John stepped away and held me at arm's length. 'What is it, mistress? What has happened?'

I realised John's mother and father were sitting on a log and staring at me in disbelief. I lowered my gaze, flushing. My heart was still racing as John's father got up and took me by the arm. He was a small man with a thin frame and chicken-like legs. The gentle fingers holding on to me were long and delicate and perfect for a silversmith.

'Come, Goodwife Gray. Sit down here with us and tell us what has happened.'

Doing as I was told, I sat beside the silversmith's wife and tried to stop my body from shaking. My breathing was quick and short, and I knew I needed to slow it down else I might bring on a seizure. Goodwife Smythe was a thickset woman with broad shoulders and heavy arms. I could see that John favoured his mother in build.

I glanced this way and that, but Samuel Fenton was nowhere to be seen. Lowering my gaze, Robert's words of warning came back to me. *You must be careful whom you speak to from now. Do not trust anyone.*

Taking a deep breath, I spoke carefully and cautiously. 'I am most sorry for causing you alarm,' I said, looking up at John. 'I…I went for a stroll and…I got lost. Forsooth, I knew not where I was and did panic trying to find from whence I had come.'

'You must calm yourself, Mistress,' said John, looking worried. He had witnessed my seizures before. 'I shall escort you back to your camp.'

'No. It is most kind of you, but your own family needs you now.' I stood and brushed down my skirts. 'If you could give me guidance as to the way back to the road, I will be fine.' I looked to John's parents, still conscious of how they had regarded me when I fell into John's arms. 'Your son does you credit. My husband says he will be a fine spurrier and blacksmith. Your investment in his apprenticeship will be repaid aplenty when he comes home for good.'

I set off back down the road, hurrying along, desperate to get back to Bridget. More carts and families on foot were arriving all the time. As I pushed and weaved my way past them, a hand grabbed my arm. Spinning around, I looked directly into Samuel Fenton's eyes.

'Thought you had lost me?'

The panic rose in my chest as I tried to break free of his firm grasp. I twisted and pulled, but it made the skin under my sleeve burn with pain. 'Let me go. I will scream.'

The clatter of cartwheels, wagons, men on horseback and travellers drowned out my cries for help. The crowds forced their way past, jostling us both, but Samuel held on to me. No one seemed to notice my predicament. Everyone was too busy trying to find a place to camp. He pulled me to one side, leaning into my face, teeth brown and breath sour. 'Why did you run from me?'

'You are mistaken. I did not run,' I said, frantically searching my mind for what to say next. 'I had business with my apprentice and his family.'

'Do not take me for a fool, witch woman. You were here to tell Lady Isabel you saw me in York.'

Staring him full in the face, I snapped back at him, 'Then better you leave this place before you are found out.'

He laughed, grabbing my patch and ripping it away. 'They would not believe you, a healer, an ugly witch with only one eye. I have already informed my mistress of your husband's betrayal.' He pulled me closer and whispered into my ear. 'I enjoy holding on to a woman with spirit. I could kiss you now if I wished. Gray would be pleased to hear his wife has been much entertained in his absence.' He raised my chin with his free hand, forcing me to look at him. 'What say you?'

I felt a sudden rush of fear as my head swam. It was a seizure coming on. Not now. Please, not now. I shook myself to ward off the feeling.

'How dare you?' I glared at him, my jaw set in defiance, and my teeth clenched. Inside, I was shaking with fear but determined not to let him see it. I would have spit in his face had my mouth not been so dry.

He smirked and let go of me. 'Go to your dear friend, Mary,' he said. 'Harry will be heartily glad to know Bridget is in your good care, sitting alongside the son of his father's murderer.'

'How—'

'I have my spies. Mayhap, Goodwife Gardyner is one of them.'

Samuel pushed me back into the crowd, and I tripped, landing in a heap. Yelping, I curled myself into a ball and tried to fend off the many feet that kicked and trampled their way over me. My body jerked violently as I sank into oblivion…

The bird was chasing me. I covered my eyes so he could not peck them out. I screamed and screamed and screamed.

When I came to, I was lying on the grass. A young woman, carrying an infant on her hip, was kneeling over me.

'Do not move. You were knocked down, and I asked someone to carry you here. I could not wake you.' She was staring at my cloudy eye. 'I recognised what was happening to you. My mother used to shake and disappear into a world not of this earth. I could not bear to see you trampled so.'

I was dazed but managed to whisper a thank you. I tried to stand. She offered me a hand, pulling me back up onto my feet. She was still staring at my eye, so I covered it with my hand, thanking her again for her kindness. Stumbling back to where Bridget still lay asleep under the cart, I slumped down by the fire, rubbing my arms and legs. My entire body ached, and when the baby kicked inside me, I winced in pain, knowing I would be full of bruises tomorrow. The family at the nearby hearth were staring, so I raised myself and took my knapsack from the cart, delving inside to find a spare eye patch. My mind grappled with what Samuel had said. Could it be that Bridget was Samuel's spy? Willing to report everything she saw and heard to Samuel?

Later, as the daylight disappeared, Bridget and I ate our supper. We were quiet, lost in our own thoughts. I had tried to behave kindly towards my friend when she had awoken and come to sit beside me, but Samuel Fenton had left me full of suspicion. Could Bridget be a spy? If Harry was capable of treachery, surely his wife must be as true to him as I am to Robert. Mayhap that is why she cries so and cannot eat. Her guilty soul must trouble her.

'Do you miss him?' asked Bridget.

'What?' I stared at her in disbelief, the bitterness in my voice choking me. 'I miss him more than I can say. Harry's betrayal has caused this. I would never have thought Harry so cruel.' Bridget sniffled again. I wanted to slap her. What right had she to feel sorrow? 'Who are you crying for? Is it the husband that turned his back on us? On you?'

'Please do not be angry with me, Catherine. I cry for you. For the shame Harry has brought on all of us.'

'I hope you speak the truth. I could not endure more betrayal.'

The sound of riders coming along the road brought everyone to their feet. A horn heralded a vast army, led by the pennants of Westmorland and Northumberland. A great roar went up as we all rushed forward to greet our leaders. I tried to get to the side of the road but was pushed and jostled amongst the crowds. There was no way for me to look for Robert in this melee, and I sat down at the hearth again.

The riders headed straight up the road and across the moat into the Hall yard. Some of the men on foot and several horsemen split up and filled up even more fields about us. It took a long time before the carts and oxen had rattled past, carrying their goods. By that time, everyone had gone back to their fires to prepare for the coming night. Bridget and I were making up beds when a cart pulled up on the side of the road.

'Catherine.' Robert's voice came to me, and I was immediately on my feet, dashing toward him, trying hard not to cry out in pain.

'Robert. Oh, Robert!' I cried, throwing myself into his arms, clinging to him as if I would never let go again.

He kissed my hair as I breathed in his musky scent. His lips brushed my wet face, lingering on my lips. 'I've missed you, my love. Are you well?' he murmured. A shiver ran through me as he lowered his head to kiss my belly and asked. 'And you? Are you still thriving in there, little one?' He threw his arm around my shoulder, stifling a wince as the pain shot through my bruised body.

We sat down by the fire, hugging each other warmly, lost in our embrace. When I looked over Robert's shoulder, I noticed a boy sitting atop the forge cart. He looked toward me, his eyes wide, his mouth turning up slightly as if unsure whether to smile. 'Who is this, Robert?' I asked. 'Come near the fire, boy, and warm thyself. You are shaking with the cold.'

The boy jumped down from the cart and raced over to the fire, warming his hands before turning his back to the flames and sticking his rump towards the heat.

Robert laughed. 'This is my good friend Edmund. He has come with me to look after the bellows and tend the oxen and my horse. He is a good and brave lad.'

Edmund barely managed a smile as he spoke. 'I will look after your husband, Mistress. He can trust me to watch his back.'

'Thank you, kind sir.' I bobbed my head, covering my mouth to stifle a laugh. 'I say he is lucky to have you then.'

Robert saw Bridget standing at the fringes of the campfire, half in shadow. 'Why is she here?' His eyes flashed as he held me away from him, gripping my arms tightly. I steeled myself against the pain.

'She was alone. The streets of Rippon are rowdy and dangerous. I could not leave her.' I searched his face for understanding.

He relaxed his grip. 'I am not sure.' He was speaking to me, but his eyes were firmly on Bridget. 'There are few people we can trust, Catherine. How do we know who is safe to have near?'

Bridget came closer, her hands held out, palms facing up in entreaty. 'I swear. I will never betray you, Robert, but I will find another fire to bide by if you would but let me stay one more night.'

Robert looked down at me. 'What say you? Do I turn this wife of my enemy out, or do I let her stay one more night?'

I looked to Bridget, speaking stiffly. 'Go to your bed. Robert and I would not turn you away in the dark.'

Robert turned to me and spoke quietly. 'This boy has lost his father, so he will need great care for a while.'

I nodded and gazed at Edmund. *So young to lose a parent.* 'His mother?'

'She died in childbirth,' he said, pulling me closer as if to give some protection. 'You must take great care of yourself, Catherine.' For a moment, I thought he was talking about not trusting the surrounding people, but I realised he was worried about when my time came for the baby.

It was a frosty night, but as we settled down under a wool blanket by the fire, Robert fell asleep almost immediately, Edmund curled up against his back. Sleep would not come for me as I snuggled my back up to Robert's chest, so we were as three ladles cupped together in a drawer. I wriggled even closer, not only for the warmth of his body but for fear of what might happen to us all. If Samuel had been truthful when he said he had told Lady Isabel that Robert was a traitor, the master might have us both hanged or locked away. If I told Robert that Samuel had threatened me, he would most likely go looking for the steward to get revenge. And what about Bridget? Should I believe Samuel was telling the truth about her? Would Bridget pass on information if we allowed her to stay? It was all too much, and I lay awake for a long time.

I must have succumbed eventually because when I awoke, cold and shivering in the early hours, Robert and Edmund had gone. I struggled to my feet, rubbing my aching back and arms as I looked around, my breath curling in the misty air. Many people were gathering their night things together, some still sitting and eating around their fires. All about, hushed voices groaned as they struggled through the effects of last night's merrymaking. Mutton had a nose bag on and was busy munching. Robert must have fed him. Wrapping my shawl tight around me, I stoked the fire with kindling, and it was not long before it blazed brightly.

'Robert has gone to the Hall with the boy.' Bridget's voice was soft and hesitant behind me. 'He said he would return as soon as he has his orders but would not have you woken.'

My heart pounded. Would they arrest him? Why had I not told him about Samuel last night? I threw more wood on the fire.

'He did not say whether I should go. What did you decide?' Bridget asked.

I did not turn to look at her lest she see the fear. 'Robert was too tired. We will decide today.' Hoping Robert would return from the Hall soon, I stirred the pottage, waiting for it to heat. My head throbbed. I was too weary of demanding answers from Bridget about what Samuel had said about her yesterday, too tired to talk at all.

When Robert returned, with Edmund in tow, I heaved a sigh of relief. He told me we would not be moving that day, but he would set the forge ready for anyone requiring his services. Robert, Bridget, and I were sitting by the fire to eat while the kiln gained heat. Edmund took his food with him and worked the bellows to hasten the process.

'He is a fine fellow, Catherine. He makes me think how fortunate we would be to have a son like him.' I leaned into his shoulder, relieved to have him beside me again. Bridget sat on the other side of the hearth, waiting, and watching.

'I cannot send her away, Robert,' I said, looking across at Bridget's forlorn face and taking hold of Robert's hand. 'I have something to tell you later, but for now, tell me what was said to you up at the Hall.'

'Only that we are to stay here today. Why? What is it that troubles you?'

'They were as usual about you? The master was kindly?'

'As always. What? Tell me now. You make me afeared.'

I stood up. 'Come. Walk with me.' I took his hand and led him away. As we strolled among the crowds, I asked, 'When you were at Brancepeth, did you tell the master of Harry and Samuel Fenton?'

'I did. He was angrier than ever I have seen before. I think he may kill Harry.'

'What about Samuel? What has he done with him?'

'Ah, well, that is another story. Westmorland did decide to let him be a while. The master sent messages to Lady Isabel while travelling, saying we had little arms and men. It was not so, but we knew Fenton would seek out our missives and feed Sussex the false information. Now we are here and accompanied by such an army he may be dealt with swiftly.'

I knew it was time to tell Robert what had happened. 'I beg you do nothing in haste, my husband, when I tell you what I know of Samuel Fenton.'

'What? Has he harmed you?' Robert pulled me to him. 'I will tear him into pieces. Tell me.'

'I cannot until you give me your word; you must say you will do nothing foolish.'

He stopped in his tracks. 'How can I? If he has done you no harm, I will promise. That is all I can say, but you must tell me.'

I looked to the floor and took hold of the rosary beads hanging from my belt, working them through my fingers. 'It was yesterday… I went to the Hall.'

'Why? What business had you there?' He lifted my chin, his brow furrowed, as he looked down at me.

I put a hand to his face, stroking his cheek. 'I had no word from you. I was afeared and wanted to warn the Lady Isabel of Samuel's treachery. I got only as far as the gate. A guard went to fetch someone to escort me, and – it was Samuel.' I could feel the tension as the muscles tightened in Robert's cheek where I was stroking him. 'I turned away and ran through the crowds, hoping he had not seen me, but he followed.'

'I will kill the bastard.' Robert clenched his fists, his face red. He pulled me closer. 'What did he do to you?'

'Nothing. As I fled, I stumbled across John's camp. His family let me sit with them a while.' Robert's eyebrows raised. 'Do not worry,' I continued, 'I was careful, telling them only that I was lost. I did not mention Samuel.'

'Go on,' he said.

'John showed me back to the road, and I walked along until I found Bridget.'

'That is all? He did not follow you again?'

I knew it was of no use to lie. He needed to know. 'He did follow me. It was before I got back to Bridget. He caught up with me, saying he knew you had gone to warn the master at Brancepeth. He said that Bridget had told him I had followed him and Harry in York, that Bridget was of like mind and was spying for them.'

'Mercy of God. Then why do you let her stay? I shall throw her out when we return.' He marched away from me.

'No, Robert.' I ran after him, catching hold of his sleeve. 'There is more. Samuel said he told Lady Isabel that you were working for Sussex. He says she believes him. She must have told the master by now.' I knew it would be safer to leave out the fact that Samuel had tried to kiss me and thrown me into the crowd.

'What will we do about Bridget? Why do you want her to stay?'

'Because Samuel is probably lying. We cannot trust what he says.'

Robert was silent for a moment. 'I am not sure. I have never willingly been violent towards a woman, but by God, Catherine, it will take all my resolve not to throw Bridget from our hearth.'

I stood on tiptoe and kissed him gently on the lips. 'Mayhap, we should follow the earl's guide and keep our enemy close. We will watch her every movement. Mayhap we might even feign a little kindness.'

Robert put his arm around my shoulder again. 'Mayhap, my wife speaks sense.' He smiled at me, and we made our way back.

Robert and Edmund worked hard at the forge. A long queue of horses waiting to be shod would mean a profitable day. I felt more relaxed now that Robert was back by my side, and Bridget and I wandered around the campsite to listen to travelling minstrels, storytellers, and acting troupes. The entertainers sent boys around their audiences with bowls to collect money.

My mood continued to lift as the day wore on, and it was almost easy to forget that Bridget could be our enemy. I could not help but feel happy for the first time in an age as we fell about laughing at some clownish behaviour from one of the actors.

'It is good to be as normal for a little while,' I said.

'Aye. 'Tis so,' said Bridget. 'I have missed you greatly.'

'There has been so much sorrow these last days. It is hard to bear.' I reached out to her. 'I was lost without Robert. You must be miserable without Harry by your side. Do you know where he is?'

Bridget backed away, ripping off my feigned cloak of comfort in an instant. 'Why do you ask? You do not trust me at all. You wish only to know where my husband bides.'

'No. I swear—'

'Robert has asked you to do this. I will not betray my husband.' Bridget stormed away, leaving me lost for words.

I ran after her. 'Bridget, please. Wait. I did not mean any other than what I said. Please.'

Bridget stopped running; she was weeping. 'I…I do not know who to trust…anymore.'

'I know.' I put my arm about her waist. 'It is the same for me. Come, let us go back.'

We made our way to where Robert and Edmund were still busy. John had joined them and was taking a turn with the bellows. I looked into Robert's eyes, seeing the questions in his gaze. I shrugged my shoulders in answer and set about making a meal for us all. Bridget helped me and was soon chatty and smiling again. It made me wonder if the crying had been false. I hated all this mistrust. Stroking my belly, I told myself it would all be over by the time our child was born.

Thomas Markenfield

STANDING AT THE WINDOW, Thomas watched the rider gallop up the road and in through the gatehouse. Jumping down from his horse, the messenger spoke to the guard. Less than a minute later, the man was standing in front of the gathering.

He bowed to Thomas and the earls before passing the missive to Westmorland.

'Ah. Sussex has sent men to defend Hull and Pontefract.' Westmorland told the company when he had finished reading. 'Gargrave has repaired to Pontefract Castle and is guarding the Aire crossing at Ferrybridge.'

'Then we must attack York post haste while Sussex has fewer men at his side,' said Thomas. 'If we act with speed, it will be ours for the taking.'

Anne agreed. 'Thomas is right. If we can take York, we will have the whole of the north behind us.'

Thomas was grateful to have her as an ally. He loved a woman with strength. A pity his own wife was not as support-ive. Isabel was made from the same mould as her family, the Inglebys. They were all supportive in words, but their deeds belied them. Her family had fled to Knaresborough castle from their home at Ripley, along with several other local landowners, and locked themselves away the night Sussex's pursuivant had paid a visit to Northumberland at Topcliffe. Isabel's father, William Ingleby, said that someone in the village had immediately tolled the bells thinking the pilgrimage had started. So they had repaired immediately to Knaresborough to make a stand against Sussex. Thomas did not believe it. His spies knew Ingleby to be a royalist.

Anne raised her glass of wine. 'Let us drink to certain victory.'

'Victory,' they all chorused, getting to their feet.

Thomas led the way to the small chapel to hold a private service before setting out to Rippon and St Wilfrid's, where they intended to take High Mass for all the rebels.

Catherine

Markenfield Hall, Yorkshire,
Thursday 20th November 1569

THERE WAS EXCITEMENT IN the air. Everyone was getting ready to leave. Most had never travelled further than their own villages before, and it would be a glorious adventure to be told around the fire for many years to come. Priests walked among the people, saying prayers and blessing any who knelt before them.

Bridget and I bundled up the blankets, pots, pans, and leftover pottage, putting it all in the cart. Robert harnessed the oxen to the forge cart, and Edmund harnessed Mutton for me.

Robert pulled out his purse and gave John some coins in payment for the help he had given yesterday. 'We will leave soon. Join your family. You can come and find me when we make camp this evening. There will be plenty of work for you then. You are a good apprentice, John.' He patted the young man's shoulder, and John left.

A great cheer erupted as Richard Norton rode his stallion through the gatehouse and out onto the road. The earls, Thomas Markenfield, and other leaders of the rebellion followed him closely. We watched the parade pass along the road and on towards Rippon.

I noted that Northumberland's wife rode at his side. She looked magnificent in her Murrey-cloth cloak, the shimmer of a silk dress peeking through, her starched ruff lifting her chin high, giving her face a regal frame. Her pale primrose-coloured hair was adorned with a red velvet cap decorated with a thick band of creamy pearls and a web of delicate silver chains across the top. I was drawn to her beauty and stared but was taken aback when she looked down and nodded at Robert before resting her eyes on me. She smiled, so I curtsied and dared to smile back. 'Doth the countess know you, Robert?' I asked.

'We met at Brancepeth when I went to see the master. Methinks she is a powerful woman. I had heard it said the earls did listen and take heed of her when they wrote the proclamation.'

When they had passed, I climbed up onto the cart next to Bridget, ready to set off with the rest of the army. Young Edmund drove the forge cart.

Robert mounted his horse. 'I will see you all in Rippon. We will take Mass together at St Wilfrid's before the day is out.' Smiling, he headed off to join his master.

I could hardly contain myself. I relished attending Mass again. As a young girl, I would go with my mother and father – and my brother Jack, albeit no one ever sat in the same pew as my family. Tears pricked as I remembered Robert and I had gone to visit them the week after the wedding. The sight and stench made us retch. I had wanted to hold my mother, but Robert had stopped me, saying that we too would die of the terrible disease the beggar had brought into the house. For a long time, I had cursed my father for being a kind man, one who could not allow a beggar to pass his home without offering charity, and in doing so, brought death to them all. Later, I had cursed myself for thinking ill of him, for not turning back and warning my family when Robert and I had passed the beggar on the road. The funeral, if you could call it that, was brief, and the bodies cremated before we buried their ashes in a pot in the churchyard.

I still missed them, but smallpox cares not who it takes or leaves behind to grieve. It still claimed its prey occasionally, but only a few. Thinking about the funeral of my family brought Samuel Fenton to mind again. He or the Lady Isobel could not have told Master Markenfield that Robert was a spy; otherwise, he would have been arrested by now. Had Fenton been lying to scare me off? Did that mean he had been lying about Bridget too? Catherine hoped so as she looked at the woman standing beside her. Bridget was smiling and also appeared excited about going to Mass.

Thomas Markenfield

The Road to Rippon, Yorkshire,
Thursday 20th November 1569

THE SUN SHONE, THE trees were cloaked in amber and gold as if a royal procession were passing by. Thomas Markenfield turned to look behind him. The swelling in his chest at the sight of so many men willing to march alongside them made it difficult to breathe. His dreams, since coming back from the Holy Land, had been fulfilled. His Holiness Pope Pious would be amazed and thrilled to see so many of his subjects on the rise. When the Spanish fleet arrived at Hartlepool to join Westmorland's son, Christopher Neville, there would be nothing to stop them. He knew it was vital they took York with speed before the queen's army, heading north, could reach them.

Northumberland and Swinburne were keen to free Queen Mary first. They thought it would add more credence to their cause, they had said this morning, adding that York was vital to their plans, but they would miss their opportunity for freeing the Scottish queen if left too long.

Robert

The Road to Rippon, Yorkshire,
Thursday 20th November 1569

I RODE A FEW lines behind but had seen the look of pride on my master's face when he turned to survey us all. I also relished being part of something so huge and so important. My mother and father had been devout Catholics and their parents before them. I edged my horse forward to ride more closely to Thomas, hoping for an opportunity to speak with him about Samuel Fenton. Going around the edge of the riders in front of me, I tried to find a gap ahead.

Before I could find a way in, a voice yelled at me. 'Get back in line, churl.'

I turned my head as Shinclyffe appeared beside me. He was riding a black stallion that fought against the bit, jerking its head back.

'Get back to where you belong, serf. Who gave you leave to ride with gentlemen?' Shinclyffe was wearing a corselet and a metal helmet. He lashed out at my head with the butt of his dagger.

My hand instinctively went to pull my father's sword from its sheath but instead found myself flat on my back on the ground, winded, my head sore and spinning.

Before I had time to get any thoughts in order, Shincly-ffe dismounted, pulling his sword, and pointed it at my neck. 'Dare to threaten me, churl?' He grinned down at me. 'Ah. The servant who thought to dissuade me from having some entertainment at Northallerton. You have a habit of getting in my way. Mayhap—'

'Shinclyffe. Hold off.' Master Thomas looked down at me from atop his horse. 'This is my servant. I will be the one who decides his fate. What has he done?'

Shinclyffe sheathed his sword. 'The varlet tried to ride in front of his betters. I was about to teach him a lesson.'

'Is it true?' Thomas demanded. 'Get up, Gray. State your business here.'

'Gray, you say? Well, that explains everything,' said Shin-clyffe, leering at me.

I looked at him, mind in a whirl. Why had he said that? What did my name have to do with what happened? For the second time of meeting up with this fellow, I scrambled to raise myself from the dirt. A man of lower status would have found himself unable to rise after attacking me so. It was difficult to temper my rage. 'I was trying to reach you, Master. I have news—'

'Then spit it out, man,' said Thomas. He sounded impatient.

'The news is of a private nature, Master,' I said, finally on my feet. My master tutted loudly.

'Very well. Get to your horse and ride with me a while.' Thomas wheeled his horse about and set off.

I mounted hastily and cantered off behind him, still puz-zling on Shinclyffe's words. His voice still ringing in my ears: *'That explains everything.'*

Having left my master's side, I made my way back to Catherine at the back of the procession and took over the reins. It was late when we arrived in Rippon, and I unharnessed Mutton and tied him up in the yard behind the house and shop. Making space for Edmund and the Oxen, Catherine and I left him to tend the animals. Bridget offered to stay behind and set a fire to make a meal for when we returned from Mass. We hurried through the passageway that led on to the market-stede. The rebels, who had set up camp in surrounding fields, were making their way to the obelisk as instructed by Richard Norton and the earls. The square was so packed we had to inch our way through.

It was impossible to hear what was being said, but the horsemen turned from the square and led us all along Kirkgate and to St Wilfrid's church. The oak doors were wide open, ready to welcome us. The leaders rode straight in. It was not long before we saw a line of people passing heretical prayer books outside, thrown into a heap and set alight. High Mass was being celebrated within the church walls and out in the courtyard and streets as well. Priests walked among those who knelt before them, readily hearing confessions and offering absolution. Women wept with joy to behold the sight.

Along with the mighty crowd who could not enter the packed church building, we were more than happy to kneel there and then on the cold cobblestones to be blessed by many priests that passed our way. The comforting sound of prayers spoken in Latin in the church and on the streets of Rippon made me feel I was finally home. When it was over, we made our way back to the shop. After eating together, we gladly lay down in our own bed. The hessian bag and ticking were still untouched, apart from a few mice that had nested in them, and I was grateful that Catherine had hired the watchmen to make our shop and home secure before she came to meet me at Markenfield. Edmund had bedded down with the horses. He said it made him feel at home, and Bridget had laid a blanket by the hearth. When I took Catherine to me, I was careful not to be too rough because of her condition, even though we were equally desperate and hungry for each other's body. We clung to each other as never before and when we had sated both our needs, fell swiftly into a deep sleep.

The following morning, I stayed with Edmund on the forge cart, travelling at the back as the army set out for Boroughbridge. The master had not been best pleased with me for getting myself into trouble with Shinclyffe. I had tried to explain but was shouted down and told in no uncertain terms that I must stay with my own kind when we marched. He did not seem interested in anything I had to say about Fenton.

Thomas's attitude hurt me after all I had done for him. Perhaps Catherine had been right when she said that he had only been kind to suit his own ends. Mayhap it was because my master no longer trusted me. Had he been drawn in by Fenton's lies? Was I being sent back to join my own kind for fear I might pass on information? I did not know which way the wind blew now. The only thing for me to do was to prove my loyalty and once more gain my master's trust. In the meantime, I would stay at the rear and avoid any more face-to-face contact with Shinclyffe. I did not know the man, but it was plain he knew who I was. I was still puzzling over what he had said to me as I lay in the dirt on the road to Rippon. I needed to be wary of a man like Shinclyffe. Not only him but perhaps my master too.

Despite my protestations, Catherine had insisted on travelling with me, saying that it was best to keep Bridget close to us both. I had reluctantly agreed as I could see Catherine was tiring quickly with the baby growing so well inside her. I thanked God she had made it thus far into the pregnancy without problems. I would like it to remain that way and would let her stay with me a short while longer. It was a hard choice.

I did not want her caught up in any violent skirmishes: nor did I want her alone when her time came.

The day was cold and wet, the wind blowing down from the north as we rumbled along the roads in line with many other carts. The excitement of yesterday washed away in the deluge. The thought of coming days or perhaps even months of endless marching in such conditions numbed the chatter and laughter amongst the men that trudged along beside us.

The townsfolk came out to greet us at Boroughbridge, eager to show their loyalty. Though we had not travelled far, we held a Mass for the locals. The earls and leading gentlemen retired to a large marquee, presumably to discuss their next move and eat dinner. A small contingent of men arrived back in the camp. I heard they had been on a scouting mission to York and watched as they were shown into the marquee.

After settling the oxen and horses, Edmund and I went with Catherine and Bridget to the stables, where I had purchased my extra horse on the day Catherine and I had returned from York. I asked the owner if the women could stay the night with him and his wife. He was most happy to oblige, he said, and I thanked him by offering a haunch of the pig I had slaughtered and cured a couple of weeks ago. Edmund and I left the women there and went back to set up a hearth.

A short time later, it appeared the earls had finally come to a decision. Westmorland sent messengers around the site.

One of them arrived to talk to the carters on the fringes of the camp. Edmund and I, along with the rest of them, huddled close to listen to the news. The rain had finally stopped, and it was a clear but cold night.

The messenger stood by the nearest fire and spoke as loudly as he could.

The Earls of Westmorland and Northumberland, along with other leaders of this pilgrimage, hath decided that York is now too well defended to risk an attack despite much discussion. Royal troops, too many in number, are moving north and will be upon us in a few days. Therefore, it is decided that our main objective is to free Mary, Queen of Scots, from captivity in Tutbury. With that in mind, we will set forth at dawn.

We were all a little surprised at this decision but glad we would soon be a part of giving the good and rightful queen her freedom and accompanying her to London. I went back to the stables to let Catherine and the others know what was happening.

Catherine wanted to walk about, so I took her back to where Edmund kept the fire going. I was glad that Bridget had opted to stay with her hosts, and even though I wanted Catherine to myself a while, I could not find it in my heart to object when Edmund asked if he could accompany us. We wandered around the camp, greeting friends and neighbours and swapping stories. It almost seemed like we were a family out for the evening as we chatted merrily to everyone, making sure Edmund was introduced and welcomed at each hearth, and telling of our hopes for the new baby when it arrived.

As we approached the well-lit area where the pilgrimage leaders had pitched their tents and marquee, we stopped to watch the staff and entourages bustling about bringing food and drink. We marvelled at the entertainment, the dancers, jugglers, jesters, and musicians. The earls and their wives were at the centre, firelight making their faces glow with warmth and gaiety. Thomas Markenfield sat close by with Richard Norton and many others in their fine clothes. Because we were enjoying the spectacle so much, we lingered awhile. My master was laughing, giving me hope that the night's company would see him in a better mood the next time we crossed paths. A steward came out of one of the nearby tents, holding a tray of pewter mugs, and stopped in front of Thomas, blocking my line of sight. When the steward moved on to serve Richard Norton, I stiffened, my hand squeezing Catherine's forcefully and making her squeal. She looked up at me before following my gaze. In the full light of the fire, Samuel Fenton was conversing pleasantly with Thomas and Richard Norton. Fenton seemed to be totally relaxed in their company. We turned to leave, not wanting the master to see us.

'Good eve be with you, Goodman Gray.'

Catherine and I turned to see Countess Anne walking towards us. Edmund and I bowed, and Catherine curtsied as best she could.

'My lady, good eve be with you,' said Robert.

'You must be Goodwife Gray,' she said, turning to Catherine. 'I see you carry good tidings with you on this long journey.'

'Yes, my lady,' Catherine responded, keeping her head bowed.

Anne approached her, and Catherine looked up. The countess was smiling. 'You have the strength to care for your husband through many long winter days?'

'I do, my lady,' said Catherine, holding her belly and looking straight into the grey eyes of Anne.

Anne smiled. 'When is the child due?'

'Not until after the Epiphany of our Lord, my lady. Mayhap even later in January. It is difficult to be exact.'

'Come to see me before we leave in the morning. I have a proposition for you.' Anne walked away, back to her husband.

Catherine and I watched her go. It was not until Anne had reached Northumberland that we realised that many of that company were looking at the two of us. Among them, I could see the sneering face of Samuel Fenton. Standing next to the steward was Shinclyffe, who, grinning from ear to ear, raised his pewter mug to me before taking a large swig of its contents.

'Who is that man?' asked Catherine.

'That is the devil who knocked me from my horse on our way to Rippon yesterday,' I answered curtly.

'There is something dangerous about him,' she said, watching him all the while. 'I sense an evil spirit.'

'Of that, I can but agree,' I replied. 'We must be wary of him. He said he remembered my father's name yesterday. It was not in the manner of someone pleased to be reacquainted with such a name.'

I guided Catherine to the stable house before Edmund and I went back to our hearth and bedded down for the night. I could not help but wonder what sort of proposition the countess might have for Catherine. It took me a long time to drop into a light sleep.

Early the following morning, I collected Catherine and Bridget from their lodgings along with the horses, carts, and oxen. Asking Edmund and Bridget to make ready for leaving, I took Catherine's hand, leading her over to the marquee where Northumberland and his wife had spent the night. Catherine seemed a little nervous, her hand clinging to mine. She stopped and looked up at me, nervousness plain on her face.

'Why do you think she has need of me?' she said. Looking down at the swell of her belly, she added, 'I have not slept well, wondering what help I could be to her?'

I smiled and retook her hand. 'I am sure there must be some special need she has of my beautiful wife…as long as it includes nothing that might cause harm to you or our baby.' I brought her hand to my lips and kissed it before leading her on.

It was busy as staff were loading Northumberland's goods in readiness for the march ahead. Countess Anne was fully dressed, but her handmaid, a rotund girl with plump red cheeks, was still putting the finishing touches to her hair.

'Upon my word, have a care,' she snapped at the maid, taking the comb from the girl and throwing it to the ground. 'You would tear the hairs from my head; you tug at it so.' Without another word, the countess clapped a hand over her mouth and dashed away.

Catherine looked at me and smiled. 'I have some notion of what she may need from me.'

I had a similar thought at precisely the same moment. I squeezed Catherine's hand.

We waited until Anne returned and approached us, wiping a lace handkerchief across her mouth. A slight odour of vomit hung about her, interspersed with the heady scent of lavender.

'My lady,' said Catherine, lowering her head and curtseying.

Anne signalled for us to follow her.

Once inside the marquee, Anne settled herself on a chair. 'You may have realised my condition, Goodwife Gray. One always recognises a fellow sufferer.'

'Yes, my lady,' said Catherine.

'I would you consider attending me on this march. I am told you are a healer.' She stared at the patch over Catherine's eye. Catherine instinctively put her hand to the patch. 'Do not fret. I do not listen to tales. I have need of your healing services. My maid has little clue of how I must be feeling and has no experience in the trials of carrying a child. You, on the other hand, could provide a sympathetic and a gentle touch.' Anne turned her attention to me. 'What say you, Goodman Gray? Would it be to your approval?'

Catherine let go of my hand and took a step forward. 'I would be honoured to help you, my lady. My husband has no reason to object.'

My cheeks burned. I disliked Catherine being so outspoken in the company of others. 'It is good to know my wife is held in such favour,' I said, grabbing Catherine's arm and pulling her close. 'I give my permission on the understanding her duties may only be light in her condition, my lady.'

Anne smiled. 'Of course, Goodman Gray. You have my word.' Turning to Catherine, she added. 'Come to me this evening when we make camp. You may travel with your husband during the day.'

I marched away. Catherine had embarrassed me in front of the countess. My head was thick with anger when I turned back to see Catherine running behind me. She stopped and put her hand to her breast, obviously out of breath. It made me feel guilty, and I walked back to wait until she was ready to move on.

'You are acting like a child,' she said when she could speak again.

'And you are acting as a single woman. You showed me no respect in front of the countess,' I flung back at her.

'And you show me none when you talk as if I am one of your chattels.' Angry tears were trickling down her face.

I gave in immediately and pulled her close. 'Come. Do not cry. You know I am undone when you cry.' I kissed the crown of her head, desperate to soothe her as she settled into my chest.

We made our way back to Edmund and Bridget, who had packed everything well and were waiting on our return. I helped Catherine up onto the cart before taking my place next to Edmund.

It took over two hours for everyone to get on the road south towards Wetherby. With every mile passed, another fifty men would tag along carrying any sort of weaponry they could muster: daggers, pikes, bows. Many were from the local villages and towns of Claro Wapentake, such as Knaresborough, Sawley and Burton Leonard. By the time Catherine and I reached Wetherby, the speeches were over. Crowds gathered for what seemed like miles along both sides of the river. I could not see the earls at first and realised they must be inside the bridge chapel. I finally caught sight as they came out and mounted their horses, leading a parade through the streets.

Everyone had followed them except for the carters who were unharnessing oxen and horses, then guiding them down to the water to drink. Catherine took Mutton, and I asked Edmund to take my horse as I drove the pair of oxen. It was a strain as they snorted and pushed me along, desperate to drink. The water chilled me to the bone as I waded in with them. A strong current dragged at my feet, and it took all my strength not to lose my footing. I shouted to Catherine to stay at the edge and not to let Mutton drag her in.

Around three hours later, we were back on the road and about 8,000 strong. We continued south to Bramham Moor, where we made camp.

Catherine

As soon as I had lit the fire, I asked Bridget to tend to supper while I changed into my Sunday kirtle, the one I had worn on my wedding day. Robert had bought it for me.

I relived the moment we had stood in front of the priest for his blessing. How, when Robert saw me that day, he had kissed my hand and said the blue of the dress matched my eye colour. The kirtle was pleated at the front and fell in folds down to my ankles. Perfect for when I was with child, he had said.

Robert walked me over to where Countess Anne was ensconced. He kissed me lightly on my forehead and whispered how beautiful I looked and how lonely he would be without me to keep him warm. His body heat and the gentle touch of his hand on my breast made me groan with pleasure. Hearing a slight cough, I turned to see the countess watching us. I blushed and pulled away from Robert, putting my hand to my cheek.

'I will take good care of her, Goodman Gray,' she said, grinning widely and waving me over. 'You will survive until the morning without her?'

'Yes, my lady,' Robert mumbled before bowing and taking his leave.

When he had gone, she asked me to help her bathe and change for dinner. I followed her to a separate room in the marquee, where a large mattress was laid down and covered with beautiful, brightly coloured, woollen blankets. There were even pillows to rest a weary head. I wondered what it would be like to sleep in such luxury while on the road. I had not had time even to sew my new mattress. With good fortune, the ticking and feathers would still be there when we finally went home. The maid I had seen the previous evening was laying a dress out on the bed.

'Leave it.' The countess spoke sharply to the girl. 'You are excused. Make yourself useful to the cook from now on.'

The girl curtsied, and, though she did not speak, she turned to me. Her look was defiant, but I saw the hurt on her face as tears brimmed in her eyes. It seemed I had already made an enemy of someone in the countess's household.

'Come along now, Catherine,' Anne said. 'I must not keep my husband waiting. He cannot bear to have to wait for his food.'

I started to undress her, and another servant brought a pot of boiled water in so that I could bathe her with lavender-scented soap and a linen cloth. An hour later, she was ready and dressed in a sage-green dress of the finest wool with a triangular bodice pinched in at the waist. It had taken the longest time to fasten the sleeves she had chosen to complement the dress with the myriad of intricate laces. My chafed working hands fumbled a great deal from nervousness and fear of catching any threads of silk in the cracked skin of my fingers. The over gown was gold and patterned with silk thread, her ruff pure white and holding her chin high to support her long and slender neck. I brushed her hair until it shone, plaited, and pinned it up, and threaded strings of pearls through the soft braids. Finally, I passed her a pomander, which she fastened to her belt. Its sweet fragrance helped to mask any underlying odours in her clothing.

'You have done well on your first night,' she said, glancing at herself in a glass hand mirror. She looked me up and down. 'You'll have to do for now. I will get my previous maid, Margery, to hand you some of her work clothes for tomorrow. I cannot have my maid looking like a farm girl.'

'Yes, Countess,' I mumbled, bowing my head. I wanted to tell her how rude she was. It would hurt Robert to know what she had said. Had I made a mistake accepting her offer?

'See the cook for your supper. I will not need you again until I wish to retire.'

'May I have supper with my husband?' I asked.

'It is not convenient for you to keep coming backwards and forwards. I need you close at hand.' She looked at me and smiled. 'It will be fine, Catherine. I know we will get along well.' She pointed to a small cot in the corner of the room. 'See. You may sleep upon this bed. We will be close enough as sisters, and you will sleep much better here in a warm room. Off you go. I will call when I need you.' She waved her hand to send me away.

I walked away slowly, dreading what sort of reception I would receive from the cook and the other servants. The maid, who the countess had dismissed, would tell them all about the interloper. If the girl disliked me before, she would most likely want to kill me when she had to hand over her clothes.

It was a clear night, and a curtain of stars draped the inky darkness like a black gown encrusted with tiny jewels. The cook and other staff sat around a large fire. A spit was turning above the flames; several fowl skewered along the thin rod. A large cauldron of broth filled the air with the mouth-watering scent of meat bones, parsley, turnip, oats, and carrots. I sat on the fringes of the group, where the cook handed me a bowl of broth and a piece of bread. There was no word of welcome from anyone. The maid, Margery, glowered at me from the other side of the hearth. I decided it was probably best if I kept my gaze lowered. Northumberland and Countess Anne sat at a table close by. Westmorland and his wife Jane, Master Thomas, and Richard Norton joined them. I did not know who the other guests were but assumed, looking at their dress, that they were people of importance. My thoughts drifted as I wished I were back at my hearth when someone touched my shoulder. I startled and looked up. The maid, Margery, was looking down at me.

'Deaf, are ye? The mistress is asking for you.' She jerked her thumb in the direction of the table. 'Better get yer arse over there before she gives you the boot as well.' There was a low rumble of laughter around the fire.

I jumped to my feet, forgetting the bowl on my lap, which now spilt down my dress. I pulled a rag from my pocket and dabbed it, desperately hoping it would come clean. The laughter around the hearth grew louder as I dashed over to where the countess was waiting.

'At last. Fetch me a cloak and be quick. I am feeling a chill.'

'Yes, Countess,' I said and hurried inside the marquee. In the tent's torchlight, I could see the greasy stain all down the front of my dress. Anger rose inside me for being so clumsy. I was now sure I would be sent packing in the morning. The thought made me breathe a little easier. It had been a mistake to accept this position.

When I arrived back at the table with a thick wool cloak for the countess, she was mid-conversation with the men, so I draped it over her shoulders. Not sure what I should do next, I stood quietly at her side to await further instruction.

Westmorland held a piece of paper in his hand and announced that the queen's troops were still far south.

'How can we be sure of its authenticity?' the countess asked Westmorland.

'Our friend at Tutbury is trustworthy. He is the Scottish queen's chaplain and a true papist. I would bet my life on it.'

'Then we must use this opportunity to rescue Queen Mary,' she responded, her hand banging the table. 'This is our only opportunity.'

Master Thomas stood up then, wavering with a drink in his hand. His words slurred a little as he spoke. 'I will go. Who will accompany me?' he said, looking around the table.

'No,' said Westmorland. 'We have armed horsemen sober enough to do the job. I will select them from my soldiers.'

My master looked none too pleased as he scowled and slumped down in his seat.

Richard Norton patted his back. 'Enough time for you to show your worth,' he said in the same slurred way as he poured the master another drink.

I stood by her side for such a long time. She did not look or speak to me. My body ached from the cold; the child in my belly kicked and wriggled in complaint. In my stomach, the rising feeling of being lifted high into the air and dropped warned me a seizure was coming. If only I could lay down, curled up within Robert's broad arms and warm body – I could – 'Catherine. Are you unwell? Catherine.'

I could hear the countess's voice, but I could not see. My head hurt. Someone was carrying me.

'Lay her on the cot – hurry, man. Tell Margery to make her a hot drink. The poor girl is frozen. There now. There. You will be well soon.'

My body was shaking, and there was nothing I could do to stop it. The countess lifted my head while I sipped the fiery liquid. There was a sweet taste of honey, but of whatever else, I could not be sure. I couldn't believe it was Countess Anne herself that was tending me.

'I am sorry, Mistress, let me get up and help you undress.' I struggled to sit up, embarrassed by my position.

'No need. Margery will help me this night. Rest your head until the morrow.'

Needing no more persuasion, I lowered my head and fell into a deep sleep.

I awoke to the sound of voices. The woollen blankets were warm and soothing, so I curled myself up within the folds. It took a few moments to collect my thoughts and work out where I was. I looked across the room to see Countess Anne fast asleep on her bed. Northumberland lay on his back by her side – snoring softly. Inching myself into a sitting position, the back of my head throbbed. I put my hand up and could feel a small lump and what I assumed was dried blood matting my hair. I got out of bed and found I was still wearing my blue kirtle, the stain down the front still making it look like a beggar's dress.

The cook was busy preparing a meal of oats, dried fish, cheese, and bread outside the marquee. She glanced up when I approached.

'I wondered if I might have a little warm water to clean my head?' I asked.

'Sit there,' she said. 'I will tend it when I have a minute.'

I reached down to the log with one hand, lowering my body with care, my other hand supporting my belly as I sat down.

'I can do it.'

I looked up to see Margery. 'Thank you,' I said.

Margery dipped a linen cloth into a bowl of warm water and dabbed the back of my head. It stung a little, but she had a gentle hand. Each time the girl lifted her hand, the cold air spiked against my scalp, making me grateful for each fresh dab of warmth. When she had finished tending my wound, Margery pulled a clean linen coif from her pocket and placed it on my head.

'There,' she said. 'That will keep it warm and dry while it heals.' Her voice was soft and kind – not a bit like last evening.

I still did not look at her. 'I am sorry,' I said.

'For why? I am the one to say sorry. I was unkind when you came.' She sat down beside me as I turned to face her. She was smiling. 'The mistress can be difficult. I do not know why she is so. She was always so kind, and now she shouts and weeps all the time. I do not know how to please her.'

It was not my place to tell her why, but the cook said, 'Are you blind as well as stupid, Margery? The countess is with child. The signs are the same as when she had the girls and that poor dear boy.' She pulled a rag from her pocket and dabbed her eyes. 'He was a grand baby, always smiling until the disease came and took him away. Even before his first year was out.'

'Why? Why did you not tell me?' said Margery. 'I wou… I cou—'

'The countess needs someone who understands,' said the cook. 'That's why she brought yon woman here.'

Margery glared at me. 'Be it true what they say about you?'

'It depends on what they tell you. If they say, I am a healer, it is true.' Her eyes were still fixed on me. 'I am not a witch. I have no powers. It is only the herbs I use that have the power to soothe and heal.'

Margery stood up. 'Anyway, mayhap it is a good thing. I slept well last night. She did not call for me once to make her pillow plump. Now I will not be the girl who has to take away a bowl of vomit this morning. Ah! That is why she is sick. Methought she had a disease. I was afeared I would catch it.'

The cook smiled at me and winked. 'She is very bright is our Margery,' she said. I could hear the slight chuckle in her voice.

Margery looked pleased by the cook's words. She held her hand out to me. 'Come. Let me help you change, and then you can take the mistress a warm drink.'

I reached out to her, grateful for the show of friendship. Perhaps things would be well from now.

A short time later, Margery handed me a mirror. That could not be me – could it? With a frilled collar, the white linen shift was so soft against my skin and the woollen kirtle, open from beneath my breast, was as yellow as a marsh marigold. Margery had pinned my hair back under the coif. Passing me a fresh linen apron, she said, 'This will help keep you clean.'

'I am grateful for your help and kindness, Margery. I will not forget.'

Margery blushed. ''Tis naught. You had better hurry; the countess will be waiting on that warm drink.'

I looked to the cook, who was already passing me a pewter mug of steaming liquid. 'It is herbal. For the sickness.'

I took it from her and inhaled. I had to swallow hard as I tried to push back the involuntary retch. The drink smelled like cow dung and rotting vegetables. It was no surprise the countess was so ill-tempered and vomiting. 'Do you have some dried ginger?'

'Are you ill?' asked the cook.

'No. I find it helps me relax and sweetens my mood during pregnancy.'

'Ha. Yes. I see,' she said, chuckling. 'You may find it useful to get the countess to drink some too.'

'That's an excellent idea,' I replied.

A little while later, I entered the bedchamber. The countess was sitting up in bed while the earl was on his way to break his fast, his manservant having already got him dressed.

'You can throw that disgusting brew away,' she said. 'I keep telling the cook how vile it is, yet she sends it to me every morning. I but catch a scent of it and—'

She leaned over the side of the bed and vomited into the bowl laid on the floor. I put the two drinks down and hurried to her. 'There, there,' I soothed, stroking the tendrils of her hair from her face. 'Soon be over. Soon be done.' It was what Robert always did in the early stages of my pregnancies. His soft voice and soothing hands ever made me tolerate the sickness calmly.

When it had passed, the countess sat up again. 'Thank you,' she said, wiping her mouth.

I retrieved the mug of ginger tea and brought it to her. 'Here,' I said. 'Try this. It will settle your queasiness and calm you.'

The countess sniffed it cautiously and then took a small sip. 'Mmm. Ginger?' I nodded. 'It is good.'

As she raised the vessel to her mouth again, I stayed her hand and smiled. 'A little at a time. Less haste is better.'

She leaned back into her pillows, watching me as I prepared her clothes for the day, occasionally asking questions.

'Have you more children?'

'I have been pregnant before, but with no success. I – that is, we both hope for a boy. A blind woman said my miscarriages were girls, so it is likely that I only give birth to boys.' I turned to hold up a pair of sleeves for confirmation and saw the distress on the countess's face. 'Oh. What is it, Countess? Have I upset you?' I went over to the bed and took her hand. This was not the same woman who took command of the meeting last night.

'My ba— I had a son. Thomas. He did not live long – but long enough to steal my heart.' She began to cry. 'I pray this child will be a boy,' she said, stroking her slightly raised belly.

'I am most sad to hear it,' I said, still stroking her hand. 'And…there are no other children?'

She sniffled and wiped her nose with a lace handkerchief. 'Three silly daughters who scream and shout and argue until my head hurts.' She stared over my shoulder for a few moments before continuing. 'I have sent them to stay at Wressel a while until this pilgrimage is over.' She laughed. 'I have charged my most trusted servants to tend them. They would give their lives in an instant should any be in danger.'

I encouraged her to tell me more about her daughters as it was cheering her mood.

'What are their names?'

'Margaret's the eldest. She is like me. She cannot bear being left out of anything. I pity whoever she marries.' Her voice was light and happy. 'Lucy and Joan adore her but fight with each other all the time.'

I envied her such a large family. Mayhap, if the child I carried survived, there would be more – hopefully, a daughter one day.

The countess was compliant as I dressed her and pinned her hair before escorting her to the breakfast table. A sumptuous array of bread, cheeses, fruit and even some dried fish awaited her. The earl was still eating and drinking as he chatted to a priest who had joined them at the table. It was likely his chaplain. Both men stood as the countess took her seat but slipped back into their conversation with mouths full of food. I stood by her side and waited to be dismissed. My stomach growled loudly enough for the countess to turn to me.

'Away, Catherine. Have your meal, and then you may go to your husband and tell him you will be here with me today as we will not be breaking camp.'

'Yes, Countess,' I said, curtseying and then hurrying over to Margery and cook.

Margery was already laying out my blue kirtle over a bush to dry. Her kindness brought a smile to my face.

'You are most welcome,' she said, smiling.

Anne Percy – Countess of Northumberland

Bramham Moor, Yorkshire,
Sunday 23rd November 1569

ANNE WONDERED ABOUT CATHERINE. She was around twenty years, but her husband seemed much older. Still, what did that matter? Goodman Gray seemed to have chosen well. Plenty of time for her to produce children to carry on his business as he grows old. She smiled, remembering the look on Gray's face when Catherine had answered for herself in taking up this position.

The girl was not afraid to speak her mind, and Anne liked that. It reminded her of herself as a young girl. Anne's father, Henry, the Earl of Worcester, would not know what to do with her when she stood up to him over the slightest difference of opinion concerning politics. He always said it was unseemly for a daughter to behave in such a manner. 'Women and girls should be seen and not heard', he would bellow, but Anne only had to smile at him, and he would relent, clearing his throat and muttering, 'Well…get on with you…can you not see I have important matters to attend', then he would wave her away, and she knew she had won the argument yet again.

Marrying had not changed her; Thomas Percy was as easy to manipulate as her father had been.

Robert

Bramham Moor, West Yorkshire,
Sunday 23rd November 1569

THE LINE OF MEN and horses seemed to get longer. Edmund worked hard feeding the kiln and working the bellows. John worked his way down the line, removing the old or broken shoes from the horses while I hammered out new ones and nailed them on. Shoeing horses was far from crafting beautiful spurs, but it brought coin for food for now, and that was all that mattered. Bridget fetched buckets of water from a nearby spring for dousing the hot metal. I had to admit she was working hard and appeared genuine in her support, but it clearly tired her. I wished Catherine were here, not only because I missed her so, but because another pair of hands would help a great deal. The thought had barely formed in my mind and she was there, looking up at me. One night away, and I hardly recognised her. She wore a yellow kirtle that shone like the sun and made her cheeks look bright and shining. She smiled at me, and I was transfixed. I lowered the horse's foot from between my knees and went to her, my arms ready to embrace. She stepped back.

'Your hands,' she said, holding her palms up to stay me. 'I cannot get my clothes dirty.'

My arms dropped to my sides. She had never turned from me before. 'Catherine?' I wiped my hands with my leather apron and tried again, but she moved backwards as if I had the plague. I felt a sudden rush of anger. 'Too good for me now? One night in good company, and I am nothing?'

'No. Do not be so foolish. It is the countess. She has already had to give me these clothes to wear while I attend her.'

I heard a roar of laughter and turned to see Shinclyffe and some of his gentlemen friends standing and watching Catherine and me.

'Methinks your wife likes much better company than a lowly smith, Gray. Who can blame her?'

I wanted to teach him a lesson. I wanted to flay him with my belt. The blood rushed into my head, pounding and thumping. I could barely see. I made my way back to the forge cart and picked up my hammer.

Shinclyffe drew his sword. 'Ready for another beating? Come,' he said to his companions. 'It is time we taught him a lesson.'

'No!' Catherine stood in front of me. 'Please, Sir. My husband has not threatened you or your companions. He has merely picked up the hammer to continue his work.'

'Catherine. Step aside.' I growled through gritted teeth. How dare she embarrass me this way?

Shinclyffe lowered his sword and doffed his cap at Catherine. 'For you, I would lay down my arms. Only an idiot would resist your words. I would not fancy my chances against a woman with powers such as yours. I have heard you are the daughter of a witch.' I took another step forward as Shinclyffe turned his eyes on me again. 'You had your master to thank for saving you the last time. Now your wife is your bodyguard.' Turning his back, he laughed and walked away with his fellow cronies.

I could not say a word to her and went back to my job. The silence in the line of men, waiting for their horses to be shooed, remained. It was as if someone had struck them dumb. Picking up a bar of iron, I fixed it in a pair of tongs and thrust it into the blazing furnace. The next time I looked up, Catherine was gone.

Around noon, I told the still-lengthening queue we were stopping work for one hour. Bridget had made sure the pottage was ready and waiting for us. My temper still simmered, and I was not in the mood for talking to anyone. I shovelled the food in my mouth, and everyone crept around me for fear I would become angry with them. It was not their fault, and I felt guilty but unable to trust myself enough to speak kindly or even whether I could talk without the anguish I felt about Catherine showing itself in my voice.

When I had finished eating, I left the three of them beside the fire and went for a walk. Catherine had shunned me and then embarrassed me in front of Shinclyffe. Rather, he had killed me than be sheltered by a pregnant woman who was barely a foot taller than Edmund. The entire camp would have heard the tale by now, and I was sure I heard sniggers as I trailed around the hearths, barely looking where I was going. Before I realised it, I had left the camp behind and was walking through the woodland. The beech still held on to their cloaks of yellow and gold, their leaves crunching underfoot. It was peaceful apart from the occasional birdsong. I stopped to listen and was transported back to the times I would go hunting with my father; to a particular day, when I was around six years, that has always stayed clear in my mind. We had gone into the woods to practise archery and spotted some wild boar tracks. Loading our bows, we had followed them. Eventually, we came across a clearing and there they were, a large sow and her piglets. My father put his finger to his mouth and we both pulled our string back hard on the shaft before letting the arrows fly. My father's aim was true, and he downed a piglet. My arrow glanced the side of the sow and dropped limply to the floor. Within a second, the clearing was empty bar the piglet my father had felled. It squealed loudly, like a gale whistling through the roof rafters in a winter storm until my father took out his knife and slit its throat. "Kill only the young, and the sow will keep you fed for many years", he had told me.

I walked on until I felt calmer. I was thinking again about what Catherine had done. She had been so brave. I could not believe she had stood in front of him. Willing to give up her life for me. No. She was a fool. She had put our baby's life in danger too. But she thought she was helping. I turned and headed back to camp; I would go and see her. Talk about it. Make things right again. As I came to the edge of the woods, the trees grew thinner, the grass now soft and long where the sun still found its way to the earth. I was about to step out when I heard voices.

'Take it quickly and tell your friend to ride hard to Bowes.'

I stepped back and tucked myself behind a tree. Peering out, I saw Shinclyffe. He had given a missive to Samuel Fenton, who now ran towards the woods and disappeared into the trees a little further along from where I was hiding.

Shinclyffe looked around and then strolled back in the camp's direction. I turned and went back into the woods, listening hard for the sound of crunching leaves. I moved quickly and soon heard Fenton's boots running. I picked up my pace, knowing that as long as he was moving forward and I kept my distance, he would not hear me following. As the sound of his feet slowed, I paused, waiting until the sound disappeared, knowing he had stopped a little way ahead. Then he moved again. He was coming back towards me. I kept quiet until he had passed and then made my way to what turned out to be the other side of the wood. Looking across the open fields, I spotted a horse and rider in the distance. I could not be sure, but it looked like the rider was wearing a red cap sporting a long feather that pointed up to the sun.

Back at camp, I made my way over to the countess seated at a table alongside her husband, Northumberland. Westmorland and his wife were with them and several other high-ranking men. What to do? Who should I tell? My master had made it quite clear; he was not interested in anything I had to say about Fenton. If I now told him that Shinclyffe was a spy, I would likely get flogged or worse. Who would believe me over Shinclyffe? Where was Catherine? I paced up and down a little distance away until Catherine appeared from within the marquee, carrying a silver cup that steamed in the bright cold air. She placed it in front of the countess, who looked up and smiled at her before cupping it in her hands and sipping it slowly. Catherine then stood behind her mistress and waited. I lifted my hand slowly in hopes that she would see me. She seemed oblivious to her surroundings and stared straight ahead, so I made my way around to her line of sight. Keeping a goodly distance, I stayed there until, eventually, I saw the spark of recognition. I signalled for her to make her way around the marquee and meet me there. She looked over the countess's shoulder and then towards me. I understood she could not move until her mistress had finished the drink. I nodded and made my way around to where we should meet and waited.

It seemed an age before she appeared.

'I am sorry I was so—'

I put my finger to my lips before taking her hand and pulling her further away. 'No matter. Can you walk a little way with me?'

She looked back over her shoulder before turning to me again. 'Only for a short while. The countess will wish to rest soon.'

We walked further away, keeping out of the line of sight. 'I have seen something bad and don't know who to tell. I do not think the master would listen.'

Catherine squeezed my hand. 'What is it? Can I help?'

I looked down at her and smiled. Her beautiful face was lined with worry. I wanted to draw her to me and breathe her in, but I knew it would sully her clothes. The countess would be furious if she appeared with the dirty handprints of a black-smith all over her. The thought of where the handprints would be, made me chuckle under my breath, but this was serious. Catherine listened without interruption as I explained what I had seen.

When I had finished, she said, 'Mayhap, we should tell the countess. She is well heard by the men. They listen when she speaks. What do you think?'

'Would she listen to us…to me?'

'She always seems interested in what I have to say. I will not reveal your business but ask if she would see you privately. I think she would listen, and even if she is not sure about what you tell her, I think she would not betray you.'

'Mayhap, you are right.'

'Robert. This morning – I—'

I put my finger to her lips gently. 'It is of no matter. You thought you were protecting me, lest Shinclyffe put me to the sword. I would rather he had done me ill than you and our precious child were killed. You must promise never to do such a thing again.'

'I promise,' she said. 'I must go before I am missed.'

I watched her hurry away before making my way back to Edmund and John. My customers would likely be queued as far as the eye could see by now.

Catherine

Bramham Moor, West Yorkshire,
Sunday 23rd November 1569

I FINISHED DRESSING THE countess, and she joined her husband for breakfast. Having slept little, I could barely stay awake as I went over to join the cook and Margery. The air was damp with a heavy mist, and my thick woollen cloak soon sparkled in the firelight with beads of moisture. Every sound seemed muffled and low, and I was grateful for the peace as we ate in silence.

My thoughts travelled back to the previous night when the countess had retired from the men. I had asked her if she would see Robert over an important matter. Although she looked pale and tired, she had agreed and asked me to fetch him....

My mistress listened carefully to all he had to say, waiting until she knew everything before speaking.

'This is grave news, Goodman Gray,' she said, looking closely at him. 'Some might say it aggrieves you with the manner he has treated you and would wish him ill. What say you?'

I stiffened at her words. Robert surprised me when he showed no sense of outrage. Instead, he nodded his head and looked the countess squarely in the face.

'I can understand you thinking such, Countess, but I swear to you on the child's life that my wife is carrying what I tell you is true.'

My mistress looked quizzical for a moment and then smiled.

'I do believe you,' she said. 'You came at speed to warn us all at Brancepeth of Sussex's muster at York. You warned us then of Fenton and your supposed friend Gardyner, and so this does not take me by surprise.' Her eyes were red with tiredness as she sank down on the edge of her bed. 'However, your news of Shinclyffe shocks me much. He marched alongside Robert Aske himself during the great pilgrimage of '36. It is hard to believe him a traitor to our cause.'

'It is not my place, but I would hope you think me not too outspoken when I say you should not trust him. He knows my name somehow and seems to dislike me greatly for that alone. I have wondered if it might have something to do with my father, who also marched in the pilgrimage.'

The countess sat quietly for a moment and then said, 'Let me think on it. I will make enquiries about our friend Shinclyffe. We will speak again soon, but now I am tired and must rest.'

Robert bowed, and I went to see if the coast was clear so he might dash away unseen. The men were busy drinking and appeared not to notice as he slipped away into the night......

'Catherine.' A hand shook my shoulder, and I looked up to see the cook with a bowl of oats in her hand. I blinked and realised where I was. I was perfectly dry, but the water from the drizzly air made my cloak heavier by the minute. 'I think you were asleep again,' she said. 'Come now. Break your fast before the mistress calls for you.'

I took the oats and forced them down. My back ached from the weight of the child I carried. I must not complain; the longer he stayed inside me, the more chance he would survive.

I put my hand to the crown of my belly and felt the solid shape of a heel. It kicked me thrice and brought a smile to my face.

We had not long eaten when I heaved myself up and took my place behind the countess. I was about to ask if she wished to rest when there was a disturbance nearby. A few screams shattered the silence, and I could hear the muffled sound of horses' hooves approaching. Someone shouted, 'Make way! Make way!' In full armour and carrying weapons, a small group of horsemen gathered outside Westmorland's marquee and dismounted. The earl welcomed the rider, who seemed to be in charge, inside for a private discussion. Three stable hands led the horses away. The rest of the men made themselves comfortable by the fire, and Westmorland's cook served them hot food and flagons of ale. My mistress and her husband Northumberland hurried over to join them, so I went inside the marquee to dry off and wait for news.

It was not long before the countess was back. She was scowling, her anger plain to see. 'Hurry, Catherine. Pack my clothes. We are in retreat.' Picking up her jewellery, she began throwing pearl and gold necklaces, several pairs of gold earrings, enamelled brooches, and charms into a leather pouch along with her comb, hairpins, and a box of white face powder. What did she mean? In retreat? It made little sense, but, for now, I must do as she says. I opened a large trunk and placed in her nightclothes and the dress and sleeves from last evening. She threw her powder box at me, which I had to grab and hold close for fear it would fall from my grasp. The edges dug into my belly, making me gasp and my baby kick and wriggle. She realised what she had done and put her hand to her mouth.

'Oh, my dear Catherine. I am sorry, as such I can be. Are you hurt?' she asked, coming over and touching my arm.

'It is nothing,' I said, pulling away quickly and continuing my work. There were times I could hate this woman, but I knew only too well how early pregnancy made a person act in a way that made her appear quite mad.

'Forgive me. I am in a sour mood because of the news that has arrived at our laps.'

I stopped what I was doing and turned to her. 'Do not fret. I am made of stern stuff. What is this news that troubles you so?' I asked, even though I knew it was not my place. 'I ask only for fear of it making you ill.'

The countess flopped down onto the bed and put her head in her hands. 'It is the young queen. They have moved her further south. We have no time now to set her free.'

What did that mean? No time? 'What is it that leaves no time?' I asked, praying to be told we were all going home.

'Elizabeth, that evil heretic, has sent an army of over twenty thousand men. They are gaining ground and will be in sight within days. We must retrace our steps and try to gain more supporters.'

When I had finished packing for my mistress, she said I could return to Robert and travel with him until the evening. I changed into my blue kirtle and packed the yellow dress in a small wrap along with my belongings. Tucking the cover under my arm and beneath my cloak, I was ready to go and stepped out onto the now-muddy earth. As I made my way through the crowds, the news she had made me privy to was washing over the camp like a wave. The men who had come back from Tutbury said that Elizabeth had issued a pardon to all those who would return to their lands within three days. Every hearth I passed seemed to talk about it. Many grumbling that the money promised by the earls had still not materialised, so why should they remain loyal?

Others believed it would come when all the fighting was done. Many had already decided they had travelled more than they ever wished. Women prayed they would make it home before the queen's army caught up with them. There were men desperate to tend to their animals and winter crops. All eager to take up life as usual in their towns and villages. Of course, some could not think of leaving if their masters were still intent on fighting the cause. I prayed Master Markenfield would be of the same mind as I and missed his wife and home comforts. The drizzle and mist pressed down and soaked everyone. The acrid, choking smell of woodsmoke from doused fires clung to everything and burned the back of my throat, but I felt my heart soar as I pushed through the mayhem and fought my way back to my husband. We could go home.

Robert was almost ready to start out when I found him. Putting my wrap on the back of the cart, I reached up to his wet face and held it in my hands, kissing the rain from his mouth. He lifted me from the ground and swung me around, our lips never parting. The world was spinning, and I felt dizzy, but it did not matter. We were going home.

At last, he sat me atop the cart and climbed up beside me. Bridget came over and looked up at me.

"'Tis good you are back,' she said. 'We have all missed you.'

I smiled and nodded. "'Tis good to be with you all.' It surprised me to find I truly meant it. Then I remembered what Robert had told me yesterday, and my face clouded. Had Fenton brought Bridget word from Harry? Did she know he had been here? No, I told myself. I will let nothing spoil this day. I squeezed her hand and said, 'Get you up, and we will away.'

I looked to Edmund standing in front of the forge cart. He grinned and waved his hand, waiting for Bridget to climb up and take the reins before tugging on the oxen harness. The field had become a quagmire, and the mud sucked on his small feet and ankles, making it difficult for him to move the beasts on. Robert jumped down and went to help the boy and soon had them back on the road. He came back for Mutton and me and set off at a sedate and steady pace. I leaned into Robert as the mist cleared, and a weak sun drifted in and out of view in the cloudy sky.

Over time, the earls and other horsemen overtook the carts and men on foot. The countess acknowledged us as she passed by alongside her husband. I nodded in return, knowing it was unlikely our paths would cross again. Sitting up, I turned to Robert.

'How long is the journey to Rippon?' I asked.

'It depends on where we make camp. One or two days, I would say.'

'Is it possible in one day if we do not stop?' I hoped it was. I could stitch the ticking for my new mattress and stuff it with the feathers. It would be good to prepare for the birth.

'We can only go as fast as our leaders. My guess is that we will camp at Wetherby.'

'Rippon is not so far from Wetherby, and I do not mind the extra hours if it gets us home sooner. There are many travelling that way so we would not be alone.'

'Why would we travel with deserters?' he asked sharply. 'All of us who believe in the cause will continue to follow our masters. I will not be called a coward in this time of change.'

It was difficult to find my voice. 'I…we are not going home? The queen offers a pardon. We—'

'A pardon? We did not come thus far for a pardon.' He glared at me, eyes wide with surprise. 'Why do you speak so, Catherine? We – I will serve my master to the end. The queen offers neither him nor the earls any such pardon. We must hold fast with them and see this through no matter what.' He paused for a moment, and then his voice softened. 'I understand your needs. Of course you must go home. When we are back in Rippon, I will see you safely there with Bridget before moving on. You should prepare for the birth.'

I swallowed, trying to remove the pebble in my throat, but it would not budge. My words would have to wait until I could speak again.

Robert

Knaresborough, Yorkshire, Monday 24th November 1569

WE DID NOT STOP at Wetherby or Rippon. It was late and dark when we reached the ruined castle at Knaresborough. The morning promise of a dry day had not lasted. Everyone was soaked through to the skin. The earls and their entourages had set up camp within the crumbling castle walls for the night. Catherine had barely acknowledged me on the entire journey from Bramham Moor, furious that I would not countenance stopping when we reached Rippon. How could I? My belief in the cause, my loyalty to my master, had not diminished. The fact we could not rescue the Scottish queen was a setback, I had explained to her, but it did not mean the pilgrimage was over. I had given my word to the master, and I could not, would not let him down. Catherine had not spoken or kissed me before she left to go to the countess, and now she was disappearing behind the bailey walls. 'There is still a wrong to be righted,' I growled under my breath. Turning back to the cart, I climbed up and crawled on all fours inside the hooped canvas cover. Bridget and Edmund huddled beneath blankets. Both held a bowl of cold pottage balanced on their knees and each a wedge of rough rye bread. Bridget handed a bowl to me once I settled in beside them.

'It will be a long night,' I said before breaking the bread into the soupy liquid to soften it. I wondered if Countess Anne had told her husband about Shinclyffe. I feared they would not believe me, as the man seemed well known to all of them. He drank with them every night. I thought about the first time I had seen him attack that poor young girl. The earls and gentlemen had seemed content to watch him play with her as if she were a mouse, waiting for him to pounce and swallow her up. The memory turned my stomach. I could only wait and see what would happen.

We ate in silence for a while, my thoughts again wandering to Catherine. She had a cot of her own and more than enough blankets from what she had told me. I could not help wishing I could share them with her. There were ways a man and his wife could keep the cold at bay. I smiled to myself before putting the bowl down on the cart bed and settling down on my side. A minute later and Edmund was spooning me from behind as usual.

'You can wrap yourself around my back, Bridget, if you wish,' the boy said. 'You will stay warmer.'

There was some shuffling about, and then it was quiet. Edmund was clever. He would have the warmth of two people now. I patted his hand as it rested on my side, and soon, listening to the hammer of rain, I fell into a deep sleep.

The weather was kinder the following day. Bridget built a hearth and lit a fire. Edmund and I loaded the forge with our stock of kindling and logs. By the time we set the forge up, the sun had risen pale in the washed-out sky, and I could see the river mist had lifted as I looked down the hill. We did not light the forge, as it was unclear whether we would stay here or move on to Rippon. Sitting around the fire, we broke our fast on cheese that Bridget had cut the rind from and the last of our bread.

Bridget would make some more if it were decided we would stay in Knaresborough another day. She had been nothing but willing since Catherine had taken up her post with the countess. It became more and more difficult to believe this woman was anything but honourable in her deeds and actions. Although her presence reminded me constantly of Harry's betrayal, I felt myself warming to her more as each day passed. She seemed more concerned for mine and Edmund's welfare than Catherine. My thoughts were broken by a sudden commotion and raised voices. I looked up to see a rider coming into camp. He jumped down from his horse and was quickly ushered inside the crumbling walls of the castle.

The response to his arrival was soon apparent as the order came to break camp. The queen's army must have gained ground.

We were set to go when Catherine arrived. I caught her hand as she placed her things on the cart, but she pulled away, feigning busyness. Her mood had not improved from the previous day. Let her be stubborn, then. What care I? Throwing the last of the pots and pans up beside her things, I climbed up and took the reins, not offering her any aid as she heaved her heavy body up beside me. A sense of guilt filled me as I pretended not to notice or care. I had welcomed her back, and she had rejected me yet again.

Back on the road, and Catherine at my side on the cart, the guilt got the better of me. I attempted to lighten the mood.

'It is a fair-weather day and good to see familiar land around us. We will be at Markenfield by the noonday if the roads allow.'

Catherine did not look at me but said in a quiet voice, ''Tis a pity we do not intend to remain on familiar ground.'

'One day soon,' I said, reaching for her hand. 'I promise.'

She did not respond, but neither did she take it away this time. 'The countess asks that you attend her and the earl when we are settled and dined this evening. I will come and fetch you when they are ready.'

My heart raced a little as the blood pounded through my veins. What if Westmorland had not believed my story of Shinclyffe? 'Did she appear kindly when she spoke?'

'It was difficult to know. The countess seemed a little distracted and not in good humour when she awoke. She was sickly and seemed to have a slight fever. I will go to her as soon as we arrive at Markenfield.'

It was likely the countess, and her husband would reside in the Hall with Master Thomas. The thought of being presented to them by Fenton made me clench my fists and grit my teeth so hard, my jaw ached. I let go of Catherine's hand and took hold of the rein so that I could manage Mutton, who suddenly seemed skittish. The horse amazed me how he could carry on day after day when I had thought him finished not so long ago. Now he had reacted as if he could read my thoughts. I could feel his tension through the reins.

We travelled the ten miles with little trouble and arrived at Markenfield with the sun having another three or four hours to shine before the moon would take its place in the sky. The master and the earls had all arrived well ahead of those of us on foot or by cart. Catherine maintained her silence and seemed lost in her own thoughts. As soon as we arrived at the Hall, she got down from the cart and said, 'I must go directly to my mistress. I fear she will be in a sorry state.' She took her bag containing all her treating herbs and hurried up the road to the gatehouse. Watching her go filled me with the dread that I may lose her, either to this countess who had turned Catherine's head to finer things, or to the determination she had in staying in Rippon.

Edmund pulled on my sleeve. 'Shall I set up the forge?' His eyes were wide, his voice hesitant.

I forced a smile and patted his shoulder. 'Good lad, Edmund. I can always rely on you.'

The boy's face broke into a wide grin before he raced back to the forge cart and got to work.

'She is worried about the countess.' Bridget's voice penetrated my thoughts. 'Do not fret so. You know how she disappears into that world of medicines and cures as soon as a body shows signs of illness.'

I turned to Bridget as she busied herself unloading the cart. I thought it was more than that, but I did not want to share my thoughts.

'You are right. Catherine is afeared of anyone dying in sickness. She still bears the pain of not being there to help when her family died of the pox.'

Bridget came close and pressed my arm; her eyes clouded with concern. 'We must support her. I will look after you and Edmund so that she may attend to her duties with the countess. Better she does not have to worry about her duties here as well.'

I placed my hand over hers. It was soft and warm. 'Mayhap, you are right. I thank you, Bridget, for all your help.'

The afternoon was busy with customers, and Edmund and I were pleased to stop and sit by the hearth that evening. Bridget had made fresh bread and a pottage flavoured with dried herbs and mushrooms. The earthy taste was strong but flavoursome and a welcome distraction from thinking about my audience with Countess Anne and the Earl of Northumberland this evening.

As we finished our supper, Bridget related stories to Edmund from her childhood at the Hall. Of how her mother was a servant to the old master. She told of a particular day when a gander had chased her because she had dared to go near the young goslings he and his goose were taking to the moat.

Standing up, she re-enacted the scene, lifting her skirts and running around the fire, screaming. Edmund had rolled around the floor with laughter as Bridget proceeded to tell him that Harry had tried to come to her rescue and had ended up in the moat himself, the goose flapping her wings and beating him. The memory shone in my mind too. I remembered dragging him out, all three of us children lying on the grass and holding our bellies and laughing most heartily. My stomach ached, and I threw my head back. Bridget, sitting down on the dirt floor, knelt up and placed her hands on my knees. Her face was red from exertion.

'Do you rememb—'

'I see you manage well without me.'

I looked up to see Catherine, hands on hips and glaring at Bridget and me. I threw Bridget's hands away and scrambled to my feet, feeling the heat rise in my cheeks. 'I… We remembered something from childhood.' I said. 'The time a gander chased Harry into the moat at the Hall.'

'I am glad you have such fond memories. A pity I was never privy to any.' Her eyes seemed cold. 'I came only to say the countess is too ill to see you this eve and asks you to wait until she is in better health.' She looked at Bridget and added, 'I will leave you to your merriment.' Without another word, she turned and walked away.

I chased after her. 'I will walk you back. You should not be out on your own in the dark. They should have sent someone to escort you.'

She stopped walking and faced me. 'I am capable of walking a short distance on my own. Mayhap it is you who needs a chaperone,' she snapped.

'Do not talk such nonsense.' I grabbed her arm, appalled at her suggestion. 'You are being ridiculous.'

'Let me go, Robert. I have nothing more to say to you.'

Her face was twisted with hurt, and the set of her chin told me she would not listen while in such a state of mind. I let go and watched her walk swiftly away and over the bridge into the Hall courtyard.

Edmund and Bridget were sitting in silence when I returned. They looked to me for reassurance.

'It is time to sleep.' I said and went to lay down under the cart.

Catherine

Markenfield Hall, Yorkshire,
Tuesday 25th November 1569

I COULD BARELY SEE as I rushed into the courtyard. My mind
was on fire with the sight of Robert and Bridget laughing so
heartily. Her hands were on his knees. I had thought of her
almost as a mother and my dearest friend. I stopped to take
some time to calm myself. I could not appear in such a state
before my mistress. Pushing my anger to the back of my mind,
I went to the kitchen to make a soothing brew of feverfew to
ease the countess's temperature. It was good to see Goodwife
Green, the cook, and she asked after mine and Robert's health
as well as enquiring about the condition of Countess Anne. I
painted a smile on my face and willed myself to speak kindly
of my husband. She did not appear to hear any doubt in my
voice as I praised him. Not wanting to linger long enough to
break down in front of her, I begged her leave as the countess
would be waiting on my attendance.

When I entered her chamber, she was as I had left her
earlier, half sitting and propped up with several feather pillows.
Her eyes were closed, and her cheeks glowed ruddy against
her pale skin; her hair dark with sweat and clinging to her
brow; her breath shallow. Dried spittle clung to the corners

of her mouth, and her lips were dry and cracked. I placed the steaming brew on a small table at the side of the bed and put my hand to her forehead. Her fever was still high. I took a linen cloth, wetting it in a bowl of cold water before pressing it on her brow. She stirred and looked up at me.

'Dearest, Catherine,' she said, lifting a limp hand and touching my sleeve. 'What would I do without you?'

No matter my wish to go home, I could not leave her afore she gained her strength and was well again. I would approach Master Thomas to plead we stay at Markenfield another day before moving on. I held the brew to her lips, and she took small sips for me. She sat up a little more when she had finished. She was gasping for breath and did cough up foul-smelling green phlegm from her chest. I had made a tonic from elfwort earlier in the day to ease her condition and now gave her a spoonful to stave off the coughing. The thick, aromatic medicine had a glutinous texture which allowed it to remain in the throat for a while and soothe the irritation. When she seemed calmer, I lifted her sweat-drenched night shift over her head and bathed her body in lukewarm water. Finally comfortable, and after dressing her in a clean linen shift, she fell into a deep sleep.

I lay on the hard floor by her bed and covered myself with a blanket. Sleep was impossible as I tossed and turned. The baby inside of me protested at the lack of comfort, kicking and wriggling. The image of Bridget and Robert still filled my mind. I could not, would not, believe they might betray me further, for to do so would be too painful to bear. It was, as he said, just a childhood memory that had given them pleasure. Even so, it was difficult to know he had memories to share with another woman. The countess coughed, and I sat up, waiting and ready to tend her, but she moaned only lightly and soon settled. I allowed my mind to think only of what plants and herbs I needed to collect to ensure I had plenty in my bag for the coming days.

Sleep came at some time during the night before I was startled awake by the sound of a man's voice.

'Wake up, girl.'

Something was digging into my side. I rolled away a little. It took me a few seconds to realise the earl was pushing his booted foot into me.

'How is your mistress? How did she fare this long night?' Northumberland was now leaning over his wife but did not touch her.

'She has slept well, my lord,' I said, struggling to my feet. I walked around to the other side of the bed and put my hand on her forehead. It felt considerably cooler, and her cheeks were not so flushed. 'Her fever has broken. I am sure she will recover fully in a day or two.'

'Good. Good,' Northumberland said, already walking away. 'Tell her I asked after her.' Then he left the room.

'Thomas? Is that you?' The countess stirred and tried to open her eyes. She moaned and put the back of her hand to her forehead.

'It was he, my lady,' I said. 'Stay rested now. I will fetch you a drink.' I had hardly spoken, and she was sleeping again.

Once in the kitchen, I was offered bread and soft cheese by Goodwife Green, which I took gratefully. I had not eaten since early the previous day. The cheese was thick and creamy against my tongue. A hint of chives added a tang which made the saliva rise in my mouth.

'I am told she favours manchet bread and have made some fresh for her,' she said, busy rolling pastry for a pie.

We chatted amiably while I ate, and then she made up a plate of soft foods and pottage for my mistress. I made a peppermint tea and took them upstairs.

When I returned to the bedchamber, my mistress was sitting upright in her bed. Her eyes were wide and shiny with exhaustion, but she smiled at me.

'I have brought food to lift your strength a little,' I said, putting the tray down on the table.

'I do not think I can eat. I feel a little nauseous.' She coughed and put a hand to her mouth. 'My throat and head doth hurt much.'

'Your fever is broken, but your chest is still much congested. I have made a tea from peppermint, which will help you breathe easy. The cook has prepared some manchet bread, especially for you. The earl did tell her it was your favourite.'

She smiled at this. 'Did he come to visit? I think I heard his voice?'

'Yes, my lady. He came. He would not disturb you while you rest.' I did not say that he could not wait to be far from her sickness and had fled the room as a dog might when fearing a kick from its master.

I did not need to ask if we could delay travel another day as no one came to say it was time to move on. Countess Anne had slipped in and out of sleep for most of the morning and, after eating a little around noon, insisted I went to visit my husband.

'He will miss you much,' she said. Her voice was hoarse from continuous coughing, but her fever was no more.

'Yes, my lady,' I said dully. Miss me? It seemed unlikely.

The countess frowned. 'What is it? Are you ill?' She patted the bed. 'Sit. Tell me, Catherine. Have I infected you?'

I sat on the edge of the coverlet, tears ready to fall. My voice was almost a whimper when I spoke. ''Tis Robert. I fear he is more than friendly with a woman who travels with us. Last eve, when I ventured out to tell him you were ill and I would stay here with you, I…' it was hard to say as a picture of the two of them came to mind yet again. 'I came upon them laughing and gay…and she was kneeling before him, her hands on his knees. He told me they were laughing at some memory of childhood.' I looked at my mistress, who squeezed my arm. 'They were children here at the Hall and…' A tear spilt down my cheek, and I tasted the salt of it on my lips.

'My dear girl. You must not be jealous. I believe your Robert is no gandermooner. I only have to see the way he looks at you to know his heart is wholly yours.' She passed me a clean lace handkerchief from her bedside table. 'Get thee to your husband. He will be most pleased to see you.'

'But who will care for you?'

'I will. Am I not without fever? Do I have a pillow to lay my head on and sleep until your return?' She smiled, and I could see a little of the spark I had come to know about her. 'Tell him I have not forgotten his words of warning. I have not been able to speak with my husband about the matter we discussed, but as soon as I am up and about my business, I will see to it he knows.' I left with her words of comfort filling my mind. The countess was right; Robert would never betray me.

I kept a little distance, watching him working hard at the forge. Robert wiped his forehead with the back of his hand in between hammer blows, the streaks of dirt adding to the grimy rivulets of sweat pouring down his face. Even his father's sweatband could not keep it from running down his cheeks, culminating at the square set of his jaw and dripping onto his shirt.

Bridget was scouring plates with salt after their noonday meal and stacking them on a stone. She then poured some water from the cauldron hanging over the fire into a large basin before shaving a little soap and adding it. When she picked up a couple of Robert's shirts, I walked over and took them from her hands.

'It should be a wife that washes her husband's shirts,' I said curtly. 'Mayhap find another chore to occupy your hands.'

She did not speak but picked up a basket and walked away; her head hung low as she made her way through the campsite, no doubt looking for food such as eggs and flour for sale. I doused the shirts in the soapy liquid and took much satisfaction in pummelling them until the water turned black. I was busy rinsing them in several bowls of clean water when Robert approached.

'It is good to see you.' He spoke softly, his eyes gauging mine to interpret my mood. 'How is the countess? Does she fare better?'

Continuing to wring the water from the clothes, I answered him sharply. 'The fever is no more, but she coughs a great deal.' I wondered if he asked for her health honestly or did but need to know her response to Shinclyffe's deeds. I laid the shirts on the stones surrounding the fire before speaking again, my resolve to be distant disappearing by the second. When I had done, I looked to Edmund, who was hard at work feeding the forge. 'Is there time to walk a little?' I asked, my voice gentler this time.

'Edmund,' he shouted. 'Take some rest. I will be back soon.'

We walked in silence through the crowds. There seemed to be even fewer people than when we had left Knaresborough. Still a goodly army but occupying a smaller number of fields around the Hall. Robert, as usual, could read my thoughts.

'Many have deserted and gone home. They expected to be riding behind Queen Mary by now. For them, the Scottish queen was the principal reason for the pilgrimage.'

'That and the lack of pay from the earls, I shouldn't wonder,' I replied.

'I am sorry for not seeing this the way you do, Catherine. I must follow my master. Upon my life, I would not hurt you willingly.' He paused for a moment before lowering his voice and adding, 'There is nothing between Bridget and me.' He sounded sincere, and I reached for his hand. The touch of his palm against mine sent a ripple of sweet ecstasy through me and caused the baby to kick out. I let go of Robert, and my hand automatically flew to my belly to stroke the protruding heel. Robert saw and covered my hand with his before kissing my cheek. His lips were like a gentle breeze caressing my skin.

'I love you, my heart,' I whispered, and he took me in his arms and kissed me soundly on the lips – the welfare of my clean dress forgotten in my haste to hold my husband close.

As soon as I returned to the hall and made my way to the kitchen, Goodwife Green helped me to sponge down my dress before I went up to Countess Anne's bedchamber. She was sitting in a chair by the window, a wool blanket of sage green covering her legs. I placed a fresh peppermint tea beside her. She was smiling as she looked me up and down, and I could see a definite improvement in her pallor. 'I see you have made peace with your husband.'

'Yes, Countess,' I said, cheeks colouring, my hands brushing down my kirtle.

'I am feeling much revived,' she continued. 'Will you tell my husband I will be ready to travel tomorrow? I know he is eager to move on.'

'Are you sure? You have been sorely ill, my lady. I would not advise travelling so soon.' I was concerned for her, but she waved me away.

'Nonsense. I am perfectly well. Do as I ask, Catherine.'

'But Countess—'

'You must not question me. I know you mean well, but I am your mistress and, as such, know what is best. Now go.'

'Yes, my lady.' I bowed my head and went to find Northumberland.

Robert

Markenfield Hall, Yorkshire,
Thursday 27th November 1569

IT WAS DARK, DAWN still a couple of hours away, when I arrived back at Markenfield. Last eve, Catherine had asked if I would ride over to Rippon on the horse I had bought at Boroughbridge to fetch her any herbs still alive in her garden and a selection of dried ones she kept hanging in the dwelling room. I had travelled at speed in the early hours of this morning, enjoying the freedom to ride Chestnut for the short distance home. The shop and house were still securely locked, and I found a little thyme still surviving outside along with some juniper, sage, and lavender. Inside, I looked around to see if everything was well before collecting a sprig of everything hanging from the rafters. Putting my haul into a sack, I rode back to Markenfield.

It was not long before the call came to break camp. The sun rose on the horizon as we set off to follow the main army. Catherine had a thick shawl around her shoulders and snuggled close to me as the cart bounced from side to side on the rough roads. Northumberland had decided that Northallerton was far enough for his wife to travel on her first day back in the saddle, and so this was agreed as the next stop. It shocked

Catherine when I told her the journey was twenty-five miles and would take several hours. She groaned and said it would most certainly set back her mistress's recovery – if she made it that far. Knowing how Catherine fretted whenever someone was ill worried me. Ever since her family's death, she had blamed herself and now believed that any fault in the way she cared might cause death. It was not good for the baby – it was not good for her. The stress could bring on her seizures.

The countess had sent word through Catherine that she would speak to me this evening when we made camp. This was Shinclyffe's home territory and where I had first set eyes on the brute. I had pondered a great deal on the comment he had made about my name on the way to Rippon a week or more ago. Mayhap Countess Anne would discover something about the matter. I was still nervous that the earls might not believe what I had seen. Fenton seemed to have kept his head down. Catherine said she had not seen him up at the Hall while she was there. Thinking about Fenton made me angry. As usual, my thoughts turned to Harry and the childhood friendship we had shared...

I remembered playing dice with him in the yard at Markenfield while my father and Harry's had worked in the smithy. Old Master Markenfield, Master Thomas's father, had always been kindly towards us. He sometimes caught us scurrying from the kitchen, our mouths full of whatever we had managed to pilfer when Cook was not looking. He would cuff our ears and wink. Sometimes my father would inflate a pig's bladder, and we would run for miles, along with other village boys, over the fields to see who could kick it over the hedge that marked the line of the common land. The race to get it back to the Hall involved much fighting for possession. Our mothers would scold us when we came back bloodied and bruised. Later, when both our fathers had gone off to march alongside the master in the pilgrimage of '36 to see King Henry and plead for the resurrection of the Catholic church, we had less time to play and helped any way we could to earn a few pennies for our mothers.

We had been playing one such rare game out in the fields the day that the old master and my father finally came home. The pain was bright in my father's eyes when the master told Harry his father had been killed and would not be returning. Harry had run back out over the fields. Without another thought, I had raced after him. He threw himself face-down onto the grass and sobbed. I sat alongside him until he stopped, and then, helping him to his feet, I put my arm about his shoulder and led him back to the Hall and my father. The old master had ensured that Harry's mother was well looked after at the Hall and set up my father with a workshop in the town market-stede at Rippon, insisting that Harry was apprenticed there until he had grown. We had been as brothers…

Clicking the reins, I swallowed hard. The pain in my chest was sharp with emotion. What happened to change a friend into a foe so easily? Having Catherine's body close against mine, as the cart jolted and bounced, comforted me. If Harry's betrayal caused harm to her or the baby, I would make him pay. I would kill him.

The sun was already low in the sky when we arrived at Northallerton. The air itself seemed to freeze in front of our faces. The grass, trees and low-lying bushes were cloaked in a hoar frost as if all had grown feathers. Catherine, Bridget, and young Edmund were shivering with cold as they blew on their cupped hands while stamping their feet on the hard ground. I told the women to unpack and Edmund to unharness the animals and feed them. Keeping busy would take their minds off the inclement weather until I made up a hearth and lit a fire. When the flames had taken hold, we gathered around it, desperate for warmth. Bridget passed around bread and cheese. Catherine made a warming drink of ale, putting in some honey to thicken it and add sweetness. Barely finishing hers, she stood and said it was time for her to leave.

'Thank you for all your hard work, Bridget,' she said. 'It is good to know I can leave my husband and Edmund in good hands.' It pleased me that her voice held no malice. She turned to Edmund. 'You are a good lad. We are blessed to have such a hard-working child.' I watched his cheeks bloom with colour as he attempted, in vain, to wrap his arms around her waist, his head ending up resting on the mound of her belly. Catherine placed a kiss on top of his head.

'I will escort you,' I said as she turned to go.

As we walked, a sense of completeness filled me. I thanked God that Catherine got on well with the boy. I had recently harboured a wish that he might join us at the shop when all this was over. I could not think the Earl of Westmorland would object as long as I did not ask for any of the money Edmund's parents had already paid over.

Approaching the marquee, I could see no sign of the countess. She would most likely have retired to bed after such a long day travelling. Mayhap Northumberland had joined her, for none but servants were scurrying about outside.

'Wait here,' said Catherine. 'I will see if she is well enough to see you.'

My stomach roiled as she disappeared inside. Stamping my feet and batting my arms across myself to keep warm, it seemed an age afore Catherine reappeared and signalled for me to enter. She lowered her gaze as if she could not look at me. Puzzled at her stance, I followed her inside to find a table set with food aplenty, as if in readiness for several guests. We carried on through a curtained-off area to where the countess was sitting on a bed, cloaked in blankets, her face wan. I bowed my head and waited.

'I wish you good eve, Robert. My husband will not be a moment; he has gone to speak to Westmorland.'

'Yes, my lady,' I said quietly. Looking up again, I saw Catherine was unpinning the countess's hair. It tumbled down her back like a mane, silken and shining gold. Catherine brushed it softly, and the countess closed her eyes: transfixed by the gentle touch of my wife's hand moving the brush from top to bottom. There was something so sensual about it; I felt a hardening in my breeches. Flushing, I turned my gaze away and stared at the small cot in the corner. This must be where Catherine would spend the night. It looked warm and comfortable with coloured blankets aplenty and a pillow so plump I could have climbed inside and rested my head. The sound of voices in the other part of the tent broke my thoughts.

'What do you think, Markenfield? He's your servant.'

I recognised Westmorland's voice and stayed stock still, waiting to hear my master's response.

'Goodman Gray is here, my lord. Shall I send him thither?' I spun my head to look at the countess. I could not read her face, but she had definitely not wanted my master to respond within my earshot.

Northumberland came through the curtained entrance and stared at me. 'We'd better hear what you have to say. Come.'

My legs were trembling as I followed him. In the outer room, alongside Northumberland, stood Master Thomas, Westmorland, Countess Jane, and Richard Norton. I bowed my head to each one, noticing my master's glare and feeling sick. Would he deny my loyalty? Why did he look so angry?

'You will await my attendance?' the countess asked loudly from her inner sanctum.

'We will, of course, dear lady,' came Northumberland's response.

The men sat down at the table, leaving me standing in front of them without a word from anyone. Not even my master. He did not look at me, and I feared he had lost all trust. I wished for this to be over and willed Countess Anne to hurry.

'There now, gentlemen, was my presence worth the waiting?' The countess was now fully made up with white powder, her lips reddened, and her cheeks rouged so that her face showed no sign of sickness. The weakness in her voice betrayed her lack of good health. Taking a seat next to her husband, she looked to me and smiled. 'Come, Robert. You must tell all here what you related to me.'

'Yes, my lady,' I said with a slight bow of the head. I planted my eyes on Catherine, standing behind the countess. Her gaze gave me confidence and encouragement as, once again, I went over the day at Bramham when I had seen Shinclyffe pass a missive to Fenton. I explained I had followed Fenton through the woods and seen him pass it on to a rider. I said I could not be sure but thought the rider might have been Harry Gardyner. They sat quietly and allowed me to finish before Northumberland narrowed his eyes and spoke.

'Why has it taken you so many days to report this?' he asked.

'Forgive me, my lord. I did speak with the countess that evening, and she said she would speak with you.' I looked to Anne, hoping she would confirm this.

''Tis true, dear husband. Had I been well enough and not become delirious with fever, I would have spoken to you sooner.'

My master glared at me, his jaw set as he spoke. 'How do we know you speak the truth, Gray?' I could not understand his fierce stance against me. Had I not always obeyed him without question? Without a grudge, no matter the task? His voice was cold and without compassion. 'I found to my cost that Gardyner could not be trusted. Why now should I believe you?'

'Pray, believe me, master. Neither my father before me nor I have ever betrayed a master of Markenfield. We have been loyal in all things.' I could not keep the hurt and anger from my voice as I stood my ground.

He continued in the same manner. 'You accuse my Lord Shinclyffe of betrayal. Of sneaking about our persons and passing on missives to our enemies. Did you not sneak away from Markenfield Hall last eve? Riding out in the dark and not returning for a good hour or two?'

He took me by surprise. Had he been watching my movements? 'I... Yes... I did not sneak away. I went to Rippon to collect some items for my wife.'

'And how should we know you speak true? Did any person accompany you?'

The men all stared at me, waiting for an answer. I was shaking. 'Master, I went to collect herbs and medicines for my wife. The countess was ill. Catherine needed supplies to treat the countess. I swear—'

'He speaks true,' said Anne. 'He came directly to my side with them.'

I let out a deep sigh, relieved that she spoke for me. My master's face was still thunderous.

Northumberland looked me up and down. He waved a hand. 'You may leave us. We will think on your words, Gray. In the meantime, you will not leave camp again without permission.'

I was still staring at my master, unable to take in his hostile manner. 'Yes, my lord,' I said.

'Wait.' Richard Norton raised his hand to stay me. 'Are you sure it was Shinclyffe who passed on the missive to Fenton?' He seemed puzzled about something. His brow furrowed with lines.

'I am, my lord,' I replied.

'It seems strange,' he said.

'Why so?' asked Northumberland.

'Because it was he who caught out Gardyner's father in '36. He had to—'

'Exactly!' shouted my master, jumping to his feet. 'He had no good reason to associate himself with that man's son. Beware of who you accuse, Gray. I will not protect you if you persist in telling lies.'

I looked to Richard Norton. What did he mean? Caught him out? Had Shinclyffe something to do with the death of Harry's father?

The countess was staring at my master as if she, too, wondered what he meant. 'Perhaps Thomas could enlighten us,' she said before turning to Catherine. 'Go with your husband this eve. I will manage well without you until after supper. You may return then.'

Catherine bowed her head. 'Yes, my lady,' she said and came over to join me.

'You may go, Robert,' said the countess, waving us away.

I bowed, and we took our leave. Yet again, I could not turn to Master Markenfield for support. I was swift in concluding that Catherine was right. Thomas Markenfield was by no means the friend I had thought him.

Both lost in thought at tonight's events and unable to fully understand what had happened, Catherine and I walked in silence back to our hearth. Norton's words repeated themselves over and over in my mind. 'It was him who caught out Gardyner in '36. What had happened on that pilgrimage to bring about the death of my father's closest friend? The image of my father, kneeling and crying, came to me again. Had he been crying because Gardyner had been a traitor? Or was it because his friend had been betrayed?

Bridget and Edmund were eating by the fire when we got back. She jumped to her feet and filled bowls of piping hot pottage for us both. As if sensing our mood, she did not question Catherine's return.

Edmund spoke. 'Why have—'

From the corner of my eye, I saw Bridget put her finger to her mouth, instructing him to be quiet. I was grateful. I needed to think about what had been said. The countess wanted to get to the bottom of things, I was sure. That is why she sent us both away. So she could speak openly to my master and Norton.

Catherine laid a hand over mine. It was as if she had read my mind. 'She will discover the truth. We can count on her.'

After supper, Edmund asked if he could go across to the horses to help with the grooming, and I agreed. He scampered away in the dark, always pleased to spend time with his beloved creatures. He was fast becoming a natural part of my family. Understanding our need to be alone, Bridget excused herself and wandered to the next hearth to speak to a woman from Rippon who she recognised. Turning to Catherine, I saw the worry on her face. 'It will all be fine,' I said softly, now my turn to be the one to comfort.

'What do you think Norton meant?' she asked.

'I do not know. I hope the countess can fathom his meaning.' Whatever it was, it would open the door to what happened in '36; to what had made my father so sad he had – no, it was not true – Mother said it was a lie. My father did not take his own life. It was the greatest sin there could ever be. 'The thought of Shinclyffe being behind Harry's father dying worries me greatly,' I said.

'Should we tell Bridget?'

'No.' I shook my head. 'We must say nothing until we find out the truth.'

A tap on my shoulder woke me long before dawn. A woman stood over me, holding a torch aloft. She looked incredibly young to be about in the dark.

'What is it?'

'My lady wishes you to come. She will speak with you.'

The girl's voice woke Catherine and Edmund, who lay on either side of me.

'Margery? What are you doing here?' Catherine asked, raising up onto her elbows. 'Is the countess ill again?' She was already getting up to her feet.

'No, Catherine. She has been up all night, as far as I can tell. She and her husband and Master Norton wish to speak with Goodman Gray and yourself.'

Catherine and I followed Margery back to Northumberland's tent and waited outside for permission to enter. Catherine looked tired, and I squeezed her hand to reassure her. All this travelling was not doing her and the baby any good. She should be resting over these last weeks. It would be useless to demand she do so; the woman was strong-willed and would not give in to her body's demands, always declaring that she was strong enough to carry on her work until the day the pains would tell her it was time.

Margery came back out and ushered us into where Northumberland, Anne and Norton were waiting. Master Thomas was not there.

'Goodman Gray. Come, sit with your wife,' said Norton. 'I would ask a few more questions of you.'

We sat across the table from them, and my stomach groaned, betraying me as usual, as I looked over the remains of last night's supper. There was enough food left to feed a poor family for a week.

Countess Anne smiled. 'You may partake as soon as we have finished speaking with both of you and Catherine. Now, Catherine. Tell us once again, from the beginning, what you saw and heard that day in York.'

'Yes, my lady,' said Catherine. Norton watched her intently as she went over the events at York and what Harry's wife had said when they came upon her after travelling back to Rippon.

Norton's face appeared to show no doubt at what Catherine had said. He turned to me.

'Is this what you reported to Westmorland and your Master at Brancepeth, Gray?'

'Yes, my lord,' I replied.

'Now tell me again what you told us last eve. Slowly so that you do not miss any detail.'

I repeated what I had said before. Catherine found my hand under the table as we waited to see what would happen next.

Norton spoke again. 'Countess Anne has told me of your concern over what Gardyner's mother claimed about your father. I realise you were but a small boy when your father and old Markenfield returned from the pilgrimage. They would not make you aware of what happened. I do not know everything of the night Gardyner died, but I will tell you what I remember. The pilgrimage was a most holy protest about the king's break with the Catholic church and the pope so that he could wed our current queen's mother, that whore Anne Boleyn. We protested about the barbaric way all our monasteries were dissolved. It left us without all the religious customs that have served this land for many centuries.'

Norton's face blazed with anger as he recalled everything. 'It resulted in many poor people starving, as it was our beloved monks who fed and schooled them. My dear friend Robert Aske led it after the Lincolnshire uprising failed. Aske was insistent our pilgrimage was peaceful and only wished the king to have an ear for our grievances. There had been talk around the camp of someone spying at our meetings and relaying messages to the king's chief minister, Thomas Cromwell. One evening, when old Markenfield was at supper with Robert Aske, I and several other earls and gentlemen discussed who the spy might be when one of Markenfield's servants came to him. He reported having seen Shinclyffe meeting a man on horseback on the outskirts of the camp. The servant also said that Shinclyffe had passed a message to the rider. That servant was Gardyner.'

Now I was confused. Harry's father had seen almost precisely what I had come across in recent days. It made little sense. I felt Catherine pulling her hand away. I had been squeezing it too hard. I slackened my grip and stroked the back of her hand with my thumb in apology.

Norton continued. 'Shinclyffe arrived on the scene. When he saw Gardyner talking to the old Master Markenfield, he became angry and pointed at Gardyner and denounced him as a spy. Shinclyffe said that it was he who had seen Gardyner handing a message over to a rider. Of course, Gardyner had pleaded his innocence and begged Markenfield to believe him, saying that all he had reported was true. Shinclyffe insisted Gardyner lied. He demanded to know who among us did not trust him, a gentleman. He who was as eager to march on the pilgrimage as all his fellows sitting around the table. He insisted Gardyner hang for his treacherous act.' Norton paused for a moment to quench his thirst.

'When he heard what Gardyner had been accused of, I believe it was your father who rushed forward to say it could not be true. He said that his friend had not been away from camp that night. I couldn't believe that was the case, or how else could Gardyner have seen Shinclyffe?' He looked at me solemnly. 'Old Markenfield had your father flogged for his lie, and Gardyner was dragged to the nearest tree and hung. The details are so similar to what you are saying now they have made me return to that sorry night. I remember feeling uneasy at the time. Shinclyffe had seemed too quick to point the finger when he arrived at our table. Mayhap he had spotted Gardyner returning to camp and wanted to get his version of events told before anyone had time to digest what your father's friend had to say.'

The image of my father on his knees, tears in his eyes, flooded my mind. Now it made sense. In his effort to help his friend, he had condemned him to death. He had borne the guilt for the rest of his life. No wonder he took such care of Harry and had shown the love of a father to the boy. It was his way of repenting for what had happened. A thought occurred to me, and I puzzled over it for a few seconds.

'My lord,' I said. 'Forgive me asking, but there is something that troubles me. If the old master had Gardyner hung and my father flogged, why did he act so generously to him when they returned from the pilgrimage? He set my father up in the shop at Rippon. I cannot fathom his reason.'

'I can only say that the old fellow was full of regret at the hanging of Gardyner. He told me that both he and your father had always been loyal, and it was hard to come to terms with such a betrayal. He carried much grief about what had happened and decided that you boys had no reason to pay for your fathers' sins.' Norton now rose from the table, and Catherine and I followed suit and stood up. 'The question now is, what are we going to do about the current situation?' He looked to Northumberland and Countess Anne.

Northumberland did not respond immediately. He turned to his wife for answers.

'Markenfield has been keeping a close eye on Fenton,' she said. 'But not close enough, it would seem. I suggest we set our own person to spy on Fenton. Someone who would shadow his every move.' Finally, she spoke to me. 'That boy who travels with you. Is he trustworthy?'

'I – I am not sure he is old enough to be involved in this matter, my lady,' I answered. The thought of Edmund getting caught out by Fenton or Shinclyffe made me shudder.

'Nonsense,' said Anne. 'He has been working as a pot boy for Westmorland, has he not? He could do the same in Markenfield's camp. I will clear it with your master.'

'No need, my lady. I travel with Markenfield. I need some-one to fetch and carry for me.' Norton smiled. 'I will take good care of him, Gray. He can report back to me if he sees Fenton disappearing. I will say nothing of our suspicions to my nephew just yet – the fewer people who know of this, the better.'

'Good. Then it is agreed. Catherine, you may return with Robert to break your fast and come straight back here with the boy when you have finished.'

Bowing, Catherine and I retreated. I trusted Norton, although I could not stay my fear for Edmund's safety.

Catherine

Northallerton, Yorkshire, Saturday 29th November 1569

WE DISCUSSED THE MEETING on the way back to our hearth and decided not to tell Bridget yet of our discovery concerning Harry's father's death. It did not excuse Harry's betrayal, but it made them both feel some sympathy for him. Shinclyffe had lied to Harry and Fenton about what had happened on the pilgrimage. He had somehow laid the blame at the feet of Robert's father. I wondered if it also meant that Fenton would be set up to take any blame should Shinclyffe find himself cornered.

Joining Edmund and Bridget by the fire, we sat down and ate. Robert explained to Edmund that he would have to work for Richard Norton and Master Markenfield for a while. The position he would take on would help the cause and be of great importance. Edmund was as excited as a young foal when first set out in the field with his mother. He raced down the food that Bridget had prepared and gathered his pitiful belongings into a hessian sack. I ate slowly, knowing in my bones that this would not end well. A vision came into my mind, fast and bright as Edmund pranced about, impatient to be off. I could not wipe away the image of Robert carrying Edmund's limp body, and I swiped away a tear before any of them could notice.

Robert snapped at the boy. 'See to the horses while you wait, Edmund. Do not rush Catherine. Her time for rest is short enough.'

Edmund dropped his shoulders and let his sack fall to the ground. 'Yes, Sir,' he mumbled before running at a pace to where the horses and grooms camped.

'I am uncertain of the sense in this, Robert,' I said when he had gone. 'I am sore afraid for him.'

'Norton will take good care of him. He will let naught happen, I am sure.'

Bridget glanced at me. 'What position has he that would put him in danger?'

'The position is not dangerous,' said Robert. 'Catherine worries he will be in close contact with Fenton when he is in the master's kitchens.'

'But why is he needed in the kitchens? They seem well staffed over there.' Bridget frowned and stared at me, and I hoped she did not see through my discomfort.

'Norton wishes a servant to fetch and carry for him – that is all. Nothing more. Now let us eat in peace. I will have much work today at the anvil without Edmund here. You will work the bellows instead, Bridget.'

We made our way back to Northumberland's marquee. Edmund snapped about my heels, chattering on about what his duties to Richard Norton might be. He had never been a personal servant before. 'Not in all my life', he had said. I could not help the smile that rose to my lips as he carried on as if eight years was a lifetime. 'Your new master has lived for many years. He marched alongside Robert's father in the pilgrimage of '36.

'And he is still alive?' Edmund's eyes widened in astonishment.

This time I laughed out loud. 'He could hardly be your master if he were dead, could he?'

'No. He must be old. Does he use a stick to help him? Will I have to help him into his bed at night?'

'Master Norton is a powerful man. Robert says he led the horsemen from Brancepeth Castle when the march began. He is well-loved by all the men who come to fight alongside him.'

Edmund's eyes lit up again. 'And I will be his chief servant.' He jumped and shook his fist in the air. 'I will protect him with my life.'

'You had better contain yourself before we get there; Master Norton will not want a childish boy as a servant. You must stand upright at all times. No fits of giggling or running off to see your beloved horses.'

Edmund stopped in his tracks, shoulders drooping, chin nearly touching his bony chest. 'No horses?'

I stopped and took his hand. 'You will see your horses again soon enough. For now, you must be a brave boy and be loyal to your new master in all that he asks of you. Can you do this? For Robert – for the cause?'

He lifted his shoulders and straightened himself out. Taking a deep breath, he lifted his chin and said, 'I will do it.' His little face was stern as he tried to convince himself, as much as me, that he was up to the job.

'Good lad,' I said. My heart cracked a little, knowing I could be placing him in grave danger.

Many of the march leaders, including Master Thomas, were there when we arrived at the marquee. They were discussing plans for an attack on Barnard Castle. Edmund and I waited in the corner until they had finished speaking. Westmorland said that his son Christopher would take some horsemen and get back to Hartlepool to make sure they held the town long enough for the arrival of the Spanish ships. Master Thomas would ride with him and sail to Spain before accompanying the Spanish forces back to Hartlepool.

'I will take cannon and sling, but I will march towards Barnard and make Bowes think he is already under siege while you carry out our other plans,' said Christopher Neville.

Northumberland agreed. 'I will send a skirmishing party to travel directly after you to keep that wretch Bowes pinned down while some of my men lay claim to his cattle herds over at Darlington. They can forage them around Stockton.' He laughed. 'I am sure the Bishop of Durham and Master Bowes will not mind us helping ourselves to their hay and corn. The men need some action, and they certainly need some food in their bellies.'

Norton agreed to take some men and cut off the castle's water supply from the river Tees. 'I will take the river on the north and south sides. They cannot survive without water.' He looked about the room, and, as I followed his line of sight, I saw Shinclyffe amongst the crowd. He was following Christopher Neville from the tent. 'Shinclyffe? Will you come with me? Your knowledge of this area will be of great help.'

He turned slowly and faced Norton. His face was red, and his voice broke a little as he spoke. 'I had thought to ride with Christopher and Thomas. They may need help to secure Hartlepool.'

'Christopher is well furnished with horse and artillery. I would be most grateful for your company.' Norton's eyes were steely as he stared at Shinclyffe fixedly.

Shinclyffe made a sweeping bow. 'Of course, my lord,' he said. 'I will ready myself and my men at once.'

Soon there was only Norton and a couple of guards left in the marquee. Norton now spotted us sitting in the corner. Edmund's mouth was still wide open as it had been the whole time we had been here. Norton beckoned the boy over.

'Well now, young Edmund. I believe you are to be my manservant for a while. How say you?'

'I – I will be a dutiful servant, Sir.' I could see Edmund's legs were shaking as he tried to stand up straight in front of his new master.

'I am sure you will. Let us away. I have some important work for you.'

There was no time to wish the boy well as Norton hurried away, and Edmund had to run behind him to keep pace.

Countess Anne was in her bedchamber. I went to see if she required my attendance.

'You can help Margery pack my clothes. We are breaking camp and heading for Richmond. My husband and Westmorland have already left with some horsemen. Go to Robert, and I will see you this eve.'

I rushed back to Robert, who had already been told of the move. I helped him and Bridget finish loading our goods and took my place with Bridget on the cart. Robert drove the oxen, and we were soon on our way.

We settled in Richmond in the late afternoon. I hurried to Countess Anne as soon as possible. There was much merriment outside the earl's marquee. Celebrations were in full swing for many of the gentlemen as Cook and Margery waited upon them. The earl and Anne must still be inside. News had arrived that the rebels had successfully cut off the water supply and taken over all of Bowes' grain mills apart from one near the castle, which was well guarded. Others who arrived back at camp were in high spirits, having spent the day baiting Bowes. They still shouted the rhymes they had used to taunt him.

Coward! A coward of Barney Castle.

Dare not come out to fight the battle.

The celebrations spread around the whole camp as news of Barney passed from hearth to hearth. The men and women were finally doing what they had set out to do in the weeks past. A few of Bowes' cattle were slain and roasted on spits. Barrels of ale appeared for all to take a jug and drink heartily.

I dared to look to Master Markenfield's tent before going to my mistress. There was no sign of Master Thomas, and I assumed he must still be at Hartlepool with Christopher Neville. Westmorland was having his evening meal, and I could just make out Edmund, standing close behind him. The little mite was standing stock still, his back straight as a staff, his chin high and looking straight ahead. I had not realised I had been holding my breath until a great sigh escaped. Norton had not taken him to the battle site. I thanked Jesus while rolling the rosary beads, hanging at my waist, between my fingers. Now calmed and allowing a smile to break on my face, I turned to my duties and went to seek the countess.

The mood was a little less buoyant in the Northumberland tent. Word had come that the earl's secretary, Christopher Lockwood, and two gentlemen from Wardell had been taken prisoner and now residing in Barnard Castle's dungeons.

Robert

WE HAD SET OFF before dawn from Richmond and had reached Brancepeth Castle by mid-afternoon. We had passed several horsemen, cannon, archers, and pikemen travelling south and toward Barnard Castle on the road here and through Darlington. The main siege would happen soon. Harry was likely among Bowes' men. The thought of Shinclyffe using him had been playing on my mind. Would Harry have betrayed his master and the Catholic cause if his mother had not fed him those lies? He had always been a devout Catholic, just as I was, and, indeed, my father. If I could speak with him and tell him of what I know, would he return to me as a brother once more? Would we fight side by side against a common enemy? He would forgive my father, who had acted in defence of his friend, I was sure. There was no way my father would have known what they had said before he rushed to give Harry's father an alibi.

As soon as we were settled, I walked Catherine to the castle gates where she was escorted, by a guard, to where Anne's rooms lay. It seemed a lifetime ago since I had first brought the message to Westmorland and Master Thomas. I kissed her farewell and headed back to where Bridget had lit a fire. She had unpacked all and was feeding the pottage with beef strips saved from our feast at Richmond.

I saddled Chestnut. I had given him a nose bag as soon as we had arrived. 'I will take a few strips of that meat with me. I have not time to eat.'

'Where do you go?' she asked.

'To join the siege at Barney Castle.' Checking my quiver was full and taking my bow over my head and across my shoulders, I mounted the horse. 'I do not know when I will return; the siege may be long. Keep safe, Bridget, and tell Catherine not to worry when she next comes.'

I did not say that I was intent on finding Harry. Mayhap he would accompany me when I returned. God willing, I hoped it would be so.

Chestnut enjoyed the freedom to stretch out his legs, and we galloped across many fields, avoiding the roads where we might come upon some of Bowes' men. It seemed strange but finding out the truth of what happened to Harry's father had lifted my spirits. The facts were dire but discovering them had taken a weight from my shoulders and left me with the hope of a reconciliation with my childhood friend.

Within a couple of hours, I was near enough to hear the shouting and sound of cannon. On reaching the brow of a hill, I looked down at the scene. Cannon fire crashed against the castle walls, sending small boulders and shards of stone tumbling down to the grass.

Thousands of men camped in the fields at the rear of the castle, and, on the steep banked side leading up from the river, the gatehouse bridge supports had been half destroyed. There was not a great deal of response from inside the castle – it was mainly in defensive mode. A few archers and harquebusiers manned the walls and fired sporadically down into the jeering troops. I approached our men, holding up a pennant to show my loyalty to Northumberland for fear they thought me one of the enemy. Once arrived, I handed Chestnut to a groomsman and went to take up a position close enough to fire my arrows at the guards atop the walls. They were soon spent, and I went in search of ones that had fallen, undamaged, among the crowds before seeking the fletcher, who was some distance away. Every once in a while, the crowds cheered as a man would leap down from the walls to join us, crying long live Queen Mary. Some made it unscathed, others had broken limbs, and some were severely injured and near death. One or two had been shot in the back by Bowes' men as they fell. Each time a man came over the wall, I raced over to check if it was Harry. Relief washed through me whenever a man who was either dead or injured did not have his familiar face. A tent had been set up for those who had survived but had suffered an injury, and I helped carry and lay them down. There was not much to be done, only splint their broken limbs and hope they would heal.

That evening, Norton arrived back in camp. He was in good spirits, having discovered the secret underground water supply to the castle and blocked its access. There was lots of back-patting as he and his men retired to a marquee. Food and drink, laid out in plenty, awaited their arrival, and it was not long before they were merry. I approached cautiously, but, seeing Shinclyffe seated next to Norton, I turned and walked away. At least Norton was keeping his enemies close for now.

A restless night amongst so many men who lay around the same hearth did nothing for mine or their moods the following morning as dawn cast a pale light over us. My stomach groaned, and I held my dish out eagerly as women walked from hearth to hearth doling out rough bread and stale cheese. I barely chewed on the vile stuff, swallowing chunks whole as I tried to fill my empty belly. I swilled watered ale down between bites to wash the acrid taste from my mouth. Still hungry, I wandered amongst the hearths until I found a family I recognised as neighbours from the market-stede at Rippon. Richard Sutcliffe was a butcher, and Catherine often bought her meat there. They welcomed me and offered a place at their hearth when I told them Catherine was looking after the countess at Brancepeth. It was when my belly growled loudly at the wonderful aroma coming from the pot over their fire that Goodwife Sutcliffe finally offered me some broth. It scalded my mouth and gullet as it went down. As soon as I'd finished, she offered more, which I gladly took along with a wedge of excellent rye bread. This time I ate slowly and savoured each bite.

When I had satisfied my hunger, Richard and I took our places by the wall again and kept Bowes' harquebusiers busy dodging our arrows and unable to fire down at the men.

More cannon, horse, pikemen, and bowmen arrived as the day went on, and it became more apparent that Bowes would stand little chance against us once the rest of the troops arrived from Brancepeth.

Anne Percy – Countess of Northumberland

Brancepeth Castle, Northumberland,
Tuesday 2nd December 1569

ANNE AND NORTHUMBERLAND ATE a hearty breakfast with their hosts and fellow rebels. Anne was pleased that Catherine had calmed her fever, and she was enjoying food again. Though a little unsteady, she was raring to go with her husband and the Westmorlands down to Barney Castle. Westmorland's son, Christopher, had returned from Hartlepool along with Thomas Markenfield the previous eve. They said it would be impossible for the Spanish ships to dock at the port because of tidal flows, and King Philip had been unwilling to support Queen Mary as she had too many ties with France. The earls were furious, knowing how difficult things would be without their help.

'Damned Spanish,' Christopher had wailed over his plate of rollmop herring. 'Cowards. The lot of them.'

Markenfield spoke little, taking the blame upon himself for not bringing the Spanish fleet back with him.

Anne reached across the table and pressed her hand over his. 'Do not blame yourself, Thomas. You have shown courage throughout. Christopher is right, the Spanish are cowards, but we will not give up. We will fight on.'

Thomas nodded. 'Thank you, my lady. We are not done, and we have many supporters.' His brief words and dull tones did not instil confidence.

Christopher stood and raised his glass. 'To victory,' he shouted. All stood and followed suit. 'To victory,' they chorused.

Last night, Christopher, his brothers, and all other rebels of high standing sent out riders to order every man from their jurisdictions to answer a muster to arms and be at Barney Castle by ten of the clock on 3rd December.

Anne returned to her room, where Catherine was packing the countess's clothes. The girl was frowning. She looked worried about something.

'We will march to Barney as soon as we are ready. You will travel with me, Catherine.'

Anne saw Catherine's face relax. She knew the girl would want to be near her husband.

'My lady.' Catherine turned to face the countess. 'What news of young Edmund? Is he to stay here or come with his lordship the Earl of Westmorland?'

'Of that, I am unsure. I would think come as the lad is to be Norton's manservant.'

'Thank you, my lady,' Catherine said and continued to pack.

Within the hour and with 1500 horse and 3000 foot, they set off in a grand procession to Barnard Castle. Anne rode out with Northumberland, looking for all the world a picture of health. She ordered Catherine to travel with her entourage. Anne's smile did not falter the total distance. She would always show strength of character to her followers. Weakness was something she despised.

Catherine

Barnard Castle, Northumberland,
Tuesday 2nd December 1569

I SAT ALONGSIDE MARGERY and Cook as we travelled on to Barney Castle, hardly able to keep my impatience from showing. I was so desperate to see Robert again. He could lie dead amongst the other fatalities or in a hospital tent somewhere. It could take days to find him in the mayhem of battle. I clutched the bag that contained all my herbs and tinctures. I was sure I had everything I needed to treat the injured. Margery was chattering away so much, I wanted to tell her to quiet herself, but she had never been part of a siege before, and her questions were incessant. I told her several times that I had no experience of warfare either, and my only use would be my ability to help the sick and wounded.

I left Bridget behind, at Brancepeth with the other women and elderly men. It relieved me. If she thought, for one minute, that Harry was inside Barney Castle, she would be frantic to see him. I had enough people to worry about for the moment. I had seen Edmund on a cart belonging to Westmorland and his entourage, so I knew he was safe for now. I would go to him when we arrived to find out how he had fared at Brancepeth. There had been no sight of Fenton since before Richmond. I was unsure of where and what he was up to right now. Edmund, I was made to believe, was to monitor both Fenton and Shinclyffe, but Shinclyffe was with Master Norton at Barney.

I was brought out of my thoughts by someone speaking my name.

'Catherine?'

'Yes?' I looked behind me to where Cook passed around rye bread and some cheese.

'Here,' she said. 'You need to eat now, for there will not be much time when we arrive. We will have much to do setting up camp and little time for our own needs.'

'Thank you,' I said. Food was not on my mind, but I realised she was right, and the only way to get through this day was to make sure I was not hungry. I stroked the round of my belly. My skin was so taut now it hindered my movements. The weight pressing down on my bladder made me pass small amounts of water almost continuously. Woollen rags helped to soak up some, but not all, and the inside of my thighs were chafing and had become red and sore. I put a soothing balm on them each morning to quiet the stinging sensation.

After what felt like many hours, even though the position of the sun told me it was not, we came to see the castle from a distance. The thousands of men and horses were a sight to behold. I almost felt a wave of sorrow for the man trying to defend his property against this mighty force. Robert had told me that Robert Bowes had been on the Catholic side during the pilgrimage of '36, but his nephew, George, who now owned the castle, was a Loyalist. It had made the earls angry to have such a man in the centre of the northern territories. They had expected his support.

It took another hour to work our way down to the fields outside the castle walls and then the long afternoon of unpacking, setting up the marquees, and cooking a meal for the earls and other staff. I had to ensure Countess Anne had somewhere to rest and somewhere to dress. Along with Westmorland and other leaders, she and her husband paced out the outer perimeters of the castle walls to see that every section was covered. When they returned, Anne was flushed and excited.

'That poor fool Bowes does not know what he is up against; otherwise, he would have mustered more men and horse. He probably tried, but Sussex does not appear to be in any hurry to send reinforcements.' She laughed and removed her hat, putting it on the bed. 'Catherine, will you make a soothing tea for me? I feel quite tired from all this excitement.'

'I will, Countess,' I replied. 'I know what you need to help you recover from your arduous journey. Let me undress you, and you can lay abed for a while.'

'Thank you. I would welcome the rest.'

I began unbuttoning her dress and disrobing her, making sure she was comfortable before making my way to the kitchen area outside. Cook was busy shouting orders to her staff, and the mouth-watering aromas spiralled up into the sky with the wood smoke from the hearth and filling the air. I was desperate to get back to the countess with her drink and then beg her leave to find Robert.

When I returned, the countess was curled up beneath her wool blankets and was grateful for the warm chamomile drink I had made. Smelling the brew immediately took me back to the summer, picking the flower heads on a bright July day before laying them out on cheesecloth to dry in the warm dark place by the hearth at home. Oh, for the feel of that warm sun now.

I asked if she had seen Robert on her survey of the castle grounds, and she said that she had not, laughing and saying it would be nigh impossible to single a person out amongst the thousands of men. I knew she was right but still intended to look. She gave me leave for a few hours, and, though tired myself, I set off in search of my husband.

As I looked about me, I realised Northumberland's marquee was easy to find, as all the leaders' tents had a pennant flying from the roof to distinguish them from others. It struck me then that Robert could find me much more quickly than I could find him. I looked for Master Norton's pennant and made my way over there to see if I could come upon Edmund.

Edmund was outside the marquee. He was sitting on a small stool and polishing a helmet. 'Edmund,' I whispered from a distance. 'How do you fare?'

He looked up and grinned. Putting the helmet down on the stool, he came over and laid his head atop my belly as he had done many times before. The coldness of his cheek burned through my dress.

'I miss you,' he said. 'Is Master Robert near?'

'Perhaps,' I said. 'I have decided to wait until he finds me. It is difficult to search among so many people.'

'Oh.' His face was sad, and his mouth turned down as if ready to cry.

'Fear not. He will show up soon enough. Look up there,' I said, pointing at the pennant. 'He will look for this flag to find you, and he will look for Northumberland's flag to come to me.' I put my hand under his chin. 'Worry not about Robert. He can take care of himself.'

We walked back to his stool. He offered it to me, knowing how difficult it would be to lower myself to the ground. 'Tell me how you spent your time back at Brancepeth. Did they treat you well?' I asked. Sitting cross-legged on the cold grass, Edmund took up the helmet again, polishing while he told me of his days at Brancepeth, of how he had helped the cook as he had done before until the day Robert had come and found him all those weeks ago. The cook, Mistress Oswyn, had made sure his every minute was taken up with tasks. He did not mind. He said it kept him busy, and it was warm by the kitchen fire. He thought they were pleased to see him and made merry with him and cuffed his ears gently in jest. I was glad to hear his news.

'I wish I were back there where it was warm. The cold seeps through my bones until I ache,' he said. Poor boy, I took my wadmol cloak and put it around his shoulders. 'No, Mistress Catherine,' he said, trying to take it off. 'You and the baby need to keep warm. You need it more than I.'

'I have another. You will put my mind at rest if you take the cloak.' I placed it back around him. 'I worry enough for Robert. To fear for you as well is no good for me or my baby.' Squeezing his shoulder, I added, 'Besides, who will help me care for this child when we all go home to Rippon?'

He leaned into me, not looking up as he rubbed furiously at the helmet. 'I would like that,' he croaked.

I asked if Master Norton had given him much instruction as to what his work would be here, and he said little except that he should busy himself with polishing the armour.

'Have you seen Master Shinclyffe?' I asked.

'Yes. He is inside with Master Norton. They are discussing tomorrow's plan.'

I was pleased that Shinclyffe's whereabouts were known, but I shuddered at the thought, kissing the crown of Edmund's head before leaving him to his duties.

I strolled around for a while, sticking close to the walls just in case I might come across Robert. Edmund was much on my mind. I could not reconcile myself to the thought that Robert and I had put him in such danger. This was where Edmund would be told to follow Shinclyffe and see if he passed information to the enemy. It would be easy for the traitor to slip away in such crowds. On my travels, I came across a large tent. The moans and groans from within told me it was a hospital. A young woman came out carrying a bowl of bloody water. She emptied it on the ground and filled it with clean water from a barrel before disappearing inside again. I followed her. The stench of blood and death had been about me as I had wandered about the camp, but, in here, it was so thick I could taste it. My stomach turned, and I tried to hold back a retch as I covered my mouth and nose with my arm. An elderly man pushed a bowl into my hands. His apron was scarlet with blood.

'Do not stand about, woman. Fetch me clean water,' he said and turned away from me.

I hurried away and filled the bowl as the woman had done. When I returned, the man was kneeling by a young boy who looked no more than twelve years. It was clear the man was a doctor, as he pulled on the boy's leg expertly. The jagged end of white bone, which had been protruding through the skin, now disappeared as the doctor manipulated it back into place. The boy screamed and screamed in pain before falling away into a dead faint. Kneeling beside the doctor, I placed the bowl by his side. I looked around for something to bathe the ragged wound. A pile of linen rags lay nearby, and I grabbed a handful.

'You do not sicken more?' the doctor asked. 'When I came across you, I thought you would keel over.'

'I am well, Sir. Sometimes my child decides whether or not a smell is pleasant.'

He smiled. 'Children may be small, in some circumstances, even unborn, but they let themselves be heard enough to get our attention.' The doctor was now stitching up the gash in the boy's leg with a bone needle and gut thread.

'I have knitbone in my bag. Shall I fetch it?' I asked.

The doctor looked at me curiously, his eyes resting on my patch as most people found themselves doing on first meeting me. 'You are a healer?'

'I am, Sir. My mother taught me.'

He smiled again.

'You could be useful to me here. Go. Fetch your bag, also fetch eggs and flour for a cast if you can find some. We have run out thanks to all who believe they can jump from the castle walls without injury.'

'Why do they do such a dangerous thing?'

'In their hearts, they know we are just in our cause. They are true Catholics.'

I wondered if Harry was among those who risked their lives in this way. For Bridget's sake, I hoped he might be. I got to my feet. Excited about helping the doctor, I almost forgot about my duty to the countess. 'I am unsure if I can work here, Sir. My mistress, Countess Anne, may not allow it.'

'Anne? Northumberland's wife?' I nodded. 'I am sure she will. I prescribe for her when she resides at Topcliffe.' He turned back to his stitching. 'Hurry now. Tell her Doctor Bartholomew requires your services.'

I was still watching his stitchwork. It was neat but not as tidy as my own. We were in the middle of a battlefield, and there was no time for care. Men were being carried in and laid down every minute.

'What are you waiting for, Goodwife…?'

'Catherine, sir,' I said. 'Catherine Gray.'

'Then hurry, Catherine Gray. I do not have all day to wait upon your return.'

I hauled myself up off the ground and hastened back to my mistress.

The countess had reluctantly agreed that the doctor needed my services more than she. Margery was called to attend and told she would see to her mistress during the day while they camped here. 'But,' she had said to me, 'you will return in the evenings to tend to my needs.' I had agreed, picked up my bag and hurried away to the kitchen.

I got back to the tent as quickly as I could, pulling a small handcart filled with sacks of flour, a large basket of eggs, and my bag of herbs and tinctures. The doctor sent me to the boy he had been stitching earlier, asking me to put a compress of knitbone on the wound and make a cast to hold it in place. The boy came in and out of consciousness as I made up a poultice of comfrey leaves. I gave him a tincture of laudanum to ease the pain while I mixed up several egg whites with flour to make a cast. He seemed more comfortable when his leg was made stiff and secure and drifted into a deep sleep.

Looking about me, I went to anyone who appeared in need of help and was soon lost in tending the sick – stitching wounds, serving herbal drinks, cutting out musket balls that were buried deep in the flesh. I knelt beside those ready for death and needing prayer and a hand to hold while waiting for a priest to give them their last rites. I talked soothingly to a man while I pulled an arrow from his shoulder. I could tell from the shaft and fletching that it was a bodkin arrow and not barbed. I removed it delicately and swiftly to cause the least damage before closing the hole with wadding. Finally, I bound his chest and shoulder with linen bandages and prayed the tip had not been poisoned.

Dr Bartholomew had little time for words but pointed out another patient who required my help. I was happy to do what I could. I had not been needed so much in a long time, and it was good to play my part. A sudden rush of familiar guilt swept over me as, once again, I remembered the terrible death of my family. If only I had not left on that day. If only I had made sure they did not welcome that stranger into their home.

It was dark outside the tent, and I knew I should get back to the countess. I searched out the doctor and told him it was time for me to go. He looked exhausted, his face pale and grey.

'I thank you, Catherine Gray. You have been a great help to me this day. I look forward to the same tomorrow. Give my good wishes to Countess Anne.' He turned and helped a soldier guide another wounded man to a gap on the floor. It was at that point I realised how utterly exhausted I was too. I also realised I had not eaten since the cheese and bread on the cart as we travelled here.

When I got back to the marquee, the countess was changing for her evening meal. Margery seemed to have things under control as I entered the bedchamber.

'Good Lord in Heaven,' said the countess. 'What on earth—' She was staring at me in horror. I looked down at myself and saw that my apron was covered in blood and was filthy. My hands were caked in dried blood too. 'I am sorry, Countess. I will go and change.' I turned to leave, suddenly finding it difficult to put one foot in front of another.

'Catherine. You look exhausted,' said Anne. 'Wash yourself and put on your nightclothes.' I wanted to say I was fine. 'Margery will bring you some food.'

'But I—'

'Do as I say. You need to eat and sleep. No arguments.' Her voice was stern. 'Margery. Help her before she falls.'

Margery sat me on my cot and undressed me. She wetted a rag and cleaned my hands and face before pulling a nightdress over my head. My body shook. 'I will be back with a broth as soon as I can,' she said. I felt myself falling...

The bird was gaining on me, the sharp talons curled, ready to pin me to the ground. Not the ground? A wall? My screams flew silently into the feathers of its beard.

Robert

Barnard Castle, Yorkshire,
Wednesday 3rd December 1569

I WAS TIRED, BUT I had to see Catherine. After eating, I made my way amongst the hearths and tents where torchlight and open fires lit the way. Many men were on night duty, guarding the walls in case of a surprise attack from inside. It took little time to come across Northumberland's marquee and the revellers still making merry and drinking outside. Northumberland and the countess were there, and Master Thomas had joined them along with one or two other gentlemen. I looked to see if Shinclyffe was about. Half of me hoping he was not, but half afraid he was out in the dark somewhere, passing on messages to Bowes and being followed by Edmund. My stomach lurched.

I had expected Catherine to be standing behind the countess, but I could not see her. I made my way around the edges of the party until I came to the kitchen area. Cook and her servants were busy at the hearth. I scanned the group until I found Margery's familiar face as she took her supper on a log by the fire. I approached her, and she recognised me, beckoning me to sit beside her.

'Robert. Come,' she said, patting the log. 'Sit beside me.'

'I come to see Catherine, but she is not here.' I hoped she might have a suitable answer as a feeling of panic rose inside. Thoughts of her lying dead from giving birth too soon flooded my mind.

'Worry not,' she said. 'Catherine sleeps.' She patted the log again, and I sat down beside her.

'She sleeps? Does she not need to attend her mistress?'

'She has been helping the injured and dying. The countess gave her leave to do so. She was so tired when she returned, and the countess ordered she be put to bed and given some broth.'

'I must see her,' I said, getting up from the log.

'Wait a moment. I will fetch the broth. She was sound asleep afore I could get it to her an hour or two ago.' She went to Cook and brought back a fresh bowl of steaming broth. As usual, my gut growled as I took the bowl from her. She laughed. Then, looking over to her master and mistress, she ran and fetched a second bowl for me. 'There,' she said, smiling. 'You can eat supper together. I will take you to her.'

'Thank you kindly, Margery,' I said, grinning.

Margery ran ahead and whispered in Anne's ear. The countess looked up at me and nodded.

Inside the tent, it was warm and dry. Catherine was sleeping in her cot in the countess's bedchamber. Margery left us both alone.

I sat at the cot side and put the bowls down on the packed earth floor. She looked like an angel lying there in the torchlight, her face calm, a slight smile on her lips. I removed a wisp of hair from her face and stroked her cheek as gently as I could. Her eyelid fluttered for a moment, then opened wide. She looked up at me, her face puzzled and frowning, and then she smiled and lifted her arms. I snuggled my face into her neck, breathing in her scent and kissing the soft, silky skin.

'Robert,' she whispered. 'Thank God you are safe.' Her arms wrapped around my shoulders, pulling me close.

'Look,' I said, sitting upright again. 'Margery has given us some broth. We can eat together.'

She pulled herself up onto her elbows and looked down at the steaming bowls.

'You are most certainly my husband,' she said, half laughing. 'When it comes to love or food, your mind is always on the food.'

I kissed her nose and helped her to sit up properly. 'You, my dearest wife, know me too well.'

I passed Catherine a bowl, and she ate ravenously. She had clearly not eaten enough this day. 'Margery tells me you have been helping the injured.'

'Yes. I asked the countess for leave to do so. I was with a Doctor Bartholomew from Topcliffe.' Her face saddened. 'There are so many injured, Robert. I could not stand by when my skills as a healer were in desperate need.'

'I agree. Our men need the best help they can get. But...' I stroked her face again, trying to wipe away the worry there. 'You must not tire yourself too much. You have yourself and our baby to think of.'

'I will be careful, I promise,' she said. 'Have you seen, Edmund?'

'No. I have come to see you first. I will find him when I leave you.'

Her face clouded over again. 'I saw him this afternoon, cleaning armour for Richard Norton. He told me Shinclyffe was inside the tent discussing plans.' She put her hand on my arm. 'Did we do the right thing, Robert? Have we placed the boy in too much danger?'

'I hope not. Norton is a good man, and he will look after him. Now, if you have finished your supper, settle back, and I will leave when you are asleep.'

I waited until her breath was sound before I left the tent and went in search of Edmund.

When I arrived at Norton's tent, Edmund was nowhere to be seen. Norton and his sons were eating supper. I checked to see if Shinclyffe was among them, and, as he was not, I approached the men and bowed.

'Good eve, sire,' I said to Norton. 'I am sorry to disturb your supper. I wondered if I might have a word with young Edmund.'

'He is on an errand for me, Goodman Gray. He should not be long.'

Norton turned back to his sons and continued eating.

'Can you tell me where he is gone, sire? I would speak with him. My wife is concerned about his welfare.'

Norton took the piece of fowl from his mouth. 'I am sure he will be back shortly. You need not trouble yourself regarding his welfare. He has but gone to fetch a fresh barrel of ale from my stock over yonder.' Norton waved his chicken leg toward a store tent some twenty or thirty yards away.

'Thank you, my lord.' I replied. Finally, having received the answer I was looking for, I bowed again and took my leave.

The tent was dark as I approached, save for a soldier standing guard by the door. I nodded and smiled. 'Is the boy still inside?' I asked.

'Boy?'

'Yes. Master Norton sent him to collect a barrel of ale.'

'No boy here. Nor has there been this eve.' The soldier narrowed his gaze. 'What are you really here for?'

'Master Norton has this minute told me he sent the boy. Ask him if you do not believe me.'

'I cannot leave my post, Goodman. Are you sure he said here?'

I could feel the bile rising in my throat, the anger making my blood hot. 'Damn it, man. Of course, I am sure. Has anyone else been here tonight?'

'Only Master Markenfield's servant. Come to think of it. There was a boy. He was hiding behind the tent. The servant grabbed him and clipped his ear. The lad was probably slothful and not wanting to work.'

'What did this servant look like? Was he tall and wiry?' I swallowed the panic down.

'Aye. The servant told the boy he had been too long and that his master was looking for him. He marched him away.'

I strode back to Norton. Without waiting for permission to speak, I bellowed. 'Fenton has the boy. What time did you send him? Jesus Christ, he could be dead by now.'

Norton got to his feet and gave orders to his sons. 'Search around Markenfield's hearth. Scour his tents,' he shouted. 'You come with me,' he said. 'We will search out Shinclyffe.'

I followed him swiftly to where Shinclyffe's tent was situated towards the perimeter of the wall. 'His hearth had been set up here by his servants. It was too late to get him to move it closer to mine.'

'You said you would take care of my son,' I blurted without thinking.

'Your son?' he asked.

'Not my blood son, but as near to being a son as he can be. Catherine and I have grown to love the boy much.'

'I am sorry, Gray. I am at fault and beg your forgiveness.' He walked at my side now. 'He has not been gone long. We will find him.'

Shinclyffe was not at his hearth or inside his tent. There were but a few servants.

'Where is your master?' asked Norton.

'He is gone to eat with his lordship, Westmorland, Master

Norton,' said a fair-haired woman who was scouring a bowl by the fire.

'Was he accompanied?'

'No. Goodman Fenton and a boy came to see him. I told them the same, but they did not go to my master.'

'Why do you say this?'

'Because they went towards the bridge and the gatehouse.'

We left them and raced towards the bridge. 'What instructions had you given Edmund?' I asked.

'That if he saw Fenton, he should follow him and report back to me.'

'God's blood. Let us be in time.'

There was no one on the bridge apart from a sentry. We asked if he had seen a gentleman and his servant pass this way with a small boy. The sentry shook his head. I wondered if Shinclyffe's servant had been told to lie if anyone questioned his whereabouts.

'We will go to Markenfield's hearth and see what my sons have found,' said Norton.

Again, I followed, hoping with all my heart that Edmund was safe and had escaped Shinclyffe's clutches.

There was no word of Fenton or Shinclyffe at Master Thomas's marquee, but after Norton had spoken to him, he joined the search. My master sent out his servants to look about the camp, and Norton did the same. I knew there was not much hope. It would be too easy to hide a small boy in such a vast camp.

I spent the whole night looking in and around as many hearths as I could, even though I knew it was hopeless. Where could he be? He could be lying dead in a ditch, or they may have thrown him in the river. Fenton or Shinclyffe would despatch him without a second thought. I had to find him, no matter what. I dropped to my knees and prayed that God would save Edmund.

When it was light enough, I went to find Catherine. She was not with the countess and had already broken her fast and gone to Dr Bartholomew's hospital tent. I could hear the cries afore I reached it and went straight inside. Catherine was kneeling beside a man with a sword wound to his arm. She was preparing to stitch the gash that ran the length of his forearm. The man moaned and groaned, lashing out at her as the pain came in waves. The blood refused to stop while she stitched his arm as if it were a smock or a kirtle. I knelt beside her, held the man down, and placed a piece of wood between his teeth. Her patient bit down hard on the wood as Catherine completed her task with speed. She smiled at me without speaking.

When she had finished, she bandaged the arm and gave him something for the pain.

'I cannot take time to talk. There are many more men await-ing treatment,' she said, wiping the back of her hand across her forehead. 'Can you come and find me when the sun is high, and we will walk together for a short while.'

'I cannot wait that long. I have grave news, my love. Edmund has been taken by that evil lout, Fenton.'

Catherine's hand went to her throat. 'Dear Lord. Where is he? Oh, God.' She pulled her apron off. 'I will come with you.' She walked ahead of me.

'No,' I said, grabbing her arm. 'These men need you. I will come back each hour if I can and report my findings.' A solitary tear ran down her cheek, and I pulled her to me. 'Take heart. I will not stop until I find him. I must continue the search. It will be easier to search by day.'

Catherine looked up at me. 'Promise. Promise me you will find him. I could not bear to lose him.'

I kissed her forehead. 'I promise. I will bring him back to us, I swear.' I hurried away before she had time to come after me. I would find him. I would not stop until he was returned safely to us.

I made my way to Master Thomas's tent. As soon as he saw me, he came to my side.

'What news, Robert? Have you found the boy?'

'No, Master. I came to see if you had any news.'

'Damn, Fenton. I have allowed him a rope to hang himself, but he has not taken the bait so far. Until last night, of course.' He looked as worried as I was, and I was pleased to have his support again. 'Norton says we should wait and see if the boy turns up.'

'Has there been a sighting of Shinclyffe?'

'I am not sure. We ought to check his tent,' Thomas said, and we made our way there.

As we approached, we saw Shinclyffe enjoying a hearty breakfast. I wanted to tear him apart. Thomas stayed me with his hand. 'Wait here,' he said. 'If he sees you, he will not be open. Wait until I walk away and then get as close as you can without him seeing you. I want to see what he does.'

I agreed, although reluctantly, and watched as Master Thomas strode over to Shinclyffe and sat beside him. Shinclyffe grinned, offering my master some food. They ate and talked for a while. Why was my master wasting so much time? I could see Shinclyffe's eyes widen as if surprised at what he was being told. Then he frowned and patted my master's shoulder, feigning sympathy.

When Thomas walked away, I moved in closer. Shinclyffe was quickly up on his feet and left his hearth. I followed discreetly, hoping he would not catch sight of me. Master Thomas was close behind. Before long, I realised he was heading for the bridge. Had we missed something last night?

Shinclyffe walked across the banking below the wall until he reached the castle gatehouse. He looked around to see if anyone was following him before disappearing down the banking at the side of the bridge to the river below. We waited a moment or two before following him. Shinclyffe was lurking in the shadow of one of the bridge's enormous stone supports. It was still standing in the main but blasted away by heavy ordinance in parts, making its strength now questionable. We watched as Shinclyffe whistled the first bars of a tune, and it was not long before Fenton appeared.

'What have you done with him, fool?' Shinclyffe said through gritted teeth. 'I have a pack of gentlemen and earls on my tail. They do not hold with the kidnapping of small boys. Especially one that even gullible Markenfield is fond of.'

Thomas looked shocked. He had been sure that Shinclyffe was a loyal friend. The knuckles on his hand turned white as he gripped his sword and stepped out from the shadows.

'Wait,' I whispered, pulling him back. 'Please, Master. I need to know what has happened to Edmund.' I thought he might barge in there, but Thomas stopped short, nodded, and stayed beside me.

'He's in the hollow down here,' said Fenton, sneering. 'He was following me. No doubt put up to it by Gray. He should take greater care of the boy. Little boys get themselves into a lot of trouble, wandering about on their own.' He snorted with laughter.

'Show me,' said Shinclyffe, and they both disappeared under the bridge. We followed them, taking great care to be quiet.

Fenton's voice echoed in the darkness as he continued speaking. 'I'll give the little bastard his due. He would not tell me anything about why he was following me or who had sent him. His mouth has been as tight as a beer barrel.'

Now it was Shinclyffe's turn to laugh. 'I think it is time we closed his mouth for good – after a little sport, that is. Small boys are almost as delectable as small girls.'

Now it was my turn to unsheathe my sword. Let them harm a hair of his head, and I will chop them into small pieces. Their own mothers will not know them.

Thomas touched my arm. 'Go around to the other side,' he whispered. 'Come at them from behind.'

I was unsure. I needed to be where I could see them. What would happen to Edmund if I did not follow their every move? I shook my head, but my master pushed me. 'Go,' he whispered. 'It will be fine. I will let nothing happen.'

I slid away, running up the banking before crossing and hurrying down to enter the underside of the bridge from the opposite side. Shinclyffe was still talking.

'I have news to pass on to Bowes. When do you meet Gardyner next?'

'Soon. He will meet me here this eve at eight,' said Fenton.

'Good. Tell him that the Spanish will not come. Tell him he needs to get to Sussex and join him. The queen's army will be in Wetherby within a day or two. Over 12,000 horse and foot, I am told.'

'That is good news, sire.'

The two men were walking towards me. Edmund must be somewhere close by. I peered into the dark but could neither see nor hear anything. I waited. They were getting closer, so I moved back until I collided with stonework, my back pressed against it. It was at that moment I heard a slight moan to my left. Fenton and Shinclyffe appeared and walked over to where I could now see Edmund hanging from a rope by his wrists; his mouth gagged; his head lolled to one side. Rage took complete control, and I flew at the two men, sword in hand. Fenton was taken by surprise as my sword entered his chest, and he fell to his knees, still clutching the blade, blood seeping through his fingers. Shinclyffe leapt over and thrust his sword into my side. There was no pain in the first two or three seconds, and I grabbed him by the throat as he twisted the blade and withdrew the weapon. I felt a rib break as he wrenched it out, and though the pain shot through my body, I still held on to him.

'Hold off, Gray. I want him alive.' Master Thomas held his sword to Shinclyffe's cheek, so I let him go and collapsed back against the stone. Master Thomas continued to back Shinclyffe up against the wall. 'Get the boy down,' he said to me, 'then tie this traitor up.'

I pulled myself upright and went to Edmund. My dagger soon sliced through the rope that strung him up, and I lowered him to the ground. Untying the rope around his wrists, I used it to tie Shinclyffe's hands behind his back. Making them as tight as I could to cut off the bastard's blood supply, I took pleasure in hearing him wince.

My master led Shinclyffe away, and I followed, carrying an unconscious Edmund in my arms. All thought of my wound disappeared as I raced to get my poor boy to the hospital tent. Tears streamed down my face, but I did not care. The boy's face was a mass of purple bruising, his body cold as stone. They have suspended him up there all night. Dear Mary, mother of God, I prayed. Please let this child live. Take me if you wish it so, but let this boy live.

Catherine

Barnard Castle, Yorkshire, Thursday 4th December 1569

It was difficult to concentrate on the tasks in front of me. I was so worried about Edmund I could not think straight. The man I was tending screamed as I bathed his wound until I realised I was kneeling on his arm. I had not seen the twisted shape of it in my hurry to deal with the gash across his chest – a near miss from a sword that was not deep enough to have pierced his heart. I apologised and took a better look at the arm. The displaced elbow had almost turned his forearm backwards so that his hand was facing the wrong way. I carried on with the chest wound, cleaning and then stitching the skin back together. I was not strong enough to handle his arm and went to find Doctor Bartholomew.

The doctor took hold of the man's arm while I held him down. We had just finished putting the elbow back in place when Master Thomas came running into the tent, swiftly followed by Robert. Edmund lay floppy in Robert's arms, and I hurried over.

'Lay him down here, Robert,' I said, crying out when I saw the damage to Edmund's face.

It did not surprise me to see that Robert's eyes were bloodshot and swollen with grief. 'Fenton had him strung up under the bridge all night. He is frozen to the core.'

The doctor came over and felt Edmund's forehead. 'He has a fever. Collect blankets and cover him well.'

Robert stood there as if in a trance, unhearing. 'Fetch hot water, Robert,' I said. 'Now!' I knew he needed to be busy.

It woke him from his daydream, and he started. 'I – I – What?'

'Fetch some hot water. I need to make him a drink.' I pushed him towards the entrance. 'Bring a bowl of thin pottage. He can drink the broth as well.'

Robert shook himself and dashed off to do my bidding. I did not know if the boy would drink any of what I was suggesting, but if it kept Robert occupied while the doctor looked Edmund over, it would help.

'What do you think?' I asked the doctor. 'Will he survive?'

He took hold of Edmund's wrist. 'His pulse is weak. He has no strength to generate his own heat.'

'Then I will warm him with my body.' I climbed in beside him and held him close, the icy touch of his skin making me shiver. My baby wriggled in discontent as I prayed, my rosary beads playing through my fingers.

'Pray as hard as you can; the cold is through his very bones,' the doctor said. 'I think only God can save him now.'

When Robert returned with water and a bowl of pottage, I asked him to take a turn under the blankets while I made a medicinal drink of yarrow tea to quiet the fever. I noticed that Robert winced as he got down to do my bidding.

'Are you hurt?' I asked, kneeling down beside him.

'Tis naught to worry about. Just a nick from Shinclyffe's blade. It will soon heal.'

I felt sick at the thought. Lifting his shirt, I could see the small wound where the sword had entered. Already a bloom of purple bruising had spread out across his side. I searched his side with my fingers, and he let out a small yelp as my hand landed on a lower rib.

'I think it is cracked. I will strap it for you when we have settled, Edmund.'

Robert held Edmund's head up as I fed him the liquor with a small spoon. When it was gone, I did the same with tiny drops of the broth. The poor boy coughed it back out of his mouth.

'Lie with him a while,' I said. 'I will fetch some linen and bind your wound.'.'

Robert's eyes were dark with worry as he cradled Edmund. 'Will he live?'

'Only God can decide now. Hold him close and get some sleep.' I passed Robert the bowl of thin pottage, which he drank down thirstily before lying back.

Robert and Edmund slept soundly for a few hours. Each time I came back to check on them, they were still resting quietly together. Robert had turned over in his sleep, and Edmund had spooned himself to Robert's back. Seeing them in this position was a good sign. Edmund loved to sleep against Robert in this way, which meant he was feeling better. I knelt and touched his forehead. It was cooler – another good sign.

Darkness fell by mid-afternoon, and the gentle sound of prayers filled the tent. Priests walked about the wounded, saying prayers and anointing each patient. The smell of wood smoke and scented oils filled the air, dampening the sickly smell of death. It brought a settling and calm that filled everyone's hearts and minds. I passed a man who lay with his hands pressed to an open wound in his belly. The light had gone from his eyes, and a priest stood over him, chanting the last rites. I knelt beside the man and took his bloody hand. His eyes flickered open, and he looked at me. There was the faintest smile on his grey face, then he took one deep breath and stilled. The priest crossed himself as he continued to pray. I struggled to my feet and went out of the tent.

The air was sharp with frost, and the new moon shone like a tipsy smile, tilted up at one side in the black face of the sky. Pulling my shawl tight around me, I made my way over to Norton's marquee. He and Master Thomas were sitting at the side of a blazing hearth. My master saw me and hailed me over.

'Come. Tell us of the boy. Is he recovered?'

'He is asleep, but the fever has broken. I come for some more broth for him and Robert, Master.'

'Of course,' said Norton. 'See the cook. She will give you what you need.'

'What will happen to Master Shinclyffe?' I asked, hoping the news would be of his imminent death. The two men looked at each other. I sensed that something was wrong.

'He got away from me in the dark,' said Master Thomas. 'Someone clubbed me from behind as I led him back.' Master Thomas rubbed the back of his head. 'He obviously has others working for him as well as Fenton. We think he has gone to ground. There has been no sighting since we found Fenton and the boy,' he continued. 'He is keeping his head down. We must keep a close eye on Edmund and make sure Shinclyffe or one of his men does not get close enough to despatch him before he speaks.'

'Then he must be brought to you and put under your protection, Master. He is in great danger in a tent full of men coming and going.' I tried to keep the fear out of my voice, but it was hopeless. 'Mayhap, I could fetch him straight away?' I looked at Master Thomas, hopefully.

'Mayhap it would be for the best,' he said. 'We will need to speak to him as soon as he is able. Fetch him now.'

I raced back to the hospital where Robert was sitting up, and Edmund was awake and on his lap. I felt Edmund's forehead. It was still warm, but he managed to smile at me and croak a grunt of greeting.

'Come, Robert. We must bring Edmund to Master Thomas, where he can be guarded. Shinclyffe has escaped and has not been found yet. The master thinks he will try to silence the boy.'

I settled Edmund in a small cot in Master Thomas's bedchamber and fed him some broth. He ate a little and was soon snoring. A guard stood outside the tent, and, satisfied that Edmund was safe, I went outside to find Robert.

He was sitting with Norton and the master, and they were discussing what they were to do next in their search for Shinclyffe.

'Fenton told Shinclyffe he would meet Harry at eight of the clock this eve,' said Robert. 'I will wait under the bridge for him.'

'He will only be there if Shinclyffe could not warn him,' said Master Thomas. 'We do not know if he has arranged for another spy to meet him.'

'I will still go. I need to speak to him.'

'Then I will come with you. The filthy traitor needs to be taught a lesson.' Thomas looked almost glad to be given an opportunity to make Harry pay for his actions. He withdrew his sword and began polishing it with an oiled rag. 'He will soon feel the wrath of—'

Robert jumped to his feet and interrupted. 'I do not believe he would have betrayed us if it were not for Fenton and Shinclyffe's lies. We must see things from his side.'

'His side? Do you support Gardyner ahead of your master?' He was glaring at Robert now, his eyes full of rage.

'Do not be so hasty, Nephew. I think we need to talk.' Norton put a hand on Thomas's arm. 'There are things you do not know about. I almost understand why Gardyner betrayed the cause.'

Robert relaxed as Norton nodded for him to sit. Then we listened again to what Norton had told Robert about the Pilgrimage of Grace. I could see Master Thomas's face change when he heard what Shinclyffe had done and how his father had done nothing to stop the hanging.

'Why did you not say something at the time?' Thomas demanded of his uncle.

'Because we did not suspect, Shinclyffe. It was not until Robert came to tell us how he had followed the scoundrel that it occurred to me. I think Shinclyffe would have handed over Fenton and Gardyner if I had questioned him; he would have blamed them, saying he caught them in the act.'

Master Thomas was silent for a few moments, and then he turned to Robert. 'I will still come with you. Gardyner needs to explain himself; he still betrayed me.'

I nodded at my master but knew that mine and Norton's words were not quite enough to bring him around. Still, Harry would give his side to the master, and, in return, Robert could explain to Harry what had happened to his father.

I should be at the countess's side by now. My heart said I must stay with Edmund, and I asked Master Norton if he could send word to my mistress to say that I would stay with Edmund this night if she would allow. He agreed and sent a man directly.

Robert took my hand and kissed it gently. 'I will come to see you as soon as I return from my meeting with Harry.'

'May God keep you safe,' I said and returned to Edmund's side. Lying down beside him, I knew I must not let him out of my sight.

Robert

I SET OFF TOWARDS the bridge. Master Thomas walked beside me. I could not see his face well in the dark, but he was not in a good mood. I wondered if he might go back on his word when he set eyes on Harry. Master Thomas had a violent temper and could not be calmed easily when his rages were at full tilt.

'Do you think he will turn up?' I asked.

'What should I know? I am no sorcerer.' His tone was as brittle as twigs snapping underfoot. 'Mayhap, you should have asked your wife. She is supposed to be able to work magic on the sick. She perhaps knows the future as well.'

I swallowed the fury that rushed up and into my mouth, threatening to explode in a torrent of angry words. Antagonising him now would not do any good. 'Why do you speak so, Master? Catherine has ne'er shown you anything but respect and kindness.'

'Let us get this deed done. I need the truth of the matter. My uncle seems to put my father's memory in disgrace.'

'Shinclyffe has done the same of mine. We both have reasons to be aggrieved.'

We walked on in silence, coming to the bridge a little before eight of the clock, according to my master's timepiece.

'We will wait until it is the hour,' said Thomas, sitting on the ground by a small bush, his back pressed into the perimeter wall. 'It will be easy to hear if someone comes or goes.'

I sat alongside him, and we waited but a few minutes before a voice came loud from under the bridge.

'At last, traitor, you show your face.'

There was no doubting who the voice belonged to – Shinclyffe. The master and I jumped to our feet and raced down the banking and under the bridge. Shinclyffe held Harry from behind, his arm around his throat, a dagger pressing into Harry's back. He turned his head towards us, a broad grin on his face. 'Ah. You have arrived in time to see me skewer this betrayer of our cause.'

Thomas and I drew our swords. 'Hand him over, Shinclyffe,' said Thomas. 'You do not fool me. You are the traitor.'

Shinclyffe's eyes widened in mock disbelief. 'Thomas. I swear to you. I only went along with the rogues until I could get enough evidence to be sure of their guilt.'

Thomas put the tip of his sword to Shinclyffe's chin. 'Then why did you run from me last eve?'

'I was afraid you might kill me afore I had explained myself. I thought to come back here tonight and capture this villain and make him confess his guilt.'

Thomas pushed the blade a little further into Shinclyffe's neck until a pinprick of blood trickled onto his ruff. 'The same trick never works twice, Shinclyffe. Even a fool would know as much. You should know that. You tricked my father into believing you when you said Gardyner's father was a traitor after he caught you spying against Robert Aske.'

Harry's face bore a look of puzzlement. I could see he was trying to make sense of everything.

'He was the reason your father died,' I said to Harry. 'Your father caught Shinclyffe passing messages to the enemy, and when the evil wretch saw him telling old Master Markenfield what he had been up to, he claimed it was your father who had been the traitor and insisted he be hanged there and then.'

I watched as Harry slipped his dagger from his belt.

'No, Harry. You will hang for it.'

Harry paused, unsure of what to do.

'Drop it, Gardyner, and I promise Shinclyffe will pay,' said Thomas. Harry obeyed his master, and I let out the breath I had been holding.

Thomas pushed his blade a little further into Shinclyffe's neck. 'Now let loose of him, or I will drive this sword right through you.'

Shinclyffe waited just a second before thrusting his dagger into Harry's back. Harry slumped to the floor as Thomas pulled Shinclyffe away.

'Search him,' Thomas demanded, and I did as he asked, finding a sealed missive in Shinclyffe's pocket, which I passed to my master.

I knelt beside Harry and pulled the dagger from him. The blood only seemed to trickle at first. I took off my shirt and tore it to make a bandage.

A moment later, Shinclyffe ran out from under the bridge and disappeared into the darkness. Thomas had been knocked to the floor but scrambled to his feet and ran after him.

I strapped up Harry's wound and cradled his head on my lap. 'You will be safe soon,' I said softly, 'I must get you to the doctor quickly,'

Thomas returned and put one of Harry's arms around his neck. 'Shinclyffe has disappeared,' he said. 'I think he must have gone to Bowes now we have discovered him.'

I took Harry's other arm, and together we hoisted him up and dragged him along between us, the toes of his leather boots scraping along the ground.

Harry had lost a lot of blood by the time we got back to the hospital tent. The doctor and a helper took him from us. I told him what had happened and stayed to watch the doctor tend and stitch up his wound. Master Thomas left us and went back to see Norton. I knelt beside Harry as he lay face-down on a thin bed of straw. The doctor had given him something for the pain, and he seemed to be comfortable.

'I will come back to see you when you are rested,' I said.

He grabbed my hand and whispered. 'No. Please stay. Is Bridget here?'

'No,' I said. 'She is at Brancepeth. You will see her soon enough.'

'I am sorry for what I have done, Robert. I was so angry with you and the old master. When Shinclyffe told me that your father had caused my father's death, I wanted to destroy you and your family – destroy Master Thomas for what his father had done.' His eyes misted. 'I was a fool. Can you forgive me?'

'There is nothing to forgive. I would have acted the same in your shoes.' I told him what had happened the day his father died on the scaffold. 'My father did cause his death in a way,' I continued. 'He thought he should give your father an alibi, but it was untrue. The old master flogged my father to within an inch of his life as punishment. Norton told me that old Markenfield had given my father the chance of a workshop because he felt sorry for his actions. He paid for your apprenticeship and set you up with your own workshop when you were old enough. I think the old man sorely regretted what happened that day.'

Harry was crying. 'We are pawns in these war games, Robert. Neither side care much for the lives of people like us. I lost my father because of their quarrels.' He rubbed his eyes with the back of his hand. 'I want to find Bridget and go home.'

'You are not fit to travel just yet. We will talk about it when you are feeling stronger.' I got up to leave, then turned back to him. 'Tell me one thing. Tell me you had nothing to do with young Edmund being strung up like a rabbit and left to freeze under that bridge.'

Catherine appeared at my side and threw her arms about me.

'Thanks be to God,' she murmured into my ear. 'You are safe.'

I returned her embrace and breathed in her scent, musky from a night lying beside a hot and sickly child. I could smell the aroma of horse sweat, which I knew came from Edmund's clothes. 'How is he?' I asked.

'Much recovered,' she said. 'I have left him abed with orders not to move until I return.' She laughed a little. 'He will find that most difficult. He is already asking to see Chestnut.'

In truth, I had not seen Chestnut since yesterday. I was sure he was well cared for among the hundreds of other horses in the nearby field. There were stable boys aplenty to tend and feed them. It would be good to have Edmund tend him again. The boy had such a way with animals.

Catherine realised it was Harry lying on the ground at their feet. She was wary, and that was to be expected. The last time she had seen Harry was in York, and he had set Sussex's guard upon them.

Her voice was sharp when she spoke. 'How do you fare? Are your wounds severe?'

Harry looked about him, unable to face her head-on. 'I am most sorry for my deeds, Catherine. I hope you can forgive me.'

She snapped back at him. 'What part did you play in Edmund's torture?'

'I do not know anyone called Edmund. Who is he?'

My face burned with anger again as I spoke. 'He is a small child, and we found him hanging under the bridge by his wrists. Fenton put him there.'

'I would never hurt a child. God's blood, Robert, how could you even think such a thing?' He fought to sit up, but the pain set him groaning in agony, and he lay back. When he spoke again, his voice was tight. 'You know how much Bridget and I have longed for a child. I would give anything for a son.'

I looked at him and then turned to Catherine. 'We will take your word, for now, Harry, but I warn you, if you are lying, there will be no forgiveness.'

'I swear it to be true,' he said.

'Then we shall forget about it. When Edmund is feeling better, I will fetch him to see you. That will settle the matter.'

'Is he important to you both? How is he so close to you?' Harry asked.

'He has been helping me at the forge,' I said. 'He has become as a son to both of us.'

Harry lay back down, but as I turned away, he spoke again.

'Robert. Inside my doublet. There is a missive. I was supposed to give it to Shinclyffe.'

I leaned over him and searched for the document. It had Bowes' seal. We left Harry to sleep and went back to see Edmund. He was still abed but playing with two miniature carved horses.

'Look,' he said, beaming from ear to ear. 'Alfred made these for me. This is Chestnut, and this is Mutton.' He held them up for us to see.

'Who the blazes is Alfred?' I asked.

'He's the guard,' said Catherine. 'He has been whittling the little horses all night. The poor man must be sorely in need of rest, but he has not left his post for one minute.'

'Come and look,' Edmund pleaded. 'You can hold Chestnut, Robert.' He held the horse out, and I winced seeing the angry red gouges in the boy's wrists. If Harry had anything to do with this, I would make him pay. I took the wooden carving from him.

'He is a very handsome horse,' I said. 'You must take great care of him – and Mutton, of course.'

'I will,' he said. 'I will guard them with my life.'

Catherine and I laughed. The boy was definitely over the worst. I would take him over to meet Harry later.

My head was spinning. One minute I was so grateful to have my friend back, and the next, I choked with fury at what had happened to Edmund. Harry had sounded truthful, but I could never take his word for anything again without proof.

The three of us ate together and took great comfort from all being close again. I wallowed in the precious moments, knowing I would soon have to go back to the wall and lay siege on the castle once more.

I left them for a short while and went over to Westmorland's marquee. Master Thomas, Richard Norton, Countess Anne, and Northumberland were discussing the situation concerning Shinclyffe. I interrupted them and handed the missive to Westmorland. He waved me away, and I backed to the fringes of the company. I could still hear the earl's words. 'It is addressed to Sussex,' he said before reading the words aloud.

> *Even now, the rebels, with the two earls, have surrounded me. Your lordship knoweth the state of this house, but if I had the 300 shot, to come from Berwick, here, I should beat them out of the towne which they have taken. We view their horsemen to be about 1200, all of which stand within falcon shot, which we lack, and keepeth that we have carefully for fear of further lack. We look for release at your lordship, whose setting forth but one day's journey out of York, I trust would fear them, and Yorkshire is now sweeped clean of them. Notwithstanding, many of those that came home from them receiving their vitals, and getting such money as they could, are returned to them again; but if some soldiers were shown, I fully hope it would do much good. Finally, I have, and shall serve dutifully, and so long*

as I shall live, I shall keep my faith and truth to our good Queen Elizabeth unspotted...

Westmorland now addressed the group. 'It is probable that Bowes would duplicate his missives and send several by various means to ensure at least one would find its recipient. Likely, the message Thomas found on Shinclyffe's person is also a duplicate. I assume it is only to reassure Bowes that something is being done concerning his plight. I will not read it out, but Sussex signs it, and the Council asks Bowes to continue sending word on where we are and where others from our number are staying so they are kept abreast of happenings. They ask Bowes to send messages to the Borders wardens, asking them to send him horsemen forthwith.

Catherine

Barnard Castle, Yorkshire, Friday 5th December 1569

I TOOK EDMUND WITH me to the hospital tent. Robert walked with us and headed straight over to Harry. Harry looked weak as he struggled to raise himself onto his elbows. His face was grey, but his cheeks burned with fever.

'Edmund,' Robert said. 'This is Harry Gardyner.'

We both watched Edmund's reaction to the sight of Harry. He appeared to be completely relaxed.

Edmund bowed his head politely. 'Good day, Sir,' he said.

'Good day to you, Edmund. I hear you have been in the wars,' said Harry.

'I have, sir, but Master Robert did save me and carried me all the way until we reached the doctor.' Edmund beamed at Robert.

I ruffled his hair, pride bursting out of my chest.

Robert's shoulders relaxed. 'You do not know Goodman Gardyner?'

'No. Have I forgotten him?' Edmund looked down at Harry. 'I am heartily sorry if I should remember you, sir. Mayhap the pain I suffered stole my memory.' He looked worried that he might have let Robert down in some way and offended Harry.

Robert laughed. 'Your memory is fine, Edmund. Harry Gardyner has been a friend of mine since childhood,' he added, looking kindly upon Harry's limp figure. 'He is Bridget's husband and will stay with us for a while once he has recovered.'

Harry looked up at Robert with disbelief. 'Thank you, Robert. I am grateful for your kind offer.'

'Bridget will be pleased to see you,' I said. 'Edmund will sit by your side a while. I will get you something to eat and something to cool your fever.'

I walked with Robert outside to make up a tincture from ingredients in my medicine bag. 'It is good that you have made peace with your friend. It will ease both your minds.'

'Time will tell. It is hard to trust again when someone you care about betrays you.'

I reached up and stroked his cheek. 'You, my husband, are the kindest man I know. Your heart is full of love and forgiveness. Things will become right soon. Your history will bind you together again.'

Robert kissed the top of my head. 'I will see you at nightfall,' he said before walking away.

†

The day passed swiftly as I tended new patients and regularly checked on Edmund and Harry. Harry sent Edmund outside to collect small stones, some to be round and others a different colour or misshapen. By the afternoon, Harry's fever had subsided, and he was teaching Edmund how to play draughts in the ground next to where he lay. Harry pretended to be cross as Edmund took his pieces, time and time again. I could hear the boy laughing from the other side of the tent.

It seemed for the first time in quite a while that I felt more relaxed. I found myself humming a little ditty as I worked away, bandaging, making poultices, soothing brews for pain and other ailments. Doctor Bartholomew commented on my high spirits and dedicated effort to heal the sick and wounded. All the while, Edmund's voice and laughter drifted over the top of cries and moans of pain. When the sun had set and the torches and candles lit, the priests prayed over the sick. The atmosphere in the tent settled, and I wandered over to Edmund and Harry. The game of draughts lay to one side, and the pair had drifted off to sleep. Harry was still pale and breathing heavily. Edmund was trying to sidle up to Harry's back. He must have thought it was Robert. My heart surged at the sight of the boy. My hand unconsciously went to my belly. Another son to look up to his older brother would make our family complete. As I looked down at Edmund, I knew he could not be more of a son to us than he already was. We had lost our hearts to this thin little boy who clung to us like a puppy. Losing his father had broken the boy badly, and it was only our care that had brought him back to life again.

I knelt beside him and stroked his cheek, brushing the thick, wayward hair from his face. His cheeks shone pink in the candlelight, and I placed the back of my hand to his forehead. His fever was only slight, but a chill now would set him back. I stood up and fetched a blanket to cover him. It would be a shame to disturb him now. He would most surely be safe with Harry so close and Shinclyffe hiding behind the walls of Barney Castle.

Leaving the tent, I made my way over to Countess Anne. She was already at the evening meal with her husband, the earl. She looked magnificent in the torchlight. All signs of sickness disappeared. Her face was painted white, and her lips were as red as ripe cherries. I wondered what she made of a woman like me who never troubled to put on her make-up or paint her cheeks and lips. My face was ruddy from working outside for most of my life. A memory of helping Mother in the herb garden, Father in the fields as he gathered crops, and spending time with the monks at Fountains Abbey, rose inside me.

Anne smiled as I approached.

''Tis good to see you, Catherine,' she said. 'How fares young Edmund? Has he recovered from his ordeal?'

I bowed my head in deference. 'He is much better, my lady. His fever is now only slight, and sleep will provide the best medicine.'

'And our wounded men? Are there many fatalities?'

'There have been several who have gone to sit with God this day,' I answered. 'But there are many with only flesh wounds that will heal speedily.'

'I hear there are many who jump the walls to join us,' said Northumberland, his mouth full of venison as he spoke.

Countess Anne put a handkerchief to her mouth and turned her head away.

'There are some, my lord, but the walls are high, and some fall to instant death. The lucky ones have broken limbs. Of those, we have saved a few.'

'That is well,' said Anne, turning back to me. 'See Cook for some supper. Then rest. You will be much busy again tomorrow.'

I thanked her and made my way over to the kitchen fire. Robert would stay with the other men tonight. At least he was nearby. Cook and Margery greeted me, and we sat in companionable silence while eating our supper. My mind drifted to Bridget. What a wonderful surprise for her it would be when we returned to Brancepeth.

At that moment, I realised that I desperately wanted to go home. I was tired. Tired of travelling, tired of fighting this feeling of fear over Robert's safety, Edmund's safety, my baby's safety. Sick and tired of not knowing who to trust in the world around me. I felt the tears well once again, and I remembered the days of happiness with my family at Markenfield. What I would not give to feel my mother's arms around me, her lips kissing the top of my head. The sweet smell of lavender and baking and baby milk.

The hand that touched my shoulder was warm and firm. I would have recognised it out of a thousand hands. Without looking up, I placed my hand over Robert's, and he sat down beside me.

'You were as in a dream,' he said softly. 'Where had you gone?'

'Home,' I said simply. 'I need to go home.'

He nodded and placed an arm about me, pulling me close. I leaned in and breathed his familiar smell of metal, leather, and sweat.

'We will go then,' he said. 'As soon as this siege is over, and we have been back to Brancepeth and collected Bridget.' I squeezed him, grateful for his agreement. 'Mutton will have grown lazy in our absence. We may have to put his old bones on the cart and get Chestnut to carry us all home.'

I laughed, realising it was the first time for an age. Once I had started, I could not stop. Robert was laughing too. A deep belly laugh as we both imagined the scene. Mutton lazing on the flatbed of the cart, poor Chestnut snorting as he tried to pull it along. Although not knowing what we were laughing about, Cook and Margery could not stop themselves from joining in. The noise we were making soon became riotous and drew the attention of Countess Anne and Northumberland. She frowned at me, more puzzled than in admonishment. I put a hand over my mouth to stay my laughter, and, soon enough, the mood quieted, and everyone turned back to eating and drinking.

Robert stayed, and we lay close to the fire until the early hours. My head was resting on his arm, but I only stirred briefly as he got up and went back to join the other archers up by the walls.

Robert

Barnard Castle, Yorkshire,
Wednesday 10th December 1569

THE DAYS HAD PASSED quickly. Each day had left Bowes more isolated and without food and water. More and more men jumped down off the parapets to join our cause. It was sad to hear them scream in agony as they fell on the hard earth and rocks and boulders, breaking their limbs. Some smashed their skulls open, and the ones who could not possibly survive their injuries were despatched quickly to save them from cruel agony before death would come and set them free. We were relentless in our siege. The walls were crumbling under cannon shot and sling.

I went in search of Catherine and found her in the hospital tent. Even the wounded seemed in good spirits, knowing they had not to go out and fight once they had healed again. Edmund and Harry were in the middle of an argument. I could tell that Harry was trying to look serious as Edmund stood up, hands on hips and yelled at him.

'I did not cheat. I am honoura – hono – I do not cheat. Ever.'

'What have you been doing?' I demanded in the firmest voice I could muster. Edmund spun round and was about to protest his innocence once more until he saw the grin on my face. 'What is my friend Harry teasing you about?' I asked.

'He says I cheat to win.' His voice was still indignant, and a frown creased his forehead.

'I was only pretending, Edmund,' said Harry. 'I know you would not cheat. You are an honest young man. I would trust you with my life.'

Edmund relaxed a little. 'Well. I would cheat no one.'

'Of course, you would not. You are my son. My son is an honest person.'

Edmund ran and put his arms about me. 'I love you,' he squeaked.

As the days turned into night, and we were reducing the castle to ruins, much merrymaking carried on well into the early hours.

Anne Percy – Countess of Northumberland

Barnard Castle, Yorkshire, Thursday 11th December 1569

ANNE MISSED HAVING CATHERINE around but, now that the dreaded sickness seemed to have dissipated somewhat, she needed her soothing brews and potions little. Her strength had returned, and she felt ready to face the world again with vigour.

As Margery helped her to dress, a messenger arrived. He had ridden from Wetherby. He reported that the queen's army had rested there and had now set out to meet with Sussex and all the men he had mustered at Darlington. Anne's appetite for everything, including food, had returned with a vengeance, and she finished dressing as quickly as she could in order to join her spouse at the table.

Her husband and Westmorland called a meeting to discuss what the news would mean, and it was soon decided that there was little hope of facing so many trained soldiers. Anne agreed with their suggestion that they finish up at Barney and move back to Brancepeth to regroup and plan how they would tackle the situation.

A second message arrived from within the castle walls. Bowes was asking for safe passage to leave the confines of his castle with the few starving men he had left.

'Have we not rid ourselves of all traitors?' I asked. 'There must be another in our midst who informs Bowes of the approaching army.'

Thomas Markenfield was quick to reply.

'Shinclyffe is obviously in there. I will send someone to fetch Harry Gardyner if he has survived his injuries. He may have heard of others who would betray us.'

'Was he not questioned when brought to the hospital?' Anne asked now. She wondered why Markenfield had not thought to glean every bit of information from the man.

Thomas reddened at her question. 'My lady. He was much injured at the time, and I doubt he made a recovery.'

'Doubt? Doubt, sir?' Westmorland bellowed. 'Then go and make sure immediately.'

Anne looked at Westmorland in admiration. His black eyes were glistening with anger, his hand gripping the handle of his sword. He always looked much more handsome when his temper flared. She turned her eyes on her husband and sighed.

Westmorland spoke again.

'While we await Markenfield's return, what conclusions are there about Bowes' request?'

Richard Norton got to his feet and addressed the company.

'It would serve us best to let him go without a fuss. If the messenger from Wetherby is correct, we need to move back in haste. We do not have enough men to hold Barney or face Sussex head-on.'

Anne's husband was quick to agree. 'Now we are sure the Spanish are not coming; we must head north with speed to muster troops from the borders.'

'It does make sense,' Anne added. 'There are many in the borders still loyal to our family and yours, my Lord Westmorland.' It was a great pity they were in precisely the position her husband had feared when first setting out on this pilgrimage.

By the time they had agreed on a plan, Markenfield had returned. The man Gardyner was on a stretcher, carried by Catherine's husband Robert and a priest who presumably worked in the hospital.

Thomas addressed Westmorland. 'This is the man, my lord. He will tell you all he knows.' Thomas looked down at the injured man, who was as pale as a linen sheet. 'Speak, churl.'

Harry lifted himself onto his elbows. 'My Lord,' he said. 'Shinclyffe did not tell me of others involved; I swear upon my life.'

'He may not have told you, but you have eyes and ears,' snapped Westmorland. 'You must have heard rumours about the castle, seen people coming and going?'

'I spent most of my time on the walls,' he said. 'I am an archer.' Gardyner looked at the ground, then, just as quickly, he looked up at Westmorland again. 'I beg your pardon, my lord. There was someone – a man came to see Bowes one night. He was a gentleman, I am sure.'

Westmorland's eyes narrowed as they gazed over the surrounding men. 'What was his name? What did he look like?'

'It was a strange name. Not belonging to any place near here. Str – Stee— I am sorry, my lord. I cannot remember. He appeared to be a gentleman of money, Sir.'

'Captain Strelley. The bastard has been staying at Raby for some weeks.' Westmorland called one of his soldiers over. 'Send riders to Raby. Drag the traitor here. He will pay for his treachery with his life.'

Robert

Barnard Castle, Yorkshire, Friday 12th December 1569

OUR LEADERS GATHERED, ALL dressed in their finery, pennants held aloft, and making a great occasion of the downfall of Bowes and his men. The castle gates opened for the last time as the depleted, bedraggled troops, led by Bowes' sorry figure, shuffled out of the shelled and broken walls of the castle. Westmorland and Northumberland rode up to face him.

Bowes held his head high and spoke; his voice was slightly shaky.

'I ask leave to pass peacefully and travel to York without delay. My men direly need food and rest. I give you my castle in return.'

I wondered what might happen next. Would Westmorland deny the request? Would he order the slaughter of Bowes and his men? We waited in silence as Westmorland seemed to consider the proposal.

Westmorland backed his horse away and to the side. Northumberland followed suit.

Bowes set forth; his head bowed as we watched him slink away like a dog with his tail between his legs. I searched among their number for a sight of Shinclyffe, knowing Master Thomas and the earls would do the same, but did not get sight of him. He could be in disguise, and there were so many riders that it would be easy to miss one figure amongst them. Men spat as Bowes rode past, while others jeered or laughed. It was over. The siege was over, and we could enjoy a few days respite. I joined the others, raising my fist, and, before too long, the whole of our army was cheering and laughing and dancing.

The air was misty with a freezing fog the following morning, but nothing could dampen the men and women's spirits as they packed up their belongings. I heard many saying they had done enough and were now returning home. This sort of news made me worry that the earls would have little enough forces to continue this pilgrimage. It was definite that the Spanish would not be coming to our aide, and, even now, I had gleaned that the pope still had not sent word declaring Elizabeth a heretic. Without that news, they would try us for treason should this cause fail. I wondered whether now was, in fact, the right time for me to take Catherine home. She would be devastated if I changed my mind, but if my master still needed me by his side, I could not desert him.

Catherine spent the morning in the hospital tent before joining me back at Northumberland's marquee. She had been preparing the patients for travel back to Brancepeth. They left those who could walk to their own devices and helped those whose wounds were too severe, assisting them in lying down on the straw-covered flatbeds of carts. Harry, still not well enough to make his own passage, was included in their number. The carts had arrived at Barnard Castle full of supplies but now were empty, and the oxen would take them back to Brancepeth full of wounded men. The countess was bustling about her staff, screaming orders, and making sure everything they had brought had been packed away properly when Catherine appeared. After kissing me on my cheek, she wasted little time and immediately got to work along with Anne's other staff.

We were on the road by midday. The fog had lifted, and the winter sun tried to deceive us into thinking its rays cast warmth upon us, but its bright face served only to light up the ice on the rutted road and the newly formed icicles hanging from the boughs of the trees. I rode alongside Catherine's cart for a while as she took her place with the injured men, taking pleasure from her face as it lit up with joy at the surrounding spectacles. She saw only the beauty of the landscape instead of feeling the bitter bite of the air around us. I knew it was because she was thinking about home in Rippon. It would not be easy to tell her I could not travel with her. I must find others that would be going back and ensure she travelled safely. The news of the queen's army gaining ground on us was worrying. If anyone met those soldiers on the road home, they would surely be captured or killed. I tried to put the thoughts from my mind and treasure our last days together back at Brancepeth. I moved further up the troops and nearer to my master to gain information about what might happen to Harry once we were back at Brancepeth. He had been good enough in rescuing Harry, but my master could be cruel in his revenge on anyone who had betrayed him. Yet, if he had a mind, he could be most benevolent towards his staff. My master had not asked after Harry since he had been brought to Westmorland from the hospital tent, but neither had he made any suggestion of punishing him. I needed to find out what was on his mind.

I made my way through the horsemen until I could make out Master Thomas in conversation with his uncle, Richard Norton. I rode nearby so that I was in their line of sight, and when their conversation took a pause, I approached the two men.

'Good day, Master Thomas, Master Norton,' I said, bowing my head. 'I wondered if I might speak to you.'

I was now riding alongside them.

'Speak,' said Thomas, still looking straight ahead.

'I wondered about Harry Gardyner, Master. Have you come to a decision about his future?'

'What business is that of yours, Gray?' he said.

'What do you intend for him, Thomas?' asked Norton.

Thomas thought for a moment. 'He betrayed me. Betrayed the cause. He cannot walk away without paying for his deceit.'

I had hoped this would not be his response. 'Master—' He held his hand up to quiet me.

'Be silent, Gray. I will think on the matter.'

Gray? Why was I not Robert anymore? I felt a flush of anger colour my face. 'Master—'

'Hush,' said Norton. 'Be patient and give your master the time to decide. Go about your business, Robert.'

There was no use saying more. I turned Chestnut about and rode to the back of the procession, where Catherine still tended the sick. My thoughts whirled again around my duty to my master and my commitment to my wife and closest friend. Master Thomas did not make it easy to be loyal.

As we arrived back at Brancepeth, the men and women who had stayed behind came out to meet us. Westmorland's wife, Countess Jane, stood at the entrance gates. Her ladies-in-waiting gathered about her as she placed a light kiss on her husband's cheek as soon as he dismounted. Countess Anne and Northumberland followed them inside the castle walls. I sought out Bridget, who was camping outside the gates. She had joined the silversmith, Goodman Smythe, and his wife during the days we had been away. I broke the news of Harry's return, and she cried with happiness that he was not dead. I explained he was travelling with Catherine and the hospital staff, who were setting up a tent for the wounded inside the castle grounds. She set off through the gates, almost running in her haste to see her husband.

The men and women of the pilgrimage spent the evening merrymaking again. Catherine spent her time with Edmund and Bridget packing up the cart with as much as it could carry, leaving space for Harry, who was still not recovered enough to walk. Bridget had not stopped talking since being reunited with Harry. I wished I had not told her, as her voice became higher and higher with tales of what she and her husband would do when they got back to Rippon. John, who had also taken a stand at Barney castle, was now back with his parents, and when he heard from Bridget that we were all returning to Rippon, he was glad and asked if he and his parents could travel with us. I agreed readily. If I decided to remain, I would be happier that Catherine and Bridget would not be travelling alone. I would send Edmund with them and ask John to train him up until I returned. He had faced enough danger in his brief life. My heart was a little lighter at this thought.

When we had eaten supper, Catherine and Bridget made their way back to the hospital tent, and the welcome silence washed over me.

The following morning seemed odd. Everywhere quiet. The damp air cut through my clothes and deep into my bones. Having the time to sit was not good. After several days at Barney castle, amid hundreds of men laying siege, it was difficult to pause. I watched over Edmund in his slumber. Deep-red ridges still scarred his wrists.

Leaning over, I shook him gently. 'How are you faring?' I asked. 'Do you think that you and John could help me set up the forge? There will be many horses in need of shoes and no doubt several weapons to be mended.'

Edmund almost leapt from his bed to join me.

'Steady now. There is no rush,' I said, grabbing his arm before he fell over. 'Break your fast. You will need hot food inside of you afore you do anything.'

John was already at the hearth with his mother and father, enjoying a bowl of steaming broth that Catherine and Bridget had heated over the fire an hour ago. The two women had since gone to the hospital tent. Edmund sat down beside John, and I loaded the kiln with kindling and substantial logs before placing a few nuggets of coal atop them. The blaze was soon high as I worked the bellows in between, adding more and more fuel.

It felt good to feel the hammer in my hand again. The air rang out with the sound of metal upon metal, and customers formed a queue almost immediately. John and Edmund joked amiably, and the atmosphere felt familiar and safe as if we were all going about our daily business. The dream of once again crafting spurs was almost tempting enough to make me want to go home alongside my family and friends. I worked hard, the hours disappearing in a haze, and when I looked up, I was surprised to see Catherine watching me from the hearth. It was only then I realised the sky was darkening. I looked to Edmund, who was almost asleep at the bellows. 'This be the last shoeing for today,' I shouted to the queue that had hardly shortened. 'Come back tomorrow.' There were a few growls and groans, but people left and soon, there were just mine and John's family.

As we ate, the atmosphere became a little uneasy again as word spread around the camp that Bowes had joined Sussex and his troops at Northallerton, where they expected the queen's forces to be with them within a day or two. Soon after, messengers sent by Westmorland, round and about the camp, asked for volunteers to prepare to march to Newcastle within the hour. A rider had brought news that John Forster, the Commissioner of the Marches, was gathering forces at Newcastle. We were to take a party of five hundred and attack at dawn to catch him unawares.

The whole camp was in turmoil again as we collected weapons and gathered in formation by the main gates. Catherine tried to persuade me to remain behind, but my nature would not allow me to stand by and watch the men go off to fight without me.

'I will be back soon. Do not worry,' I mouthed into her hair as I held her close to me. 'John and Edmund will take care of the forge in the morning. They are both capable.'

There were 100 each of pikemen, archers, and light cannon. About 200 in number, the horsemen included the harquebusiers and were led by Richard Norton. I saddled up Chestnut and joined them. Catherine watched me go, a sad look on her face. I blew a kiss to her and then turned to follow the other men out into the night.

Anne Percy – Countess of Northumberland

Brancepeth Castle, Northumberland,
Monday 15th December

MESSAGES CAME BACK AND forth during the day. Anne noted how good it was to be comfortable again within the safety of Westmorland's castle. Not as comfortable as the Neville's Raby castle by any means, but well-furnished compared to the cold marquee she had called home for the last few days. Still, she missed the danger, the daily battle cries. Anne sometimes thought she should have been born a man. She looked at her husband, who was marching about the bedchamber.

'For goodness sake, come and sit down,' she said to him. 'Pacing the room will have no effect on your snake of a brother, Henry. He will still kowtow to the heretic Elizabeth if he thinks it offers him a chance of a place in the inner court and more riches.' The thought of being betrayed by a sibling must be so hard to take.

'I should have gone with them,' he replied, finally coming to sit beside her. 'But – to take arms against my own flesh and blood—'

'Do you think he would hesitate in striking you down? You are a fool if you think thus. He would kill you without a second thought and take your title tomorrow. If we had a son, it could not be so.' The vision of her poor baby son, who died within a year of his birth, filled Anne's head. The pain of that time, so real, she felt faint. Her hand rushed to her belly. Without looking up, she spoke again. 'I am with child, Thomas.' Her husband's head jerked up, and he reached a hand out to her.

'Will it be a boy? Will God have finally answered our prayers?'

Anne laughed. 'Do you think I can foresee the future? I am no soothsayer, but I pray each night for the son we have both longed for these past years.'

His face lit up, and he pulled her to her feet. 'You should have said something sooner. I could have added my prayers to yours. Our voices in prayer together would carry a stronger message.' He got up and strode towards the door to their bed-chamber. 'I must send for Father Mudde. We will all pray together.'

Men and priests crowded the room as before when we first arrived in Brancepeth when the Pilgrimage started. An hour or so later, they took their place in the Baron's Hall with Jane and her husband. Westmorland had received word from Newcastle and was relaying the messages as they came. He told everyone that Forster and Percy had many soldiers from Berwick and the skirmishes were bloody. The enemy had chosen a piece of high ground, and it was impossible to use the cannon. The men were giving of their best, but it was not an easy fight.

As Anne ate and drank and made merry, she thought about the troops out there fighting their cause. Looking about the room, she could see many men who were more than capable of joining them. It made her angry. She wanted to ride out at the men's side and show them they were all in this together.

'Have we sent reinforcements?' Anne asked.

'We cannot send more, my lady,' said Westmorland. Anne's heart fluttered as usual when he stared directly into her eyes.

'We need to keep a reserve in case the fight goes into a second day. Besides, we are waiting to hear about the progress of the queen's men from the south. There is no point trapping ourselves in Newcastle if we need to push further north in haste.'

There were murmurings of agreement from around the room.

Anne stood and took her leave. She would walk about the people outside, let them know their masters were still there for them.

With a small entourage, she made her way to the hospital tent. The smell of death was thick in the air outside the tent, where many men, who could not be housed inside, were out in the cold air with only thin blankets to cover them. They, at least, could be offered words of comfort from their leaders. Anne knelt beside a young man who looked barely old enough to be here. She thought he must only be thirteen years at most. The side of his head was split wide open, and blood and pus oozed from the wound. She could already see maggots feeding on his rotting flesh.

Taking hold of his hand, Anne smiled down at him. 'Hold on to me, and I will stay and pray with you. For you are the truest of men and have given your life in the name of our Lord Jesus.' She felt his fingers cling to her hand as he opened his eyes.

'Are you an angel come to take me?' He gazed at her face for a moment; a smile trembled on his lips. Then his hand became slack in hers, and his head lolled to one side. His eyes stared into the next world.

'You are in God's care now,' Anne whispered, crossing his arms over his chest. She got to her feet and turned away so that her guards may not see the well of tears ready to spill down her face. 'Come,' she said, without looking at them. 'We will take some time with the injured inside the tent.'

Anne saw Catherine almost immediately, her hair pinned back, her coif stained where she had pushed strands away from her face with bloodied hands. The pallor of her cheeks told Anne the girl was tired, but there was an air of quiet about her. The same calm she had seen when Catherine tended her. There was nothing rushed in her actions as she knelt beside a man and tended his wounds. Anne could see her lips moving, but not what Catherine was saying. The man's eyes were closed, and she worked deftly, bathing and bandaging his arm. When Catherine had finished, she placed the used piece of linen into a bowl of red-stained water and stood up. Her hand reached to her back as she arched and stretched herself out again, her belly as swollen as a large pumpkin. She saw Anne watching her and came over.

'Good morrow, Countess,' she said, bobbing her head in deference. 'I hope you fare well this day.' Her smile was wide, and there was warmth in her voice.

'You have been at work long?' Anne asked, unsure of what to say. The question felt foolish. The sight of her told Anne she had been up and working many hours already.

'A while,' she said, looking down at her apron. 'Do you have need of me?'

'Nay. I come to see our good men that are wounded.' Anne looked around. 'I need – I wish to make myself useful. I do not rest easy when our brave men are fighting without their leaders by their side. What can I do to help relieve some of the suffering? I am at your service.'

Catherine looked at the number of guards that had accompanied Anne. 'It may be difficult with so many at your side. The tent is full, and the walkways narrow.' She looked into Anne's eyes. 'The men will be honoured that you thought to come and see them.'

Anne felt as if she was being dismissed. A spark of anger curled up and into her throat. 'I am of no use? You think me incapable?'

The colour rose in Catherine's cheeks. 'No, my lady. That thought never crossed my mind, but I cannot ask you to stay unguarded. It would be remiss of me.'

'I will make that decision,' Anne said, turning to her entourage. 'Leave me. I will stay and help the wounded.' They looked uncertain, blinking and looking at each other. 'I said go. Have you but cloth for ears? Go.'

They left her, tripping over each other in their haste. No doubt hurrying now to inform her husband. Anne turned back to Catherine, detecting a brief smile on her lips. 'Now, Catherine. Do with me as you will. I will not turn away.'

Catherine passed the bowl to her mistress. 'Please, Countess. Take this outside. Wash the rag and put fresh water in the bowl. Come and find me when it is done.' And with that, Catherine moved away and toward the sound of a man crying out for someone to help him.

As she did Catherine's bidding, one of Anne's guards returned to say that her husband had insisted she return to him immediately. She sent him away again with a flea in his ear. He did not return. Anne spent a goodly time fetching and carrying for Catherine, the doctor, and the priests. She watched with interest the way each one tended a patient. How they bathed a wound, pulled an arrow if it was not barbed, broke one and left the head in if it was.

When she left the tent some hours later, her body ached, but her mind filled with joy, knowing she had been of service to her people.

Back inside the castle, Anne went straight to her bedchamber. She looked a fright, covered in blood and mud. The servants gawped in horror as she strode past them. A few moments later and Margery came panting up the stairs and into the room.

'My lady,' she gasped. 'Are you injured? Shall I send for the doctor?'

'I am not injured. I have been helping the wounded and dying. Help me undress and bathe, for I am hungry enough to eat a table full of food this day.' Her head was light with happiness; her mind danced at the thought of her actions. She would attend the hospital tent again on the morrow. It felt good to be of use.

Anne's husband frowned and growled as she related her tale of blood and gore to the party sat about them. He was furious with her for lowering herself to such drudgery and fetching and carrying for the humdrum of society. Westmorland, on the other hand, goaded her to tell more. His black eyes were dancing with mischief and amusement at Northumberland's discomfort.

It was late in the evening when they heard the return of Norton and his men. The rumble of the cannon over the yard cobbles brought everyone to their feet. They made their way outside to hear of the success of the skirmishes. What they heard was anything but. Norton insisted he came inside to relay the day's events. He was grey with exhaustion and hobbled to the table. Grabbing a flagon, he drank as if he had not quenched his thirst for many days. After waiting a few moments, Anne could see the impatience in Westmorland's face as he told him to 'Get on with it'.

Norton told of the disadvantage of being caught at Chester Deane at the bottom of a steep hill where a broad brook divided them from Forster and Northumberland's brother, Henry Percy.

'It made it impossible for us to convey the ordnance and, being a good distance from the foe at that point, unable to fire any of the cannon. We had to cross the land whereby as soon as we reached the foot of the hill, arrows rained down on us.' He ripped the gloves from his hands as he spoke of the one-to-one armed conflict with pike and staff men thundering down the hill. Pausing for breath, he took another great draft of ale before telling us of the number of dead and dying they had to leave behind.

Westmorland let the man alone then, and Norton ate ravenously, surrounded by many suggestions on what our next move might be. Messages arrived over the next couple of hours with word of Sussex's progress since he had joined forces with Lord Hunsdon and Ralph Sadler and the royal troops in Darlington. There was no time to lose. Knowing that Forster and Northumberland's brother Henry had their own men and the soldiers from Berwick virtually on our doorstep, everyone agreed they could not travel with any speed encumbered by footmen and carts. Westmorland sent his messengers out amongst the crowds outside the gate to say they must scatter and make their own way. All men who owned a decent riding horse were to remain and be ready to accompany the earls when they left the castle.

Anne's thoughts travelled to Catherine, who, she knew, would still be helping the wounded. She slipped away and went to find her.

As Anne had thought, Catherine was still tending the men who had put themselves in mortal danger for the cause and God himself. Why, then, was God not standing beside them in their hour of need? Why did he not drive the heretics into the soil and be rid of them? Why were all these godly and pious men dying?

She hurried over to Catherine and took her aside.

'Catherine, you must come with me to the castle. The earls and all the horsemen will make haste to leave within an hour or two. You will be in danger out here. Countess Jane will not be travelling, and she is at once sending a message to Sussex to say that only she and servants remain here and begs his mercy when he arrives. It will be the safest place for you.'

'But – I cannot leave these men. They need my help,' she said, already turning away from Anne.

Anne grabbed her arm. 'You cannot help them. Can you not see? Sussex will order their slaughter. He will not leave men alive that may recover and creep up behind his back in the coming days.' She stared at Catherine, who looked defiant. 'If not for yourself, then for your child and the boy who has stolen your heart.' Anne felt the determination dissipate as Catherine's body softened, and she stopped pulling away. 'Take the boy and your friend over there,' she said, pointing at Bridget, 'and go to the kitchens. Tell the cook I have sent you to help her and her staff. The boy already knows how to carry out his duties, and I am sure you will be of much use.'

Anne left Catherine and hurried back inside, shouting for Margery to help her dress for the journey. She and other women servants would ride with them and attend to their needs.

When she was ready, Anne paid a last visit to Jane in her room. She was still at her desk, penning the letter.

'Dearest Anne,' she said, her eyes wide with fear. 'Please read my letter and tell me if you think it will compel Sussex to be merciful. I am in dread fear for my family.'

Anne took the papers from her hand and read them out loud for clarity and meaning so that she may judge for herself the tone and substance of what Jane had written.

Good My Lord: Have consideration of my desolate and comfortless estate lacking both quietness of mind and health, neither being able to fly to any place, nor knowing where to have any refuge: and, besides all other miseries, I am in great fear of the cruelty of the rude soldiers; and, therefore, albeit my trust is that your lordship and other of the nobility will not, of your honours, deal otherwise with me then samely; yet I must heartily beseech your good lordship that

*such order may be given that neither I nor my children, nor
such poor servants as are left about me, may be put in fear,
or have any bodily harm...*

Anne could read no further. Her stomach curdled at Jane's cow-
ardliness when she should be at Westmorland's side through
these times. She curbed her anger, looking at the crumpled
wretch before her. 'It is bound to appeal to Sussex's honour and
his assumption that all women are gentle but foolish creatures.
I am sure he will look kindly on your requests.'

Jane took Anne's hands, hope kindling in her eyes. 'You
think so? He will consider my children, my home?'

Anne forced herself to smile. 'Of course, dearest friend.
Sussex is not a barbarian. He will remember who your brother
is. He cannot harm the sister of Thomas Howard, the Duke
of Norfolk. Hasn't the queen forgiven him many times over
the rumour of him wanting to marry our beloved Mary, the
Scottish queen for whom we fight now? He is back at his
family seat and in favour again.'

'Is he truly? Has Elizabeth forgiven him? I feared his execution.'

'Rumours, Jane. Silly rumours,' Anne said, turning from
her, knowing full well her words were lies, but Jane's manner
was servile, and she despised her for it. 'Pray to God, and all
will be well.' Anne left her to her own devices and went to
find her husband.

Catherine

Brancepeth Castle, Northumberland,
Tuesday 16th December

IT WAS A LITTLE after midnight. I was tired and had hoped to retire soon, but now we were all in flux. I gathered what I could of my herbs and tinctures and placed them in my bag. It was mayhem outside as families gathered their goods together and packed carts, if they had them, before setting off into the surrounding woodland. Doctor Bartholomew persuaded some to take sick men onto the backs of their carts, but many refused, saying they could not risk being slowed down by the dying. Had it not been for my baby and Edmund, I might have stayed with the doctor. My heart was sickened with the thought of deserting these poor men, but I had to save my family. Bridget and Edmund had helped Harry to his feet. With the aid of a stick, he hobbled his way from the tent. There had been no sign of Robert for a while, and I feared he might prepare to leave with the earls. I chided myself for thinking such. He had promised to take me home. He would not break a promise, I was sure. Where was he?

Once inside the kitchens, Edmund and I explained the situation to the cook, Goodwife Oswyn, but she already knew and welcomed us.

'You sit down and take a few minutes to eat, and then Edmund will show you what you must do. He is a good little worker, and I am glad to have him back.'

Edmund beamed. 'She has never spoken thus before,' he whispered as we all took a place at the table. 'It is good to know I have been missed.' I patted his head and gave him a look of mock reproof before squeezing his hand and standing up again. 'There is one more to join us,' I said to the cook. 'I will away and find him.'

Barely had I reached the door when it flew open, and Robert stood before me.

'I have been searching everywhere,' he said. 'The countess told me you were here.' He pulled me close. 'I need to speak with you,' he added.

I looked up at his face. He was scanning the room. I knew Robert's eyes must have alighted on Edmund when he sighed.

'Can we talk outside?' he asked. Without waiting for an answer, Robert took my hand and pulled me out into the chilly night air. When the door was closed behind us, he took hold of both my hands and spoke again. His eyes were cloudy, his brow furrowed.

'What is it? Is something wrong?'

'The countess has asked me to ride with her as part of her personal guard. She says she would trust no one better to ensure her safety.'

'You promised,' I said, already knowing he had agreed to go. 'You cannot break your promise to me.' I fought to hold back the anger and tears. 'What about my safety? Edmund's safety? Do we mean naught to you now we are all in mortal danger?' I pulled my hands from his and turned back to the door.

'Please, Catherine. Master Thomas has given his word to her. He has pledged my support.'

'Then damn him. He knows you have a wife and a child on the way.' The tears were flowing freely now, and he put his arms about me. I tried to shake him off, beating his chest with my fists, but he held me tight until I could struggle no more. 'Harry and Bridget will take good care of you and Edmund. Please try to stay calm. You know it may bring on a seizure if you get too distressed.' I was sobbing into his shirt, my heart breaking knowing he was slipping away from me. This might be the last time I would see him, and I grabbed on to him, lifting my head as his lips came down to meet mine. Finally, holding me at a distance, he looked at my reddened face and wiped the tears away. Before I could find the strength to say another word, he was gone.

The feel and taste of his kiss on my bruised mouth remained. I put my fingers up to touch where his lips had pressed against mine. I did not go back inside for several minutes, waiting for my face to cool in the night air, waiting for the sobs to subside entirely.

When I entered, all faces flew to mine, searching for a response. Edmund was attempting to look behind me to see where Robert was. I shook my head, and he ran over and clung to me, his head buried in my skirts.

Harry, who had been quiet since we entered the kitchen, looked up at me.

'He has gone with the earls?'

I nodded, unable to speak for fear of breaking down once more.

'He promised,' wailed Edmund, still holding on to my skirts. 'He promised we would all go to Rippon with Goodman Smythe and John.'

'He did,' I mumbled. Only then did it occur to me that John and his family were not among us. How could Robert let all these people down? My grief, suddenly overtaken by anger, dissipated. 'We must find them before they leave. We can still go home.' I turned back to the door, and without looking back, I added, 'Come. Bridget. Help me finish loading the cart. Edmund will hitch up Mutton.'

Harry got to his feet, leaning on his stick, a smile on his face. 'I will go to find Goodman Smythe. We have talked long about the route we must take to avoid Sussex and his men.'

I addressed Goodwife Oswyn. 'We thank you most kindly for feeding us. Please tell Countess Jane we are forever grateful, but it will be easier to explain her number of servants if we leave. God keep you all safe.'

Goodwife Oswyn came to the door and saw us out. 'God bless you all,' she said before closing the door behind us. I heard the bolt hammer home and knew they were glad we had gone.

Doctor Bartholomew was still in the hospital tent. One or two priests tended the poor souls who cried out in pain. I went over to him and asked what he would do.

'These men are too ill to move,' he said. 'Their suffering would become much worse if I forced them to take the journey. Besides, they are near to death and will be in our saviour's care before too long.'

'Will you leave them?' I asked, worried about his safety. These were all good men who had stood by their masters only to be left, like bits of garbage, outside the castle walls. My heart raged at the earls for leaving us to die at the hands of Sussex and his army. My heart raged at Countess Anne for taking Robert away from me and putting him in grave danger. Of all people, she should have understood how much I needed him, how much Edmund needed him. I prayed he would come home safely in the end.

'I will stay here,' the doctor answered. 'I will do what I can for these poor souls, and I can be of service to Countess Jane. She is in great distress. Mayhap Sussex and his men will treat her kindly and give me quarter for having tended her.'

Harry was in the back of our cart with Bridget. Edmund sat beside me, not saying a word as we passed through Brandon.

I realised he must be thinking of his father, who had raised him in this village, and now he would never see it again. I took the reins in my right hand and held my arm out to him. He shuffled closer so that his head rested against my side. 'We will be fine,' I said. 'We will all be fine.' His head was warm against my dress as I wrapped my arm around his thin body and took hold of the reins in both hands again. Goodman Smythe's cart was directly behind us; his wife and John sat beside him.

The road was packed, farmers, shopkeepers, and families who had followed their men on this pilgrimage. Some travelled on horseback, some on carts, some walking.

While most travelled towards Sunderland Bridge and crossed the River Wear, our group of two carts turned off the road and drove south towards Willington and Bishop Auckland, a small market town sitting in a valley where the River Wear and River Gaunless joined. We assumed the southern army were travelling the great north road from Darlington, and, not knowing how far north they were by now, we wanted to travel west and take the less travelled route. Harry said Bishop Auckland was the seat of the heretic Bishop of Durham, James Pilkington. A vision of Robert filled my head; his face lit up with laughter as he told me about his journey to Durham cathedral with the earls. I repeated the story to Edmund, telling of how Dean Whittingham was hiding when they arrived at the cathedral; how Westmorland had made fun saying he would like to see the dean bound and rolling down the hill from the cathedral and into the river. Edmund laughed loudly. Harry was quiet. I realised it must be hard for him to relax and join in, having fought on the enemy's side all these weeks.

The country tracks were dark and quiet at night, which helped us to listen out for anyone coming in the opposite direction. Dawn was creeping over the horizon by the time we reached Bishop Auckland. The castle and grounds were on the edge of the town, and we skirted around the total area to avoid being seen. In a nearby copse, we rested a while and let the horses graze on the frosted grass. The morning mist was rising slowly, and I could hear birdsong. My mind, as usual, turned to Robert and home. When would life return to normal? Would he be home to celebrate Christ's Mass?

Edmund came and sat at my side. 'When will we reach Rippon?' he asked.

'It may take several days. We are travelling on back roads. It will be hard but better than being confronted by the Queen's soldiers.'

'I have my dagger,' he said in a serious voice. 'I will protect you.'

I kissed the top of his head. 'I know you will. You are my brave lad.'

He smiled at that; then his face fell as he said, 'I hope Robert comes home safe.'

'He will,' I said, pulling him to me. 'He will.'

Back on the road, we passed two carts coming in the opposite direction. They appeared to be farmers taking goods to the marketplace.

The man in the front cart doffed his felt hat. 'Good morrow,' he said.

I smiled and replied. 'Good morrow. It is a good day for the market. I wish you well with your fare.'

'Aye, 'tis well. Snow's a coming, though.' He looked at the rising sun.

I nodded, and we continued on our way.

'How does he know that snow is on the way?' asked Edmund, scanning the sky above us.

'Because the sun paints the clouds the same colour as a lady's blush,' I said with a smile.

We passed through the village of West Auckland and continued south. Mile after mile of fields and woods until we reached Piercebridge. Exhausted, we sat at the river's edge, tucked in the shadow within the underside of the bridge and near the small chapel. The horses drank their fill from the shallow waters. John's mother, Hannah, passed around a jug of small ale for us to share, and Bridget unpacked some dried beef, bread, and cheese. There was a coaching Inn nearby, but we thought it better not to mix with the locals. We could not be sure of their faith or their leanings when it came to the pilgrimage. The days were short now, and it would soon be dark. We decided to stay here the night and continue our journey tomorrow. We did not light a fire for fear of attracting unwelcome guests and huddled close under the carts, using each other for warmth. Lying there in the dark, I wondered Where Robert was and what he was doing right now.

Robert

Hexham, Northumberland, Tuesday 16th December 1569

I RODE BESIDE THE countess, my heart still in Brancepeth, but my determination to keep the countess safe, along with three other able men she had chosen, kept me vigilant and wide awake. The pace was fierce to Hexham, which we reached in the early hours. We were welcomed most heartily by the local villagers, who were all staunch Catholics, and led inside the Abbey. The local priest was holding Martins, and the soft voices of singing echoed around the cavernous building. The thirty-mile journey exhausted the horses, and we took rest while they recovered in the capable hands of two local men who fed and watered them. Countess Anne had brought two ladies with her, and I stood guard while they fussed about her and brought food and drink to her side. She bade me sit with her and break my fast. I ate the piece of dark rye bread and cheese, a bowl of thin broth and a wrinkled apple that local villagers had provided. Northumberland had found a seat with Westmorland, Richard Norton, Master Thomas, and several others. I recognised the Swinburnes and Tempests and most of the other gentlemen, having spent a great deal of time in their company over the last days and weeks.

'I am most grateful for your company, Robert,' said Anne. 'I need only those I would trust with my life about me.'

'Yes, my lady,' I answered dully, my mind flooded with thoughts of Catherine and our last embrace before I left Brancepeth.

She stumbled a little over her next words. 'I – I feel – I know you were reluctant to leave Catherine. It was well that you did not stay behind. Sussex would not have believed that you were a house servant. It was better only women and children remained.'

'She is in the care of Countess Jane,' I answered. I heard myself say the words, but I did not believe them. Countess Jane and all about her would be at the mercy of Sussex, or, God forbid, that tyrant Forster and his men. It took all my strength not to jump up and ride back to her that minute.

'The countess has written to Sussex,' she said, as if already reading my thoughts. 'There is no danger from anyone. Your wife is in safe hands.'

I did not answer. Let her convince herself if she must. I prayed she was right and finished eating my meal. 'Will you rest now, Countess?'

'I will. You may rest for an hour or so with Duncan, then Alfred and George will take your place a while.' Duncan, a tall, heavy-set man with a mop of red hair and matching beard, in a leather jerkin and carrying a halberd, nodded at his mistress and joined me on the nave floor. The other two men stood guard by the doors. We could almost pass for brothers with the colour of our hair and the same stature.

Westmorland and the others spoke in whispers as the priest offered the sacrament. I hoped I would have opportunity for the same. It was only my belief that kept me going through these dark times. That and my hope to return home with all my family intact before too long. I lay down and closed my eyes. An image of Catherine hovered about me as I fell into a deep slumber. She whispered to me, and I reached up and pulled her face to mine, where her kiss was soft and full of love. I groaned with pleasure until a fist thumped my chest and woke me.

'Save your dreams for when you are alone. Your noises are keeping me awake.'

I opened my eyes to see Duncan's ugly brute of a face about an inch away. Sitting upright, I chased out my dream. 'I am sorry, friend. It was a dream of my wife. I meant you no harm.'

Duncan laughed loudly. 'We all miss our wives, but I was not in the mood for kissing someone as ugly as you,' he said. A broad grin appeared from under the red beard he sported.

'Then we shall lie back-to-back, and I will refrain from sharing my dreams with you,' I answered, returning the smile.

We settled down once more, and, in what seemed no time at all, I was being woken again by one of the other guards.

'Your time to take watch,' he said and lowered himself to the floor.

Duncan and I got to our feet and took our positions by the great wooden doors at the abbey chapel entrance.

A couple of hours later, and everyone was up and busy. The countess and her ladies were eating a meal of oats and dried fruits. The men were holding court and discussing the next move. A messenger had arrived to say that John Forster was close behind with up to 1,000 horsemen. Westmorland gathered us to say we needed to make haste to Brampton afore Forster and his men arrived.

It took little time to saddle the horses and be on our way. The countess, with the help of her women, was dressed in splendour as usual. We set out on the road again. I was sorry the priest had not given me the sacrament and could only hope there would be an opportunity at our next stop. The feeling of knowing we would soon be at Naworth Castle and behind its defences lifted our spirits as the magnificent building came into sight ahead. Westmorland stopped as a rider approached. He and Norton rode up to meet him and, within a few moments, were riding back. Westmorland's face looked like thunder as he came and told us that Dacre had refused shelter.

'The treacherous dog has switched sides. There is nothing for it but to return to Hexham and take shelter at the abbey again until we can resolve our next move.'

We returned to Hexham for another night, where at last I received the sacrament. The earls sent some horsemen to discover Forster's and Sussex's plans. The following morning news came that Forster had turned to Alnwick to attack the men Northumberland had sent there to waylay Sussex.

Catherine

Richmond, Yorkshire, Wednesday 17th December

THE FOLLOWING MORNING, ALTHOUGH still dark, I awoke to the sound of Harry harnessing Mutton. Bridget was helping him, and they whispered to each other. I was glad for their reunion and that we could be friends again. In my loneliness, I could now understand what she must have gone through all these weeks. Seeing Robert and I embrace must have been torturous for her when she did not know if Harry was alive or dead. Now it was my turn to wonder for Robert's safety. I ached all over with cold, and it took a while to haul myself to my feet. Seeing how I struggled, Edmund offered me his hand and heaved and pulled until I was upright and panting with effort. The ground was wet underfoot, and I realised it had snowed in the night. A light wind pinched my cheeks with its icy touch. I shivered.

'I will take the reins today,' said Harry. 'You must rest. I can see how tired you are. You must take care that you and the baby come to no harm, Catherine.' As he spoke, I felt the soft lick of a snowflake on my cheek.

I did not even try to argue with him. I had reached the end of my strength. My body welcomed the thought of not having to do anything at all for a few hours. We still had a long way to travel, and the roads, now covered in a white blanket that did hide all the ruts and dips, would be treacherous under the cartwheels. I climbed up onto the flatbed and gathered blankets around me, feeling as though my bones might never be warm again. Edmund climbed up beside Harry, and Bridget joined me. She pulled me close, and we hung on to each other for comfort and warmth.

We arrived at the town of Richmond as the sun had reached its peak. People crowded the streets on this wintry Wednesday. The steep roads were ankle-deep in snow, which had turned into a muddy sludge. Richmond had been faithful to the rebels, and we thought it would be a haven to stay awhile. Harry said he knew of a tavern that served hot food, so we made our way over and put the carts in the courtyard at the back.

Robert

Hexham, Northumberland,
Wednesday 17th December 1569

THIS MORNING EDWARD DACRE, who had quarrelled with his older brother, Leonard, for turning us away at Naworth, arrived with the news that Sussex and Hunsdon had changed direction and were heading our way. Westmorland sent half the horsemen back the way we had come, attempting to hold off Sussex, whom we heard was nearing Newcastle. A rider had ridden both day and night from Hartlepool. He told us there was no hope of defending the town, and the men had left and were headed to Alnwick to support our fighters there.

We set off towards the Scottish border as soon as we had broken our fast, heading first to Brampton and then, Edward and his cohort leading us, north where we were to meet with friends of the Scottish queen in Liddesdale in two days. Snow had fallen during the night and had settled thickly on the moors, but the sun was bright against a cloudless sky. My cheeks burned from the icy wind, and my hands were stiff inside my leather gloves, making it difficult to hold on to the reins. Progress was slow, and the higher we travelled, the thicker the snow became until we had to dismount and lead the horses as they struggled to move forward. We eventually stopped to rest in the lea of a craggy rock.

It felt good to be out of the wind for a while. Anne and her ladies looked cold and exhausted. I wondered if it had been a good idea for them to be travelling with us at all. I could see the countess was struggling for breath. The cold seemed to have taken hold and was squeezing the life from her. The ladies gathered about her to shelter her body, but I was not sure it would help. I went to Northumberland, who was in conversation with Richard Norton and my master.

'Pardon me, my lord. The countess appears dreadfully ill from the cold. Is there anywhere we might take shelter for her and her ladies-in-waiting?'

'Blast the woman!' he snapped. 'I knew it was ill judgement for her to travel with us. She will not listen.'

Northumberland got to his feet and went to see his wife. Master Thomas offered me a drink from his flask. 'Here,' he said. 'this will chase the cold out.'

I took it gratefully and swallowed the fiery liquid, which must be, I presumed, the famous Scottish drink I had heard of before. My throat was on fire, and it took great fortitude not to spit it out. 'Thank you, Master,' I squeaked, handing the flask back. He roared with laughter.

'Never tasted whisky before? It will keep your innards warm for a while.'

Northumberland came back to us. 'We best keep moving. Countess Anne is succumbing to this blasted cold. We must also ensure we avoid the queen's troops at Bewcastle.' We all knew of their determination to keep the reivers in check. Sussex's scouts would have informed them of our whereabouts. 'We will find shelter up at Newcastleton before too long,' he added.

I hoped he was right; none could survive a night out in this weather.

We carried on, heading north-west in the biting wind and snow for another hour, and came to a small homestead called Roadhead and took shelter in the church there. The priest was wary of us but welcomed us inside. When he saw the countess in dire need of warmth, he opened the door to his little cottage at the back of the church, where a fire blazed in a small hearth. He took the thin blankets from his cot and gave them to one of the ladies-in-waiting. She draped them around Anne, who coughed and wheezed constantly. Duncan and I stood guard under the church porch while the women took shelter. Westmorland and most riders were itching to move on, and they allowed Anne only a short time to rest and warm herself before we continued our journey to Newcastleton.

Jack Armstrong and his men came upon us when we were not much further along the road. Duncan and I immediately drew our swords and rode in front of Countess Anne, ready to defend her, Westmorland and the others quickly followed suit, but Jock Armstrong and his men seemed to think we were ridiculous and laughed. Edward Dacre held up his hand to stay us, smiling as he rode up to greet them. After a short discussion, he came back to Westmorland.

'They offer you shelter. They welcome anyone who is on the run from the English.' He laughed. 'They also enjoy the idea of making any of the English troops lives a misery if it suits them. And this they say suits them.'

We were still wary of them, knowing their reputation for robbery and violence, but, with no other options available, Westmorland accepted their hospitality. I could not help but keep my hand on the hilt of my sword for the rest of the journey. Once we reached Newcastleton, Anne and her ladies, who could travel no further, were offered shelter up on Kirk Hill by a rough-looking fellow in a filthy kilt and nicknamed Jock o' the Syde.

One of the Scottish lords sniggered loudly, saying, 'His house is a hovel. Not fit for a dog kennel, never mind a countess.' The others around him laughed.

'Beggars canna be choosers,' said Jock, grinning. I was furious at his discourteous manner, but we had no options left and could not turn down his offer. I looked to the countess, who did not appear to have heard the comment. Her head was hanging, and she was ready to slip off her mount and fall to the ground. I helped her down, almost having to carry her the few steps to the 'hovel' entrance, where the ladies took her inside. Duncan, I, and a half dozen other men were to remain here with them, and we settled the horses in a low stone stable before joining them in the warmth.

Hector Armstrong took Anne's husband, Northumberland, and several men, including Master Thomas and Richard Norton, to his house at Harelaw around seven miles south. Jock Armstrong offered sanctuary to Westmorland and the balance of the riders at nearby Puddingburn Tower.

Inside the thick walls of Jock o' the Syde's house, it was dark and cold. A sparse fire burned in a colossal grate where Anne was sitting on a large, padded chair; her ladies huddled on the floor about her. At least we were out of the biting wind.

The dark walls displayed no hangings, but the heads of several stags stared down at us. 'All shot by my own arrowheads,' said Jock, pride in his voice. 'I'm a canny wee hunter. Nothing escapes me when I set my mind to hunt something down.' His eyes were taking in the countess and her ladies. 'Tis dreich the day. Best coorie by the fire under a wee blanket or two.' Duncan and I stepped closer to the women. He laughed and shouted for a servant to fetch some whisky for his guests.

Looking at Anne, I wished Catherine were here to tend her. She would know the best treatments. An elderly woman in dirty clothes that looked as if they had never been off her back in years brought a tray of small pewter mugs and a bottle of dark liquid. It was difficult to see what it was in the dim light, but the smell was the same as the drink Master Thomas had given me on our journey. I remembered the sharp burn in my throat, followed by a warm sensation inside my chest. It would probably do us all good to have a swig of this fiery potion, especially Anne. The room was poorly furnished with a large oak table in its centre, long benches down either side. There was only one decent chair at either side of the grate, and Jock was sitting opposite the countess. As Jock's men filled the long benches, the rest of us were told we must make use of the stone floor to rest and take a drink. I lowered myself gingerly down onto the stale rushes, the smell of urine and decaying food filling my nostrils. Duncan did not seem to notice the stench at all as he joined me on the floor. Neither did any of Jock's men as they grabbed a mug and held it out to be filled. The same burning sensation hit my throat, and I waited for the welcome warmth that was to follow. It did not disappoint. The old woman brought bowls of oats and more drinks, and as our bellies filled and our insides warmed, the dismal room and the stale rushes did not seem to matter at all. We all became glad to be in such pleasant company. My head was swimming a little, and I could barely see the ladies helping Anne to her feet and leading her away to a bedchamber. The drinking and laughter continued far into the night and disappeared before my eyes as I succumbed to the sleep I had been craving.

Catherine

Leyburn, Yorkshire, Wednesday 17th December 1569

EVEN THOUGH IT HAD been six years since the devastating plague outbreak in Leyburn, we were still cautious about entering the town. The population was small, and there were many abandoned buildings that, although damp and overrun with vermin, allowed us to shelter for the night. The town was not on the route we had intended and took us further west and into many vales and hills, but on hearing word that troops were camping a few miles south of Richmond, there was not much choice. It had taken a few hours to get here through the snow-laden roads, and we were all exhausted. We found a large barn and so drove the carts inside. There were one or two mounds of hay so old they were black, and upon touching, disintegrated like wood ash in our hands. The wind echoed in the rafters above us, and the sudden screeching of a large bird startled everyone. I screamed as it sailed past my shoulder, almost catching my cloak with its sharp talons. I began to shake uncontrollably as I looked for somewhere to hide. Running for the door, I was almost outside when Bridget grabbed my arm and pulled me close. Her voice was soothing.

'It has gone. Do not worry. I have you.'

'Where? Where is it? It will catch me. Please do not let it take me.' I was sobbing now. My heart raced, and the barn was swimming around me. I broke free of Bridget's hold. Her voice grew distant as I dropped into a black hole where I knew the bird would find me.

Running. Running. I can hear its wings beating. Feel the power as they rise and fall. Rise and fall. I'm falling. He's here; he's caught me. Please! No!

I was cold and shivering. I could see a faint light. A candle? I could see people sitting close by. My mouth was dry, and I couldn't swallow. My head hurt as I tried to lift it, and a weak moan escaped my lips.

'Hush now. I am with you.' It was Bridget's voice. I put my head back and felt her lap beneath my head. We stayed as we were for a little while. Edmund came and sat beside me, his hand taking hold of mine.

'I must get up,' Bridget said, looking down at my face. 'Do you think you could sit now?' I tried again, and this time I sat up. She helped me shuffle back and lean against the wheel of our cart. Edmund took a blanket from off the cart and placed it around my shoulders. I smiled at him in thanks, pulling it close.

Bridget got to her feet. 'Stay where you are, and I will fetch a drink.' When my gaze followed her, I could see that the candle was, in reality, a small fire in the middle of the stone floor. I remembered where we were and looked about frantically for the bird that had screeched at me. The enormous doors had been closed and offered a little more protection, even though they hung loosely and had missing batons.

John's parents watched me closely, but as I returned their gaze, they looked away quickly. I wondered if they thought me some kind of witch. They always seemed on edge when I was near them.

'Where did it go?' I asked.

'Outside. 'Tis only an owl, Catherine. It will not harm you.' said Harry, from where he was sitting by the fire. Bridget and Harry had known for years that I had feared falcons since my accident as a child. It was the sudden shriek of the owl that had set me in a spin. That and the wings flapping so close to my ear. I took deep breaths until my heart slowed, and I felt more comfortable.

We ate a little bread and cheese bought in Richmond before we left, and Bridget warmed some ale. Then she examined the lump on my head. 'The skin is not broken. Your head must be very hard. I heard the crack as you hit the floor.' I laughed and winced at the same time, grateful that she was here to watch over me. A flash of anger raced through my head as I wondered about Robert and where he was. Mayhap the countess did need him, but I needed him more.

A little while later, and after eating, Bridget lay our blankets across the flatbed of the cart, saying it would be better than lying on a floor full of owl pellets. Looking around and seeing the litter everywhere, I realised this must have been the home of the owl for years. It made me feel guilty for evicting the poor creature out into the miserable night.

Robert

Newcastleton, Scottish Borders,
Friday 19th December 1569

'GET UP, YOU LAZY dog!' someone was shouting from very far away. The voice was distant but became louder and louder until it was a roar. It was difficult to open my eyes, and my head hurt as if someone had hit it with the hammer I used to make my shoes for the horses. Bang. Bang. Bang.

'Please. Stop hammering. My head—' I forced one eye open slightly and squinted at a pair of feet beside me. My gaze followed the line of the boots to a pair of thick hairy legs and the edge of a pleated kilt. I sat up with a jolt. My head exploded, and daggers of pain stabbed at my temple. I could barely see and put my hands over my eyes, rubbing them slowly, desperate to ease the pain.

'Up, Robert. Up.' Duncan's voice gnawed at me, his feet still poking my thigh. I wondered where I was for a moment, but the raucous laugh of Jock o' the Syde and the pungent smell from the surrounding rushes reminded me quickly of my whereabouts. I struggled to my feet and felt my stomach roil as if I were at sea. My head swam, and my legs did not understand what my mind was telling them. Duncan took hold of my arm and dragged me outside, where I promptly gagged and was sick, repeatedly, my stomach doubled up and griping.

When I finally got control of myself, I sat in a heap on a boulder close to the house wall. 'I am ill, Duncan. Some devil has entered me and is twisting my insides.' I shivered uncontrollably. 'I think I have a fever, an ague.'

'You suffer from drinking too much.' He laughed. 'The fiery stuff can do that to a man when he's not accustomed to it.'

I tried to stand up and slumped down again, putting my head in my hands. 'Will I recover?' I felt as if I might just die and never see my Catherine again. 'My wife – she is having a baby soon. I need to be with her. Who will—'

'Stop your blether,' he said, 'You will not die. You will get up and come to the stables with me. We have horses to tend.' Duncan marched away from me as I tried once more to stand. I waited until nausea and dizziness passed before following him across the yard to the low stone building that housed the horses.

'Christ Almighty!' Duncan swore. He had opened the door to the stall where Anne's and the women's horses were sheltering. 'Mary, Mother of God,' he shouted again as he opened the door to the next stall where Chestnut and the men's horses had sheltered last night.

I tried to quicken my pace, thoughts of my poorly condition disappearing. Something was wrong. What had happened? I reached the entrance and looked inside the first stall, then to the second where Duncan was standing. There was no sound; not a neigh, not a whinny – not a single horse. 'God's blood!' I swore.

Countess Anne still looked weak as she sat by the hearth, shaking her head in despair. I had never seen her as low as this. Even so, I could see the spark of anger in the flames that reflected and danced in her eyes. She wrung her hands and stared into the fire. 'Will someone go and fetch my husband?' she asked.

'I will, my lady,' I said. 'Is it far?' I turned to Jock.

'I'll send one of my men,' he said, putting his hand on Anne's shoulder. She brushed it away.

'Send someone after them,' she hissed. 'We need those horses.'

Jock sniggered. 'They'll be away o'er the border by now. Selling them on to many eager customers.' He sat in the chair opposite the Countess. 'Dinna worry, madam. Ye can stay here as long as ye like.'

Anne glared at the oaf. Had she the strength, I thought she might take a sword or a whip to the brute.

I could not do much else, so I went outside to clear my head from this damned fog and endless throbbing that sat there.

The earl arrived with Hector Armstrong riding by his side. Master Thomas, Richard Norton, and several other riders, I had travelled beside on our journey here accompanied them. The earl went inside to see his wife accompanied by Hector, and when he came out a good hour later, he told the men and me we were to stay and guard his wife. He did not say what, if anything, he was going to do about our missing horses. With that, the entire party turned and rode away, leaving us with no option but to stay put in this dreadful place with these appalling men. What a strange feeling it was to be at the mercy of so many robbers and villains. How safe would the women be here among so many savages? I went back inside to seek the countess's wishes of what she would like of Duncan and me and the rest of her entourage.

She was still sitting by the fire with her ladies at her feet.

'My lady,' I said, bowing before her, 'has your husband, the earl, planned for you and your ladies to travel on to somewhere – a little more comfortable?' I looked around at the men in the room. They were at the table drinking and eating what I presumed to be venison and some sort of fowl.

She did not raise her gaze but said, 'It appears this will be our home for the present. My husband will furnish us with horses when and if he finds the means of doing so. Meanwhile, we must press ourselves on this – this good man's hospitality a while longer.'

'Very well, my lady.' I responded, bowing and turning to our host. 'Are there horses to be had nearby?' I asked him. His companions roared with laughter.

'We'll be gan hunting for some soon enough. You'd better fill your belly afore this lot wipe the plates clean.'

By 'hunting', I presumed he meant waylaying some low travellers and stealing their horses. Mayhap they would rob them of their lives in the process. I hoped Northumberland would provide for us before it came to that. Now, there was nothing for it but to stay put in this rank house with its stinking floors. Duncan and I grabbed a plate and filled it with meat. There were jugs of whisky and ale on the table. I chose the ale to wash down the taste of the pungent-smelling game on my plate. We sat on the floor with our backs against the cold, stone walls. The meat was tough and poorly cooked, but better than nothing. While we ate, the ladies removed themselves from the room. Anne still looked pale as she stumbled away, and I could hear a persistent cough coming from behind the closed door of the bedchamber when she had gone.

One lady came back and asked the old woman who had fed us last night and appeared to be the only other female in the house apart from those of our party, if she would make a tea that could soothe the countess's ailments. The old woman disappeared into the kitchen, soon coming back with a pewter jug that steamed. The smell was very like that of the whisky we had drunk last night. Remembering how deeply it had made me sleep, I thought it would be good for Anne as long as it was not so much as to cause her sickness and headache as it had done to me. My stomach roiled slightly at the thought. Through the small windows, I could see great flakes of snow falling, and I had the feeling of being in a coffin where it was dark and cold – a place where no sound came in from the outside world. The silence covered me like a thick blanket, and I neither heard nor saw anything as my head dropped to one side, and I fell asleep.

Later that day, Duncan and I stepped outside for a short while. The snow had stopped, and the sun was low in the sky. It did not seem to stay light for many hours up here, and we could see the moon was already rising. It always seemed strange to me that the sun and the moon could be in the sky at the same time. It was a peculiar sight, and one day I wished to learn more about the things that hung in the sky and did not fall on us while we stood and looked up at them. We walked over to the stables, and I lit a torch before sitting down on the straw. I asked Duncan where he was from and how long he had been fighting alongside the earls. He told me he had travelled down to England a few years ago from his home on Scotland's west coast. His family had been fishermen. He did not want to go out on the seas and drown like many of his family afore him. Deciding to find work on a farmstead in the low countries, he had walked there over many days but, having no luck, had kept walking until he came to Durham. There was work in the coal pits near Burnhope. The pay was not much, but the work was steady enough. He enjoyed working for the Tempest family at Holmside Hall. They were a good Catholic family like his own back in Scotland, and he was happy to join them in their pilgrimage against the English queen. I asked if he had a wife waiting for him, and he smiled.

'Joan is a kind woman,' he said. 'I left her with our three children. They are too small to be travelling about the country. Her parents will make sure they have enough to eat. Her father works at the corn mill near where we live.'

I told him about Catherine, how her parents had worked the land, how they had died of plague soon after we married. How brave and caring she was. I told him how she was a healer and had helped the wounded at the siege of Barney Castle. I talked about my father and Harry's father; about what had happened during the Pilgrimage of Grace, how it caused a great fallout with Harry, who had been like a brother to me.

When it was fully dark, we went back to the house. It felt warm after being outside for so long, and we were grateful for the fire in the hearth. The old woman had built it a little higher tonight, and I thought that was probably for Anne's benefit. She also brought food out to the table again, and Jock's men, who had been drinking the whole day and fallen asleep, woke up long enough to shovel some of it into their mouths and drop off again. The snoring was like a swarm of bees in springtime. Anne did not come out from the bedchamber. The women took it in turns to come for food and drink for themselves and their mistress. They hurried back behind the door of theirs and their mistress's room as soon as their plates were full.

Jock o' the Syde was sitting in one of the chairs set the fire, but he would let no one sit in the other in case the countess relented and came to warm herself.

The next morning, a loud hammering on the door woke us. I stood quickly, my hand on my sword. One of Jock's men shouted out, asking who was there.

'Martin Elliott,' came the reply. The man who had shouted opened the door, and in stepped a tall man dressed in plate and a steel helmet. Jock o' the Syde welcomed him and offered him a seat by the fire.

'What brings you here, Martin?' asked Jock.

'You know why I am here.'

I wondered who this man was. Looking out of the window, I could see what appeared to be a large group of horsemen, most in plate and helmet. I turned my attention back to the two men facing each other from each side of the hearth.

Jock smiled. 'You know all are welcome at my hearth. I canna turn a body away. Especially those who are on the run from the bastard English.'

'Then we have a problem,' Elliot said. 'I have sworn an oath to help the regent, Moray.'

'Ah. I see. We do have a problem. I wouldna want to fall out with you, Martin. T'would be a pity to take arms against a friend.'

'I knew you would see it my way.' Elliot smiled at Jock and stood to leave. 'I'll be sure to call back again the morrow and find all peaceful in your house.'

Anne entered the room at that moment. She was coughing pitifully but held her head high.

'Who is this, Jock?' she asked, her stare firmly on Elliot. I stepped a little closer and put my hand under her arm to support her. Elliot removed his helmet and bowed.

'Martin Elliot at your service, my lady,' he said.

'What is your business here?' she asked, not a trace of fear crossing her face.

He grinned at her, his eyes taking in her beauty. 'I am about the Earl of Moray's business, my lady. I have heard of your husband's travels in this area, and I bring a message to my friend Jock o' the Syde.'

'And the message would be what?' Anne's face had remained stony toward the man. Her arm was shaking as I supported it, and I helped her to the chair by the hearth.

The smile disappeared from Elliot's face. 'I come to tell my friend he would do well to ask his visitors to depart the morrow before the regent has cause to travel this way in search of traitors to the English queen.'

'We will gladly go if someone could find and return our horses. They have been stolen, and we have no means of transport.'

Elliot looked sharply at Jock. 'Is this true?'

'Aye. Methinks it be Black Ormiston.'

'Then, my lady, you must look to your husband for transport.' Elliot walked back to the door and opened it. He looked around again. 'Take care, Jock o' the Syde. It would be a great shame to bear arms against each other.'

We all, apart from Anne, went outside and watched him and his party ride away. The snow flew high under the galloping hooves as they disappeared into the distance. I looked up at the dull white sky and could see the weather was closing in again.

Jock called to one of his men. 'Ride out to the Armstrongs and let them know that Martin Elliot is joined with Moray and will come here tomorrow in search of the earls.'

Back inside, the countess was sipping a hot brew. She looked a sorry sight, and I knelt at her skirts. 'My lady. Is there anyone in these parts who might take you in?'

'I know not anyone here, dear Robert—' A coughing fit stopped her from saying more.

'Come,' I said. 'you must away to your bed.'

She did not argue, and her ladies guided her back to the bedchamber.

It was a few hours before the sound of riders, once again, pounded the courtyard outside. At first, I did not recognise the men who looked, to all intents, another gang of reivers in their dirty apparel. It was not until the leader spoke I realised it was

Northumberland, Master Thomas, Norton, and several horsemen gathered there; their faces dirty, their hair matted, their clothes ragged. Countess Anne was once more seated by the fire as Northumberland dismounted and came inside, immediately going to his wife's side. Master Thomas and Richard Norton followed him. Anne recoiled at his appearance, pushing him away.

My master did not acknowledge me but spoke to Jock sharply. 'We will need more heavy clothing against this weather. Can you supply cloaks for the purpose?'

Jock laughed at him. 'Och, yes. Anything to help you sneak away. What can you pay?'

I saw Master Thomas's hand automatically reach for the hilt of his sword. Norton put a hand out to stay him.

'My nephew is quick to anger,' he said, looking at Jock, 'We would be much obliged if you could furnish us with such. So we can blend in a little more with the local population.'

'Aye, I ken your need,' he replied, looking at my master's hand. 'I have plenty of old garbs I intended to throw to the beggars and the poor the next time I go to Glasgow.' Jock's men did nothing to hide their amusement. Master Thomas marched outside, the sound of their laughter following him. A sudden feeling of shame flushed my face. Why did my master have to succumb to a temper like a child? He had no control over his manner, jumping to the quickest way of retaliation whenever something displeased him. His father would be ashamed of his petty son, who stamped his foot so readily at the slightest adversity. I wondered what his uncle thought of his behaviour.

The old woman came outside with a bundle of ragged cloaks and blankets. She tossed them on the floor and hurried back inside out of the cold.

'I see you and your friend have a fine set of spurs on your boots,' said Jock, looking down at my master's and Norton's boots. 'I think they would be a fair price for warm clothing.' I looked to Thomas's and Norton's feet. I was thrilled that they still wore the spurs I had made them.

'You can have them,' snapped Thomas. 'Much use they have done me.' He knelt and unstrapped them, flinging them at Jock. Jock spat on the dirty silver engraving and polished it with his sleeve. The pattern shone in the sunlight.

Norton passed his spurs over with more grace.

'I pass them over, but I have not yet paid the maker for his work,' he said, nodding in my direction. 'It is this man who owns them and made them. He deserves some compensation for his skill.' Jock looked at me but said nothing. Northumberland then appeared. He thanked Jock for taking care of his wife before mounting his horse.

'Ye can all help yourselves,' said Jock, pointing at the heap of dirty clothes on the ground before leaving them to it and going back to his hearth. Two or three riders gathered up the cloaks and handed them around.

I approached my master. 'Will I stay here with the countess?' I asked.

'You must,' he answered, without even looking at me. Pulling himself up onto his horse once more, he looked down, his face with a pained look, and added, 'I am sorry to leave you, Robert, truly I am, but I would be executed if caught now. You have been most loyal, and the countess could not find a braver man. God take care of you.' Wheeling his horse about, he set off with the other riders without a backward glance.

'God speed,' I whispered after him.

The rest of the day and night passed solemnly. Duncan and I wondered how we would get the countess and her ladies to safety before Elliot returned and arrested us all. Jock said he was sorry, but we had to leave in the morning, on foot if necessary. He could let the countess have an old nag that he kept only for its service to him over many years, but for the rest of us, he could spare none. I could not sleep. My mind was going over our predicament – the anger at Northumberland for having little regard for the fate of his wife. He could have left one of his men behind so that his wife could ride with him. He had told her that Elliot would not hurt a lady but handle her with respect and courtesy. I would have gladly given my life for Catherine in a heartbeat. But was that true? Had I not left her back at Brancepeth at the mercy of Sussex? Did I not tell her the same, that she would be safe with Countess Jane? I felt ashamed and wished, more than anything, that I was home with her. That all this was over; that I had not set out on this pilgrimage in the first place.

We awoke to a snowstorm. How would the few men here get the countess to a safe place? She could not travel in this weather. Jock would not change his mind.

'I am sorry to turn you out,' he said to Anne and the two women. 'I canna afford to be arrested with you. Mayhap you should set off when the storm is a little quieter. Elliot told me he would not return until after noontime. The weather may have improved by then.'

Anne thanked him for his kindness. Her voice was hoarse from coughing, and her cheeks burned red with fever. The old woman looked out a thick blanket that she had held back from Northumberland's men.

'Dunna cover yourself with it until you leave. You'll not feel the benefit otherwise.'

Anne nodded at her and placed the blanket on the floor in front of the fire. She called me over. I knelt before her, and she reached a hand out to me.

'You have been true and loyal to me, Robert. I cannot ask you to stay longer. Catherine will be afeared for your safety, and the baby will come soon.'

I answered her, holding back my genuine feelings on the matter. 'I cannot leave until you are safe, Countess. Catherine will understand my absence.' I wanted to leave. I wanted to hurry back to Brancepeth and be by Catherine's side when my son was born. Of course, she had Bridget with her, and Countess Jane would say they are servants and plead for their security. Sussex surely would harm none of them.

'I will surrender to the Scottish regent. He will not harm ladies. Go now while you may.'

I stood. Could I? No. I knew I would never forgive myself if I walked away and left her to her fate. 'I will not leave, my lady. Not until I know you have reached safety.'

Jock was watching me as I refused to go. 'I like you, Robert Gray,' he said. 'You stand by your mistress. Others might scurry away at the first chance.' He picked up the spurs that Norton had handed over. 'Here. Take these. I will not cheat on an honest man. You can sell them. You may need the money on your travels.'

'Thank you,' I said, taking them quickly afore he changed his mind. These would help me start up my business again when I got home.

Jock and his men jumped up at the sound of horsemen. 'Elliot has come early,' he said and pulled out a dagger. 'We will have to fight them. He will not accept that I did as he said.'

A voice I recognised shouted clearly to us, asking for Lady Anne. I looked through the window to see Westmorland with several horsemen. I went to the door and opened it warily.

'Fetch the countess. We will take her to safety at Ferniehirst,' he said. 'My good friend here, Sir Thomas Kerr, has agreed to shelter us. I have extra horses for you all.'

'Thank you, my lord,' I said, smiling. At last, someone who would help us flee from here. Sir Thomas, dressed in plate and helmet, slipped down from his horse.

'I would speak with the countess,' he said. 'I have some grave news.' I stood aside as he entered the house. He went straight to Anne and bowed. 'My Lady Anne, I carry news of your husband.'

Anne looked up, fear evident in her eyes, 'Sir Thomas. What? Is he dead?' she asked.

'No, my lady, but the regent has taken him. I have heard that Hector Armstrong led him into a trap. Elliot and some of the regent's men were hiding in wait for them. Markenfield and Norton slipped away, but I heard there were at least thirty captured.'

We did not take long to prepare ourselves for the journey, glad to be leaving. We were all given good war horses to ride. The countess mounted with help and lifted her head high for the first time in days. She was still ailing but tried to hide her suffering. I felt a certain pride in this strong woman. She had more right to be riding alongside these men than many of the so-called gentlemen I had met since this journey commenced. Duncan and I flanked her as we rode along. The biting wind was blowing from the east, and sleet stabbed our faces like shards of glass. Westmorland told us it was a journey of twenty-five miles, and in this weather, would take at least eight hours. He was not wrong. The journey over Saughtree Fell was arduous as we rode higher and higher, the wind and snow making every mile seem like ten. After around three hours, we had not travelled very far but pushed on as we were told that we would reach a great forest soon and could take some shelter there. Anne was barely holding on, and Duncan and I held on to her as we inched our way forward. By the time we reached the forest and could get out of the wind, I feared the countess would not make it. I lowered her down from the horse and laid a blanket beneath a tree. She curled up, and I covered her with the blanket I had been wearing about my shoulders. I fetched Westmorland to see the pitiful state she was in. He squatted down beside her.

'My dear,' he said. 'I fear you are suffering a great illness. We will rest a little while, and I will think of some way to make your journey more comfortable.'

'My lord,' I said. 'If it be a possibility, she could ride with me. She could lean into me and take the heat from my body.'

He pondered for a moment. 'Yes. That may work. The countess will have to rest a while longer first.'

Anne's ladies-in-waiting were not faring much better, and we agreed they would travel the balance of the journey in the same way. We rested for another hour; then, as agreed, the countess was seated in front of me, bound together by a blanket and lengths of hemp rope. Her back soon felt warm against my chest. That was a good sign, although she did not speak at all.

There were several paths through the forest, and I followed the lead group of men. The wind was calm while we were among the trees; the only sound was that of falling snow from the branches when it thudded onto the forest floor or the path on which we rode. Not a bird sang, nor a pheasant called. It felt as if we were travelling through a secret world of silence. Occasionally, a horse snorted, and clouds of white breath billowed into the still air. We travelled this way for two or three hours, and as the trees thinned and the sound of the wind grew louder, we could see the open moor once again ahead of us. Sir Thomas called a halt, and we rested again before going on. Someone untied us and lowered Anne down from the horse. She sat on a blanket with her back to a tree, the air making her cough relentlessly. One of her ladies passed her a drink, and she sipped until the coughing ceased. We ate bread, and a little dried meat, savouring the food, batting our arms across our bodies to keep warm. Once more, we mounted and made ready to move on. The sun was low in the sky, and it would soon be dark.

'Lean into me, so the wind does not catch your breath,' I said. She made a muffled groan in response as we set off again and rode out onto the open hills.

We had ridden high above a stretch of water and into some tall trees.

'Get the women inside,' shouted Westmorland as we came to a stop in the courtyard of Ferniehirst Castle. Several servants had come out to greet us and ushered Anne and her women inside the great wooden door where family crests were carved into the stones above. Grooms took the horses to the stables, and we made our way inside. We climbed the stairs, which strangely ran counter-clockwise, and led us above the under-croft and into the Great Hall.

The hall was vast, at least ten men high, and I gazed in awe at the wall coverings and a hearth large enough for several men to stand inside if it were not for the enormous fire that burned therein. Everyone made their way over to feel its warmth and comforting glow. Countess Anne was not there. I assumed she had been taken directly to her bedchamber to recover. The floor, thickly strewn with fresh rushes, did not smell, and there was a jake in the corner. In amongst several men, who were already ensconced in front of the fire, were Master Thomas and Richard Norton. It pleased me they had escaped capture, and Thomas even smiled and lifted a glass in my direction when he saw me. I pulled the wet blanket from my shoulders, and a servant immediately took it from my hands and hurried away with it.

Catherine

Rippon, Wednesday, 24th December 1569

LOOKING DOWN INTO THE street and across the market-stede, it felt good to be in my home again. I could hear the hammering in the workshop below, almost imagining it was Robert at work on a normal day. The shop fronts were being decorated with holly and ivy and mistletoe in readiness for Christmas celebrations, and merry music floated up as I watched a small band of minstrels playing by the obelisk. John and Edmund were working hard. Since we arrived back three days ago, Bridget had insisted I stayed abed and rested. I did as I was told, and soon, I would even have the luxury of my new feather mattress. Bridget and I had been working on it together each day. It was likely we would complete it today.

Bridget returned from downstairs carrying a jug of chamomile tea and two drinking cups.

'There is plenty of activity on the market,' I said, turning back to stare down at the people about their business. It would be the first Christmas I had spent without Robert since we were married. Bridget came and stood beside me. 'Have you decorated the spinning wheel?'

'I have. I think it looks better than any other on the street,' she said, beaming from ear to ear. 'Young Edmund is so excited to see the mystery plays. I am sure he will burn himself in the workshop; he dances about so to the music of the minstrels.' She laughed, her voice warm as she spoke about the lad. It was good to see my dear friend back to her usual self. If only Robert were here too. I sighed and walked back over to the bed. Sitting on the edge, I took the cup of warm sweet tea from Bridget.

'Do you think he will get home safely?' I asked as if she might truly know the answer.

'I know he would do anything to be by your side, and, if that is so, it will take the whole of the queen's army to block his path home.'

I smiled. Bridget was right. Robert would face anything to get back to our child and me. I stroked the tight ball of my belly and wished him beside us.

Bridget turned from the window. 'I will make the mynst pye and a wassail bowl for our celebrations.'

'I will come and help,' I said, following her from the room.

'You must not tire yourself.' Bridget stopped to bar my way.

'I have had enough time in this room; I need to do something.' I spoke purposefully, making her relent almost immediately. She continued down the stairs, and I followed on, my legs a little shaky on the wooden steps.

We had made enough money from the workshop in the last couple of days to buy a little meat to put in a mynst pye, and I used the dried apple and plums from my store to add extra flavour. We were not in a position to dine like gentlefolk and lords. When Bridget had gone to the butcher this morning, he had looked kindly on her, putting a little powdered beef in with the mutton. I wondered if Lady Isabel would sit down to a Christmas feast fit for a queen, as she and Master Thomas usually did. She had provided some food for her villagers up at Markenfield Hall but could not cater for the town. It was unlikely she would have a home there much longer. She must have the same fears as I. Only the Lord knew whether either of us would see our husbands again.

I made a simple pastry of flour and water, adding a little marrow that the kind butcher had also thrown into the parcel Bridget had brought home. Bridget mixed the balance of the marrow with the apples and plums, an egg, adding a little dried saffron and dried spices from my herb store. It would not make one large pie, we had not enough flour for such if we wanted biscuits as well, but it would undoubtedly make enough chewets for all of us. Cutting my pastry into little rounds, I put a large spoonful of the mixture in the middle before stretching it up and about the mince before pinching the top and popping them into the oven Robert had made above the kiln in the workshop.

I made the biscuits simply by mixing dough and adding mace and a few caraway seeds and honey to sweeten. I rolled them into long fingers and plaited them into knots before dropping them into boiling water for a few seconds each. I lifted them out and drained off any excess water before placing them in the oven. Within minutes, the workshop smelled of sweetness and charcoal.

Robert

W<small>HEN</small> I <small>AWOKE, IT</small> was to the sound of neighing and snorting and the sweet smell of fresh hay mixed with the sour tang of dung. I thought I was at home for a moment or two and had fallen asleep in the stable with Mutton. I opened my eyes to see Duncan lying alongside me; his mouth was slack, and I could see the blackness of his teeth. I sat up and stretched. We may be sleeping in a stable, but it was warm, and no draught came through the walls or doors. The horse looking down at me was the one I had ridden from Newcastleton, and I lifted my hand to its muzzle. The horse drew its lips back and nuzzled the flesh of my palm, searching for a titbit. It pulled its head away when it realised there was nothing there.

'Ah! You love only when there is something in it for you,' I murmured. 'Wait until you have met the woman of your dreams. You will love her regardless of what she offers you. Your heart will be lost forever.'

'God's blood,' came a voice from the black-toothed mouth. 'You'll have me weeping in the hay. You great soft Sassenach.' Duncan laughed loudly and sat up.

I pushed his shoulder hard. 'Do not tell me you have no such feeling for Joan. I hear the way you speak of her.'

'Aye, well. 'Tis a natural thing. Were I in a bed with a soft woman rather than a great ugly brute such as you, I wouldna be pouring tender words on a horse.' His eyes lit up with mischief.

I stood and brushed the hay from my jerkin and hose. 'We best away and ask after the countess. God willing, she will be recovered after a night in a soft bed and thick blankets.'

'Aye,' he said, 'then mayhap we can go home.'

'I truly hope so.' We walked across the courtyard and into the kitchen. It was bustling, and I immediately thought of Edmund. I half expected to see him fetching and carrying as when I first met him at Brancepeth. I felt a sudden pang of longing for my family, although it was almost immediately replaced with a sudden desperation for food. My mouth was practically dripping saliva at the rich smells of meat and game, slow roasting on a spit in front of the fire. A great cauldron of broth hung on an iron hook above the hearth, and fresh bread, the best smell of all, seeped up my nostrils until I could almost taste it on my tongue.

'Sit, lads,' said a young woman whose face was red from the heat. Sweat trickled down her forehead and the sides of her face. She swiped it away furiously with the back of her hand. We did as we were told and sat down on a long bench alongside others who had shared our arduous journey yesterday. Barely a second passed afore we were grabbing at the bread, shovelling it into our mouths. Bowls of broth appeared in front of us. A serving girl placed plates of beef and poultry at intervals down the wooden table. I thought I might be dreaming. It had been a long time since I had seen such food. Duncan and I ate as if it were our last meal on earth, and, when we had room for no more, we stuffed our pockets with bread and meat, for chance it was the only meal we would get for a while.

I asked if anyone had been upstairs to Countess Anne's room. A young maid said she had taken breakfast to her, but the lady had not eaten and was gravely ill. I prayed she would recover. She had been the bravest among us and did not deserve to die. Surely God would spare her.

When I left the kitchen, I found a priest and asked if I might pray with him for the swift recovery of Countess Anne. We knelt together, and I found myself praying for not only her but Catherine and Edmund, Harry and Bridget, and my apprentice John's family. Let them be safe, I begged. Let them be unharmed and waiting for me back at Brancepeth.

†

It was not until the last day of December that a servant came to inform us that the countess, although still weak, was feeling better and eating again. I was relieved to hear the news and thanked God for his mercy. Mayhap I could go home now. I sought an audience with my master.

Master Thomas was in the Great Hall where a servant ushered me over to where he conversed with a small group of men.

'Now here, my honourable gentlemen is the finest spurrier in England,' he said, raising his glass to me. He appeared slightly unsteady on his feet; his speech was slurred, and his hair matted and unkempt, which suggested he had been drinking through the night. His group of friends were not much better in appearance as they raised their glasses too. 'I am sadly,' he continued, 'not in…not…not in a position to show you his work. Some vile reiver stole mine from me.'

I was at a loss how to respond when the morrow may not remember whatever I asked now.

'Good morrow, Master. I had wished to speak with you about going home, but it can wait until—'

'Home?' He reached out and put his arm about my shoulders, almost toppling us both. 'Home?' he said again, 'There is no home, Robert. There will never be home again.' He let go of me and slumped to the floor, his back against the wall. 'We can never go home now,' he groaned. 'I can never see my wife again. My children. What will happen to my children? Even my dear brother John is captured and in prison at Carlisle.' He was whining now. His companions laughed, then, realising Thomas was crying, turned their backs and drifted across the room. I squatted down in front of him.

'Come, Master,' I said, taking him by the hands and pulling him to his feet. 'Let us away and find the cook. Methinks you need some of her excellent food and a hot drink to put you to rights.' He did not protest and allowed me to lead him from the room. Norton followed us to the door.

'Thank you, Robert,' he said, patting my back. 'You serve him well – despite his sometimes foul humour.'

'Yes, my lord,' I replied. 'I will fetch him to cook. He is not himself this morning.'

'Pickles and fish,' he said, laughing. 'It will scour his stomach of the accursed drink.'

The cook served up what she called her cure for such gentlemen in the kitchen, asking me to take him outside the minute he had drunk the foul-smelling liquid she had put in his hands. Master Thomas, assuming it was more wine or whisky or some such other evil concoction, threw back his head and downed it in one. I took him outside as the cook had suggested and watched as he, bent double and hands on his knees, unloaded himself on the cobbles. The stench was worse than a pig pen that had not been cleaned in weeks, and I had to put a hand over my nose and mouth to stop myself from joining him in his delicate state. When he had done, he wiped his mouth with the back of his hand and once again slumped to the floor. I picked him up and put him over my shoulder before carrying him across to the stables and lying him down on the straw floor. He was best left to sleep awhile. I remembered how I felt after my drinking whisky session back at Jock o' the Syde's house and pitied my master the headache to come.

Back in the kitchen, I asked if anyone had taken food to the countess this evening. I was told that a plate was being prepared for her. One of her ladies came in to collect the dish of manchet bread, cheese, and an apple.

'Could you ask her if she was well enough to give me an audience for just a few minutes?' I was not hopeful but wanted to see for myself that her health was improving. The thought of walking away and deserting her when she was so ill pricked at my conscience.

The countess's maid nodded stiffly and left the room. I offered to make myself useful to the kitchen staff, but they bade me sit and help myself to whatever was on the table. I did not need telling twice, the stench of my master's vomit already gone from my nostrils and replaced by the wonderful aromas of a well-served kitchen.

Anne's maid returned a few moments later, just as I popped the last of the manchet bread in my mouth.

'The countess will see you now.' Her face was still blank and showed no sort of emotion. 'Follow me,' she added, already walking back outside.

Climbing the stairs, I followed her through the Great Hall and into a passage where several doors led off to bedchambers. The maid tapped on one of the doors, and a woman opened it and bade us come in.

Anne was sitting up in a high bed, someone had tied the heavy drapes back, and several bolstered pillows supported her. Her hair was lank upon her shoulders, her face small and pinched. A goodly fire blazed in the hearth, and the air was thick with a mixture of sweat and the sweet perfume of rose powder.

'Come, dearest Robert,' she said, pointing out a chair beside the bed. 'Sit here.'

I bowed and crossed the room. The chair was small, and, on sitting, I found myself having to look up to the countess.

'My lady,' I said. 'I would come to see for myself that you are recovering well. Duncan and I have prayed for your swift journey back to health.' She held a hand out to me. I let my lips barely touch the papery veined skin before sitting back in the chair.

'I expect to be up and about in time for the epiphany of our Lord,' she said, 'which brings me to a most important matter.' I waited expectantly, wondering what this vital matter might be. I dearly hoped it would not be something that would detain me here too much longer. 'I am aware that Catherine expects to deliver her child around that time. I cannot keep you from her longer, Robert. It is time you went to her.'

I breathed a sigh of relief. 'Thank you, Countess. I am grateful for your release. I have worried for Catherine these last few days. Babies do not always follow a timetable when it comes to being born. It is a dangerous time for her, and I wish to be at her side.'

Her voice became serious now. 'It will not be a straightforward journey. You must take great care. Westmorland tells me that many of our allies are captured and imprisoned at Carlisle Castle as we speak. Over two hundred, it is said.' She leaned forward. 'Many roads will be patrolled by the queen's men as well as Forster's men. I hear of executions and hangings in many towns, of loyal constables and local men who have marched alongside us. But a little good news. Westmorland has had word from his wife to say that she is under house arrest at Brancepeth, but they have not harmed her or her servants.'

'Thank you. Thank you,' I said, grateful for the news, almost crying out loud with joy. 'I will travel by night and shelter by day. I would ask a favour, though, my lady.'

'Ask away. I will grant whatever might be in my power to give.'

'I need two horses – one for me and one for Duncan, who would travel with me if you would allow. I have the means to pay,' I added quickly, taking the pouch that contained the spurs I had crafted for Richard Norton. 'They are inlaid with silver.'

She took them from me and looked them over carefully. 'Do these not belong to your master?'

'No, my lady. I made these for Master Norton. He gave them to Jock o' the Syde. He had not settled with me for them, and Jock did give them back to me.'

Anne's mouth fell open. 'That money-grabbing oaf? That is hard to believe.'

'I was surprised too, but he said he would not take them as Master Norton had not paid me for my work.' I did not add that he respected my decision to stay with this woman when I could have left her to her own fate.

She passed the spurs back to me. 'I will not take these. You may need them if you get into trouble on your journey. They may buy your freedom.' I thanked her and put them back in the pouch. 'I will ask Sir Thomas to loan you and Duncan a horse apiece and tell him I will pay him.' Her eyelids drooped, and she lay back against the pillows. 'I need to rest now, Robert. Go back to Duncan this eve. I will send word to you in the morning.'

'Thank you, my lady. Is there news of your husband?'

Her eyes opened again. Her look pained. 'That man Moray is demanding ransom. He says he will release him to the highest bidder.' Tears flowed. 'I must look to my friends and allies to raise funds.'

'I am sad to hear that. Mayhap my spurs will raise a little?'

Her smile was weary when she answered. "Tis far more than your spurs could bring, Robert, but I will remember your kindness when this is all over. Go now.' She waved me away.

I stood and bowed. Although sad to leave the countess's side, my heart filled with excitement at the thought of going home. I would hope to meet my son in the next few days. I hurried through the Great Hall and down the stairs before stepping out into the courtyard and giving a great whoop of joy to the snow-filled, white sky.

'Duncan!' I shouted. 'We are going home!'

Before we ate, I went to speak to Master Thomas. He agreed I could take my leave. He told me he and several other men were to travel north soon to be smuggled out of Scotland and set sail to Flanders. Once there, they and their faith would be welcomed with open arms by friends. I asked if the countess would be in that number, and he assured me she would once the child had been born. In between times, Anne would go to friends further north to await her child's birth and raise funds for Northumberland's release.

Duncan and I waited for word from the countess about the horses. We could now leave knowing she was in safe hands and getting stronger with each hour. I hoped she would carry her child safely and have a good birthing when the time came.

It was late in the day when a servant came to tell us to go to the stables where two mounts awaited. We intended to travel through the night, and we had rested most of the day in readiness for the journey. We knew the general direction in which we must travel, and one of Kerr's men gave details of safe places to stop on the route, and so, with light hearts, we set off. The cook had filled knapsacks with dried meat, cheese, and bread for sustenance along the way. The sun had set, and we headed out, first through a forest, but more and more the land became moor where the wind whipped at our woollen cloaks and froze our eyebrows and eyelashes. We did not stop, heads down. My hands seemed to freeze inside my gauntlets, and my gauntlets froze to the reins I gripped. We reached Otterburn by morning, whereupon, a chaplain had told us at Ferniehirst, we would find a small enclave of monks who still bided there in secret. Looking like frozen statues, the monks helped us dismount and guided us inside a low building where a fire burned, and one monk served hot flagons of ale. Neither of us spoke a word, so frozen were we, but our saviours did not require an explanation from us before leading us into a small room with cots. The priests removed the stiff cloaks and took them away. We both lay down and collapsed from exhaustion but could not find sleep because of the pain in our fingers, hands and feet as the blood warmed in our bodies. I thought my fingers might snap like icicles as they thawed. After a while, a priest came in and rubbed ointment on our faces and hands. Initially, it burned but then soothed sufficiently enough to allow us the peace of sleep.

When I next awoke, it was to the sound of someone entering the tiny room. The slight aroma of hot broth soon brought me back to life, and in the sliver of light coming from a small window high on the wall, I could see the outline of a man in robes. I moved to sit up and was shocked into lying back down again by the pains shooting through my entire body. I heard Duncan cry out at the same time and turned to see his face. It looked like raw meat in the daylight. My hand automatically reached up to my face, my fingers were still a little numb, but my face burned at the touch. I felt a roughness that suggested that I looked as bad as he did.

'You will need rest for a day or two,' said the priest, looking down upon us. His face was thin and grey and showed a lack of good food. 'It is not wise to travel so far on winter nights across the moors.'

'We,' my voice was almost a whisper as I tried to speak, 'We had little choice, for there was no shelter.'

'You may stay and rest here until you feel able to travel further. Where is your destination?'

We spoke in unison.

'Durham,' I said.

'Blaydon,' said Duncan.

'I hear there are many soldiers in Durham.' The priest sat down on the edge of my cot, his face downcast. 'Many good men are arrested and imprisoned there. Some gentlemen who have played their part well, and are landowners, will be fined sizeable sums of money and have to give up their lands. Still, they will live.' He got up to leave the room, shaking his head in despair. 'Lord Sussex intends to hang the constables and officers of each town alongside yeomen and commoners. Even women and children are among the unfortunate souls. Many will lose their lives in defence of the true faith this day and for many days to come.' He then left us to our food.

'I pray God they have spared my family,' said Duncan. 'I canna bear to think them gone.'

'You are not alone, my friend,' I said, wondering what Catherine was doing this day. Had they arrested her and Edmund at Brancepeth? Had they hung them for their part in the pilgrimage? I could only hang on to Countess Anne's words and hope they were true.

We sipped on the thin broth in silence. It had little flavour. These priests were of good nature to share their meagre food supplies with us, and I thought it well we give them some of the dried meat we had brought from Ferniehirst. Desperate though we were to leave this place, we understood we would not make it far unless we allowed our bodies to heal.

Sleep came quickly, and when I next opened my eyes, there was no light seeping through the tiny cell window. I thought I heard the bleating of sheep, which soothed my mind, and I soon drifted off again.

Catherine

Rippon, Wednesday, 31st December 1569

I COULD HEAR SINGING on the market-stede and went to the open shopfront to listen to the carollers singing while the players acted out the scenes of Herod sending his men out to slay all babies.

> *Lullay, Thou little tiny Child,*
> *By, by, lully, lullay.*
> *Lullay, Thou little tiny Child.*
> *By, by, lully, lullay.*
> *O sisters, too, how may we do,*
> *For to preserve this day;*
> *This poor Youngling for whom we sing,*
> *By, by, lully, lullay.*
> *Herod the King, in his raging,*
> *Charged he hath this day;*
> *His men of might, in his own sight,*
> *All children young, to slay.*
> *Then woe is me, poor Child, for Thee,*
> *And ever mourn and say;*
> *For Thy parting, nor say nor sing,*
> *By, by, lully, lullay.*

Edmund ran outside and followed the players, delighting in the savage scenes as only a child who does not understand the significance can do. The last time they sang such a sad and haunting song, Robert was standing here beside me, his arm wrapped about my shoulders.

Tears ran down my cheeks. The words and scenes made me think of the children I had lost, and my hand covered my belly to protect the child within. Bridget slipped her hand in mine. Both of us mourning the lack or loss of children.

Robert

THE NEXT DAY, WE ventured from the room and into the small abbey to see where these few monks lived. It was a bleak place where some parts of the roof were open to the sky. I counted around ten men who were wearing habits and long cloaks to keep warm. A sparse fire burned in the kitchen where the good men sat at the table, breaking their fast on black bread and a meagre helping of oats. One monk was making cheese from the milk of the sheep I had heard in the night. The sheep were being sheltered in a small lean-to outside. The monk told us it had been too bleak on the moors these last few days, and they feared they would be buried in the snow. I pulled the meat from my knapsack, and our hosts took it with many thanks and gratitude. We took our place at the table and shared their food. In return for our food and drink, we offered help in whatever way we could. The weather was much calmer outside, and though we both were stiff and sore, we went out to gather

---

† *In 1569 the Julian calendar was still being used in Britain which meant that the year did not end until the 25th March, but to save too much confusion, both dates are shown as above from this point on.*

wood for the fire and even tried to patch up a couple of holes in the thatching. Neither of us was an expert but guided by an elderly monk who was now too old to climb, managed to do a reasonable job. By nightfall, the monk who had made the cheese had prepared a pottage flavoured with the dried beef we had brought, and now with our bellies full and warm, we were ready to continue our journey. When we stepped outside, we realised the snow was still falling heavily, with all signs of the ground covered in a thick white layer. We realised with heavy hearts that it would be foolish to continue the journey and resigned ourselves to another night here.

The snow kept falling for several days and lay too thick on the ground to travel. I was desperate to leave but knew it was impossible. The monks were kind and shared all they had with us. They did not ask our names, saying it would be safer if they did not know, and therefore could not tell if anyone came asking. Most of what we ate had been pickled or cured in the weeks leading up to the foul weather. The taste was much the same, regardless of what we were eating. One day, when the sun shone, something they had seen outside while collecting wood for the fire excited the monks. A deer had wandered nearby. It was busy scraping away the snow with its hooves to reach any sort of green fodder beneath. The monks took out some linen cloths for us to drape over our jerkins, and Duncan and I crept outside, keeping as low to the ground as we could manage. The deer's ears pricked forward as it lifted its head. We stayed stock still until it set to graze once more. We could not afford to move much nearer, so I drew my bow, loaded an arrow, and drew the string back slowly. Duncan did the same, and we waited. The deer's head shot up again, and I let the bolt loose at the same time as Duncan. I aimed my arrow directly at the heart of the deer, and Duncan sought to lame it so that it could not run far if I missed.

It staggered for a moment and then dropped like a great stone, the blood ribboning across the soft white snow. We raced towards it, and Duncan sat on the animal's neck, slicing its throat swiftly to ensure no suffering. We tied the beast by its feet to a long pole that a monk had brought us and carried it back triumphantly. The monks butchered and hung the meat swiftly and efficiently, making broth from the blood, adding herbs and spices for extra flavour. We ate like kings that night and slept well; replete, and comfortable.

Our cloaks were warm and dry again, having been hung close to the fire since we arrived, and the night air was still. The moon helped to light our way, and we travelled fast. We wasted little time with idle chatter; both our minds firmly on the goal of reaching our families. We soon reached the Pictes Wall and knew we had to be extra careful from here. In the distance, we saw the town of Newcastle, lit up by torches. Duncan was familiar with this landscape and led the way around the northern walls and west to Blaydon village – arriving at a cluster of simple wattle and daub shelters near a corn mill. We dismounted, and Duncan went quietly to one of the little shacks and entered. I heard a shriek and then children's voices screaming with delight at the sight of their father. Duncan came back outside, his arm about a short woman with two small children clinging to her skirts.

I greeted them and was asked to come inside. There was little room, but it was warm. The children went back to their straw beds beside the hearth, and Duncan offered me a small stool. Duncan explained that the houses, an overestimated description to my mind, belonged to the mill. They provided shelter for all those who worked there. It was not much, he said, but it was enough for him and his family. They ate bread every day, not being charged much for the flour. There was a bread oven at the end of the village, which they all shared and a small piece of common land on which they kept sheep for milk and meat. His wife, Joan, grew a few vegetables to feed the pot on the fire and, in most things, they were content. Her main employment was working in the Tempests' cornfields with the other women of the village, sowing and reaping through the season, and Duncan helped grind the flour and deliver it to local villages and towns. The wintertime was quiet, but he had found work in the Tempests' coal mines, which saw them through.

We sat and talked while the haunch of venison we had brought with us roasted on a spit before the fire. Joan told us of some villagers being arrested and taken away to the prison at Newcastle. When it was light, Joan cut and parcelled pieces of venison to distribute among their neighbours.

I left them as soon as it was dark and made my way towards Brancepeth. There was a mixture of joy, knowing that, at last, I was making my way back to Catherine, and also sorrow to be travelling alone after leaving my friend, Duncan. We had made good company for each other, and I hoped we might meet up again one day when all this was over. This journey was to be the last. Once home again, we would take up our lives as before. I could rekindle my dreams of becoming the best spurrier in England. I touched the pouch tied to my waist, feeling the cold metal of the spurs through the soft hide. They would fetch enough money to buy more silver and make another two pairs of good-quality, mayhap three. Yes. Life would be well again, and with Edmund and my son, who I hoped had not arrived yet, I would build a future for our family. I was so busy dreaming of things to come; I did not see the men ahead.

'Now what do we have here?' said a man in full plate and heading a group of around ten.

I steeled myself and rode closer, desperately trying to think of a good reason to be on the road. Were these Forster's men? Sussex's men? I could not see a pennant. Perhaps they were robbers, but then why be on the road in the open?

'Good eve, sirs. It is a fine night,' I said, looking up at the star-filled sky. Why had I chosen the road? I should have stayed in the forests. I had been in such a hurry to get to Catherine; I had put myself in danger.

'Where are you off to?'

'Brancepeth, sir. I have been in the borders these long days. My wife be servant there.'

'What did you there in the north?' He looked me up and down as if trying to decide whether I was friend or foe.

I prayed for some signal as to their loyalties. 'It seemed like a game of hide-and-seek for the most part.'

'Aye,' said another man. 'Too damned cold for such a game, too. That damned Sussex was a wily hunter. He nearly had me a few times.'

I let out a sigh of relief. 'It was so. I was with Countess Anne.'

'Is she safe?' asked another. 'We were with her husband and that traitor Hector. He sold us out to Elliott and his mob.'

'I heard such. Northumberland is caught and taken to Leven Castle,' I said, now relaxing.

'Aye. 'Tis so. We were lucky to escape.'

'I am glad to have come across you. Do you travel south?'

The lead man nodded. 'We journey home. We will travel with you a while.'

Glad of the company again, I joined their number, and we carried on our journey. One or two were from Wetherby and others from Knaresborough. One man, Jake, hailed from Brandon, and after talking for a while, I discovered he had known Edmund's father. I told him of our meeting and how we had become close.

'He comes from outstanding stock,' said Jake. 'I worked alongside his father for many years. A good friend until the cursed pox got him.'

We approached the castle cautiously, trying to glean whether any of Sussex's men were still there. There was plenty of light emanating from the windows, which made it obvious it was still in use. The question was, by whom? The door to the kitchen opened, and a young girl I recognised as one of the cook's helpers stepped outside to empty a bowl of slops.

'Psst!' I hissed, trying to draw her attention. She glanced up but did not see me and turned to walk back inside. 'Psst! Margaret,' I tried again, hoping I had remembered her name correctly. She turned towards me, and I stepped out of the trees. 'Over here.' She was not sure but took a few steps forward. 'It's me, Robert. The husband of Catherine Gray.' She stopped again before a smile grew, and she came over. I took her hand and edged back under the canopy of the trees.

'Robert,' she said, 'Why are you here? It is dangerous.'

'I have to collect Catherine and take her home.'

'But she is not here. Catherine left on the same night as you rode out with the earls. She said she was going home.'

I felt the excitement leave my body. I had so looked forward to being reunited with her. Now I would not know if she had reached home safely or been accosted on the way. 'Did she travel with others?' At least she would have afforded some protection if that was the case.

'Yes. Young Edmund and Bridget. Bridget's husband and I think another family travelled with them. There were many left that night.' She looked back at the kitchen door. 'You must go afore anyone sees you. There are many officers here to guard Countess Jane. She may not leave the castle until the queen has decided her fate.' A sob escaped her lips. 'I fear what will become of us, but the countess says we will travel with her wherever she goes. She has written to the queen to ask for pardon and the right to travel to London.'

I squeezed her hands. 'She will take care of you. Do not fret for your safety.'

When Margaret had finished crying, I asked if there might be some food for me and my friends. She asked us to wait there and hurried back inside. It was a goodly time before she appeared again with a bundle of muslin in her arms. 'Cook said to go to the church and see the priest there. He will offer you shelter for a time.' I thanked her and took the package.

'Can you take a message to the countess?' I asked. 'say that her husband, Westmorland, is well and safe. I have been with him for some days.' She nodded and turned on her heel, hurrying back inside to the warmth.

I signalled the others to stay within the shelter of the trees as we made our way around the outskirts of the castle walls and reached the church. We gathered in the porch, swords and daggers drawn, and opened the door slowly. It creaked on its hinges, so we dashed in, trying to gain the upper hand and an element of surprise. Three priests were kneeling before the altar in prayer. One was kneeling in front of the other two, and I assumed he had seniority. They did not jump up or turn but carried on praying. We approached slowly and, one by one, knelt beside them as they prayed in the beautiful Latin language we all loved and missed.

When they had finished, they stood, and the senior priest blessed each of us as we remained on our knees, heads bent.

'You are most welcome here,' he said when we all stood again. 'I feared my time to join our saviour had come and was praying for swift deliverance. It seems he has use of my fellow priests and me here on earth yet.' He smiled, though his eyes showed deep sadness. 'I am Father Drake and lead those who are left of us. Please sit and rest awhile.'

We settled ourselves on the floor, and I opened up the parcel of food that Margaret had given us. Father Drake sent one of his priests to fetch a jug of ale from one of the outer rooms.

'What happened to all the wounded? Have they been killed or taken prisoner?' I asked, dreading the answer.

He nodded. 'When the soldiers arrived, they arrested my lady, Countess Jane, and despatched her guards. The doctor was tending the wounded alone, save for a few priests who remained to help. Those injured but able to walk left before the soldiers arrived, some families carried them away on their carts.' I told myself that Catherine must have made her way back to Rippon with these people. If I did not, then I might collapse with grief. She had to be home and safe. The priest, who continued with his story, interrupted my thoughts. 'The soldiers slaughtered those too sick to move. It was perhaps a mercy as they neared death. My fellow priests and I fled into the woods when they first arrived. We stayed hidden in the woods for several days. When we returned, the poor doctor was hanging from the parapet of the castle. We thought they would kill us, but the countess begged we be spared and allowed to provide her with comfort and prayer. The soldiers agreed, knowing we were not likely to cause them trouble. I believe some would find it difficult to harm a man of God. We cut the doctor loose when they were all abed that night before burying him in the churchyard here along with his slain patients.'

'You must come with us,' I said. 'There is nothing left here for you now.'

He shook his head. 'I am now chaplain to Countess Jane – she needs me. The others may go with you if they wish.' The other priests showed their willingness and put on their hooded woollen cloaks. The chaplain blessed them both and wished them a safe journey.

'You will find shelter in the Abbey at Fountains,' I told them. I took one priest up onto my horse to sit behind me, and Jake did the same for the other. It surprised me. 'You have family here, Jake. Do you not wish to stay?' I asked him.

His face saddened. 'I have no family now. They died of the plague a few years ago,' he said. 'There is nothing to keep me here.'

We held to the back ways until we came out atop the wild moors and felt the biting wind once more. My mind imagined Catherine travelling this same route, and I hoped the weather had been kind to her and Edmund. I was determined to make as much headway as possible without resting. My need to see Catherine was growing more urgent with every mile covered. When we finally reached Richmond's outskirts, we were all in need of rest and made camp in a wooded area on the edge of the town. Richmond had been faithful to our cause, but it was likely filled with soldiers and others of the queen's faith. We sent one man in to gauge the danger, and when he returned a little while later to tell us the town and castle were under the care of many soldiers, we moved on again. Weary though we were, we put another few miles between us and the town, stopping only at a small brook to replenish our water bags as a pink sky heralded the dawn. Nearby stood a small hamlet of wattle and daub cottages of perhaps about seven or eight dwellings and decided it was small enough to take our chance and ask for food. We stopped in the centre of the dirt track, and I called out,

'Good people, we wish no harm. We would only ask for a little food if you can spare it. We have travelled long and are in need of sustenance.'

A door creaked open. A small, bent man came out slowly with the aid of a stick. His legs were weak from a lifetime of heavy work. He bowed his head when he saw the priest at my back.

'We are but poor, sir. We have little to offer but a jug of ale and a piece of rye bread. The bread be stale but will soften in the ale.' He signalled to the door of his house, and an elderly lady appeared carrying a pitcher of ale. A younger woman followed on, a black loaf in her hands.

I dismounted and went to them. 'Is this all you have? I will not take it unless you have more for your own family.'

'Our neighbours will help us,' he said. 'We would ask only that your priests bless us afore you leave.'

The two priests dismounted and approached the old man and his family, who fell to kneel in front of them. One by one, other doors opened; the villagers were coming out and kneeling on the frozen earth. They all awaited their blessing in turn as one priest held the pitcher and another the loaf. With each blessing, the priest offered a sliver of bread and a sip of ale. I took my place and knelt to receive the sacrament alongside the villagers and the other riders. Joy filled my soul as Christ entered my body, and I knew at that moment that Catherine was safe, and life held such promise. The villagers opened their houses to us so that we might rest awhile and showed their appreciation by bringing out what little food they could spare. Our hunger was not satisfied by any means, but we were filled with the grace of God, and it was enough to keep us going. We slept fitfully for a couple of hours before moving on.

It was a strange day; the bright dawn had melted into a mist that hung over us as we travelled down the country track leading to Bedale. Nothing could dampen my spirits as we passed carts and people on foot. Like ghosts, they slipped in and out of view through the swirls of foggy air. I caught sight of a milestone on the edge of the track and slipped down from the saddle to take a closer look. The sign said we were only three miles from Bedale and sixteen miles from Rippon. We would make it by late evening. I could almost feel Catherine in my arms. We would share a bed this night.

In the dimming light and a thickening fog, we entered the town. The sound of keening was all about us, and as the mist swirled and thinned, we were aghast to see men hanging from gibbets in the main street at the side of a stepped cross. I could count at least thirty. Women and children sat around each post, mourning their husbands, sons, and neighbours. We dismounted, and the two priests approached them, offering comfort and solace and blessing the men who hung above them. I walked over to the large notice pinned to the platform. I asked someone its meaning, and an old man told us that no one was allowed, on pain of death, to take the men down. Anyone who did so would face the same fate. All people should note what happens to traitors. We left them to their grief and travelled on.

We had gone only a little way when we heard horses travelling towards us. We scattered into the trees around and about and hid. The horsemen were travelling toward Bedale. When they had passed us by, we gathered again on the road.

'They were not the queen's men. We have heard they travel in small gangs and pretend to be Sussex's men or Forster's. Most likely, robbers taking their chances for cattle and sheep,' said Jake.

'Then we must follow them back to Bedale,' I said. 'Those poor people have suffered enough without being starved out of their homes as well.'

'What do you say, lads?' Jake asked, a grin on his face. 'Anyone up for a fight? There is barely a half dozen men.'

We travelled back in haste. Tying our horses around the back of an alehouse, we split up so that there were two or three men on each side of the street. Jake and I crept inside. The innkeeper was hiding upstairs and was about to scream when I grabbed him and placed a hand over his mouth. I put a finger to my lips, and he nodded in understanding. Going over to the window, I drew my bow and took an arrow from my quiver. The mist had cleared somewhat now, and the men were beside the cross, holding up torches. As Jake had predicted, the villagers were rounding up a few sheep and three or four cows. The men held some women prisoner on the hanging platform. I looked across the square and could just make out Jake and the others looking down from upstairs windows of houses on the other side.

I let an arrow fly, and its aim was true, slamming into the chest of a robber holding on to two of the women. He slumped to his knees as the women screamed. Arrow followed arrow. The robbers tried to run but to no avail. Most were dispatched swiftly, bar two who ran with great speed into the woods.

As we came out of hiding, the townsfolk approached us with caution. No one was cheering. I realised they must think we were there to take our share now we had got rid of the competition. That is until the two priests appeared from one of the houses and realised who we were and meant them no harm. They insisted we stay, and we followed them into the alehouse where we were fed and watered, each cottager fetching a little something for the table. The innkeeper's stable lad took our horses and fed and watered them. After several jugs of ale and black bread and cheese, we were all a little tired. The innkeeper showed us the room where I had found him earlier, and we soon settled down into a comfortable sleep. I dreamed again of home, and Catherine and Edmund and our baby.

When I awoke with an elbow in my face, it took me a moment or two to remember where I was. The moon was bright through the window, and though there was no fire burning in the grate, the room was warm and thick with the smell of bodies, sweat, and urine. I fished around in the semi-dark until my hand found the handle of a jug. I sniffed it cautiously to satisfy myself that it was ale and not the nearest vessel someone had found in the night to relieve themselves. It was ale. I sat up and drank deeply to wet the dry coffin of my mouth. Someone lit a candle, and the room became clearer. Jake and one other had claimed the sizeable wooden bed that had a mattress stuffed with straw, plenty of which was protruding from every corner. There was a rough wooden chest beneath the window where I had positioned myself when shooting at the robbers. Other than that, there was naught for comfort, no chair or washbowl. Looking at the thatch above us, I could see that it was riddled with insects and other wildlife and almost appeared to be rippling like a pond's surface when whipped up by the wind. I was keen to be on the move again. It was a clear night and suitable for travelling. I got to my feet and kicked a few sleeping bodies to stir them. They got to their feet, muttering and grumbling. 'Where's the jake?' one moaned before pushing the window open and sticking his member out. I hoped there was no one in the street below.

After a bowl of oats the innkeeper had afforded us, we collected our horses from the inn stable and set off in good spirits. The stars were thick in the sky, the moon as big as a barn door. My heart sang, knowing I would be home by daylight.

We did not hear them. They had been waiting in the woods that lined the road. They fell upon us in a flash, surrounding us – a troop of queen's soldiers. There was no point putting up a fight; there were too many of them. My mind slipped to the memory of the two robbers who had got away from us at Bedale. They most likely had sought the soldiers and informed them of our whereabouts. The commander approached, wearing a gleaming breastplate and riding a large warhorse. I would have recognised the man who had ridden out of Barney Castle in shame without the need of seeing the Bowes pennant held high. George Bowes was a heavy-set man with a thick moustache and bushy beard. Riding alongside him was Shinclyffe on his black stallion.

'It looks like we have found ourselves a band of Papist traitors,' Bowes said to his men. A few sniggers and laughs filled the air. 'The queen will be pleased with our haul, methinks.' Shinclyffe rode up to my side. 'Well, what have we here? If it is none other than my good friend Gray. A good haul indeed.'

Forced to dismount, we were tied together, hands behind our backs. The soldiers added us to the end of a line of captives they had collected on their travels. Some were men dressed such as we, but others looked like townsmen and constables. Riders at the back of Bowes' troops led us along like cattle. I wondered where they might take us. Mayhap they were scouring the countryside and gathering prisoners before taking us all to Durham for hanging. No. that could not be. If that had been the case, we would not have seen people hanging at Bedale. We could be only ten miles from Rippon, and I prayed we would be taken there. I did not want Catherine wondering and waiting for years in case I came home. Better she knows my fate than living in hope of a reunion someday. Tears stung, thinking that I would not see my son born. I would not see him and Edmund grow into strong men. Who would care for Catherine now? I had come so close to being with my family, and now all was lost. I would never hold her close to me again.

My head was bent as I looked down at the road we walked on. Now and then, the hemp rope was pulled harder, and we stumbled to stay upright and manage the fast pace that was expected of us. I felt a hard tug as an elderly man further up the line fell forward, his face hitting the dirt and stones. The man behind was pulled atop him, and several men followed suit. It took a great deal of strength for Jake and me to stop ourselves from joining the chaos. As we came to a complete stop, the rider jumped down from his horse and beat all that had fallen. Jake leaned into my back, whispering that he had undone his tether. He untied me, and I wriggled to free myself. It took barely a moment before we made a run for the woods. No one seemed to notice that we were gone at first, but it wasn't long before the shout went up, and several riders entered the woods in search of us.

I looked down from the giant oak tree we had scrambled up as the riders shot past us and rode in circles about the trees. We hardly dared breathe as we lay flat and nestled in amongst the enormous bare branches. They did not look up, beating away at the shrubbery and ferns with their swords – shouting for us to show ourselves. As they moved further away, their voices became softer. We realised they had made their way back to their troops when we could hear George Bowes yelling at them. We grinned and grasped hands in joint celebration.

Not daring to come down, we stayed put through the night and all the next day until darkness fell once more. If Bowes had left any men behind to wait in ambush for us, they would certainly have given up by now. We were both stiff from sitting up there so long, and Jake fell to the forest floor from the last branch. He had hurt his foot and could hardly walk. I looked about for a fallen branch to serve as a crutch for him. The journey would be slow from here. *No matter*, I thought. *We would take our time as long as we got there in the end.*

The sky was a thick blanket of cloud above us, with no moon or a single star to guide us. We walked on in silence; both lost in our thoughts. We came to Tanfield, a hamlet I knew well from visits with my father when he came to shoe horses for the Parr family at the manor house there. The memory of my father was as bright as day in my mind. I could see him in the courtyard, his leather apron scarred from the burns of the iron. I could hear him tapping the nails into the shoes as he held the hind leg of the horse between his knees – his red bandana around his forehead to catch the sweat that beaded across his forehead. I remembered racing about with the cook's lad. What was his name? No matter, it was not important. There were only six miles from here to Rippon.

From then on, we followed the sound of the river, knowing it would guide us. When in need of a drink, we stopped to rest. I knelt on the bank and drank the clear waters of the River Ure before dipping a rag and passing it to Jake, who could not lower himself into a kneeling position. The excitement rose inside me, and the moon had finally come out. We were almost home.

'Will you stay in Rippon?' I asked Jake. He was limping badly now, and I suggested we sit for a while.

'At least until this heals,' he answered, sitting down and rubbing his foot.

'Catherine will sort it out. She is a healer,' I said. 'You can stay with us as long as you want.'

Catherine

THE BED WAS WARM, but it was impossible to lie still. I could not sleep. The pain in the rains of my back and gutters gnawed at me until I got up from the feather bed and walked about the room. My thighs ached, and I felt a sharp stab in my privy parts with every step. I should have lit the fire earlier; my head felt hot, but I shivered in the icy room. It was my time, and Robert had still not come home. Last night, I had been filled with an absolute dread he was in danger. More and more these last few days, I had imagined him captured or set upon by robbers or lying in a ditch somewhere, buried in snow.

Edmund was standing in the doorway of my bedchamber. He must have heard me walking about from the kitchen downstairs where he slept.

'Can I help?' he asked tentatively.

'I wish it were so, but Bridget is probably better placed. You are a good lad, Edmund.' I paced the floor as I spoke. 'Mayhap, you could go over to Harry's shop and wake her for me, but not yet. It is too soon.' His face was sad as he bowed his head and turned to go. 'I would take great comfort from one of your teas, though,' I added. 'You know how much comfort they bring me.'

He turned to look at me and smiled. 'I will prepare it straight away,' he said and ran back downstairs.

Edmund had been so helpful since we had come back to Rippon. He knew all the right words to comfort me for such a young boy – always understanding when I was anxious and bringing me soothing teas. Edmund told me he often had to take drinks to Countess Jane when she was with child, so the cook had taught him and was now an expert. He knew which of my herbs to use without my telling him. He seemed to enjoy helping me with tinctures and potions, taking great care with his measures as I instructed him. It was wonderful to think my adopted son could be a doctor when he grew up, or at least a healer like me. I was unsure where he might train as a doctor, or even if he would be allowed as a commoner to practise, but even if he became only a healer, it would be a way to carry on mine and my mother's legacy.

'Thank you,' I said when Edmund returned with a mug of hot tea. 'That is exactly what I needed. Would you fetch some kindling and set a fire for me? I feel a chill.'

He disappeared once more but soon returned with some kindling and an iron spade with a few burning embers from the kitchen hearth. It took very little time until the room came to life with the roaring fire – no longer dark and grey but alive with shadows dancing across the walls. The heat seeped into my bones as the pains increased, twisting, and burning, so it felt as if my whole insides were afire as well. A sudden warmth erupted down my thighs as the slightly sweet-smelling water soaked into the rushes on the floor. I let out a gasp and lowered myself onto the bed. 'It is time for Bridget.' I groaned, trying not to frighten the boy. 'Can you fetch her now?'

He ran from the room as I writhed on the bed, wishing I had let him go and fetch her sooner. I cried out for Robert. 'Where are you? I need you so. Your son is coming.' I thumbed the rosary beads, praying with all my might that God would see fit to send my husband home soon. 'God keep you safe, Robert. God keep you safe.' Another pain ripped through me and made me scream. Something must be wrong. Never, even when I miscarried my other children, had I felt discomfort such as this. Would my baby survive? I was in so much pain; I felt sure that I would not survive either. I leaned over the side of the bed and vomited. This blessed sickness had returned with a vengeance in the last week, and it made me afraid. Was this a sign of malign spirits inside me? I felt my body shake and jerk, and my world began to disappear. 'Where are you, Robert?' I whispered before everything went black.

The falcon was tearing me open. He was eating me alive. Someone help me. The pain was too much to bear. I knew I was dying. Dear God, have mercy upon my soul.

Robert

Rippon, North Yorkshire,
Tuesday, 20th January 1569 (70)

We sat on the cold shores of the river once more. Jake's leg
looked severely swollen, the pain making it almost impossible
for him to walk now. I collected water in my hands and poured
it over his misshapen ankle. He groaned, lying back and closing
his eyes. His face burned with fever, and I tore a piece from
my shirt, wetting it in the river and putting it to his forehead.
The cold bit into the bare patch of my skin around my waist as
I tried to tuck my shortened shirt into my breeches. I kept on
wetting the strip of linen and squeezing it so that Jake could
take a drink. When he had drunk enough water to slake his
thirst, I wrapped the cloth tightly around his ankle, trying to
make the bones sit true as I had seen Catherine do many times,
cursing myself for not having done it sooner. When we both
had rested a while, I lifted Jake and put him across my back. He
was heavy but a burden I must shoulder. We were so close to
Rippon, I could smell it, taste it – and it smelled of Catherine
and home and comfort. I must be delirious, too, for I could
have sworn I heard Catherine calling my name over and over.

We plodded on along the rough track for what seemed
like miles until, far ahead, I saw the bridge. I was so tired, my

legs buckling under me. Finally, we had made it. I felt the relief spill over. My vision had become blurred, but I was sure I saw people, lots of people up on Gallows Hill. My mind was muddled. *What were they doing there?* I lowered Jake down onto the roadside and wiped away the sweat. Someone was coming towards us. Several men. The metal of breastplates glinting in the morning sun.

'You take him, I'll grab the one on the ground,' a voice said. I tried to struggle, but they were too strong, and I was too tired. I closed my eyes and let myself relax as they dragged me along between them. I was travelling uphill, over grass, white with frost that sparked sharply against my face. The men strode on, hauling me by my arms until they were almost torn from their sockets. Voices grew louder and louder. I opened my eyes to see legs all around me. So many legs. Where was Jake? Had they taken him to Catherine? He needed to go to Catherine. My face hit the hard ground. I groaned before sinking into the warm fug of nothing.

The hammering was beating a hole in my head. Who was making the shoes? Was it John? I could smell freshly cut wood. Why was that? I squinted into the bright light of day. I was sitting on the icy ground, leaning against a tree, my hands tied behind my back, the damp seeping through my breeches. Slowly, I let my hands fall. All about me, soldiers, and men in working clothes were sawing trees, cutting posts, and con- structing – gibbets. I placed my hand against the tree behind my back, soon realising it was another gibbet, and I tried to stand, pushing back hard against it.

Where was Jake? I looked about me and found him lying on the ground next to another hanging post. I stepped out and fell flat on my face. My foot had caught on something. Of course, they had wrapped a small length of hemp rope around my ankle and tied it to the post. They were not likely to have left me free to walk away. A woodsman looked over at me. He did not speak but turned away and continued with his job. His face was familiar. Mayhap someone from Rippon. I understood his reluctance to acknowledge knowing me. I called out to Jake. He did not move initially but eventually lifted his head and raised his hand before lying down again. His ankle must bother him still. The longer his ankle was left, the more chance it would get infected, and he would die. I shouted to one soldier. He glared at me and sauntered over.

'What do you want, rebel?' he asked.

'My friend,' I said, nodding towards Jake. 'He is injured. I fear he may die if a physician does not tend him soon.'

He laughed loudly before sneering and saying. 'You think I give a shit? Look around you, fool; of course, he will die.' He turned and walked away to continue helping another soldier carry logs from the nearby wood.

It was dark before the work stopped. The woodsman and his fellow workmen lit a fire and settled down to eat and talk. When it was dark enough, he crept over to me and handed me a jug of ale and a wedge of rye bread.

'Here,' he whispered. 'Get this down you.' He stuffed a small amount of bread in my mouth and then put the jug to my lips. I gulped, half choking on the welcome drink. He placed another piece of bread in my mouth and repeated the actions until the bread and ale were gone. I was about to ask him what was happening in the town, but he crept back to the fire before anyone could notice his absence.

'My friend,' I croaked, but I was not sure he had heard me.

I slept in fits and starts and was woken yet again by the now-familiar sound of hammering. It was barely dawn, and more gibbets were being raised and put in place. It was not light enough to see Jake, and I closed my eyes again, not to sleep as there was too much noise, but to think of Catherine. I was so close to her; I could almost imagine her calling to me in the darkness. Had my son been born? I prayed I might get to see him. Pulling myself up onto my elbows, I looked over to where Jake had lain all night. He was not there. I scanned the hill, but my friend was nowhere to be seen. I looked to the woodsman, staring at him so that he would understand my need to speak to him. He knew what I was trying to ask and shook his head. The sadness in his eyes told me that my friend was dead. I had travelled with Jake little but knew him to be a good man. I mumbled my prayers, hoping he would not spend long in Purgatory afore taking his rightful place with God.

The hammering and sawing went on for most of the day until I could see but a mass of gallows stretching across the hill. The woodsman brought me bread and drink again when he and his fellows were comfortable by the fire. My hands were so numb with cold; I could not hold either the bread or the ale. He fed me slowly, then rubbed my hands to warm them. Pain shot through my fingers as the blood warmed beneath my skin. Memories of my father doing the same when we had been out to hunt in the winter months, bringing home a hare or pheasant. I spoke slowly to this man, telling him the story of how my father would not let me sit near the fire until he had rubbed my hands and feet, saying I would have blisters on my fingers and toes if I did so. When I had finished, the woodsman smiled. He crept back to the fire and brought two blankets, folding them around my shoulders. I thanked him. I was so cold, every inch of me from my head to my toes, but the blanket might allow me to live through one more night.

I massaged my hands every few minutes. My legs felt numb. I feared sleep; sleep would mean death now, I was sure. After two or three hours, the woodsman came and sat beside me, his thick blanket about him. He pulled me close and let the heat of his body seep into mine. I could not have been more grateful. It was difficult to speak, but he hushed me with his hand over my mouth. We stayed like this for another hour or more before he left me his blanket and went back to his fellow workers. I watched as he built up the fire in the hearth, and the other men roused themselves and made ready to work again. Once more, the woodsman brought me food and drink.

Catherine

Rippon, North Yorkshire,
Wednesday, 21st January 1569 (70)

A VOICE BROUGHT ME back from the darkness. 'Robert,' I mouthed.

'No, dearest,' said Bridget. 'I will tend you. Your son is on his way.'

'I thought—' I said but gasped as the pain grabbed me from the inside and tore through my body. 'God in heaven. Please make it stop.'

'It will. It will.' Bridget's voice was soothing as she gripped my hand through the pain.

'I think I am dying, Bridget.'

Bridget was lifting my kirtle and undergarments. 'Lift your knees for me.'

She put her head between my legs. Her fingers were like sharp spikes of burning metal. I moaned and tried to break away. A vision of my father helping one of the sheep that was struggling to lamb came to mind. I felt like an animal as I writhed with the pain. Sheep were so much less vocal about birthing, and I felt slightly ashamed of the noise I was making.

Bridget came out from under my clothes. 'The child is breech. I will away and fetch a doctor.'

'No,' I screamed, grabbing her arm. 'A doctor will cut me wide open to get the baby out. I cannot survive such a thing.'

'I cannot do this, Catherine. I have no experience.'

'I do. Let me guide you.' I was determined to do this now. I put the pain to one side and concentrated on what needed to be done for my baby and me. I tried to remember how my father had delivered my sister when my mother's time came. Her baby had been breech too. 'It's just like helping one of the ewes,' he had said to her. I watched in fascination as he cut my mother and put his hand inside her. She did not cry out once. I could do this. I knew there would have to be some cutting, but it could be small if Bridget did what I told her. All thoughts of dying disappeared as I talked her through the steps.

'I will probably scream, but you must ignore me. First, I want you to get Edmund to boil some water and place a sharpened knife in it. He must place a hard piece of wood in the water too. Everything must be clean.' She disappeared, and I lay there, groaning. I must save this baby, even if it meant losing my own life. Robert's son is the most important one.

Robert

Rippon, North Yorkshire,
Wednesday, 21st January 1569 (70)

I<small>T WAS STILL DARK</small> when the soldiers got up from their hearths and readied their horses. It seemed there was to be no more building of gallows today. We remained still while the soldiers gathered in a formation in front of us and set off at a walking pace. One of the soldiers dragged me to my feet and, using a length of rope, tied one end around my waist and the other to the back of the woodsman's cart. I stumbled as my legs tried to move forward, but I fell to my knees almost at once. The woodsman stopped the cart. He came to me and helped me up again. 'Sit on the rear of the cart for a while. If I stop the cart, it will be because a soldier is coming. You must jump down and feign weariness from walking.'

'That will not be difficult, dear friend,' I said. 'I shall probably fall over as soon as my feet touch the ground.'

His smile was not glad but pitying. ''Tis a pity you joined the pilgrimage. We could have been friends, I feel.'

I nodded as he helped me onto the cart.

Catherine

Rippon, North Yorkshire,
Wednesday, 21st January 1569 (70)

I HELD MY BREATH and bit down on the wood as the knife sliced through my flesh. A roar escaped my gritted teeth. 'Now put your hand inside and turn the baby until it faces down.' I screamed. The torture of her hand entering me was even more excruciating than the knife's blade. The whole of my body was one writhing mass of torturous pain, and I felt myself disappearing into a black place where Hell and the Devil lived. It scorched my mind so that I was blinded. I hung on, trying not to leave the actual world behind. I could hear a small voice from afar telling me to push. I felt too weak, but the voice was insistent.

'Push, Catherine. Push!'

I gave an almighty roar and felt something sluice down my legs. There was a timeless silence. The pain had gone, and I waited – and waited – and then it came, the sweet mewling of a child. Bridget laid the infant in my arms, covered in mucus and blood.

'A few more pushes, and you will be done.' Bridget's voice was brittle with wonder and tears. 'Then I can stitch you up.'

I pulled my shift to one side and laid the baby against my full, leaking breasts, guiding his heart-shaped lips to my nipple.

He latched on immediately, and the sweet pain of his suckling began. *Where are you, Robert? You promised me you would be home in time for the baby coming.* I stroked the baby's head and felt the slight fuzz of hair covering his crown.

'Can I come and see?' It was Edmund's voice.

'Soon,' said Bridget. 'I need a few minutes more.' The needle pierced my skin, but I was almost numb now and happy for her to stitch me back into a whole person again.

When she had done with me and wrapped the afterbirth in a linen sheet, I took a small shirt that I had made for him and pulled it over his head. Bridget took a breechcloth and packed it with moss before wrapping it around his tiny bottom; then, she made sure the tender twigs of his limbs were straight before tightly binding and wrapping him in the woollen swaddling bands. She signalled for Edmund to come and look at the child, and he flew to her side. I watched his face turn from a grimace of fear to a flush of pleasure as he looked down upon the baby's face. His smile was wide and open. Edmund would be my son's big brother. He would teach him to play games, ride a horse, handle a bow—

A sudden fear took hold of me. What if the baby was not as strong and healthy as he looked? Many children died soon after birth. I held him out. 'Take him, Bridget. Take him to the priest and have him baptised.'

Bridget understood my urgency. No matter to me, if I should leave this earth now, the priest must baptise my baby quickly to ensure God will accept him into heaven if he did die in the next few days – or hours. Thoughts of my dead babies who had come too soon filled my mind. None were buried in holy ground. None had lived long enough to be baptised. The thought brought a wave of anguish. Already he was more than life to me.

When Bridget had gone, I beckoned for Edmund to sit on the edge of the bed. 'You will make a fine brother, my son,' I said, taking hold of his hand and looking directly into his glossy, shiny eyes. 'We will make a fine family and prosper. I was a lucky person indeed when you and Robert crossed paths. To gain such a son as you has been a blessing.' He leaned forward and put his head against my shoulder.

'I love you as a mother,' he sobbed. 'I did not know my own mother. I was afeared you might die of childbirth too. I could not bear to lose the only mother I have known.'

I stroked his hair, holding him close and squeezing him to me. 'I will not leave you. Of that, you can be sure. Robert will be here soon. I can feel his presence close by. Why don't you check the roads to see if you can welcome him home?'

He seemed glad to have a purpose and jumped up. 'Is he nearby? You can tell it is so?'

'I can,' I said, not letting him see yet another fear wash over me. I prayed I was wrong. 'Go now. Bring him home to us.'

Edmund hurried away, and I settled down under my blanket.

Robert

'GET HIM ON HIS feet.' A man's voice penetrated the silence. I was sure I recognised it, but the noise of so many people shouting rushed back inside my head until I thought it would burst. I remembered the soldier had taken me from the back of the cart as we came over the bridge and tied me to the saddle of his horse. I couldn't quite recall his face. My head pounded as I was dragged along, my legs wouldn't work, and the ground kept rising to meet my face; my arms were being pulled from their sockets. I tried to look to the side to stop my nose from cracking as it bounced from the ground. The smell of human shit filled my bloodied nostril as my body slid through snow and excrement and waste food that littered the street. My stomach roiled, and I almost choked on the bile in my throat. I thought I heard someone call my name, but I slipped into the darkness once more.

Catherine

Rippon, North Yorkshire,
Wednesday, 21st January 1569 (70)

THERE WAS A COMMOTION outside. I could hear screaming
and shouting. I got up and went to the window. The crowds
were thick. Soldiers. Mary, Mother of God. The soldiers were
rounding up men by the score and tying their hands together,
using a rope to join them like a string of onions, then marching
them to the obelisk on the market-stede. My heart raced as
fear enveloped me – ropes pulling men along. I scanned the
soldiers on horseback – that's when I saw him, right below my
window. I looked down on the helmet of a soldier who had a
taut rope fastened to his saddle, a limp body trailing through
the dirty street behind him.

The door to the workshop bang closed, making me jump.
What had I just seen? Edmund raced up the stairs. He was
weeping wildly.

'Robert. He is being dragged along the road at the end of a
rope.' He spluttered the words, his face contorted, snot running
from his nose. 'His face is covered in blood!' he wailed. The
boy buried his face in my night shift, making me wince as I
pulled him close. My head was spinning. I could not think; I
had to get to him. I went to the stairs.

'I must go to him. Robert! Robert!' I shouted his name as I made my way down the stairs and through the door to the workshop. John stared at my bloodied night shift. A man stood nearby, waiting for him to finish fashioning a crook from a length of twisted iron. I realised I must look like a madwoman in my bloodstained shift and tried to cover myself. I went back inside and shouted for Edmund to bring me a long cloak which I wrapped about my shoulders and pulled close about me. When I stepped through the door again, the man had gone, and another had entered from the street.

'My horse needs shoeing,' he said. 'Take a look.' His manner was brusque as he ordered John. John hurried outside. When he turned toward me, I realised it was Shinclyffe. I looked away for fear he might recognise me, but it was too late.

'Goodwife Gray.' There was a particular triumph in his voice. ''Tis good to see you again.'

I returned his gaze, desperately wanting to leave him here and find Robert. I took a step forward and tried to pass him. 'I have no time for idle chatter, sir. I have business to attend.'

He grabbed my wrist. 'There is little you can do for him now. If he survives the day, they will hang him in the morning.' I stared at the floor, determined he would not see the fear on my face. 'Methinks you are as guilty of treason as he. Mayhap I should tie you up with him and take you to the gallows the morrow as well.' He lifted my chin, and as he did, my gaze fell on the tunic he was wearing. Emblazoned across his chest was the image of a falcon in full flight, its eyes staring right through me…and I remembered…

'It was you…'

Catherine

November 1558

MOTHER AND FATHER WERE inside the workshop, talking to the smith. People were saying that Queen Mary had died. Everyone seemed angry that we would soon have a new queen. We had come to town for the market, and Father had brought his ploughshare to have it sharpened. There was a crowd on the market square, and I crossed the street with Jack to get a better look. We wormed and wriggled our way to the front of the group and saw that the crowd had gathered around a falconer as he showed his beautiful birds. He was auctioning them, and the public was eager to buy. One, fastened securely by a leather jess, was sitting atop the man's gauntlet and tearing at a morsel of meat. Others were chained inside wicker cages on the back of his cart. The falconer asked if anyone would like to hold the bird, and Jack laughed, pushing me forward, knowing I was afeared. I squealed and stepped back into the crowd. A man was standing close enough that I backed into him. I turned to beg his pardon. He was tall, my face reaching only halfway up his chest. He wore a tunic embellished with a large falcon's head, the bird's eyes piercing as they stared into mine. Eyes that seemed to look right through me. The man pulled me to him; my face pressed into his clothing, I couldn't breathe. I felt the heavy cloak he was wearing fold around me until I could see no light at all.

He hissed through the thick folds of wool. 'Do not cry out, or I will have to kill you, little bird.' I was screaming, but no sound emerged. My heart pounded so fast I could hear it thudding in my ears. A pain shot through my chest, and I thought it would burst open and tear in two. He was dragging me through the people, taking me away from Jack. From my mother and father. Why did they not come? Why did they not try to stop him?

My back pressed hard against the wall. I tried to catch my breath. I was suffocating, his hand pressed against my mouth and nose while he tore at my undergarments – and then a shout. 'What's going on down there?' The voice came from high above us. Suddenly I was free. I ran and ran…

Robert

Rippon, North Yorkshire,
Wednesday, 21st January 1569 (70)

MY EYES CRACKED OPEN, a red mist blurring my vision, and the pain in my nose and cheeks told me something or someone had hit me several times. Through the red haze, I could see a crowd about me. Women were weeping on their knees, their arms in the air as if praying. I looked up, finally realising where I was. The obelisk rose above me, and I was lying on the steps below. I was home, but not in the way I had hoped. I remembered being tied to a horse as we left Gallows Hill, but little more. There were many other men bound together and even young boys. I could not see them clearly enough to know if Edmund was among them, praying he was safe with Catherine.

'Can you help me stand?' I asked the well-dressed man who was standing nearby. He was with the crowd that had gathered about us. He leaned forward and put one hand behind my elbow before taking hold of the rope between my hands. I gritted my teeth, wincing at the pain as he tried to pull me to my feet. I was too weak, and he lowered me back to the ground, guiding my back so that it leaned against the steps of the obelisk. 'I cannot.' My breathing was laboured as I felt near to death.

'You are the one I saw dragged through the streets,' he said. 'You must be in much pain.'

'The smell is worse than the pain,' I replied, pulling a face. The man's accent was not from these parts, and I wondered why he was here.

He laughed. 'You are right. The smell makes a fellow gag, but I would not shun you.'

I was grateful for his help. 'It would be good to wipe the blood away from my eyes. It is difficult to see.'

He took a linen kerchief from his pocket and wiped my face. My sight improved a little, enabling me to look around. The people were thick about, so it was difficult to see anything other than feet and legs.

'What brings you to these parts?' I asked, my voice barely a whisper. 'Do you have business here?'

'Indeed, I do. I am in search of a particular man. I have heard tell he is a spurrier of great skill.'

I looked at him curiously. Was he playing a game with me? 'Why would you search out this man?'

'I have a large shop in London. I wish to see his work. They say he crafted the most beautiful set of spurs for two local gentlemen, Papist rebels.' He leaned into me and whispered. 'As am I.'

'What would you of him should you find him?' Could I trust him? I coughed and wiped a gobbet of blood from my lips.

'I would see if the story were true and, if it is so, I would likely offer to put some business his way.'

'I wish you luck in your search then, sir.' I had to trust him. 'I would ask a favour of you, sir. My shop. It is the one in the far corner.' He turned to look in the direction I was pointing. 'My wife – I – Could you tell her where I am? I can pay.' He raised an eyebrow as if dubious of my ability to fulfil my promise. 'Come close,' I said. He drew near, squatting on his haunches, and I put my mouth to his ear. 'Put an arm about me and pull me close, then put your hand inside my jerkin.'

He stared at me for a moment, then did as I had asked. He smelled of fine perfume and wine as he put his hand inside and felt the pouch, pausing when his hands touched the soft leather, and then he smiled. Thankfully, it had survived the journey. My stitching had served its purpose.

'You will need to cut it free,' I whispered.

He fumbled at his belt and withdrew a small knife. I felt the pouch loosen and then come away from the lining of my jerkin before he stood up and put it in his pocket. 'Is it the window with the sign of the spurs and horseshoe hanging above?' he asked, looking directly into my eyes.

'It is,' I said, nodding. 'Her name is Goodwife Gray. Give the pouch to her and tell her I am alive. She will pay you for your kindness.' I coughed again, my head foggy, my breath shallow. 'tell her not to come out. She is near her time, and I would not want her in such a crowd of people. It would be dangerous.'

He nodded and headed away from me and towards the shop. I had to take the chance. Mayhap he would look in the pouch and walk away with the spurs. I hoped he was an honest man, but I had not much choice.

I could feel myself drifting away. Every bone in my body hurt as I let myself slump once more. The shouting faded away as I welcomed unconsciousness.

Catherine

Rippon, North Yorkshire,
Wednesday, 21st January 1569 (70)

SOMEONE WAS SCREAMING, THE sound piercing. I was beating someone's chest.

'Witch. You'll join your husband on the gallows for this.' A fist hit my nose, and the screaming stopped. I realised it had been me as I dropped to the floor.

'Leave her. Leave her alone.' I could hear Edmund shouting. Shinclyffe would hurt him. I tried to speak, but my jaw hurt when I opened my mouth.

'What on God's earth is happening here?' Another man? I startled, wincing, and looked into a round face and kindly eyes. 'Keep still. Do not move.'

'Get her on her feet. She is coming with me.'

Shinclyffe. It was Shinclyffe. I struggled to get up. 'It was him. He tried to...' I couldn't find the right words. 'He stole me and... I was only a child... The falconer. I had been watching the falconer.'

'What is she talking about? Stupid whore,' said Shinclyffe.

'She is delirious,' said the man, bending over me. 'Look at her, the blood on her shift. Can you not see she has only now birthed a child?' He took me by the elbow and lifted me to my feet. 'Let me help you.'

Shinclyffe grabbed my arm. 'She's under arrest for treason and witchcraft.'

'No,' said Edmund. 'Please, sir. She is unwell.'

I found my senses and glared at Shinclyffe. 'If I am a witch, I curse you. You will be dead afore this day is done.'

He was now unsure, his hand dropping to his side as he stepped back, his face losing the blush of anger, and he suddenly appeared afraid. 'You…You heard her,' he said to Edmund. 'She…She admits to being a witch.' His voice trembled.

'No, sir. She knows not what she is saying. She needs my help.'

'Get from my shop,' I said in a low, threatening voice, pointing my finger at Shinclyffe. 'The Devil is on your tail.'

He turned and ran into the street. I clung to the stranger who had said he was a doctor as my legs buckled under me.

I heard the clatter of a horse's hooves. The horse whinnied, and there were shouts and curses. John came back inside the shop, his face puzzled, his eyes wide.

'The man… Shinclyffe. He ran in front of a horse.'

'Is he dead?' I asked.

'I could not tell. He did not move when they carried him away.'

Bridget came upstairs in a hurry; my baby held tight against her.

'They have Robert. I saw him at the obelisk. I think he is dying—' She stopped dead in her tracks when she saw the gentleman standing by the window.

I reached out to her from my bed, and she passed the baby to me. 'I…this is Master Bright. He has brought me news of Robert – and these.' I added, handing the pouch to her. 'It is the spurs Robert made for Master Norton.'

Bridget took them from the pouch and looked at the intricate workmanship. She had heard of their splendour, but it was the first time she had seen them. Putting them on the bed, she backed towards the door. 'I need to go, Catherine. I do not know where Harry is. He may have been arrested along with all those other men who are being held hostage.' She disappeared, and I heard the slamming of the outside door as she left.

Turning back to Master Bright, I thanked him once more for saving me from Shinclyffe downstairs earlier.

'It was not me, Goodwife. You fair scared me for a time when you cursed him.' Master Bright took a spur in his hand again. He turned them over and over, inspecting them. 'I have a proposition,' he said. 'It may be possible to bribe the hangman. At least I could try.'

'Why?' I asked. What did this man want from us?

'Why what? Why am I offering to help?' He smiled, holding a spur up to the light. 'Your husband is highly skilled, and I could make a great deal of money from his talent. Also, it is because I have met him and think him honest. He trusted me, a complete stranger, to fetch you this pouch, and, for that, I wish to help him. If I am successful, he and you would come and work for me – in exchange for his freedom.'

'I must go to him,' I said, trying to stop the tears. 'If he is dying, he needs to see his son.'

'No,' he said, gently touching my arm. 'He asked that you do not go outside so soon after giving birth. You will only give him more to worry about. He has been through much and is weak. I will get him to you soon enough. Have no fear.'

What he said made sense. Any chance of getting my husband returned to me was worth taking. 'Take them,' I said without hesitation, picking up the other spur and pushing it into his hands. 'Take them, please. Anything, if there is the slightest chance it will save him.'

I asked him if it was possible to save Harry as well. He was not eager and asked about Harry's skills. I told him he had many years of experience as a smithy and sometimes made spurs. Mayhap it was the forlorn look on mine and Edmund's faces; mayhap it was because I said that Harry Gardyner was Robert's dearest friend. I do not know, but eventually, Master Bright said he would try offering one spur for Robert so that he had a bargaining tool for Bridget's husband.

I turned to Edmund. 'Give Master Bright some of my tincture for calming a fever.' Edmund ran downstairs and returned quickly with the medicine. Master Bright took it, nodded, and turned to leave. 'I cannot promise anything,' he said, his face grave, his hand resting atop mine.

'May God help you in your endeavour,' I said as he left.

Robert

THE PRISON WAS NOT of a size to contain all the men of Rippon they had rounded up for hanging, so we were all kept where we were. The night was clear and cold, but it felt almost warm enough to have been indoors with so many people huddled together. The downside was the crush as the men on the group's outer fringes tried to push their way into the centre. I wondered why the soldiers were waiting. Why had they not marched us back to Gallows Hill and hung us this night? My answer came as the sun rose and the sound of horses' hooves drummed along the street and into the square. I was stepped on, tripped over, and trampled several times. In my head, I could hear Catherine calling me. I was not sure if I was dreaming or not as my head spun. I tried to raise myself, using the obelisk as support, but it was hopeless. The man who had taken my spurs appeared at my side; I recognised his boots.

'Please,' I whispered, trying to grab hold of his leg. 'Help me. Please.' Another man helped him as they put my arms about their shoulders and hoisted me so that I might see what was happening.

'Did you see her?' I asked.

'I did, and she is well,' he said. 'She is thinking of you.'

George Bowes sat atop his black stallion and looked the captives up and down. I looked for Shinclyffe but could not see him. Now I remembered it was he who had dragged me behind his horse and through the streets. I watched Bowes' eyes land on a man on the fringes of the crowd.

'So, there you are, my trusty messenger.' He was smiling down at someone, and I knew at once that it must be Harry. 'You survived then? Did you join the other side?'

Harry spoke, his voice strong and defiant. 'They caught me delivering your missive. I was a fool for turning my back on my faith.'

'Feeling brave, I see,' said Bowes. 'As brave as you were when you watched me leaving Barnard? You and your friends were brave enough then, surrounded by the Papist dogs. I wonder how brave you will be when you're led to the gibbet and hung.'

'That is my friend, Harry,' I whispered. 'I wish he were at my side. We could face this together.'

'Harry Gardyner?'

'Yes.' I frowned. 'You know of him?'

'A little,' he replied. 'I must away,' he added before getting another man to take his place in holding me up. I wondered at his haste and was sorry to see him disappear into the crowd. I had not had the opportunity to ask more of Catherine.

Bowes turned to his men. 'I will break my fast afore taking these treacherous souls to their deaths. Make them ready.' He made his way through the crowd and over to an alehouse before dismounting. I could barely see his head as he disappeared inside. Many of the surrounding men were from other towns, dressed in the clothes of constables, aldermen, and even men of God. Bowes was going to take his pound of flesh. How many hundreds were there here? We would lose many good

Catholic lives this day. The two men lowered me back down to the ground.

The soldiers split the groups of men in readiness to march back through the streets and on towards Gallows Hill. Women and children gathered alongside, weeping as they offered ale and bread to the prisoners. Soldiers loaded men who were infirm or lame onto carts confiscated from the local tradespeople. I was told to get to my feet, but I was too weak no matter my efforts. The soldier who had commanded me kicked me in the side. It made no difference; I would die here where I lay. Then I heard someone speaking to the soldier.

'I have orders from Master Bowes to take this man I have here, and the one at your feet, over to the prison,' said a man authoritatively as I lay there. It was the stranger back again. I recognised his voice and wondered who the other captive might be. 'They have information on the whereabouts of the traitors in Scotland. I am to get the information afore we put them to the noose.' I felt the sky brighten under my eyelids as they made space. 'Help me get him up,' the stranger said again, and I felt myself being hoisted up and lifted over the saddle of a horse. The voice whispering in my ear belonged to Harry. Of course, Shinclyffe would have ordered this. No matter, I was ready to die. I drifted in and out of consciousness as my head bounced against the rider's knees.

'Catherine,' I whispered. 'Catherine.'

Catherine

MASTER BRIGHT SENT A note along with a suitable travelling horse. The message was brief:

> *Your nag looks too old, and we need something that can move at speed. I will see you on the hill around three of the clock. No sense in going earlier. The prisoner's in gaol will be the last to be transferred up to Gallows Hill. Be prepared to leave Rippon without attracting attention from anyone.*

It was two of the clock when Edmund harnessed the fresh horse while Bridget loaded the cart with food and blankets. Mutton would stay with John at the shop. I handed the keys to him and wished him well. I swaddled the baby in thick woollen bands. It was dangerous to take him outside in the cold for long, but there was little choice. John had affixed a canvas cover to hooped bands over the cart to provide shelter for the long journey ahead. My hands shook from nervousness. Had Master Bright been successful? He had told us to be ready to move quickly and quietly when the time came.

I busied myself feeding the child. The sensation, each time his mouth nuzzled against my breast, filled me with such love I could cry with joy. I looked around my home of the last few years, longing for a reason to stay. *No use longing*, I scolded myself. We would say goodbye to Rippon for many years. Mayhap for the rest of our lives. I looked again upon my baby's face. It was a price worth paying.

We arrived on the hill at three of the hour, as Master Bright had suggested. My son was sleeping in my arms, wrapped in many blankets, I was desperate for him to meet his father, so I took him with me. Leaving Edmund to watch over the cart, Bridget and I pushed through the weeping crowds to reach the prisoners who were waiting for the moment they had to step up to die. Scanning their faces, we could see neither Robert nor Harry amongst them, but there were so many it was hard to tell if they were there or not. 'Robert!' I shouted. There was no reply. Had Master Bright been lying? Was he, at this moment, riding back to London with Robert's spurs in his bag?

I took hold of Bridget's hand. 'We must be brave,' I said, squeezing it tight. We walked among the gibbets, barely able to look up. Each time we stopped and steeled ourselves before gazing at the ghoulish faces with bulging eyes and tongues lolling from their mouths. The smell of piss and human excrement filled the air about them. It took a while to cover every post, but we had to be sure. My son mewled from cold and hunger as we made our way back to the cart. I could not weep, not until I had seen his body, his gentle face, and touched him for the last time. Bridget was hanging on to me, her feet barely able to carry her in her grief.

As we approached the cart, I thought I could make out Master Bright sitting atop his horse, his head bent low. My breath juddered. He had come to tell us he had failed. The pit of my stomach jerked in pain, and I leaned over and gasped, determined not to be sick. Bridget fell to the ground and curled into a ball.

'Get up!' I hissed. 'Get up now.' I no longer had time to comfort her. My grief was about to swallow me up. 'Get up and walk. I will leave you if you do not!' I snapped. I forced myself to walk on, back to the cart – back to a life without Robert. The tears were hot on my cheeks now, scalding and salty as they ran over my lips. The baby was howling wretchedly. He wanted to suckle. 'Robert. Oh, Robert. Why did you forsake me? Why—'

'Hurry,' whispered Master Bright as I reached the cart. I ignored him and climbed aboard, intent on getting under the hood to feed the baby. Robert, my baby Robert. I would name him for his father. I stepped up and hoisted myself aboard before turning to climb inside, and then I saw them. Two dark faces wearing women's caps, but I would know that face anywhere – while it was red raw, bruised all over and awash with blood. I knew that smile. I knew my Robert was here. I gasped, crawling into the warm space between the two men. Edmund leaned over the side and pulled and dragged a sobbing Bridget up into the seat beside him before snapping the reins, and we moved off. The cart was tossing and swaying over the grassy mound, Master Bright riding alongside.

'Do not cry out, Bridget,' said Edmund. 'You may find what you have been looking for in the back of the cart.' Bridget held on tight as she turned her head, her hand jumping to her mouth as she made out Harry alongside Robert. She cried even louder. Anyone watching us leave would assume she had been successful in finding her husband dangling from a noose. We were back on the road and moving quickly now, making it difficult to suckle my baby and stop him from crying. Robert stroked his son's tiny head.

The cart slowed as we approached the outskirts of Rippon. We did not want to draw too much attention. Edmund turned the cart off to the left as we came to the bridge, and we did not cross. My heart raced, praying no one would stop us. No voices called out as we rode on into the dark night. We would never set foot in our home again, never hear the bells of St Wilfrid's. It did not matter; we were together, and I clung to the man at my side. I swore I would never be parted from him again. We were free of Master Thomas, free of Shinclyffe, free to begin a new life. Robert's head slumped to one side, his hand sliding away from my baby's crown, eyes closed.

The Aftermath

IN THE REBELLION'S AFTERMATH, the Crown ordered the execution of over 600 of the common rebels. The intention was to make an example to deter future uprisings. Rather than execute the wealthier men whose children would automatically inherit all their wealth, the crown fined them a goodly portion of their property and money in exchange for a pardon, thus gaining their support for future rebellions. The Crown confiscated all lands and property from the main instigators of the uprising before executing all those they managed to capture.

Anne Percy, Countess of Northumberland, stayed in Scotland until the birth of her daughter, Mary. Friends smuggled her out of Scotland, and she arrived in Bruges on 31st August 1570. She spent the rest of her life as an exile in Flanders, King Philip of Spain, having provided her with a pension. Her daughter Mary joined a Benedictine monastery in 1599 and became abbess in 1616. The daughters left behind in England were brought up by their uncle, Henry Percy.

Thomas Percy, 7th Earl of Northumberland, was held captive at Loch Leven Castle. His wife spent the next two years trying to raise money to pay the ransom asked by her husband's captors but to no avail. His captor, the Earl of Morton, sold him to Queen Elizabeth in 1572 for an agreed figure of £2000. While being escorted to London, the party stayed overnight in York, where he was taken to The Pavement and beheaded. They buried his headless body at St Crux Church in York.

Charles Neville, 6th Earl of Westmorland, was smuggled from Orkney to Flanders, where he received a pension of fifty crowns a month from King Philip of Spain. He had several attempts at raising forces against the Crown to no avail and died in poverty in Nieuport in November 1601.

Jane Neville, Countess of Westmorland, was put under house arrest at Kenninghall, Norfolk, where she lived out the rest of her days.

Richard Norton also escaped to Flanders. In 1585, English soldiers in Flanders took him, prisoner. They injured him during the arrest, and he died of his wounds while on the ship during his return journey.

Thomas Markenfield escaped on a ship to Bruges, where he lived in abject poverty and was found dead in a small cottage in Brussels in 1592. The Crown confiscated Markenfield Hall and his lands, but his wife Isabel remained nearby, living on a small pension her brother William Ingleby provided.

Bibliography

Forster, B. (2018). *Ripon Cathedral: Its History and Architecture, Second Edition.* Ripon: The Chapter of Ripon Cathedral 2018.

Goodman, R. (2016). *How to be a Tudor.* London: Penguin Random House.

Kesselring, K. J. (2010). *The Northern Rebellion of 1569.* Palgrave Macmillan.

Macculloch, A. F. (2016). *Tudor rebellions.* Abingdon, ORoutledgexon.

Mortimer, I. (2013). *The Time Traveller's Guide to Elizabethan England.* Vintage.

Norton, E. (2017). *The Lives of Tudor Women2017.* London: Head of Zeus Ltd.

Sharp, S. C. (1975). *The Rising in the North THE 1569 REBELLION Being a reprint of the Memorials of the Rebellion of the Earls of Northumberland and Westmorland edited by Sir Cuthbert Sharp 1840.* Shotton, Durham, England: J. Shotton, 3b Old Elvet, Durham City.

Speed, J. (1995). *The Counties of Britain A Tudor Atlas by John Speed.* London: Pavilion Books Limited.

Wilson, D. (2010). *Tudor England.* Oxford: Shire Publications.

About me

I AM CJ RICHARDSON
    I live in a small village in North Yorkshire with my husband. This is the second time around for both of us and we have six grown up children and fifteen grandchildren between us.
    I started writing when I retired in 2008. Firstly joining a beginners class and then forming a writing group with some fellow students. We meet regularly to share our work and also to critique and help each other.
    I completed my studies with the OCA and gained a BA (hons) in creative writing in 2020.
    I released my debut novel NORTH SEA SHELLS in May of 2016 and you can find a link for it on the website if you would like to know more.
    I released my second book HOME TRUTHS in 2018

Website: www.cjrichardsonwriter.com
Twitter: cjrichardsonwr2
Instagram: cjrichardsonwr2

Printed in Poland
by Amazon Fulfillment
Poland Sp. z o.o., Wrocław

83355788R00204